Also by Sierra Simone

Co-Written with Julie Murphy
A Merry Little Meet Cute

Priest
Priest
Midnight Mass: A Priest Novella
Sinner
Saint

Thornchapel
A Lesson in Thorns
Feast of Sparks
Harvest of Sighs
Door of Bruises

Misadventures
Misadventures with a Professor
Misadventures of a Curvy Girl
Misadventures in Blue

New Camelot

American Queen
American Prince
American King
The Moon (Merlin's Novella)
American Squire (A Thornchapel and New Camelot Crossover)

Co-Written with Laurelin Paige

Porn Star
Hot Cop

Markham Hall

The Awakening of Ivy Leavold
The Education of Ivy Leavold
The Punishment of Ivy Leavold

London Lovers

The Seduction of Molly O'Flaherty
The Wedding of Molly O'Flaherty

American King

Sierra Simone

Bloom books

Content Warning: *Chapter 22 of this book contains a depiction of suicide by drowning. This chapter can be skipped and its events inferred from later chapters.*

Cover design by Hang Le
Cover image © Braayden Penrod
Internal design by Ashley Holstrom/Sourcebooks

Published by Bloom Books, an imprint of Sourcebooks
P.O. Box 4410, Naperville, Illinois 60567-4410
(630) 961-3900
sourcebooks.com

Originally self-published in 2017 by Sierra Simone.

Cataloging-in-Publication Data is on file with the Library of Congress.

Printed and bound in the United States of America.
VP 10 9 8 7 6 5 4 3 2 1

For Laurelin Paige, Melanie Harlow, and Kayti McGee. We'll always have the lake.

A threefold cord is not easily broken.

—Ecclesiastes 4:12

PROLOGUE
ASH

> When I was a child, I talked like a child, I thought like a child, I reasoned like a child. When I became a man, I set aside childish ways.
> For now we see through a glass, darkly, but then we shall see face-to-face.
> Now I know in part, but then I shall know fully, even as I am fully known.

THERE IS A CERTAIN FATALISM IN THE OLD MYTHS AND legends that I've always relished. This idea that our paths are preordained by some external hand—by God or by the universe or by fate or by some mixture of the three. That from the moment I took my first breath, the date and time of my last were already stitched into determined existence. Why this idea should fascinate me, I don't know, but it does. I suppose it promises meaning. And meaning, above all, is what I seek.

I want to know this isn't in vain.

I want to know my life wasn't in vain.

I keep having this dream about a lake. Mirror still, glass clear, fog wisping over the surface. There is a boat there, and women, and there is someplace to go. A better place, over the water.

My Greer is there. And my mother, and Morgan, and strangely enough, Embry's mother, Vivienne. They cry over me like they would cry over a body, and the boat cuts through the water like a knife, swift and smooth.

There is a better place over the water.

It's no easy thing, knowing the day. Choosing it. Fuck fatalism because it's still a choice. I still have to put on this armor I've chosen—cuff links, tie bar, flag pin—and I still have to pick up my weapons. I still have to face a man I love and hate—a man who loves and hates me in return—and choose to lay down my life, hoping that everything I fought for, all the fragile peacetime work of a tired soldier, will still stand when I no longer can. I have to trust—so much trust—that this sacrifice has meaning. That on this wicked day, when I fall to my knees, I will fall knowing that the world has shifted that much closer to peace and goodness. I will fall knowing the people I love are safe.

I will die and go to a better place over the water.

Now I know in part, but then I shall know, even as I am known.

The Sword

CHAPTER 1
ASH

THEN

I PULLED A SWORD FROM A STONE WHEN I WAS TWELVE years old.

A carnival had come to town, all lights and cotton candy and generators whirring in the summer heat, and Althea had given Kay and me each ten dollars to spend there. Kay, too cool and too old to be bothered with the rides, bought a soda and spent the evening flirting and showing off her new yarn braids, bright blue and just finished after midnight the night before.

But me, I spent every last dollar at the same booth. Sandwiched between the ring toss and the place where you shot metal ducks with cork guns was a small canopy strung with lights and carpeted by grass so trampled that the dirt showed through. It was a strength game, much like hitting a giant hammer on a scale—pull the sword from the stone and you won the blinking plastic crown hanging from the ceiling. If you could pull the sword up halfway, you won a stuffed animal.

The stone was, of course, molded concrete, and the sword wasn't a real sword. Just a piece of stamped metal rigged with bolts and slides to keep it from moving up all the way out of the stone. It was a money trap, exactly the kind of thing my adoptive mother Althea would refuse to let me spend her money on if she were there.

But she wasn't there, and for some reason I was determined. I think I had this idea that the crown would look good perched on my sister's new braids. I'm sure part of it was an adolescent desire to show off. And part of it still lay beyond the realm of explanation; I couldn't articulate why I wanted to do it, I just knew that I did. And so on a hot summer's day, thunderclouds piling up like cars, I spent ten dollars for ten tries at the sword.

I failed nine times.

On the tenth, the sword pulled free.

A bolt must have broken, something sheared loose with a rattle and a snap, and all of a sudden I was staggering backward, holding a sword-shaped piece of metal too heavy to keep upright.

"Holy shit, kid," the carnival worker said. "You broke that thing right off."

I was too stunned to answer, holding the sword-shaped metal like it was the answer to every question in the universe. Up until that moment, I'd been a good but unremarkable boy—I got good grades; I played a decent game of baseball; I got along with almost everyone. But holding that rusted, dull metal, the hilt cool in my hand, the humid air hot on my face, I felt the thrill of possibility. The insistent tugging feeling that I needed to be doing something, going somewhere, finding someone. The enchanting itch that there was a better, richer world just out of reach, that I could stretch out my fingers and part the very air like a veil, and that behind that veil would be a place that was *more* than my own mundane life. The trees leafier, the sun warmer, everything just *more.*

Now I can look back at that tug or itch and call it destiny—or the beginning of my adult consciousness, depending on how pragmatic I'm feeling. But I had no words for it then. One moment I was an ordinary boy throwing his money away on a cheap carnival trick, and the next I was a young man on the precipice of something dizzying in its depth.

I've never told another soul what happened next.

The carnival worker, still swearing in a mixture of disbelief, annoyance, and admiration, reached up for the plastic crown and held it out for me to take…and someone else took it before I could.

It was a man—well, barely a man, really—early twenties and thin in a way that reminded me of birds or a sapling in winter. He had pale white skin and near-black eyes, and it could have been his sharp and delicate face or maybe his shabbily elegant clothes, but I suddenly felt very aware of myself. Of my youth, of my ordinariness. Of my well-worn T-shirt and jeans and church-sale sneakers.

He held the crown in his hands, studying the plastic as if it were finely beaten gold, his head bowed in thought. "Is this yours?" he finally asked, glancing up at me from under dark eyebrows. He had a lilt that I mentally fumbled to place; it was Welsh, and I'd never heard a Welsh accent before. What a man like him was doing in a hot city park in Missouri, I had no idea.

"I, uh, I won that crown," I explained pointlessly. I lifted the hand wrapped around the cheap metal hilt of the sword. "For pulling this thing from the stone."

He nodded, looking down at the crown with something like reverence, and then held it out to me. "Then I suppose you should take it."

There was a moment as I wrapped my fingers around it. Short, wordless, jolting. Like we'd done this before, this very thing. That I'd stood with a sword in one hand and this man had handed me a crown and I had taken it, knowing nothing would ever be the same.

But the moment blew away in the electric, pre-thunderstorm wind, and the man gave me a small smile and turned to leave.

I wasn't ready for him to go. I felt a sudden anxiety I couldn't name.

"What should I do with them? The sword and the crown?" I asked the stranger. It seemed so important that I ask, that I know, and that he be the one to tell me.

The man stopped, looking thoughtfully up at the dark, rain-laden sky. "The most important part of wearing a crown and using a sword is knowing when to set them down."

It was cryptic. And yet perfectly clear, somehow.

"And until then?" I asked.

"Why, until then, you use them. Goodbye, Maxen."

He knew my name.

He left, and I stood there with a fake sword in one hand and a plastic crown in the other. Then the storm broke and the rain started pouring down.

CHAPTER 2
ASH

NOW

WHEN EMBRY MOORE LEAVES A ROOM, THE AIR CHANGES. The molecules of oxygen and nitrogen and argon rearrange themselves into something stale and listless, something only barely life giving. You can drag in lungful after lungful and never get enough because it's not enough. There's not enough to fill your chest and push into your blood. Systems start shutting down. The world fills with static, goes dim.

And now here I am, each breath grating in and out, bringing me no relief, no mercy. Because I am alone, and everything I've ever done wrong has made sure that Embry will never breathe the same air as me again.

That's not even the worst part.

No, the worst part is learning that I've never breathed the same air as my son.

Greer is away, Embry is gone, and I have a son.

Whom I've never met.

Whose mother is my sister.

Fuck.

I scrub my hands over my face, over the hair that Embry kissed not ten minutes ago. I try to breathe again, try to stop the way my ribs keep jerking with choked sobs, try to stop the tears burning their way past my eyelids. It hurts, my entire body hurts, my chest, my throat, my eyes. I've been carved up and I'm bleeding out.

I slide out of the chair I'm sitting in, right onto the floor of my study, pressing my face into the carpet, and I cry. For a young man named Lyr that I've never met. For Embry, pressed by Merlin to refuse my love, pressed by Abilene to hurt Greer in order to protect me. Pressed by his own conscience to fight me at long last.

I cry for Greer because she's not here, because she doesn't know, because I don't know how she'll look at me when she learns that I got my own sister pregnant.

How could I not know?

I roll onto my back, pressing the heels of my palms into my eyes. It's all there behind my eyelids—the fires at Glein, that fateful village during the war. Morgan's limp form as I carried her out of the church. My child was inside her then, saved from incineration by moments, by luck. If he'd died, it would have been my fault.

And all these years—how can my son ever forgive me for all these years apart? How can I ever forgive myself?

There's more. Embry breaking and betraying me…but broken and betrayed himself.

Greer, with new shadows in her eyes, publicly shamed and taken by force when I couldn't protect her.

Everyone I've failed. Embry and Greer. Lyr and Morgan. Countless others…soldiers and civilians, American citizens and Carpathian villagers. The line of people I've let down is numberless, and I have no one to blame but myself.

I stay there for a long time, stretched out on the floor,

my hands pressing into my eyes until the tears stop and I see stars. I can't remember the last time I've cried this hard. I can't remember ever feeling this lonely, this alone. This… rudderless.

What am I supposed to do? When the man who is supposed to love me hates me? When I can't protect the woman we both love? When I have a *son*?

What am I supposed to do?

"Morgan."

Her name from my lips results in silence on the other end of the line. Finally Senator Morgan Leffey speaks. "Mr. President."

"Don't do that."

"Do what?" my sister asks in a tired voice. "Be respectful?"

"Put distance between us." I close my eyes and think of Prague. Not with lust, obviously. But with a sort of fondness. She'd been the first lover to show me what I needed, both that time and then again after Jenny's death. Even when she hated me, she'd still helped me.

I couldn't discount the debt I owed her for that. Not in the face of this new, terrible debt.

"Why are you calling, Maxen?" she asks. "Is this about the VA overhaul? Because I told you that my committee won't budge on—"

I interrupt her. "It's about Lyr, Morgan," I say. "It's about our son."

I hear a small intake of breath, then careful stillness. "Who told you?" Morgan asks in a voice of glass pretending to be stone. "You weren't ever supposed to know."

"That's not true though, is it?" I'm walking around the empty Residence feeling just as empty as the rooms. "You wanted to tell me once. Before Glein."

"Yes," she admits. "Before Glein."

I rub at the spot in my chest where my heart used to be, before Embry tore it out. "Fuck knows you don't owe me anything Morgan, but why? Why couldn't I have known?"

"I thought it made us even. You left me to die, and I hid the new life we made from you. It seemed fair at the time."

"And now?"

Morgan lets out a breath, and I can picture her running her thumb along her forehead, just like I do when I'm thoughtful or stressed or sorrowful. "And now I don't know."

"I grew up thinking I had a father who didn't care about me. And then you told me the truth about my parents at Jenny's funeral, and I knew for a fact that my father didn't care about me. All I ever wanted was not to do that…not to *be* that. And now that's what you've made me. The same kind of man."

Morgan's voice is sharp when she answers. "You want to pout about not having a father? What about my mother, Maxen? The one you killed when you were born? You think I don't miss her? That I wasn't scarred or lost or damaged knowing that she'd gone to bed with a man who wasn't my father and ended up dying because of it?"

"Dammit, Morgan, do you think I don't know that? That I don't feel her loss too? That I don't feel the karmic weight of being born under such a fucking cloud?"

"Don't try that with me. You had Althea. You *had* a mother. I only ever had Governor Vivienne Moore, and even as stepmothers go, she was fucking cold. My father was a husk. I grew up alone."

"You had Embry," I point out.

"You had Kay," she retorts.

I stop at the window in the dining room, looking out on the night-dark lawn. Past the fence, headlights and taillights move through the district's streets, lamplights glow, window squares of yellow light point to where the brightest minds of Washington are burning the midnight oil on policy and lobbying and diplomacy. "This is pointless," I say. "This who-had-it-worse game."

She sighs. "Fine. But you have to understand why I wanted something different for Lyr. Vivienne suggested Nimue raise him instead, and Nimue is happy and kind and undamaged. She's not like us, Maxen. There's no stain on her. And I knew she'd be a better parent than either of us."

I listen to her. To the pain in her voice. And something in me cracks. "Was it hard? To give him to Nimue?"

She lets out a noise that should be a laugh but sounds like a sob. "There isn't a word for how hard it was. When he was born, he was so, so quiet and so stoic, like you. He didn't even cry when I put him in Nimue's arms. He just looked at me, resigned and silent. Like he'd been waiting for me to let him down all along."

There's silence for a long time, for both of us. Each of us lost in our own pain.

"I want to tell him, Morgan. I want to meet him."

"No."

"No?"

"What good will it do? You think we're fucked up, just from sleeping with each other? Imagine what he'll feel like knowing that's where he came from!"

"And if Abilene Corbenic makes good on her threat and reveals it anyway? Which is worse, him learning it from us or learning it from the internet?"

"Maxen, everything I've built has been to protect Lyr. After I learned the truth about us, that protection became more crucial than ever. Even my ex-husband, Lorne, didn't know about him."

I move away from the window and into my bedroom, taking a moment to straighten my well-thumbed Bible on the end table before I wander into the dressing room. There's a small picture on the vanity of me as a child with Althea and Kay. There is no picture of my birth parents. I don't have any pictures of Imogen Leffey. And while I wouldn't have to search the White House too hard to find a portrait of Penley Luther, I'd rather not.

"My real parents were kept a secret from me too," I say finally. "It didn't make it any easier to learn it at thirty-six than it would have been to learn it at fourteen."

"I don't want him to carry that burden at all," she says. "Can't you see that? It's better that he never know."

Then I'll never know him, a selfish part of me cries. God, how much I've wanted a child to hold and raise and love, and now I find I already have a son of my own, unfolding into manhood, and the idea of not knowing him *ever* slices at me.

But it's not only about my selfish need to know him; I recognize that. It's about what's best for him, and while I disagree with Morgan that it's better for him to believe the lies he's been told since birth, I don't disagree with her so strongly that I can't understand her concern.

"I see that too," I say. "But please see it the way I do. I've already committed enough sins... I don't want to compound them by lying. I don't want to miss any more of my son's life."

A pause.

I'm sitting down at the vanity now, toying with Greer's necklaces, running my fingertips over slender chains and delicate pendants.

"I'll think about it," Morgan says eventually. "It's not a promise. But I'll...I'll think about it."

I close my eyes, trying to make myself think like a president again. Like a soldier. And not like a man who's just been gutted by his best friend and lover. "We have to prepare ourselves too, Morgan. If Abilene goes public about Lyr, that necessarily means the world will know about us. About what happened between us."

"Right," she says, her voice once again climbing into her crisp Senator's tones. Scandal and spin. This she knows; this she is comfortable with. "I can have my chief of staff liaison with Kay and Trieste, talk through a coordinated approach to media defense."

"Kay won't be my chief of staff much longer," I say, glancing over at the picture of us as kids.

"Why on earth not?" Morgan sounds irritated. "She's the best person you've got on your team."

"Which is why I'm appointing her vice president," I explain a little impatiently. "Or did you forget that Embry is quitting the White House and planning to run against me?"

"Oh," she says. "That."

"You two will make a great team."

"As will you and Kay," she concedes.

"It makes a nice symmetry. A brother and sister on each side."

"And a brother and sister opposing each other," she says and gives a small laugh, and for a moment, I remember Prague. I wonder what life would have been like if I'd met her as a sibling, if we could have loved each other as a brother and sister should do, instead of…well.

Her laugh turns into another sigh. "It was Embry who told you about Lyr, wasn't it?"

"Yes."

"He wanted so badly to protect you from the truth. To protect Lyr and me from exposure. He must have been very angry with you to change his mind."

Behind my eyelids I see his face in the office again, wildflower-blue eyes full of pain, lines of fury and resentment around his mouth and creasing his forehead.

"I think he hates me."

"Maybe," Morgan replies. "But he'll never stop loving you. You have that effect on people."

I open my eyes, looking at myself in the mirror. Silver speckling at my temples, a serious mouth, day-old stubble. A weary ex-soldier. A man who hurts the people he loves and gets hard doing it. I don't deserve their love. I don't deserve any of it. How funny that before tonight I never doubted anything about what I deserved, and now…

"*Do* I have that effect on people?" I ask. "It feels more like I burn people out with my love, like I use them up until they've got nothing left. No one who loves me gets a happy ending, have you noticed? Just being close to me infects their lives with tragedy."

I don't know why I'm confessing this all to Morgan. She's one of the people I've harmed, a life I've ruined simply by existing inside of it. And other than this phone call, we haven't spoken through anything other than memos and aides since I met Greer. We're not in the habit of being vulnerable with each other.

"I knew when I met you that it would end in tragedy. And I still wouldn't have done a single thing differently. Not a single thing."

There's an edge of defiance around the cold, steel core of her words, as if she's daring me to argue. And I take the dare.

"Why, Morgan? What has been the point of any of this? All this…*suffering*…and for what?"

"What do you want me to say?" she asks. "That every part of your life has been hallmarked by coincidence, that all of this was just an accident?"

Coincidence. Coincidence that the woman I got pregnant happened to be my sister. Coincidence that her stepbrother would be one of the two loves of my life. Coincidence that my father would have been a president too, that his vice president would be my wife's grandfather.

There can be a lot of coincidences in a man's life, and yet this is too much.

"No," I reply. "I don't want you to say that."

"Then you have to accept that things have happened the way they've happened and that you can't change the past. There's only the present."

"The present," I murmur. The present when my little prince is running away from me, when my little prince is running *against* me. The present when I might lose everything. And I might deserve it.

"Maxen, I..." She takes a deep breath. "For what it's worth, I never doubted that you'd make a good father. You're a good man. A great man. The best kind of man."

My fingers are tight around a necklace of Greer's; my voice is also tight with pain as I answer. I still see Embry's face. Hear his words.

The difference is that I'm not afraid to do what needs to be done. And I think you are.

"I don't feel like a great man."

"If you did, it wouldn't be true."

I don't have an answer to that. It feels both wrong and right, that idea. That great men and women are necessarily filled with doubt and jagged humility.

"You will know what to do," she says. "About Lyr, about Embry, about Melwas. You will find a way through it."

"Do you really have such faith in me? You hate me."

"My faith goes beyond love and hate, Maxen. I may join Embry in running against you and I'll fight my damnedest to win, but I'll do it because it's in my nature. Power and the winning of it. It's not because I don't believe you're a good president or a good man. It's not because I share the same delusion as Embry that you're afraid of fighting."

I let go of Greer's necklace and stand. "And what do you think I'm afraid of?"

Morgan lets out a dark laugh. "Embry thinks you've grown passive, but I know the truth, little brother. You've grown so active that it feels like sharks are swimming in your mind. You itch for the fight so much it scares you awake in the middle of the night. You're not afraid of conflict; you're afraid of what will happen when you *do* fight. You're afraid of yourself. And I think you're going to unleash a kind of storm this country hasn't seen in years when your control finally breaks."

"I won't let it," I vow. I couldn't let it.

"There's more than one way for your armor to fracture."

I narrow my eyes, even though I'm staring at a rack of ties and not my sister's face. "What does that mean?"

"It's not a threat," she says. "Just an observation."

And we're silent for a moment more before I say, "I should go. About Lyr…"

"I'll think about it."

"I recognize that's all I can ask. I'm sorry, Morgan. For Prague, for Glein, for all of it."

"It's too late to—"

"Maybe it is too late. But I want you to know anyway. There's not a night that goes by that Glein doesn't haunt my dreams…that the whole fucking war doesn't weigh on me. I failed you that day. I didn't mean to. I was trying my hardest, but I still failed. I'm still responsible, and I'll never forgive myself for it. Especially now, knowing about our son."

Morgan is quiet when she speaks. "Okay, Maxen."

"Okay?"

"Okay," she affirms.

"Thank you."

"Good night, little brother."

"Good night, Morgan."

CHAPTER 3
ASH

NOW

I DIDN'T SLEEP THAT NIGHT. I DIDN'T EXPECT TO, BUT IT STILL feels bitter when it comes. The insomnia. The restless memories. The guilt. The endless chewing questions—*what if what if what if.*

What if I'd saved everyone in Glein?

What if I'd found ways to spare more enemies?

What if I'd kept Greer safe from Melwas?

And the wave of *what ifs* would curl and hang into the future—what if I begged Embry to come back? What if I went after Melwas right now? What if I said fuck everything and caught the next flight to Seattle to meet my son?

Then the wave would collapse and crash, sucking itself back into the past. An endless, churning cycle of doubt. I only knew one way to stay the doubt, to part the guilt and the worry like a biblical sea, and that way was lost to me. My little prince had run away, my little princess was in another city. There was no one to wrestle, no one to whip, no one to kiss. No one to shove inside of and relieve every ache.

Fuck. I needed it bad too. Those moments before Embry had told me he was leaving, his jacket crumpled in my fist, his fingers warm and probing the place I'd denied him so long…

God, what I would have given. My kingdom. My soul, just to have Embry in front of me. I'd grab that jacket again and then I'd push him down, shove his face into the carpet. Yank down his pants. How the fuck dare he, how the fuck *dare he*, and I'd seethe just that into his ear as I laid my body over his. I'd pin him down with a forearm to his neck, I'd make him feel every angry pound of me. I'd fuck him right in two.

Belvedere finds me in the gym the next morning, naked to the waist and covered in sweat.

Belvedere's in his midtwenties, with medium bronze skin—and his floppy, black hair and tight cardigans and trendy glasses betray the same level of attention he gives to style as he gives to everything else, which is part of why he makes such an excellent aide. The other part is his sheer unflappability; he makes no comment on my haggard expression or sweaty body.

"Good morning, Mr. President," he says. I grunt in response, finishing the last four pull-ups of my set before dropping from the bar and reaching for my towel.

"We've got a full docket today," he continues, unfazed. Ryan Belvedere has seen me in every mood, every state of sweat and undress, every tired, snappish moment in a rented car or in the corner of a high school gymnasium or under the baking sun at a state fair. He's my body man, my personal aide—my valet if you care for such old-fashioned terms—and he's awake before me and asleep after me. His job *is* me. To manage my travel and my appointments in conjunction with my secretary. To make sure my dry-cleaning arrives at the right hotel when I've got three different events in three different cities. To hand me Sharpies when I'm signing at rallies, to carry my spare ties, to answer my phone when I can't. He's my shadow, and after last night, he's my most loyal friend.

Of course, Embry and I were never really friends. When we first met, he thought I was his enemy and I thought he was perfect. Then I fell in love with him, and he's been breaking my heart ever since.

I flex my hands just once, hard enough to feel the protest of the bones and thin tendons, to remind myself that I can feel something other than *this*. Than him.

My little prince.

"What's on today?" I ask, throwing the towel in a nearby basket and taking the folder Belvedere offers. Inside is my agenda for the day and several memos from my staff to review.

"Briefing from your secretary at eight thirty," Belvedere says, taking the folder from me and handing me a bottle of water, which I gladly drink. "Then your daily security briefing with Gawayne at nine thirty. A phone call with the new UK prime minister right after, then the televised visit with Pine Ridge High School. Merlin wants me to remind you to use it as a chance to showcase the early achievements of the education infrastructure bill you spearheaded last year."

Merlin. Another open wound that needs triaging today. I cap the now-empty bottle and drop it into the recycling bin. "I'm not going to platform on something that should have been done decades ago. It feels corrupt."

"I told Merlin you'd say that. And he told me to tell you to do it anyway."

"I won't."

"I told him that too. He said to tell you that you and Embry aren't going to get reelected on modesty alone."

Embry.

Hearing his name from Belvedere's mouth is like having my guts exposed. I rub a hand over my face, pray that the salt sting in my eyes is from sweat and not tears.

"What else?" I ask through my hand.

"Bakewell wants to meet about the Carpathian sanctions bill the House is floating around. I put her down at one. Then we've got a staff meeting in the Oval Office at one thirty. Handshake session at three, at four we've got the police widows coming in. Merlin wants the photo op to smother the latest GOP claim that you're anti-cop."

"For fuck's sake," I mutter, dropping my hand. My party had sponsored and successfully pushed through legislation to track officer-involved shootings and to provide federal funds for body cameras and racial sensitivity training. The bill had been crafted in close consultation with the Fraternal Order of Police and several key police chiefs from around the country. It's the kind of choice I would have easily made as a captain or a major in the war.

But this isn't the war, I remind myself with a sigh. *This is peacetime.* And in peacetime, even the most careful of decisions can get ripped to shreds. Twisted for political gain.

I remind myself that I chose this way of living. Or it chose me. I'm still not sure which.

"And then there's the gala for the Luther Center Honors tonight. Trieste, Merlin, and Kay have made a few notes on your speech—would you like me to squeeze in Uri this morning for final revisions?"

Uri Katz is my head speechwriter, and he's damn good. Normally, I want his input at every stage of a speech. But today is not a normal day, and today more than ever I'm feeling the bitter irony of speaking at the Luther Center—a foundation dedicated to promoting the arts and sciences that began with an endowment from my dead father, President Penley Luther. A father that only a few people in this world know is mine.

"Any word from Berlin?" I ask. "It should come through today or tomorrow, and it'll be by unofficial channels."

Belvedere shakes his head. "Not yet, sir."

"Okay." I hand him the folder back. "We're changing the day. Tell Lana to compile any information from her briefing and put it on my desk. Have Gawayne send the PDB digitally, reschedule the prime minister. I trust Uri to revise the speech on his own; I'll tweak it later if I think it needs it. Something big happened last night, and our staff meeting is first thing now, got it?"

"Got it," Belvedere murmurs, already typing into his iPhone.

"High school and widows stay, everything else gets bumped to tomorrow, please. I'll go to the gala tonight—see if I can call the prime minister from the car on the way there, now that I think of it."

My body man is nodding, tapping on the screen. "Anything else?"

"I want Merlin in the Residence as soon as possible." I glance at the window by the weight machine; the pink dawn is glowing into the hot orange of morning. "He'll be awake."

"Done."

We walk out of the gym together, making for the stairs to the second floor. "And, Belvedere?"

"Yes, Mr. President?"

"The moment my wife's plane from New York touches down, I want to know."

"Yes, sir."

I touch his shoulder, and he looks at me, his young face a

combination of honored and vulnerable and wary. It reminds me so much of a young Embry that I have to swallow.

"Thank you, Ryan," I say quietly. "For all your help. I would be nothing without you. It was true during the campaign, and it's even more true now."

"Sir," Belvedere stammers. "You know that's not true at all."

"I wish you knew," I say with a rueful smile, "how weak I really am." And then I leave him to start my first day in ten years without my prince.

I feel Merlin approaching.

It was one thing I was better at than most in Carpathia, that feeling. It's not simply seeing or hearing, it's not guessing, it's not even really deduction. The ability to feel your way through a forest, through a silent village full of blinking eyes and closed mouths. To feel your way through a battle.

When I came to the capitol, it served me well. I already knew how to be still through the bullshit, through the noise, and I could feel the lies and the plans people spun around me. It's not actually battle in the true sense of the word, and thank God for that. I've taken enough lives, killed enough enemies, watched enough buildings burn. Sometimes when my staff is caught up in the daily cycle of panic and exhilaration that defines life here, I remind them that this is not really war. What we do matters, but more importantly, everybody gets to live. There's time to fix things, time to think.

Everything terrible here can be undone. That wasn't true in Carpathia.

And if I'm honest, I crave the extra challenge. In the mountains, a person was either a friend or a foe, and there was no other option. But here the foes are friendly, and the friends are scheming. No one fits into a black or white box;

their words are layered, their intentions nuanced. It takes every neuron, every ounce of my perception and charisma and self-control to lead here. It keeps me strong. Alert.

I try to gather my perception and self-control now, using them like plaster to cover over all the new cracks in my soul. My old friend will see them anyway, as he seems to see everything, but I'd rather not make it easy for him.

"This will be short," I say once Merlin actually walks through the door. "We've got the staff meeting in less than an hour."

Merlin nods, studying me, his dark eyes taking in my undoubtedly tired-looking face, my hair still wet from my shower, the suit jacket I haven't bothered to put on yet.

"Have a seat, Merlin, please."

I stay standing as he sits. My muscles ache from my workout, my dick aches from being hard and angry all night, my chest aches from missing Embry and Greer. I take a moment to imagine her kneeling at my feet, my hand sliding through all that silky gold hair, her face turned in to rub against my thigh, and something inside me settles.

I sit too.

"Embry quit last night. The official resignation will come from his office today."

Merlin looks unsurprised, although he makes a noise that a less observant person might translate as shock. "How terrible. I suppose it's to prepare to run against you?"

"Yes."

"And his replacement?"

I pinch the bridge of my nose, a headache creeping behind my eyes. "Kay, of course. I'd like to ask Trieste to fill her spot as chief of staff."

"And your new press secretary if she accepts?"

"I don't think Uri wants it, but we'll ask him first. When he says no, we'll go outside staff. I want someone young and smart, and we've got enough white men on the team, so let's keep that in mind as we look."

"Agreed," Merlin says calmly.

"Did you know this was going to happen?"

"Of course not," he answers. He's a good liar, but not good enough. I feel the ripple of omission in his words, the studied guilelessness of his face. He knew something. He's never withheld anything from me politically, but Embry straddles the line of political and personal. And when it comes to the personal, I think Merlin's withheld many things from me over the years.

I change subjects. "You told Embry he couldn't be with me."

Merlin lifts his chin. "It was wartime, Maxen. Sacrifices had to be made."

"But that one?"

The mundane whoosh of the air-conditioning kicks on. Outside the window, the district is already a swamp of hot metal and steaming asphalt. Despite the whirr of cold air blowing through the vents, I feel the August heat trying to beat down the walls of the building, and I suddenly feel very, very tired.

"I told him the truth, nothing more," Merlin says simply. "It was always up to him what he chose to do with that truth."

"You knew him. You knew if you presented it like I needed protecting that he would protect me."

"You did need protecting."

"Goddammit, from *what*, Merlin?" I take a breath, trying to sheathe the knife of my anger. "I didn't ask for anyone to watch out for my career. I would have accepted the consequences of loving Embry, no matter what they were."

"You needed protecting from yourself," Merlin replies, "from this very attitude. You were made for that war and you were made for this." His finger comes down deliberately on the arm of his chair, indicating this room. This building. This city. "I'm sorry, but that couldn't be wasted."

"Wasted," I repeat. "Wasted on what? Love? A happy life? Have you ever been in love, Merlin? Do you even know what you're talking about?"

To my surprise, Merlin's eyes flash a hot, furious onyx. "I've been in love," he says in a careful voice. "But I always knew my life was a lonely path. I did what needed to be done, so that I could do this work with you. For you."

"So was Embry revenge? You gave up love to work for me, and I had to be denied the same thing?"

"You're tired and you're hurting, so I'll excuse the accusation that I've orchestrated the intentional destruction of your happiness. Lest you forget, if you'd married Embry all those years ago, you wouldn't have Greer."

That stops my anger cold in its tracks.

"Embry said the same thing last night," I say, looking down at my hands. "You're both right."

I wouldn't be complete without her, and neither would Embry. She was made to be my wife, and we were made to be a three.

Merlin stands up. "If that's all?"

"It's not," I say, although I wish it were. I wish I'd woken up this morning with my wife on one side of me and my lover on the other. I wish that the ghosts of everything I've ever done wrong, and everything my father did wrong too, would stop haunting me. "My son."

Merlin stiffens, and for the first time this morning, I realize I've truly caught him off guard.

"Tell me you didn't know," I nearly plead. "Tell me that you wouldn't keep this from me."

Merlin is struggling; I see it in his face. Feel it inside his mind, like a wind is blowing all his thoughts away like dry leaves on a tree. I also feel the moment he decides to tell me the truth.

"I'm not proud of it," he finally says, meeting my gaze. I see something much, much older than his fortysome years in his crow-black eyes. "I had thought…well, I'd hoped… not to repeat old sins. Not to make the mistakes of the past."

"Old sins? Are you talking about my father?"

He blinks, as if coming back to himself. "Yes," he answers, but he's lying again, and I'm not sure why.

"You don't have to protect me from Penley's mistakes, Merlin. I would have given anything not to make them myself."

"You couldn't have risen very far with a child born out of wedlock, not in politics, and I had ambitions for you even then," Merlin says. "Before we officially met, I had my eye on you. Morgan wanted to hide it from you, and Vivienne and I saw no reason why it would help anyone—you or Morgan—to stop her from hiding the truth."

"We didn't know back then Morgan was my sister, Merlin. It would have been okay."

He doesn't answer right away, and a cold suspicion tugs at me. "Merlin."

He takes a breath, those black eyes looking ancient. "I knew before then, Maxen. I've known for a long time."

"Jesus Christ." This new betrayal is like a spear through my side. "How did you know?"

"My first job out of university was at a law firm in Manhattan responsible for carrying out certain provisions in Penley Luther's will. They involved conferring a settlement on Imogen Leffey's youngest child. When I found you, it wasn't hard to see that you were his child as well. You have Imogen's coloring, but your features, your bearing…it's all Penley."

"When you found me," I echo his earlier words, staring at him.

"The fair. Do you remember? You'd just pulled a sword from a stone."

I've thought of that moment almost every day since it happened, of the tall stranger who knew my name, but time had blurred away all the details, scrubbed away the reality of the moment. It had become something like a dream. "It was you."

"I found you, and then I found Althea Colchester and left her the settlement funds. Didn't you ever wonder how she was able to pay for your college tuition?"

"She said there'd been a scholarship…" I trail off. "But it was you. And Penley."

"Yes."

"But if you knew all those years ago, why didn't you tell me? Why didn't you warn me? Why didn't you tell me never to sleep with anyone who had the last name Leffey?"

"I wrongfully thought you were too young to hear such a dire warning. To know the truth about your real parents. And so I was too late. As always." And he smiles ruefully, as if at some private joke with himself.

"How did you learn about it?"

He looks away from me, to the window, his eyes going distant. "Nimue. I offered to help her family in any way I could, and together Vivienne and I made sure Lyr's guardianship was transferred discreetly and legally. In fact, I was even the one to suggest the name. It's Welsh," he explains, his eyes still fixed on some far-off point in the past. "*From the sea*. I thought if I was going to make the mistakes of the past, I could at least make them thoroughly."

"I don't understand."

His eyes snap back to mine and clear. "You will. But not yet."

"No more secrets, Merlin. You had no right to keep Lyr from me." Pain tightens my chest again and I pause. "No more secrets."

"No more," Merlin agrees, "save one."

"No."

"I will tell you, I promise you that. But not now."

I throw my hands up in the air. "When? Next week? Next month?"

"In two and a half years."

For a moment, I think he's joking and I laugh. But he doesn't join me in laughing, and I see that his face is completely serious.

"Two and a half years," I say incredulously. "You think I owe you that? After what you've done to Embry and me? After hiding my son from me?"

"I don't think you owe me anything. I recognize that I've done cruel or manipulative things to you and the people in your life, but it's always been in your best interest—in the best interest of everyone. Which is why you will have to wait. Not because you owe me, but because you don't have a choice."

I stand up. "Tell me how I'm supposed to trust you. Tell me how I'm supposed to go into that staff meeting and turn to you for advice."

Merlin gives me a small, sad smile. "You will trust me because it's in your nature to trust. You will turn to me for advice because I've never steered you into a decision that would harm this country or its citizens. The real tragedy of your life, Maxen, is that you will never stop having faith in the people around you, even when they hurt you over and over again."

He takes his leave, and I take a breath.

You will never stop having faith in the people around you, even when they hurt you over and over again.

It feels like a curse.

I grab my jacket and follow him downstairs.

CHAPTER 4
ASH

NOW

THE STAFF MEETING IS HARD. I KNEW IT WOULD BE, AND YET sitting in that chair and looking at the faces of my friends and allies—Kay, Trieste, Uri, with Belvedere just outside the door, and Luc and Lamar outside the windows standing guard, and Merlin looking on—it all serves to underscore exactly who isn't here.

My prince.

It was always something I'd shared with him, this pipe dream of running for president. Most candidates pick a VP to satisfy the base or win over the moderates or some combination of the two. But not me. From the very beginning, I made it clear that I wasn't taking a single step forward without Embry by my side. I was with Jenny then, so there wasn't…there couldn't be what we used to have. But I needed him all the same. He was my brother in arms, my former lover, my best friend. He'd grown up in politics; his mother was a powerful governor; he understood the strategies of schmoozing and courting better than I did.

And I needed him. I just—I just needed him.

And now he's not here.

Kay accepts the position I offer, so does Trieste. Uri declines, more comfortable with screens and paper than being grilled by reporters, and we talk over our approach for finding a new press secretary. Kay and Trieste immediately plan to interface with Embry's office to see if they can get a copy of his statement before it's released, we hammer out a media strategy for his departure, and we agree to keep the gala speech free of any mention of it, although Embry's resignation will dominate the news cycle. Probably for the next month. We won't try to sidestep the narratives and we also won't assign blame. I can see this approach chafes at Trieste, who'd rather try to control the story from the beginning, but it's not how I run my administration. Embry and the press can say whatever they want—we'll stick to honesty, restraint, and dignity.

"We need to think about the next election," Kay says crisply, making a few notes on her tablet. The sunlight pouring through the windows from the Rose Garden strikes bronze notes in her deep brown skin and outlines every natural curl corkscrewing from her head. Her suit is tailored to perfection, every sharp line echoing her high cheekbones and delicate jaw. For a moment, I think of the girl I grew up with, the one with the blue yarn braids and the baggy jeans. The older sister who defended me from every bully, every raised eyebrow at the adopted brother, every busybody mother at Mass who wanted to make sure Althea was teaching me my rosaries and chaplets. And I'm overcome with profound gratitude and debt. For her undeserved affection and loyalty. For her drive and intellect and untiring work.

I stand up and give her a hug, interrupting the flow of

the meeting. I don't care. Everything is falling apart, but Kay has been here for me since I was four years old and I need to hug her. Everyone stops what they're doing to stare.

"Thank you," I tell Kay. "You're my favorite sister."

"I'm your only sister," she says dryly as I pull away from the hug.

I'm about to tell her that's not technically the truth when there's a knock at the door. I straighten up as Belvedere pokes his head inside, looking abashed.

"I'm sorry, sir, but it's the vice president on the line. He's asked to speak with you."

Something twists inside my chest. Excitement or pain, I don't know.

"To formally tender his resignation, I imagine," Merlin says, standing up. "Let's give the president the room."

My staff bustles up to leave, Kay giving my hand a quick squeeze and Merlin sending me an inscrutable look. Then I'm alone in the Oval Office with a ringing phone.

My hand shakes as I pick it up.

"Colchester."

"You know it's me" comes Embry's irritated voice. I soak up every sharp consonant, every drawling vowel. It's only been twelve hours and yet I miss him with the whining pangs of a starving dog.

Embry goes on. "Answer the phone like an actual human."

"Come over here and I'll talk to you like a man."

Embry laughs, and as always the sound unlocks every door to my heart. He and Greer, they laugh so much, and the sound of it is like joy itself. "Ash, we both know what would happen if I were in that office alone with you."

"And what would that be?"

"We'd fight. You'd ask me not to leave. I'd tell you I had no choice. We'd find new ways to hurt each other. It wouldn't be pretty."

"But finding new ways to hurt you is always so pretty to me, little prince."

A short inhale is my only answer. I picture those ice blue eyes going hooded with desire, those firm lips pouting ever so slightly with need.

I sit down behind my desk, running a palm along the smooth wood as if it were my lover's back. "Let me tell you exactly what would happen if you were here. You'd walk in here and try to stay standing, because you would think it put us on equal footing. Because you wouldn't allow yourself to relax around me. And I'd let you stand because it wouldn't matter."

"It wouldn't?"

"Do I have any less power when I'm sitting than when I'm standing? Am I a different man?"

"It wouldn't be about you," Embry says impatiently. "The standing would be for me. To demonstrate that we are different now, that *I* am different."

"But you're not, my Patroclus. How many times have you been ready to fight me, ready to struggle and bruise to prove to yourself that you don't want me, only to end up begging for my cock?"

"And you think that's what would happen this time?"

"I know it's what would happen," I say in a low voice. My cock lengthens down the leg of my pants as I imagine it. "I'd let you stand long enough to prove my point, that I still own you, sitting or standing, and then I'd make you get on your knees and apologize to me for breaking my heart."

Embry's voice is silky when he responds. "Apologize how?"

"By taking my cum down your throat."

"It wouldn't be enough. Not to earn your forgiveness."

"You're right," I say, rubbing a palm over my erection. I'm hard enough that I can feel the heavy flare of my crown through the fabric. "After I fucked your mouth, I'd haul you up by the back of your neck and bend you over the desk. I'd take off my belt and stripe your ass red for every time you've left me."

"I'd like to see you try," Embry says, and the breathlessness in his voice gives him away. He'd like to see me try as much as I'd like to see me try—which is quite a lot.

"I'd have to hold you down. Maybe you'd be able to twist away, but I'd catch you and then we'd both fall to the floor in a tangled heap. And then I'd fuck you until you sprayed the carpet with your release. Until you were spent and loose for me."

"And then?" Embry asks with a hitch in his voice.

"I'd use you until you begged me to stop."

He sounds like he can't breathe. "You know I'd never ask you to stop."

"Then I'd fuck your hole until I was done. I'd make you walk out of the Oval Office with a torn suit and my semen still hot inside you."

"Holy shit, Ash," he groans.

"Are you jerking off right now?"

"Yes. Are you?"

"Almost," I say, unbuckling my belt. My cock is hot when I pull it out, hot and stone fucking hard. I angle my chair away from the windows behind me, even though I know the Secret Service agents outside the windows won't break protocol and look in without a reason. "Now it's your turn."

"My turn to what?"

"Tell me what you would do to me if you could. Tell me what would have happened last night if you hadn't stopped it."

"God," Embry breathes. I can hear the sound of skin on skin, that pale aristocratic hand wrapped around his beautiful dick. "You would have… You were going to…"

I grunt as I close my hand around my own dick, giving it a few rough tugs. "Yes."

"I would have bent you over your desk too, only…" He trails off, as if catching his breath. "I wouldn't beat you. I'd spread your cheeks apart and kiss you where I wanted you. I would use my tongue where I want to use my cock. I'd tease you with my tongue, pull each testicle into my mouth, I'd cover each cheek with sucks and kisses. And then I'd turn you over onto your back and do the same to your belly and your thighs. You'd have your hand in my hair—because even though it's supposed to be for me, you would still remind me that you're in control. That you're the one giving it to me."

His words hook into the deepest pit in my belly, the pit that defines me. The idea of him worshipping the most hidden crevices of my body, cleaning them with his tongue, of making him do all that with my hand on his head as I deign to give him something I've cruelly denied him for years…

Fuck. I stop stroking for a moment, just so I don't go off like a teenage boy.

"Then what would you want, Embry? To fuck me from behind? Hard and mean, to punish me for wanting to keep you? Or would you want to see my face and go slow, so you can mark every moan I make as you push inside of me?"

"Jesus Christ," Embry says in a choked voice. "All of it. Both ways. Every way."

"I'd want to see your face," I tell him quietly. "I'd want to remember it for the rest of my life."

"Ash, tell me you're going to come too. I want to hear it."

I hesitate. I'm desperate to come, so desperate that my cock is swollen and leaking, but I know how I'll feel after I release into my hand. Empty. Hurt. Unsatisfied. The dark pit deep inside me still hungry and growling for something more elemental, something more powerful.

Scarier. Dirtier.

I can climax just fine without my lover's surrender, without exerting my control, and I can even enjoy it in a fleeting way. But I can't really *finish* without it; I won't be sated and replete until I get what I need.

But this isn't about what you need—or it's not only *about that.* I promised to take care of him. Which means I need to put his needs above my own.

"Please," Embry says, and I can tell he's so very close himself. "Give me this one thing."

"What haven't I ever given you?" I sigh as I slide my cock back into my closed fist. I've given this man everything I could. My heart. My Greer. My entire life.

"Then this shouldn't be hard to give," he replies jaggedly. "Oh fuck, Ash. I'm gonna come. I wish I were inside you, filling you up—*shit.*"

He gives me a broken moan as he ejaculates, and I moan as well, imagining his fantasy. His face creased in pained pleasure as he thrusts into me, the feeling of owning him completely by giving him the very last slice of myself. Coming all over my own belly as I let him use my hole and then making him lick me clean.

"Ash, let me hear you," he whispers. "It's my last day in this office and I've got cum all over me and just—please. I want to hear you."

I let him hear me, wedging the phone between my shoulder and my head so I can pull my pants down farther. I speed up my fist, tightening around my organ, beating off hard enough to make noise. The pressure behind my cock builds and builds, and it's not what I want or what I need, but I won't refuse Embry this. Not when I don't know what the future will bring.

"What are you thinking about?" he asks. "What are you going to imagine as you unload?" His words are curious, his voice hungry, and I'm hungry for his hunger, jealous for his attention. I want all of him, always, mine and mine and mine forever.

"I'm going to imagine fucking you again. Greer is there, and she's out of her mind watching us, her fingers buried deep in her cunt. You beg me to let you inside her, and you promise to be a good boy for me. The best boy."

Embry groans. "God, Ash. You're making me hard again."

"And that's how we finish, all three of us. You inside Greer's tight pussy and me inside your ass."

A wet sound tells me Embry is jacking off again, using his own ejaculate like lube. That image on top of everything else makes my stomach clench, my dick flare with sudden, heavy heat. It all flashes fast and dirty through my mind: Embry's thick organ, smeared and wet with himself; the feeling of his hole so fucking tight around me; the firm rounds of his ass against my hips every time I push into him; Greer's pussy so wet I can see her thighs glistening; her nipples rosy and needy and erect; Embry's back rumbling against my bare chest as he groans out his release; the three of us in one sweaty, needy, forceful tangle, stealing pleasure and rubbing friction.

My boy and my girl, my prince and my princess. Mine and mine and mine forever.

"Yeah," Embry says. "I'm gonna come again, I'm gonna—" He bites off his own words and gasps, and it's the image of cum spurting all over his hand and pants and tie that does me in. Yanking my pocket square from my suit just in time, I hold it in front of my cock, and I release with a grunt, ejaculating into the silk with heavy, unending spurts.

"Embry," I manage. "Fuck. Embry."

"Yeah?" he breathes. "Yeah?"

"God, it feels—wish you were here to see—fuck." It's like I can't stop coming, and I feel each contraction at the base of my spine with unabashed pleasure, watching my thick length judder and jerk as I spill my seed. So much, so much, and I want it to keep going forever, to share this sticky, dirty moment with Embry forever, just the two of us with our needy cocks and even needier hearts.

But all too soon it's over, my cock slowly going still, my pocket square ruined, Embry still breathing hard on the other end of the line. It comes faster than I thought it would—the unsatisfied restlessness, the emptiness, the heat pooling deep in my groin letting me know that I'll be hard up for it until I can slake my thirst. I close my eyes and lean back in my chair, trying to breathe through it. It's okay that it's not enough, I tell myself. It was about what Embry needed, not me, and God knows few things are enough for me.

"I'm still hard," Embry says, bringing me back into the present. "It's like you're some kind of cock magician."

"I'm not a magician," I say softly. "I'm the king of your body, and your body knows it. It won't rest until it's mine again."

And mine won't rest either.

A long-suffering sigh. "The reason I didn't meet you face-to-face is because I didn't want to end up ashamed and covered in my own semen," Embry replies. "And yet."

"And yet."

"I know I'm doing the right thing, Ash, and I'm doing it for the right reasons. I can want you and fight you at the same time."

"I know that," I say heavily. "You've been doing it since the day we met."

"Are you furious with me?" he asks.

I finish cleaning myself off and drop the pocket square into the trash can. I tuck my still-hard cock into my pants and zip up, and I buckle my belt and check my tie for stains. And then I finally answer. "I'm lots of things right now."

"But furious is one of them."

"Yes. But I'm also guilty and worried and hurt, and hurt is the biggest one by far. I love you, and you're leaving me. You're leaving me because you think I'm a coward and that I don't love my wife enough to keep her safe. And by extension, you think you must love her more because you're willing to put innocents at risk to protect her."

"Don't put words in my mouth," he says. His voice is surly when he answers, and it almost makes me smile. Still the same petulant, pretty lieutenant I pinned against a wall all those years ago. "You think you're so noble and so fucking stoic, but it just means that you choose honor over emotion every time you start to feel something."

"I just confessed to an entire list of things I *do* feel, Embry."

He sighs. "That's not what I mean. I mean that you're never vulnerable; I mean that you never bend, you never break, sometimes you're as inaccessible as the sun, and I used to worship you for it. I still want to."

"Then don't leave," I say. Beg. I'm not above begging, if that's what he wants. If he wants to see his king on his knees, weeping and tearing his clothes, I'll do it. I'll do anything. "Stay. I can't do this without you." I take a deep breath. "I never could, you know. You are my strength. My courage. And I need you."

"I can't," Embry says joylessly. "It's what I have to do in order to live with myself. It's what I believe in."

"You used to believe in me," I say, and just saying those words out loud rips open something new underneath my ribs. I didn't know how much I relied on that belief until it was gone. How much I craved his trust and his faith. It makes me want to do anything to be worthy of it again, *anything*, but then I remember that I can't. Remember that I can't say fuck everything and make winning Embry back my sole aim. I'm in charge of keeping an entire nation safe, the people who believe in me *and* the people who don't, and I can't risk war and death for just one.

As much as that seems like a good idea right now.

"Will you say goodbye to Greer for me?" he asks, breaking the silence. "I…I don't think she'll want to talk to me after she finds out I'm going to run against you."

"And that you're marrying the woman who arranged for her abduction."

He exhales as if he'd forgotten. "And that."

"No."

"Ash—"

"I won't talk to her for you, Embry, and here's why: we made vows on my wedding night. The three of us. Together. We promised each other that we would try, that we wouldn't run away."

"I also said we had to be honest the minute it stopped working."

"We said we would love each other as long as we could, in all the ways that we could, as best as we could. Maybe you've stopped loving me, but have you stopped loving Greer?"

"I haven't—" My heart jolts hopefully, but then he interrupts himself, and I feel the meaning of his next words like a halberd through the chest. "I still love Greer."

I rub my thumb across my forehead, counting one breath, then two. Yes, I'm still alive. Yes, I heard him make sure not to say that he loved me. And yes, I can do the right thing even though all I want is to storm over to his office right now and refuse to leave until we're both covered in sweat and cum.

"If you still love Greer, then I don't consider you released from your vows to her. You still owe it to her to try."

"You're not the keeper of my vows," he mumbles.

"Fine. Then I'm reminding you of them. You want to be

free of any promise to love me? You can be free. But I'm not freeing myself from my vow of loving you, and I doubt Greer will either, once she comes to terms with it all."

"What are you saying?"

"I'm saying that maybe we aren't a three right now and maybe we'll never be again. But you and Greer still have my blessing to love each other as fully as you used to."

"Are you…condoning our infidelity?" He sounds so suspicious, and that almost makes me smile too, despite everything, because it's so very Embry Moore to be suspicious. I can easily picture those blue eyes narrowed in wariness, that mouth pulling into a doubtful frown.

"I'm a jealous lover, Embry, and an even more jealous husband. I will be jealous and it will hurt, but at the end of the day I don't consider it cheating, not really. I was there in that room too; I knew what it meant to promise what we did. And to me it means that we all still try as hard as we can to love each other."

"So if Greer and me…?"

"Yes."

"And you and Greer…"

"Will continue to live as man and wife."

There's a pause before he asks it, and I feel that pause with every cell in my body. "And us?"

I try to keep my voice steady as I ask, "What about us?"

"God, you know what I'm asking."

"Not loving you isn't on the table for me, Patroclus."

Embry doesn't answer, but he doesn't have to. I didn't say it expecting an answer; I only said it so that he would know. My cell phone buzzes in my pocket and I pull it out to check it. It's Belvedere.

Mrs. Colchester's plane just landed. She'll be at the White House in forty minutes.

Greer.

Something deep inside me unlocks for the first time since last night, clicking open walls and doors that I didn't even know I'd slammed shut. Letting out mercies and honesties and tendernesses that I would have kept hidden out of hurt or guardedness just moments before.

But that hurt and guardedness has to stop. I'm here in this chair listening to Embry resign because I've taken too much for granted, his love and his faith and his loyalty, and today is the day when that changes. I'm going to do better, love him harder, prove over and over again that I deserve his devotion and trust, and I'm going to do it even if it still means he won't ever come back.

I'm going to do it even if it's the last thing I do.

"Embry, I am sorry," I say softly. "For whatever it's worth. I wish I'd known what you'd given up for me. I would have spared you that."

"I know you would have. But there's more at stake now; you understand that, right? This is about Melwas and Carpathia, about our country, about Greer—not just you and me."

I stare at my hands, scarred and big on the gleaming desk in front of me. Those are things I can't apologize for, and he knows I won't. Two good men on either side of a moral swamp, and there's no bridge. Not even my love, sure and strong and bedrock, can bridge it for us. All I can do now is try to fight for both—to be a king and to be *his* king—and to hope I get it right.

"I'll see you around, Embry."

"Yeah. You too."

And with the hollow click of the line going dead, I accept that this fight is coming whether I want it or not.

Chapter 5
Ash

THEN

How does a man end up loving two people?

As a young child—years before I felt desire as a bodily thing—I found myself fascinated with Jareth and Sarah from the movie *Labyrinth*. Him, supple and almost feline, lithe and dangerous and drenched in a kind of knowledge that I could only barely begin to apprehend, and her so clear-eyed and rosy mouthed and *strong*, this contradiction between delicacy and iron will.

Yes, both of them enraptured me as a little boy, and when I saw the movie again at the awkward, unfurling age of thirteen, watching both characters made me flush hot. I remember checking the basement—paneled in fake wood and studded with scratchy chairs and an even scratchier sofa—to make sure I was completely alone, and then I let myself feel the creeping edges of that flush all over my body.

Later that night, alone in my room, I rolled onto my stomach and pressed my hips into the mattress, mindlessly rubbing into the soft sheets. My mind was a jumble of ideas and images and thoughts: the sleek lines of David Bowie's body, oozing invitation; Jennifer Connelly's pink, pretty mouth. But more than all of those things, I thought of one scene in particular, one line. The part when Jareth says to Sarah, *Just fear me, love me, do as I say…and I will be your slave.*

Those words had rung through me like a gong, calling awake something new and sleepy-eyed and hungry and eager. I wanted to touch and be touched by Jareth, but that was only the edge of my lust; I wanted to *be* him. I wanted to find someone with a pretty mouth and demand their obedience and affection in return for my heart. I wanted to own the world like Jareth owned his kingdom; I wanted to be so powerful that I could make someone smile or cry or dance with me, not out of coercion, but because they loved me so much they'd surrender everything just to endure the whims of my attention.

And if they did that…I'd be undone. Theirs. My heart in their hands forever.

The first time I ever gave myself an orgasm, this was what I was thinking of.

Like Embry, I knew that I wanted both boys and girls in my bed from a fairly early age.

Unlike Embry, I didn't live in a city where that was common, at least not when I was growing up, and so there were several years when I didn't know what to do with my desires—both the queer and the kinky. Not because I was tormented by them; I felt too much clarity and—if you can excuse the spiritual overtones—too much *rightness* for that. Nothing in Althea's home or within myself ever painted my desires as aberrant or immoral.

If I liked boys as well as girls, then that was how I needed to live. If the idea of power seeped into me like sunlight and grew a crop of desires so fretfully preoccupying that I could barely make it through reading *The Taming of the Shrew* in class without getting hard, then that was how I was made. If I sometimes had to bite the inside of my cheek to keep from biting the good Catholic girls I dated, if I had to fist my hands as they crawled onto my lap to keep from spanking and grabbing and bruising, then that was fine too.

And if there weren't boys ripe for plucking in my working-class neighborhood, well, then I could also live with that…at least until I left the neighborhood for the greener pastures of college. It wasn't in my nature to brood or wish for something out of reach, or at least it wasn't in my nature then.

College came, and with it, for the first time, boys. A kiss stolen in the back of a liquor store, a drunken Princeton rub at a frat house—even a professor once, right there in his office, his glasses falling off his face and my skin stinging with the feel of his beard as we kissed against his bookshelf. There were flashes of connection, even something like a boyfriend for a few short weeks, but nothing stuck. I began to consider that maybe I wasn't capable of love or romantic connection—that I could fool around but not feel, that I could spend hours learning someone's mouth with my own but have no desire to learn their mind. Maybe every college boy was the same as me or maybe I was broken, but whatever the reason, I spent those years alone, the occasional impersonal fumble lighting up my landscape like a flash of lightning and then plunging me back into darkness.

That all sounds so grim, and I don't mean it to be, because I wasn't depressed or lonely. I had friends. I had fun. I didn't feel the lack of passion like a weight or a burden. It was only at night, my homework done and my eyes tired, when my mind wandered back to Jareth's words, back to the *fear me* and *love me* and *do as I say*. I wanted to own, I wanted to possess, I wanted to bruise willing flesh with rough fingers and push someone down to their knees and have them like it.

I wanted someone to look up at me with their whole world in their eyes.

In my human sexuality class, we learned the term *aromantic*, and so I thought I'd figured it out. I was an aromantic bisexual, and I could be content with my life, with friendships and meaning beyond romance, and it would be fine. Surely it was telling that I hadn't fallen in love by the time I'd finished college? Surely it was a sign that the only thing that made my heart beat faster, that made me think of things like vows and *forever*, involved kneeling and arched throats and the most sinful kinds of discipline? That wasn't romance—not at all. It was just what I had to think about in order to climax when I fucked my fist in the shower.

The problem was that the two things were—and still are—hopelessly tangled together for me: my capacity for love and my craving for power. And those in turn were, and are, tangled with my bisexuality. Did I fool around with more boys than girls in college because they liked the rougher stuff, even if it still wasn't as rough or cruel as I wanted? Did I date more girls in high school because it was so easy to indulge in small exercises of power? Picking the restaurant? Driving the car? Paying the check? All of it was rooted in culture, in how society told me the ways boys should be with boys and the ways boys should be with girls. Yet so much of it was rooted inside me as well, in this tangle I couldn't unravel and wouldn't attempt to unravel at the expense of a lover's comfort or safety. It might seem laughable for a devout Catholic to indulge so guiltlessly in debauchery but balk at power exchange—but I've always believed the heart of Christian sexual ethics was consent and respect. And so with every lover, I poured all of my energy into those two things. Negotiating consent. Engaging respectfully. Even my hottest, dirtiest encounters started with questions and answers.

Is this okay?

God, yes.

Can I see how wet you are?

Fuck, please.

Can I rub you where you're hard?

Hurry, please, hurry.

And every encounter ended with kisses and a glass of water and help cleaning up if necessary. For the baby dom in me, the after part was my favorite, because that's when my lovers were as I liked them best: grateful and pliant and so very, very sweet.

But because I took consent seriously, it meant I rarely allowed my darker side out to play. Never, actually.

Never until Prague.

The final piece grew inside of me at the same time as all of this, something just as insistent and hardy and impervious to outside damage as was my bisexuality, and it was this old-fashioned idea of honor. A sense that there was an objective standard of goodness and honesty and morality, that justice was necessary, that fairness was important, that safety shouldn't be a privilege assigned by skin color or gender. I say old-fashioned not because I believe justice and safety have ever been unpopular, but because I believed in them with such a naive, almost Victorian, zeal. I believed that honor was available for the earning so long as you did the right things, said the right things, *believed* the right things. That was how you became honorable. That was when you could feel noble.

It was an idea that died in the valleys of Carpathia.

But that's not important now. What's important is that

I couldn't escape this idea that it wouldn't be honorable to share a bed with someone if I couldn't do it honestly. If I had to pretend to be something else, to want different things, if I had to close my eyes and imagine more in order to come. I recognize now how heteronormative this belief was—even with bisexual desire—centering meaning on penetration when really sex is a spectrum of activities that far exceeds the narrow boundaries of intercourse. But back then, I believed there was a difference between the grinding, sweaty encounters I'd had and taking someone to bed to intentionally join my body to theirs. And however mistaken that belief was, it braided itself into me until I didn't think about it any longer; I didn't question it. I wanted my first time to be with all the things I'd dreamed of, and if I couldn't have it the way I wanted, then I would rather not have it at all.

Which is how I ended up a virgin in a war zone.

Anyway, I'm telling you all of this, about *Labyrinth* and Catholicism and boys and honor, so that you understand what a precise constellation of unmet desire I had become. So that you can see how I'd grown around this empty space, keeping something clear and untouched without even really knowing why. I was holding a door open to a room I didn't know I had, keeping a hidden garden free of weeds, sheltering a hollow meant for someone or something I couldn't yet see.

And then came Embry Moore.

And then came Greer Galloway.

How does a man end up loving two people, you ask? This is how.

CHAPTER 6
ASH

NOW

I'M WAITING FOR GREER WHEN SHE WALKS INTO THE Residence.

I shouldn't be, honestly. I should be back in the West Wing, I should be with Merlin and Kay and Trieste, I should be meeting and working and planning, but I'm not. Surely I'm allowed a day? A couple of hours? To come to grips with this?

But even as I think it, I feel irritated at myself. No, I'm not allowed those things; I've never allowed myself those things. I didn't allow myself sick days or rest days during the war, and I certainly didn't give myself breaks during the campaign—the only exception being the two weeks before Jenny died and the day of her funeral.

There's something about denying myself that's satisfying in a deep, purging sort of way. I'm not masochistic: I don't enjoy the pain for the pain's sake, and furthermore, I don't need pain to help me access vulnerability or emotion or connection. But the pain is proof of my discipline, and the flare of misery is evidence of my self-control. When I marched through Carpathia burning with fever, when I shook hands on the campaign trail while my wife's grave was still a pile of fresh dirt…every moment that I persevered, every second that I chose strength over weakness, was testimony to a truth I couldn't live without: that I was worthy of the life I'd built. Worthy of the trust of others. I had earned it, and I was strong enough to keep it.

Until last night, I thought being strong was enough. I thought caging all my weaknesses—anger and fear and vulnerability—meant I was a better person for it, but I see that now for what it really is, which is the pride of a man addicted to control. Perhaps I'm not boastful; perhaps I'm humble in every other respect, but when it comes to discipline and sacrifice, I've taken great pride indeed.

Fix this, goes the thrumming headache creeping behind my eyes. *Fix this*, goes my heartbeat, beating wildly still for Embry and his blue eyes. *Fix this*, goes my pulse, a staccato rhythm, reminding me that I'm alive and strong and that it's my job to keep my kingdom together.

But it's not as simple as laying down my pride, you see. If it were, Embry would be back in my arms right now. The problem is that I still know I'm right. War isn't a game; it's not a declaration of love or proof of devotion. When it is unnecessary, it is the worst sin a man can commit because it's not just death, it's the grossest and most careless kind of waste. It's rubble and fire and rape and lives forever upturned, and that's if the people are lucky—and they are so very rarely lucky.

My little prince thrilled at battle, even craved it sometimes, and so he'll never understand my reluctance. He'll never understand the ghosts that follow me to this day, the women and children and young men who deserved better. I hated the way I felt after a fight—like a live wire, exposed and sparking into the empty air, and I hated the animal I became after, undisciplined and feral with lust. *The opposite of death is desire* I'd read once in a play, and it was as if I needed to make up for every death at my hands with untrammeled excesses of depravity. If Embry remembers nothing else from the war, surely he remembers that. All the times I fucked him like I wanted to tear him limb from limb with my teeth and fingers, like I wanted to conquer his body like it was the next outpost. Those weren't fucks of victory and exhilaration. They were fucks of pure, mindless despair.

All this to say that I'm here in the Residence, somewhere between surrendering my pride and protecting what needs to be done, and when Greer opens the door to our bedroom, I do the only thing I can.

I go and I kneel at her feet.

"Ash?" she asks softly, running her fingers through my hair. I hear and feel her surprise, her gentle pleasure. Never have I done this, never have I wanted or needed to, but right now, it is undeniably right. With my arms wrapping tight around her legs and my face pressed against the sweet curve of her hip and her hand on my head like a priestess conferring a blessing.

I lift my face to hers, and I think for one crystalline, perfect moment that I could live like this forever. Drinking in her silver eyes and long, dark lashes with gold at the very tips, as if her eyelashes remembered too late that they were supposed to be blond. No one is beautiful like Greer; no one else has that same combination of regal poise and secret knowledge and fragility and joy. My young bride, with her pretty pink mouth and her yielding strength, the kind of bride I've craved since I was old enough to crave. And her hair tumbling over her shoulders in a tousled mess of light and dark gold… I revise my earlier wish. I could live forever like this if only I had her near and her hair unbound.

I close my eyes and remind myself not to be selfish. What I want is comfort, her strength and vulnerability laid bare to me, but it would be cruel to demand it after she's come straight from her dead grandfather's house. Instead of biting her thigh through her dress like I want to, I hug her tighter, still gazing up at her face.

"How are you?" I ask. "How can I help?"

Her fingers twirl idly through my hair as she gives me a sad smile. It cracks my heart open to see, that mouth curling in such a melancholy way. When I saw her last October after all those years apart, what struck me most was how sad she seemed. How lonely. Her delicate face arranged in an expression of pained reserve, as if she'd rather die than seek comfort, and I got the sense then that she hadn't smiled or laughed in years, that pretty mouth going long untouched by kisses or possessive fingertips. Nothing gave me greater delight than surprising her, than petting and pleasing her and spoiling her with every display of tender affection that I could dream up. Whenever she laughed, I felt at that moment that I could die satisfied, having made her safe and happy and loved enough to feel joy.

"I'm okay," she answers after a moment of thought. "I'm sad and it hurts knowing he's gone, but...there's something clarifying about death. It's like all the extra stuff gets swept away—anger and hurt and sharp words—and all that's left behind is what matters. And what matters is you and Embry." She shakes her head. "I've been so hard on him when I know better than anyone how cruel Abilene can be."

My chest tightens at the mention of Embry, but I don't speak yet. I let her finish.

She gives me another smile, less sad this time, more rueful. "I'm sorry for keeping us apart these last few weeks. I've been selfish and angry and I don't even know what point it served now. Punishing Embry only punished us, and God knows you least of all deserve to be punished. What was it you said to me on our wedding day? Living without the pain means living without each other? I choose the pain, Ash, and I always will. I choose the three of us, no matter what."

"Greer," I say, muffling my voice with her body as I hold her even tighter. I finally give in to that dark urge and I bite her thigh, just a little nip, just enough to make her whimper and tighten her fingers in my hair. I love her so fucking much, and I want to give her everything—every single thing she wants and needs and wishes for, and all the things she doesn't know to wish for yet—but she wants the one thing that's no longer in my power to give. The three of us.

Once again, the weight of my missteps and my pride and what I know to be right and honorable hangs on me. It feels like a sword too heavy to wield, like a crown too heavy to wear. I can't carry all of this. I can't lose my heart to save my soul. But I must. I have to. Even though, for once, I take no pride in the pain it will cause me.

I stand up and kiss my wife. "Are you really okay?" I ask her, cradling her face in my hands. "Tell me if you aren't."

My tone is authoritative, and her body responds like a flower to the sun, tilting and opening to me. Despite everything, I don't bother to suppress the tendril of satisfaction that curls through me at her response. She's always been like this. Responsive. Open. Frost on a window that you can melt and mar with a single fingertip.

She peers up at me, sliding her hands up my chest. Out of habit I take her wrists in my hands and fold her arms so that they are behind her back, and she gives a small shiver of delight. Suddenly my barely dulled need from earlier comes roaring back, and I'm hard; when I've got her like this, trapped and panting and wary, I feel ten fucking feet tall.

"What's your safe word?" I ask, wrapping one hand

around her forearms so that I can use the other to take her chin between my fingers.

"Maxen," she breathes with fear and with trust and with the whole fucking world in her eyes. She's too good to be true. Too perfect to be real.

I'm hers. Forever.

But then I feel Embry's absence like a living thing, a cold sucking of air and wind where his body should be right now; he should be shaking with need right next to us, his eyes as wild and skittish as an unbroken stallion's, just waiting for the right hand to coax him into obedience.

I was that hand once.

And that thought brings me away from the edge of my need, just enough to remember who I am. A snarled tangle of kink and honor, and honorable kink means consent. Unconditional respect. I owe it to Greer to tell her everything now because it affects her as much as it affects me, and she deserves to know. She deserves everything I can give, in fact, and this simple courtesy is the least of what I owe her.

"I want to play," I say, loosening my grip on her arms and releasing her chin. "But perhaps we shouldn't right now."

She rises up on the balls of her feet and nuzzles her face against my neck, rubbing and making noises like a needy little cat. "Please, Mr. President," she begs, and oh, she begs so beautifully like this.

"Greedy thing," I scold her with a reluctant smile. I can't resist her, and yet I love her too much not to. "We need to talk, angel."

"Can't we talk after? Sir?" She's practically purring now, her fingers seeking out my chest and my belt and my shirt buttons without my express permission, and all I want on this earth right now is to yank her over my lap, flip up her skirt, and spank her for her sauciness.

But I can't yet.

With a quick move, I scoop her up and over my shoulder, her ass up in the air and her legs kicking fruitlessly as I carry her over to the chair by the window and set her on the floor. I snap my fingers, and she drops to her knees so gracefully and gratefully, a relieved smile on her downturned face.

I sit in the chair in front of her kneeling form. "You may look at me," I inform her, and she does immediately with spots of color beginning to bloom on her cheeks. She's excited, and she wants this, and if the world were normal, I'd already be guiding her head onto my waiting cock.

The world's not normal though, and she doesn't even know it yet, which is why I can't. But there's more to this way of life than fucking and spanking, and if we both crave the comfort of the exchange, then there is another way.

"It pleases me to have you like this," I tell her. "It comforts me."

In response, she leans forward and rests her head against my knee with a contented little noise, and I allow her the informality. I enjoy it, this contact, her contentment and trust, the way she acts like there's no place she'd rather be than kneeling at my feet and resting against me. I run a hand through her magic hair, watching the sunlight glint through the strands. She could be anywhere right now—giving lectures at an academic conference or meeting with members of her grandfather's party or doing the endless publicity and charity expected of a First Lady—but for right now, she's chosen to lay all that power and acclaim aside and kneel. It's heady, what that can do to a man.

"I would prefer to talk like this," I say, still playing with her hair. "And I think you would too"—I feel her nod against my thigh, but I keep going—"but I want you to know that you can stand up at any time and talk to me as an equal. You are also permitted to speak freely and ask questions."

This sends the first arrow of suspicion through her, and she lifts her head. "Sir?"

I trace the line of her lower lip with my thumb. "Embry left me today."

I see the moment the words register, the second they transform into terrible, terrible meaning. "What?" she whispers.

Her lips are so soft, and the place where they blush from skin into plump rosiness is unbearably silky. "He visited last night actually, to tell me in person. But he called with his official resignation this morning. He's leaving so he can join the Republican Party and run against me in the next election."

She blinks once, her mouth parting, and I know that she's already grasping all the political and administrative ramifications of this news. The PR, the strategy, the math of states and votes and polls. She's better at that than I am. Better at seeing and understanding when it feels like all I'm good for right now is standing still.

"Kay and Merlin know?" she asks. Then talking mostly to herself, she says, "Of course Kay would know. You've asked her to fill Embry's role, I'm sure. Which means you would ask Trieste to be chief of staff. And what does Merlin say about the election? We'll have to—"

"*We* don't have to do anything," I say in a gentle voice. "Embry left me, Greer, not you. He doesn't have to be your enemy, and I would never ask you to help me campaign against him."

She stares at me. "You must be joking."

"I'm not," I say firmly. "I mean every word of it. Embry loves you and you love him and I love you both. It's my intention to honor that as much as possible."

"But you'll still run, right? You're not stepping aside out of some misguided nobility?"

I smile weakly at that. "It may still be misguided nobility, but no, I'm not stepping aside. I'm afraid that my disagreement with Embry is too fundamental."

She bites her lip for a moment. "Is it about me?"

"Yes."

She waits expectantly for me to elaborate, but I won't. I shouldn't. "It's Embry's story to tell," I explain. "He should be the one to give you his reasons. It would be wrong for me to speak on his behalf."

"Oh, Ash," she murmurs, pressing her face back into my leg. "Stop being so good for just a second and talk to me."

"I'm not being good," I promise her. "If I were really being good, I would have accepted his resignation without provoking him. But I couldn't do that, and we—"

I take a breath. "It got messy."

"Messy how?"

My curious little cat. Even with everything that's happened, I'm still charmed by her fascination with Embry and me. "We fought and then we came, so business as usual," I say. "It wasn't good of me to do. He wanted dignity in that moment and I made sure he didn't have it."

"He wanted whatever you wanted," she says, glancing up at me. "And you wouldn't have done it if you didn't know that he wanted it too."

"That's pleasant to think, but I'm not sure how true it is." I smooth her hair away from her face. "The most important thing for you to know is that I gave Embry my blessing to be with you. And I'm giving you the same blessing. I don't expect or want this shift in loyalty to break the two of you apart. I certainly won't curtail my relationship with you, and should the moment arise between Embry and me again, I can't imagine I would stop myself from doing what I want."

She has no answer to this, and I can see the tiny pulls and parts of her mouth as she struggles for words. "Ash, I don't think I can…cheat on you," she finally manages. "There were times when it was just me and him, but that was when we were a three. If we aren't a three anymore, then I don't know how I feel about being with Embry."

"You won't 'be' with him; you'll fuck him. And at the end of the day, you'll come home to me. My bed. My body. I will always be your husband and your king and your master, and it doesn't matter who I let you fuck, you'll always belong to me, understood?"

"Yes," she breathes, her eyes wide and open. Her body has gone hot and pliable in front of mine, practically begging to be handled.

I ignore it for the moment, ignore the angry throb of my cock against the wool of my suit pants. "This isn't cheating, Greer. We promised each other on our wedding night, and we keep our promises. That means you and Embry have my full consent and permission to be together, and that means I don't expect you to help me campaign against him or to do anything else that would divide your loyalty. I care too much for you to do that."

"But I don't want to hurt you," she insists. "And this will hurt you, I know it will."

"I choose the pain too, angel. I always have."

"And I'll campaign by your side," she says. "No matter what."

I'm touched by her loyalty—more than touched, I'm fed by it in all the wrong ways—but I don't tell her that. Instead I say, "You should wait until you talk to Embry to decide that. You might agree with him that I should no longer be president."

"Never," she vows. "There's nothing he can say that will convince me you shouldn't be in this office."

"I didn't keep you safe from Melwas."

Her mouth drops. "Is that what this is about?"

I don't answer.

"Ash—"

I shake my head. "It's Embry's story to tell. I'm not going to interfere between the two of you. It wouldn't be fair."

"Fuck *fair*," she protests, her voice rising. "What about what's fair to you? What about what's fair to me? Do I really lose the right to talk about Embry with you because you want to be *fair*? We promised, even back before the wedding, that we would talk about him with each other, that we wouldn't hold back or hide, that everything had to be completely honest."

"Princess," I say, looping her hair around my finger and tugging gently. "That was about missing him, not about anger. Not about pain. It's a world of difference."

"But you still miss him," she points out. "Even if you resent him at the same time. And I know he's going to miss you. I know he still loves you."

I sigh, releasing her hair. "That's what Morgan said last night."

"You talked to Morgan last night? She knew about this before I did?" There's a hint of insecurity in her voice, and with some shame, I realize I'd forgotten about her disastrous interaction with Morgan last year...and with even more shame, I realize I still need to tell Greer the worst part of it all.

"She knew even before *I* did, Greer. She'll be Embry's running mate." I pull my wife up into my lap, gathering her to me until she's nestled against my chest and enclosed by my arms, her legs tucked up in the chair and her head resting on my shoulder. I stroke her hair as I say as kindly as I can, "There is one more thing, though."

"About Morgan?" I can hear the wariness in her voice, and I wish I could spare her this part, so soon after finding out about Abilene and Embry's baby, so soon after finding out that she isn't carrying a child of our own. But Greer is strong; she doesn't need to be protected from the truth.

"It is about Morgan," I agree, holding her a little tighter. "There was a baby—a son. Her aunt raised him, and no one knew the boy was hers, not even Embry. Not even me."

Greer's gone completely still, her body braced for it, and I wish to God I could say anything other than what I say next. "He was mine, Greer. He *is* mine."

I expect her to stay frozen or maybe even to rage at me, to call me all the words I've already called myself—sinner, pervert, a twisted, incestuous bastard—but she doesn't. She looks up at me with eyes the color of the sea under moonlight, and then she presses a cool hand against my face. I turn and kiss her palm and taste salt—she's caught tears I didn't even know I was crying on her skin.

"Oh, Ash," she murmurs. "Is this why you knelt when I came in?"

I close my eyes. "I knelt because nothing feels real anymore. Only you."

"You didn't know, Ash. You can't be angry with yourself for something you didn't know about."

"I should have known," I say, my eyes still closed. "Before Glein, she wanted to speak to me so badly; she wouldn't leave until we'd talked, and I mistook it for… I don't even know. An infatuation I didn't have time for, maybe. Something I couldn't even entertain because I'd fallen so hard for her brother by then and the war was really starting and…" I open my eyes. "All along, she was trying to tell me that we had a child. And I couldn't be bothered to give her five fucking minutes of my time."

"You were fighting a war," Greer reminds me. "And she could have written, she could have called, she could have served you with a paternity test—anything other than melting into silence after Glein."

"I think there was no hope of anything else after Glein. I failed her and our baby too badly for her to trust me again."

"God!" Greer practically explodes. "Of all the things to hold against you! That wasn't even your fault!"

"It doesn't matter," I say heavily. "At the end of the day, a person is held to account for their choices, by history or by God or by something else, and what happened at Glein amounted to the results of my choices. I was green, I was young, I was doing my best, but I still chose what I chose. I can't blame Morgan for hating me."

I can tell by her huff that Greer disagrees, and it makes me smile. "My loyal young bride," I say, pressing my forehead against hers. But then I pull away and search her face. "I will understand if this changes how you feel about me. It is one thing to have fucked a sister in ignorance, but now that there's a son…it's a much heavier sin. You would be well within reason to divorce me over this."

She sits up in my arms, her cheeks going red with anger. "I can't believe you'd even say something like that."

I run a hand along the curve of her thigh, soothing my restless filly. "There's more to contend with than just Lyr's existence, Greer. Aren't you curious how Embry found out when Morgan hid it from him for so long?"

There's a stubborn set to her jaw. "It doesn't matter."

"It does, unfortunately. Your cousin was the one who told Embry. In fact, she was using Lyr as blackmail to manipulate Embry into dating her. He was hurting you in order to protect me and my image from the truth. You are allowed to resent me for that at least."

"Dammit, Ash, I can't resent you. Not now, not ever." She flings her arms around my neck, twists until she's straddling my lap with her forehead touching mine. "I hate her and I'm furious with him, but this is not your fault. None of it is."

"You'll find that Embry disagrees. And Morgan. And certainly the public will have a different opinion."

Greer stiffens slightly as she realizes what I'm saying. "The public?"

"Abilene's threat was to go public about Lyr. For now, with Embry thoroughly trapped and you thoroughly miserable, she might be content. Especially if she has a chance of taking your spot in the White House. However, that same chance might be too much of a temptation; she could just as easily disclose the information about Lyr in order to destroy my chances at reelection. We'll have to hope she's wise enough to see how it would tarnish Embry's ticket, since Morgan is his running mate." I lift a shoulder. "I don't know her well, not like you and Embry know her, but she strikes me as fundamentally unpredictable. And so you see why I want to give you a choice. It's one thing to forgive me such a sin in private, but it's quite another to stand by my side when the entire world knows. You'll be tainted by association."

"I'm already tainted," she says tiredly. "The video of me and Embry, remember? It doesn't matter how loudly we said it was fake, I'll always be suspect now."

"But we have to make our choices where we have them. And I hope I've done a thorough job laying out your choices, as much as God knows I secretly wish for you to have none. To stay with me. Moments like this, I feel like I'll dissolve without you."

She holds me tighter, snugging her body closer to mine and pressing down harder on my dormant erection. "I've made my choice," she whispers. "I told you before, I'll always choose the pain."

My body responds to her words and her loyalty, surging with heat and desperate need.

"You mean that?" I murmur, ducking my head so I can peer into her face. "With Lyr? With Embry gone? After all that Melwas did and with all the terrible things that might happen?"

She brushes her lips against mine, and my entire world

is the smell of her skin and the glint of her moon-sea eyes. "Yes. I choose it all."

I want to weep. And I nearly do, holding her close. I don't deserve her pain, I don't deserve her trust, but somehow she's choosing to give them to me anyway. I'm humbled and grateful with the kind of gratitude that can flay a man alive, and my entire body is trembling with the urge to reward her devotion the way I know best.

She must be thinking along the same lines because she kisses my jaw and then whispers in my ear, "Use me today, make yourself feel better inside of me. Master me. Break me."

Always and forever, my queen.

CHAPTER 7
ASH

NOW

"SIR, THE BEAST IS READY."

The Beast is my car—*the* presidential car, though there are multiple vehicles that fill the role—and it's time for the Luther Center Gala. I nod to Belvedere, indicating that I heard and that we'll be outside shortly, and he vanishes back out of the living room to wait for us.

I'm fastening my cuff links as I walk into my bedroom to find my wife panting and squirming on a chair, trying to stay quiet so Belvedere can't hear her out in the hallway. Her ball gown is rucked up around her hips, her chest flushed, her knuckles white as she grips the edge of the seat. And the wand vibrator buzzing between her legs makes an ominous *whirr* against the wood as she tries to shift away from it.

"Sir, please," she gasps.

I glance at my wristwatch; she's been on the chair for twenty minutes, forced to sit with her cunt snug against the vibrator duct-taped to the seat and not allowed to come. This is after I spent an hour teasing her with my mouth before my meet and greet, and after I spent another thirty minutes in the shower with her afterwards, slowly fucking her ass until she could barely stand up. She was not given permission to come then either. In short, she is currently a wet, writhing mess, and I plan to take her to the gala that way.

"You may get up," I allow.

She's up in an instant, a little whimper of both relief and bereavement coming out of her pretty mouth. Red lipstick tonight, immaculate and classic, just like her, and I can't wait to smear it all over her face. But for now…

"Knot my bow tie, please," I order her, and she walks to me on shaking legs, the tulle and silk of her ball gown falling back to the floor and covering up her swollen pussy. God, that cunt will feel so good to fuck later, so puffy and so wet. And when she finally comes, I'll get to see the way she unravels down to her very soul. It is one thing to break someone open with pain—some might even say an obvious thing, if not an easy one—but it is another thing entirely to break someone open with pleasure. It takes a different kind of skill and care, a different brand of attention to keep someone so torturously aroused for so long.

"You did ask to be mastered," I remind my wife with amusement as she has to steady herself with a hand on my shoulder.

"I thought you'd belt me," she admits with a breathless laugh. "Or choke me with your cock. I wasn't ready for this. It's almost harder than being worked over."

"It is harder, and you've pleased me very much," I tell her, lifting her chin with a finger so she looks up into my face. "You are still pleasing me. I'm so very proud of you for taking my cock up your ass and for rubbing your pussy on that toy. I'm even prouder that you could do it all without restraints."

She flushes happily, and I enjoy lighting her up with my praise. It's well-earned too; it's hard to endure twenty minutes of that even when you're bound to the chair, unable to move. But because of the gala and her sleeveless gown, I decided not to tie or tape her—nothing that would leave visible marks. Which meant she had to keep herself on that chair with sheer willpower; every moment she sat on the chair, she was suffering and enduring that vibrator for my sake. For me.

Her smooth, pale arms, free of any mark or stripe from my ropes, display the difference between *force* and *choice*, and while both things are delicious to me, right now the *choice* carries so much more weight. Perhaps it's because it's all a choice at its heart—even when I pretend to force her, she has her safe word, she still has a way to escape, and we both know it. But an exercise like the chair strips away all the pretenses and leaves our exchange for the naked, gleaming thing it is.

A decision. A willing surrender. A display of love.

And it's as she's slowly knotting my bow tie, her normally practiced movements made slightly fumbling by her hyper-aroused state, that I finally feel like myself for the first time today.

I am a man who loves. A man whose love demands much in return.

And I will survive this.

I mark every flutter of those long eyelashes against her cheek, every tiny furrow of her brow as she pulls the fabric around my neck into the right shape. She's so fucking beautiful all the time, but now, with her eyes glassy and her cheeks flushed and her full attention on the task I set her to, I'm so fucking in love that I can barely see straight. My young wife, my regal little queen, so willing to be unspooled at my whim.

She finishes with the bow tie, plucks the corners into sharp peaks, and then smiles up at me, all bright red lips and white teeth. I bend my head and bite the small cleft in her chin and she laughs.

"I want to kiss you," I say, biting her again. "I want to kiss all the air right out of you until the only thing you can breathe is me. But the fucking gala."

"We could cancel," she suggests with a coy smile. "Pretend we're sick."

"Naughty thing. You just want to be fucked sooner."

"I would never presume, sir," she says in a voice that says she would do exactly that.

I sweep her into my arms, honeymoon style, and carry her out of the bedroom.

"My shoes!" she protests, feet kicking adorably under all that tulle. She's also not wearing underwear, but she's smart enough not to ask for it.

"I'll have Belvedere get the shoes," I tell her with a smile. "I like having you in my arms too much to put you down."

She sighs, resting her head against my shoulder. I can smell all the sweet aromas that come with a woman—soap and perfume and the faint smell of skin and arousal underneath it all. "I love you, my Greer," I tell her. "And do you love your sir?"

She nods against my shoulder. "I love my sir with all my heart."

"Even tonight?"

"Even tonight." A pause. "How long until you let me come again?"

I laugh and pinch her ass for her impertinence, and then I carry her out into the hallway toward the limo.

There's something quite thrilling about fucking a woman in a ball gown. It's like having a secret that no one else knows, a sin that no one else can see. Of course, no one else can see us in the Beast anyway, but it still feels sweetly illicit to have Greer's skirt fluffed and bunched around us and my cock inside her underneath it all. I savor the picture she paints like this—hair coiled into perfection, makeup like art, the gorgeous gown—but she is a hot, greedy thing under her skirt, her snatch tight around me and her clit a hard, plump bud against the muscles of my groin. She's under strict orders not to come or make a single noise, and I can tell that both are testing her discipline at the moment—her fingers are digging into my shoulders and her teeth are digging so far into her lower lip that I wonder if she can taste blood.

I'm enjoying it very much.

"...and that's another year on the timeline, thanks to the coalition," the new British prime minister is saying into my ear. I'm on the phone with him, ostensibly to congratulate him and his party on their victory, but it's gone beyond congratulations into an unwelcome digression about his goals, and it's taking more than my usual reserve of self-control to listen to him fully. Not the least because I have my wife on my lap, repeatedly impaling herself on my penis.

But listen fully I do, and when I hang up the phone, I take a moment to lift up Greer's skirt and reward myself with the sight of us fucking, watching my thick organ disappear into that tight cunt and reappear again, the wet pink of her hugging me even as she lifts away, as if her body doesn't want to let me go. I lean back and watch this for a few minutes, considering rather lazily if I'd like to come inside her now or wait and savor the anticipation, and then I decide that she's been such a good wife for me today that I'll reward her at the gala itself, whisk her off into some dark bathroom upstairs and fuck her until she screams. And that is the moment I want to come inside her, when she is completely and utterly outside of herself with release.

"Up," I say with a stern swat to her ass. "We'll finish this later."

I can see a faint mist of sweat along her hairline as she nods dazedly, clambers off my lap, and reaches for her purse.

"Don't clean yourself," I say. "I want to know that you're wet."

"Yes, sir," she manages. I enjoy the effect of denying her very much, but I still give her the last few minutes of the ride to compose herself and let her mind clear a little—I always play to tease, sometimes even to test, but I would never actually jeopardize her ability to do her job—and by the time we reach the Luther Center itself, she is able to smile and wave calmly enough as we leave the Beast and trail past the red carpet into the crowd.

"Don't forget," I whisper in her ear before I go to find the event coordinator. "I want you wet and ready for me later. If I like what I find, then I'll reward my good little girl."

"And if you don't like what you find?" she whispers back a little nervously.

"Then it's going to be a long night for you," I say with a quick kiss to her temple. And I mean it. I'm not without mercy, but I always keep my word. Always.

Greer lifts her chin a little. "You'll like what you find."

"My little queen is determined to please me," I say, smiling. "And I am determined to give her everything she needs to be a happy girl."

She stops walking and turns to straighten my tie and smooth down my jacket, the flat of her palm running teasingly over my hidden erection as she does.

I catch her wrist. "Bold, naughty girl."

"Hurry, Mr. President," she murmurs, looking up at me

through her eyelashes. "I feel like I could come just from your command alone right now, I'm so wound up."

My dick, still heavy and hard and wet, jolts against my zipper at her words. I'm grateful for the concealing effect of the tuxedo jacket, but I do press into her so she can feel the ramrod length of me against her belly. "I like this idea very much," I murmur back to her. "Of you coming from my command alone."

"I'd rather have you inside me," she whispers plaintively.

"Mmm. Me too. Are you sure I have to go give this speech?"

She gives a sighing little laugh. "I suppose you must." She fiddles with my bow tie once more and rises up to kiss me gently on the mouth. "You'll knock them dead."

I kiss her back and then leave to find the coordinator.

The speech goes well—the Luther Center probably would have preferred that I had spoken mainly about the arts and sciences, but Uri and I included several sections about education as well, in anticipation of a school reform initiative I hope to push through later this year. Afterward, there is the usual array of handshakes and pictures and conversations, there is dancing, there is the expected bevy of powerful people hoping to speak into my ear. In short, it is a typical night in Washington, and ordinarily, it would take tremendous powers of focus and memory to distinguish it from any other night afterward.

But three things set it apart.

The first is—painfully and inevitably—Embry. While at the White House today, I kept myself busy and sequestered with my wife, and even with the few meetings I couldn't escape, I purposefully stayed free of my phone and any chatter from my staff. But as the night goes on, it becomes clear that the rest of the political world exploded after Embry gave his official resignation speech today.

"Did you know?" people ask. "Did you want him to leave? Did you *make* him leave?"

No and no and fuck you if you think I would ever make that man leave me, but I can't say those things. I can't deliver those honest answers with all the bitter pain they deserve. I have to make polite noises and vague explanations and benign well wishes for his future, and how do they not all see? How do they not hear the trickle of my heart's blood dripping out of my chest, how do they not see the scooped-out pain in my eyes, how can they not hear every desperate plea and every rasping sob I've let out in the last twenty-four hours?

Merlin rescues me eventually, inserting himself into a cloud of speculation and curiosity that no amount of calm, noncommittal statements on my part can clear, and he pulls me away on the pretense of discussing something confidential. But when we reach the edge of the room, he merely hands me a flute of champagne from a circulating tray and says, "Drink this."

"I'm fine," I insist.

"No," Merlin says. "You were *performing* fine, and doing a wonderful job at it, but another five minutes of that and the seams would've started to show. Take a minute to breathe."

"I feel like I've been taking a minute to breathe all day. I'm ready to stop breathing and start fixing things."

"Well, you've already stopped breathing," Merlin observes with an edged perception that makes me uncomfortable. "Perhaps you haven't breathed properly since last night. Which is all the more reason for you to breathe now. Take comfort in your queen. We can discuss preliminary election strategy later this week."

The casual way he says it strikes some new and horrible understanding into me. Embry is gone, and his leaving is now so permanent and acknowledged that it's almost mundane. Business as usual. Just one more angle to fold into the strategy. Don't worry about that hollow echo in my chest, let's just turn to item two in the handout…

"Drink," Merlin says. "Do it for me if you won't do it for yourself."

I have no energy left to argue. I drain the flute in one movement and set it on a nearby table. Merlin gives me a moment or two to compose myself, and then he says, "Better?"

I'm not actually, but I believe very stridently in not making my unhappiness or discomfort another person's problem. I'm also not a liar, so I simply say, "I will be."

"Yes, you will."

"It embarrasses me to admit this," I say, looking out over the dim ballroom, "but no matter how cautiously I spoke or thought about it, no matter how much I told myself I was prepared for the possibility of something different, beneath all that, I never doubted that I would win again. And I am only realizing this now as it becomes apparent that I might lose."

Merlin makes a skeptical noise. "I hope this doubt isn't because of Embry?"

"Why shouldn't it be? He's a decorated soldier, he's become a skilled politician, he has all the right connections. He's more charming than me, besides."

"You're looking at him with a lover's eye," Merlin says frankly. "And not looking at yourself at all. I think this reelection could be personally uncomfortable but politically quite easy."

"All the same," I say, putting my hands in my pockets and scanning the room for Greer. "I want to meet with Kay and Trieste about how much of our agenda we can get accomplished this term."

"Maxen, that agenda was calculated precisely for two terms. Even then, it's almost certainly too ambitious. There is no way we can accomplish the rest of that list in the time we have left."

I finally find Greer, a glint of near-white hair under the golden lights of the dance floor. The band is playing a waltz now, and the music is a shard of glass against my throat. How many times had I held Embry in my arms to music just like this? Can I number all the times I'll never get to dance with him again? Do I even want to try?

I was even listening to Strauss when he came to me last night, when I saw him standing in the doorframe of my office, looking beautifully brooding, as only he can. God how I love him, and it took only one blue glance before I was coming toward him, pressing against that firm, flat chest of his and guiding his long, elegant fingers to the place that waited for him. One blue glance before I was completely open and undone for Embry Moore, just as I have always been, just as I have been since the first day I saw him spoiled and scornful in the mountains of a strange land. I would walk barefoot over every jagged rock of that distant country if it would bring Embry back to me. I would crawl.

"I'd be a fool if I planned on a second term; I'm not owed it," I finally say to Merlin. "I'm not entitled to anything more than what I've earned here and now. I have to get as much done as I can in case I have to leave."

"Poverty, sexual assault, education, climate change, stability overseas—you think it's merely a matter of willpower and focus to effect those changes? No, these are projects that require huge amounts of bipartisan leverage and cooperation and favors—not even Penley Luther himself could have done it."

"I'm not my father," I say with perhaps more sharpness than necessary.

"And I thank God for that every day," Merlin responds blandly. "Nonetheless, it can't be done. Give up this idea of cramming six years of work into two, and focus on getting elected again."

I look over at Merlin, and I'm surprised to see something almost goading in his face, although it's not truly goading… A challenge, maybe? A dare?

But that's not quite right either. It's almost less like a dare and more like he's delivering lines from a script. There's something mechanical in the way he insists it cannot be done. It's cursory, an actor running through the kinds of expository lines that require little emotion or effort. Like he knows he must say these things to provoke me into saying the opposite, but when I examine his face, all of that vanishes, and he is the picture of polite and reserved calm once again.

I can't resist the script either, if scripted this moment is, and I find myself saying exactly what would have been laid out for me on the page. "I'm doing it, Merlin. Even if it kills me."

The second thing remarkable about tonight is my wife. Her dress—some strapless confection of gold and white—renders her into a shimmering vision of light, a drop of sunlight playing over water, and she draws people to her simply by existing as she does, sublime and sovereign. I catch glimpses of her face—kind, serious, almost tormentingly lovely—through the crowd as I make my way to her, and I'm reminded of a John Collier painting I saw once in England of Queen Guinevere gathering flowers on May Day. Like the painting, she is clad in white and gold and surrounded by a crowd; like the painting, there is something aching and lonely in her face.

I had once teased her that one man wasn't enough—that she needed both Embry and me to feel loved—and she had shaken her head and pressed her hand flat against where my heart beat in my chest.

Don't you see? she'd implored once. *It is because I love you that I love Embry. We fell in love with each other by loving you.*

It was just as well. My love was—and is—implacable and cruel to those it chooses. I had been glad that they could take comfort in one another, however envious the idea made me. And I feel quite the same now, although my wife's face reminds me that she may not get any comfort from Embry anytime soon. His absence has gouged a hole in our marriage just as surely as it's gouged a hole in our three.

When I reach Greer, however, and take her wrist in my hand while she's talking to the governor of New York, that lonely look vanishes and is replaced with something so warm and yielding that I have to kiss her on the mouth, lipstick and onlooking governor be damned.

"Mr. President," she says, half laughing and half gasping under my mouth.

"Mrs. Colchester," I return, lifting my head but pulling her into me. "I'm so sorry, Governor Jarrett, do you mind if I steal my wife away for a few moments?"

The governor waves an amused hand. "By all means, save me from this gorgeous, interesting woman," she says. "It was unbearable company anyway."

We laugh, we say goodbye, we make more excuses as we squeeze together through the crowd, and then Luc is escorting us out of the ballroom into the small art gallery off the north wing of the Luther Center.

"We're not to be interrupted," I tell him at the door after I send Greer inside.

"Yes, sir," Luc says, his expression betraying nothing.

I clap him on the shoulder. "Good man," I say, and then follow Greer through the doorway and close the door behind me.

Inside, the world is small and quiet. A wall of windows frames a spill of Georgian buildings and thick trees; beyond the rise of stone and leaves, the white finger of the Washington Monument presses into the purple-clouded night sky. Huge canvases of modern art stud the all-white walls, shadows leak from the windows onto the blond wood floors, the noise of the gala is a muffled memory.

We are alone at last.

When Greer hears my footsteps, she turns to face me and the lights from the city outside catch on the gold of her dress and in the gleam of her hair. She sinks to her knees in a cloud of tulle and silk as I approach, her neck arched as gracefully as a swan's as she trains her eyes on the floor.

I take a minute to enjoy her, strolling around her kneeling figure with my hands in my pockets, taking in the elegant line of her neck and shoulders, her perfect posture, the delicate curve of her collarbone. The corona of white and gold silk around her knees. The excited heave of her breasts under her bodice. The ring glinting off her finger better than any collar. A thousand possibilities scorch through me all at once—my cock down her throat; her face in the floor; the nylon tie of a stocking around her wrists. The sound of her begging voice echoing off the empty walls.

Without saying anything, I cup the back of her head with my hand as I stand beside her, and she leans her head against my thigh. Not kittenishly rubbing or bucking as before, but merely resting, enjoying the simplicity of the contact. I enjoy it too, standing above her, looking down on her with pride and pleasure. Both of us exactly where we need to be and how we need to be.

If only...

If only my little prince were here.

I allow myself the grief and the splintered hurt, even as I refuse to vent it on Greer. If only Embry were here. If only it were the three of us in this gallery, the only entrance guarded, our privacy secure. I'd make him watch me fuck my wife, and I'd fuck her slow, slick, grinding, so that he would see every slide of me inside of her, every quiver of her stomach, every gasping part of her pretty lips, and know that it was me doing it. I'd make him lick her clean after. I'd make him beg like a dog, I'd make him cry for me. I'd leave a bruise for every minute I loved him that he didn't love me back.

I'd spread him out and kiss every inch of him. I'd spread Greer's hair over his flat, muscled stomach just to see the contrast, I'd tickle the soles of his feet until he laughed, I'd press and nuzzle into every corner of him—elbows and in between toes and the hollows under his arms—until he knew that every part of me belonged to him. I'd pin Greer between us and together we would love her the way she needed to be loved. I'd spread her legs and allow him to take his pleasure there, and then when he came inside of her, I would watch and my heart would be full.

Beside me, Greer makes a small, unintentional sigh.

"What is it, pet?"

She looks up at me. "I'm missing him right now."

"Me too, angel."

"How are you so calm about it?" she asks. "How do you hold it all inside yourself?"

Hold what? I want to ask. My own fucking heart, torn into bloody tatters? My every foolish hope for a future with both my queen and my prince? My kingdom, which was built with Embry at my side?

Can't she see the broken bones pushing through my skin? The garish, crimson wounds all over my body? *What should such fellows as I do crawling between earth and heaven*; can't she see me crawl? Can't she see me weep? If I could press my fingers into my veins and claw out any acceptable and worthy sacrifice, my soul, my blood, my past, and my future, then by fucking God I would have done it.

Anything, anything, anything.

I get to my own knees in front of my wife. I see the shock on her face when I turn my palms up toward the ceiling, the backs of my hands resting on my thighs as I sit back on my heels in an unmistakable submissive's pose. This isn't the spontaneous gesture of need and adoration from the Residence this morning; this is a deliberate posture of submission and humility, and I've never assumed it in front of Greer.

Psalm 51. The adulterer's psalm. The psalm of a father mourning a son that should not have been conceived. That's what I quote. "You do not delight in sacrifice, or I would bring it."

Greer stares at me with silver eyes in the dark.

"You do not take pleasure in burnt offerings," I continue. "My sacrifice, O God, is a broken spirit. A broken and contrite heart which You will not despise."

A single tear tracks down my queen's cheek, and I don't wipe it away. I let it fall as I keep my hands open and empty. "Do good to Zion in your good pleasure; rebuild the walls of Jerusalem. Then you will delight in right sacrifices."

Another tear spills over onto my favorite face in the world, and my chest squeezes in shared pain. All the ways I've failed her and Embry, I won't fail them anymore. I won't fail her. I will love her until the stars burn themselves out and hang like cold rocks in the lightless sky.

Right sacrifices, I remind myself. The Lord only delights in right sacrifices. What a bleeding, sluggish world this would be if we all indulged in martyrdom; what a luscious fucking lure to bite—to brood and wallow and feel. But the world was not made to be bleeding and sluggish, and those lures are just baited traps for the moody and the vain. The world must spin, the battles must be fought, the grails and the quests won't chase themselves. However tempting a sacrifice for its own sake might be, however tempting self-flagellation and melancholy and grasping, needy gloom—it is not a *right* sacrifice. It would only serve me, and I'm pledged to serve so many others.

The world must spin.

And yet…

And yet for just a moment, I wonder what it's like on the other side. I wonder what it's like not to have to serve everyone else, what it would be like to chase my weakest impulses to their selfish ends. What it would feel like to give in. To yield. To—just for a moment—drop the crown and the sword to the floor and carry my heart in my hands.

"I hold it inside of me as best I can," I finally answer her. "And I'm afraid I'm not holding it very well right now. But I must, Greer, I must, even if it dissolves my bones and eats me alive. Even if I sometimes fantasize about not holding it at all."

"Let me," she begs. "Let me hold it for you. Beat me or fuck me or anything you need."

Anything I need. Does she realize that's everything right now? I need everything. I'm a gaping, sucking void of need.

"Can we try something?" I ask. My heart thumps uncomfortably in my chest; my mouth feels dry. Clumsy. I feel like a boy asking someone on a date for the first time. "Can you…can we, I mean… I want—"

I clear my throat, looking down at my hands resting on my thighs.

"Tonight I want to be your submissive," I say. "I know I prepared you to be mastered today, and I will keep my word to do so if you like. I just thought…" I falter, my words slipping away from me. I tilt my head all the way back and stare up at the ceiling. "I just want to know what it feels like. Not to be the one to carry it all."

Greer's dress rustles. I hear her breathing. "I can try," she offers. "But it won't be—I'm not you, Ash. I'm worried it will feel awkward. Like a child pretending."

I drop my head to look at her. "You're perfect," I say softly. "Anything you do will be perfect."

She bites her lip and I read every uncertain flicker in her moon-sea eyes. She's worried she'll be clumsy, that I'll inwardly be judging her performance, that she'll fail to please me. And I understand—mastering is far more complicated than being mastered. A dominant not only has to plan but to assess, to read what a submissive needs in that scene, and they must adapt and adjust and continually monitor a submissive's progress through pain and pleasure. It's a heavy weight—a joyful and pleasurable one, often—but a weight nonetheless. And here I'm asking her to trade places in the middle of a daylong scene with no warning and no chance to prepare.

But I'm ready to break and crumble, and if there's any person on this planet I feel safe doing it in front of, it's Greer Galloway Colchester.

"Please," I whisper. I bow, moving so that my palms are flat on the floor in front of her knees and then I press my forehead to the floor. "I want to feel free of it. Only for a few minutes."

"I'm nervous," she admits. "I've…I mean, with Embry I sometimes can, but you aren't him. With you, it's like all of me responds with the urge to obey. It's beyond my control."

I push aside the prideful sting that comes with hearing his name. She and I have endeavored not to have any secrets from one another, and so I know all about their times alone—Carpathia and her office at Georgetown chief among them—and I know that together, the two of them have a much more traditional dynamic. Giving and taking in equal measure, unspoken negotiations of power—the way equals fuck each other. I should be happy for them, happy that without me they can find some normalcy and intimacy in sex without resorting to degradation and a degree of suffering, and I *am* happy for them, but also I grieve. Envy curls in my chest. I got my teenage wish to become the Goblin King, but wars and sisters and lovers and my dead wife have finally planted all the guilt and shame I never used to feel about it, and sometimes I hate myself for the things I need. I resent my lovers for not always needing them. I hurt for wanting to hurt them. I want the other side of it—I want the other side of it right now.

"Pretend, then, that I'm ordering you to do this. I'm ordering you, as your sir, to take control, and you are simply obeying me."

"Okay," she says above me. And then she takes a deep breath and says clearer, louder, "Okay. Yes, sir."

I see the froth of white and gold fabric move around me, and then I hear her stand, hear the *click*-thunk of her heels dropping from her feet and the pad of her steps on the floor. Then silence.

I stay where I am, my eyes on the wood grain of the smooth floor, my body pulling uncomfortably in the unfamiliar posture. This is what it must be like for Greer. The waiting. The pregnant stillness. The creeping uncertainty. It takes so much willpower simply *not* to move, *not* to act, when moving and acting are my defaults.

At the club I'd joined after Jenny's death, they require all dominants to undergo certain kinds of training in order to play there, and I'd done them all quite willingly, because I'd been eager to learn, I'd been eager to know how to do all the things I wanted to do safely. And in order to do that, I had to know how they felt. I've been whipped, cropped, paddled, flogged, edged, bound, gagged, and once—just once—fucked in the ass with a toy.

And countless other things, but right now I'm remembering the very first time I was made to submit as part of my training, and it was something very like this. Kneeling with my head pressed to the floor for almost two hours while the dominant training me watched. I'd just won the election and I was going to be the leader of the free world and I was spending my spare time getting beaten by a man named Mark. But in that room, it didn't matter. Actual kings and queens had been there, crown royalty, billionaires, generals, dignitaries—secular power meant nothing in Mark's kingdom, which was the entire point.

Those two hours on my knees, it had felt like an academic exercise, like I was taking a tour. A visitor to the land of kneeling. And although I made notes in my head about how long it took for parts of my body to fall asleep, about the ways my thoughts wanted to stray, about what I could see and perceive from my deferential position, it never felt *real*. It never was real. It was research. A game.

This is not a game.

Every step Greer takes sends ripples of awareness through me, every brush of her dress against my legs turns into a blessing. I am noticed. I am touched. Each glance of her fabric is a gift. And when she finally deigns to run her fingers over the tuxedo jacket pulled tight over my back, I let out a ragged exhale of relief.

"I want to see your face," she murmurs. "Back up on your knees."

I raise myself back to my knees, not lifting my eyes until I'm expressly asked to, putting my hands palm-up on my thighs once again. A model submissive. It feels forced, but it feels nice as well. Nice not to have to worry about anything. Nice to be responsible for nothing but myself.

"I—" She swallows. "I want your mouth on me. Lift your face."

I lift my face like she asks, catching her eyes with my own. She looks uncertain, concerned that maybe she's doing something incorrectly, and I smile reassuringly at her. "Yes, mistress," I answer.

She nods, almost absentmindedly, and for a moment I consider taking pity on her and ending this pointless request of mine. It was selfish to ask for, and there's no reason Greer needs to suffer for my broken heart, but then she steps close to me, raising her dress, and her bare, wet pussy is right in front of my face, like something out of a dream. Framed by white and gold, the barest glimpse of pink peeking out from her cleft, and I can smell her. My cock strains against my pants, fully hard since the first time I knelt, and for a second I relish the unfamiliar sensation. To be hard and to be kneeling.

It's strange but not unpleasant. Like driving someone else's car.

"Eat me," my wife says, and I keep my eyes on hers as long as I can as I slide my hands up the back of her thighs to steady her. My instincts are still to take care of her, to make sure she's safe, and it's jolting to realize I can still do this from my knees, perhaps as well as I can as when I'm standing.

I press my mouth against the soft lips of her cunt, which she keeps bare at my asking, and then I part my lips the tiniest bit and let my tongue tickle against her clit. I feel her knees weaken and nearly collapse at the touch, and I smile to myself and do it again. Her skin is so soft, almost like satin against my lips, and she smells like the delicate lavender soap she uses until I nuzzle my nose into her and inhale. And then she smells like herself, sweet and warm, if warm can be a scent.

I press my face harder against her, angling so that my tongue can begin sweeping lines along the folds of her slit, and a whimpered *Ash* drops from her lips. I relish it, this sign of her pleasure, and I slide my hands up to her ass and over her hips and down her thighs again. She's all silky skin and garters and stockings, and then when my hands find her from the front and gently spread her lips apart, she's all wet, quivering flesh. Flesh I've been fucking and denying all day, and the thought of her carrying all that slippery need around in public, just tucked up inside her all aching and heavy, has me so fucking hard.

This position, too, has a certain kind of intimate appeal. Normally I enjoy her cunt while she's tied to my bed or perhaps bent over a table with a spreader bar between her legs. Normally, I use my fingers to part her as wide as I please, exposing her sweet hole and the firm berry of her clit and the tight pleats of her anus. I lick and taste at my leisure, I nibble and I suck at whatever pace I deem fit, all while she's wide-open for me like the good girl she is.

But this is so much more immediate, so much more desperate. Even with my hands helping, I have to nuzzle and force to get at her most secret spots when she's standing like this. There's barely any part of my face that goes untouched by her—her thighs against my cheeks, my nose buried in her mound, my chin wet and glistening, and then her hands are in my hair, yanking and pulling and she's rubbing against me, grinding herself against my face. She and Embry did this, I remember. In her office at Georgetown. I made her tell me all about it as I fucked her afterward; I made her tell me exactly how Embry looked with his face between her legs, exactly how his expensive suit bunched and strained as he stayed on his knees for her, exactly how hard she came on his tongue. How wet his face was after.

I don't like admitting to myself how much jealous pleasure I feel in overwriting this experience for her; it's a toxic tendril of satisfaction knowing that whenever she thinks of having a man on his knees, she'll have to think of both of us now. There's nothing he can do to her that I can't also do—no pleasure he can give that I can't also give. Even now, with this huge hole ripped in our lives, I'm still jealous of him. I'm still so possessive of her that my bones threaten to crack with it. She is mine. Mine against my mouth, mine on my tongue, mine as I fuck her and beat her and cherish her in every way that a man can cherish the keeper of his own soul.

I don't know how it happens, exactly, except that maybe thinking of Embry triggers it, but somehow I end up taking control. On my knees, my face buried in between my wife's legs—and buried there at her command, no less—the Jareth inside me takes over, and my hands move the way I want them to move, digging points of pain into the tender flesh, finding all the places where I can push and press, all the places that resist. The lips of her pussy, the silky skin running back from her slit to her rear entrance, the hard cords of tendon connecting her thighs to her pelvis. The firm swell of pubic bone and the plush handfuls of her ass.

She shudders above me, the slight tease of pain ratcheting her tighter against my face and wetter against my tongue, and all of her body seems to twist into me, toward me, tugged on a tide that formed between us the moment we met. She opens and peels apart when I treat her like this, and it's more than the pain—although admittedly the chemicals released by the pain help. But it's *me* she responds to—my ownership, my possession. My desire pouring over her like water, like darkness, my heart pushing up naked and needy against her own and demanding her heart in return.

And so we end up with her edged against a display case, one leg slung over my shoulder, with her barely hanging on for the ride and me tasting and touching her exactly like I know she needs. And what she needs is how I give it—a little demeaning, a little authoritative, a lot selfish...at least selfish in that imperial, demanding way she loves so much. I've got her folds spread apart, and I'm holding her open for me to lick in the way that satisfies me: deep inside to taste her, down to her anus to make her squirm in embarrassment, up to her clit to make her moan.

And then that word I dread hearing.

"Maxen."

CHAPTER 8
ASH

NOW

HER SAFE WORD.

Her escape.

Everything stops. My mouth, my hands. My heart. I lower her leg carefully and make sure she can stand, and then I drop back onto my heels, hands up and open. My stomach knotting in guilt. We have the safe word so it can be used, but the idea of having done something to force her to use it…it tears at my conscience. I'd rather eat my own liver than harm her, and normally I'm so careful about reading her body and her face when we scene, and I must have missed something, some sign—

"Ash, look at me."

When I look up into her face, I don't see the face of a woman who's hurt. Instead, she looks concerned, like *I'm* the one hurting, and she drops her fingers to play with the hair near my right temple.

"You asked to submit," she says softly. "But you weren't submitting just then."

I'm on my knees and my chin and lips are wet with her, and she's right.

I wasn't submitting.

"It only works if you want it to work," she says, twining her fingers into my hair and pulling. On instinct, I turn my head and nip at the inside of her wrist. She laughs, but her face goes serious.

"Do you want it to work?"

Did I want this to work? I thought so, but maybe I was wrong. Maybe it's impossible for me to yield, even as some sort of twisted emotional rehearsal for yielding on a larger scale. Maybe it's impossible to be any other man than I am.

Except even the thought of it being impossible stiffens my spine. I don't believe anything is impossible. Not for someone who is brave or disciplined or honorable or blessed, and I want desperately to be all of those things.

"I want it to work," I whisper. I catch her hand again, not to bite this time, but to kiss each and every fingertip, lingering long with scrapes of my teeth and brushes of my lips until she's shivering and pressing her legs together under her dress. "But you have to help me. It is hard to be anything other than what I am."

Which is why I need to feel it, I think, peering up at her and hoping she can see the reckless anguish in my face. *I have to know what it feels like, at least once.* How can I rule if I don't know what it feels like to be ruled?

Greer examines my face a moment more, her red lower lip caught between her teeth. I see the thoughts and decisions flit through her eyes like determined birds. "Okay," she says. "Stand up and undress for me."

I do.

It is a foreign feeling, to undress in front of her like this—at her command, at her pleasure. As I shuck off my jacket and toe off my shoes, I have to remind myself that this was what I wanted. This mirror of our normal lives, this reflection of our marriage, the one where she undresses and I watch. Now it is her standing, swathed in silk like armor, and it is me slowly laying my own armor aside. I tug my cuff links off with practiced care; I slide the bow tie off with deliberate focus. Like a good submissive, I take enough time to put everything away neatly, but I move fast enough for my mistress's pleasure.

And it's her pleasure indeed that I hear as I pull off my shirt and expose my bare torso. It's pleasure coming from her mouth as I unzip my pants and my cock pushes through the placket, still hard and dark and thick. It's pleasure panting through her body as I straighten up to my considerable height and permit her to see almost every inch of my naked flesh.

"We've been married for three months, and I still feel like I've hardly ever seen you naked," she says with a smile, biting that lip again. "I'll never get bored of it."

She steps forward and presses her hands to the tight flats of my stomach; she lets her fingertips trace the feathered lines of my oblique and serratus muscles. She drops kisses along the swoop of my collarbone and on my nipples, which tighten at her touch. She runs a teasing palm against the underside of my penis, causing it to thicken and swell and bob, which delights her. She does it again and again and again, until the tip is flared dark and dripping, and I've never been teased, not like this. I'm the one who does the teasing, and all I want to do is grab her arm and spin her around and kick her legs apart. Fuck the adorable impertinence right out of her.

But I don't do those things. I hold myself perfectly still. I force myself to feel it, to surrender to the sensation of being touched without touching back. To having no say, no jurisdiction over my own body. It's shocking how difficult that is. How worrying it feels.

"You are so handsome," Greer tells me, her eyes and hands all over me. My hips and ass and thighs and shoulders. "You make me so proud. I'm proud that you're mine. So strong and so…" She circles my dick and gives me a stroke that has me breathless. "Virile."

Her words help; they smooth over the awkward self-consciousness I feel at my own lack of movement, my passivity. It's hard not to feel useless, oafish even, standing tall and hulking over her as I do, but the way she handles me and speaks to me reminds me that I'm only to worry about pleasing her right now, and I've already done that, simply by being myself. It is a weighty blessing to feel, knowing that your very existence is enough to make someone happy, and it shouldn't be, because I feel that way about Greer and Embry. They don't have to do anything to earn my love and affection because my love and affection simply bubbles up for them. They've already earned it just by being themselves.

I've never considered that anyone might feel that way about me.

"On the bench," Greer says after she's done petting and purring over me. "Flat on your back."

I move as she asks, the air strange on my skin. I'm rarely unclothed like this—only in bed or in the shower—and even during a scene, I'm usually still covered, and I feel vulnerable and exposed as I walk to the low, wide bench. I feel young. I feel small. And I'm neither young nor small.

This is what you wanted. Savor it.

And somehow as I lie on that bench, the wood cool against my bare back, ass, and legs, my cock leaking onto my belly, I manage to. Find it and savor it—the freedom past the self-consciousness. I knew it was there, of course, even as a teenager I knew that was how it had to work, and as a man, I've seen the dazed rapture of my lovers more times than I can count. I've known exactly what kinds of pain and pleasure, or mixture of the two, to inflict on someone in order to peel them open and leave them shivering, and I've even visited this place once or twice before under Mark's tutelage at the club, although only briefly and with the distance of a scholar.

It's different now. The air weighs more against my skin, my blood moves differently in my body. Is it because I'm with my wife and not a near stranger? Is it because I want it, because I'm trying to feel it? Is it because Embry has already laid me so low that it takes next to nothing to blow me into pieces, like a pillar of ash in the wind?

I sink into it, let myself be blown apart, and when Greer crawls over me and slowly moves my arms above my head, pinning my wrists there and tying them with her stocking, I'm completely there. Floating, drifting. A leaf on a lake, skating across the surface with joy and fear.

"Don't move," she commands in a whisper after she finishes binding my wrists, and then my abdomen and thighs are tickled by silk as she moves down to straddle my hips. When she lowers herself, it should be impossible to keep from trying to thrust up into her, it should be impossible to endure the teasing wet rubs of her pussy along my cock, but I do, I endure it. I stay still and obedient even as my ribs jerk with jagged breaths, even as my erect cock aches with the need to release and my balls are drawn up tight to my body. I stay still and obedient as she finally puts me out of my misery and reaches under her dress to position me at her entrance. And I stay completely still as she guides me inside of her, even though it feels like the best kind of hot, wet dream.

"God," she whispers. She's so swollen that she has to work herself down on my penis, and there's a moment when I think she might not be able to take all of me like this, but she spreads her thighs wide and throws her head back and sinks to the hilt. She seats herself fully with a gasp and a shudder, goose bumps everywhere across her chest and her arms, and even I have to bite back a moan at the wet, kissing heat along my length. Her pussy is the best thing I've ever felt, the sweetest and tightest thing, and having her on top of me like this is a revelation.

I can see her face and neck perfectly, the flush creeping up past the bodice of her dress and the tendrils of hair coming loose from her updo. I can feel the needy roaming of her hands and the hungry clench of her thighs around my hips. I can see and feel exactly what she would do to my body if given unfettered access, and it's feverishly erotic to see her using me with such unabashed ferocity. It's provoking to think that this must be how she wants me all the time, to be able to bite my nipples and scratch down my abs and fuck me with brutal, grinding rolls that send the tip of me deep into her stomach and leave her quivering with unrelieved pressure.

"You're so big," she tells me, all purr and sweetness as she rides me. "My big, strong Ash."

And she makes me feel big and strong in an entirely new way, in a way where I don't have to use my bigness and my strength for anything. I don't have to justify possessing those attributes; I don't have to carefully counterbalance them with gentleness and finesse. I am the leaf skating across the pond again, simply blowing where her words take me, and I can just watch with exhilarating clarity how much she enjoys my size, my strength, my body. I don't have to worry about pleasing her with those things because she will please herself; I don't have to worry about right and wrong, strong and weak, protective and reckless, because she will worry about it for me. I can sink like a stone into my body, into my own mind, and vanish into a breathless, static fog of electric need and chemical want.

It's magic.

It's mindless, sweaty magic.

There's no country to lead, no Embry, no war to avoid, and no broken heart. There's no sword and there's no crown. There's nothing but Greer holding me as closely as a body can hold another's, carrying me far above it all and deep below, and when she twists her body down harder onto mine and orders me to let go and climax, I do it.

I obey.

I yield.

I submit.

I am nothing and she is everything, and somehow it makes me everything again just to be under her; I am alchemically transformed from a leaden man into a golden being of pure, incandescent surrender. When the orgasm comes, it comes like the swift cut of the sun across the globe; it comes bright and hard and fast, and the ecstatic surges deep in my pelvis are echoed by the clenches of my abs, the tight jerks of my hips and thighs, until my entire body is caught up in the feeling.

"Give it to me," she murmurs, riding my restlessly orgasming body like a queen would ride a steed. Her hands dig into my sides, her heels into my thighs, and for a moment, I really do feel like a stallion, proud and powerful but completely tamed at the same time. Her eyes are gentle on mine as I empty myself into her, and not only am I emptying, but I *am* empty. For just a few sweet moments, I don't exist. I'm not real. I know exactly how it would be to give up everything moral and ethical and practical and just *give in.* There's no Ash, no President Colchester…only a man who wants his lovers close and nothing else.

So this is what it would feel like.

The words come like drops of water in zero gravity, floating through the animal dark of my mind. Clear and sparkling.

This is how it would feel to truly yield.

Wild. Primal. Selfish.

Short.

And then I'm back again.

I blink up at her, my body still giving the occasional pulse, but the rest of me sated and heavy. My eyelids are hooded, my muscles relaxed. I could fall asleep right now if it weren't for this twist deep in my gut, this faint flicker of unhappiness or dissatisfaction. I try to push it away, to soak up every part of this moment.

Greer smiles down at me, laughing a little as she brushes a quick kiss along my jaw.

"What is it?" I ask, my voice sleepy.

"I've just never seen you like this. All stretched out and satisfied and drowsy." Another kiss, on my cheek this time. "Now is usually the time you're cleaning me and giving me water and asking me how I feel. It's nice to see you so thoroughly fucked that you can't even move. Maybe nice is the wrong word... It's more gratifying, I guess."

I catch her lips with mine the next time she tries to kiss my jaw. "Gratifying how?" I ask against her mouth.

"Mmm," she hums, kissing me back. "I suppose it's flattering to think that I made you that way. It feels good to look at you like this and know that I'm the reason. That I turned this tall, strong beast into a loose-limbed man ready for a nap."

"It's the power," I say. "It's the power that feels good. Can you untie my wrists, please?"

She does, leaning forward as I bring my wrists to my chest, and once I'm free, I reach up to touch her face. She's stunning like this, with shadows casting down from her pretty cheekbones and her delicate jaw and her long eyelashes. There is even the tiniest curl of shadow in the cupid's bow of her upper lip. She was formed for sunshine and pleasure, but fuck if darkness and pain don't look beautiful on her—and there is pain cast onto her features right now, even if she doesn't know it.

"You didn't come," I say, brushing her lower lip with my thumb.

"I—"

"Don't lie, angel. There's no point."

She sits up and sighs, and the movement reminds us both that I'm still inside her, semi-erect but slowly stiffening again.

"I loved being able to ride you like that," she says. "And I was so fucking close, but I just couldn't get there. I wanted to, but I… It kept slipping out of reach."

I give my hips an experimental thrust, and her pussy—still wet and wound tight—flutters in response. I do it a couple more times until I'm all the way hard, and then I wrap my arms around her waist and sit up. I move her on my lap, angling her so that her clit rubs against me every time she moves and so that my cock kisses that sweet, rough spot on her inner wall with every thrust.

"Like this," I say, using a finger to lift her chin so she has to look in my face. "Move as I am moving you."

"Are you my sir again?"

"I am."

The flush is back on her neck as she obeys and begins grinding on my cock, and I keep my finger under her jaw so she can't look away. I watch her face as I tell her to move faster, to lean back a little, to grind down in twists that leave her gasping. I watch the pleasure flit across her face like cloud shadows over the prairie, fast and ever-changing, and then I watch the relief there as I band an arm across her back and start matching her thrust for thrust, pushing up into her until I can feel her womb. I know she can come like this, but there's still something holding her back, something keeping her chained to the ground. And with heartbreaking clarity, I see what it is.

"Hold on," I breathe, flipping us both over so that she's flat on her back and I'm moving cruelly in between her legs. She twists and whines and arches.

"Is this what you need to come?" I ask a little meanly. "To be fucked like this?"

She nods frantically, her fingers fisting in the overflowing fabric of her dress. Her cunt is so wet that I can feel it on her inner thighs, on my own thighs, and it gets even wetter as I lean down and slide an arm under her back, crushing my weight on top of hers. My other hand comes up to collar her throat, my male organ below it all continuing to do its work, claiming her just as my hands do, just as my eyes do.

"Why couldn't you come earlier?" I ask gently, the kindness in my voice completely at odds with the merciless movements of my body. But I want her to see the tender patience in my face, to see all of my eternal love and concern, so that she knows I'm not asking to shame her or induce some kind of misplaced guilt. I genuinely want to know, even though I can already guess her answer.

It takes her a moment to find the words.

"I didn't feel free," she finally says on a gasp, her body wild under mine. I can tell by the shine in her eyes that she's close to tears, the admission prying open something she's avoided looking at for a long time. "I thought I would love it, and I did, but it wasn't enough."

Enough. It was what I had felt under her touch: that I was enough to please her, that I was enough to deserve her affection and love, that I was enough as I *was* without all the things I *do*. The pull in my gut right after I'd ejaculated had betrayed the truth, but if I had any doubts, they are burned away now.

My submission only showed me a lie. I'm not enough.

It's not enough for me to yield. It's not enough for me to surrender and give in. Perhaps it was never in my nature to feel satisfied with passivity, but now I see it doesn't matter. It's my actions that earn the love in my life, and I can never stop working.

The world must spin.

And maybe one day, I'll find that right sacrifice, that one act of martyrdom that will please God and save my soul, but until then, I will stand and work and earn that elusive sense of honor and probity. Even as my chest twists with jealousy when I realize that Greer has never had these problems when she fucks Embry, that she's never needed anything other than him, that he is enough as he is. But from me, she will always need more. She will always need a king. I take a moment to let the unfairness and the envy sting, and then I let them dissolve into the ocean of my love for her. I'm a better man than to resent this, and I love her too much to deny her anything.

And perhaps most importantly, I am meant to be the man she needs. I crave it. I'm unhappy without it. It would be churlish of me to begrudge her needing the exact same thing that I need, even if she doesn't need it from our other lover.

I carefully press with my thumb and fingers, squeezing the pulse points on the sides of her neck—the illusion of choking with none of the damage to the windpipe that inexperienced dominants often cause.

"Yes," she whispers, her eyes fluttering. "God, yes."

I measure every flicker of her pulse, every dilation of her eyes, every ripple through her taut body, keeping her safe as I tease her along the edge of consciousness, keeping her orgasm right on the brink. Then we are there, the two of us, my hand around her throat and her body speared on mine.

"You are free now," I tell her. "Fly."

And when I let go and all that oxygen-rich blood floods to her brain, she comes so hard that her back bows off the bench and her mouth O's into a silent gasp and I can feel every minute I spent teasing her and toying with her today as she unspools in wild, writhing loops. I let go along with her, letting her slippery rapture and the intoxicating feeling of my body over hers—broad shoulders shadowing her slender ones, my hand so large and rough on the elegant arch of her neck—tug me into orgasming inside her once again. And this time, as I fill her with my climax, there's no shadow of dissatisfaction or emptiness. I feel whole and complete, and even more so looking down at the woman below me, who's now smiling and spent.

Yes, this is the way it should be.

"Thank you," she says dreamily up at me. "That was perfect. You master me so well."

I smooth some of her hair away from her temple. "Thank *you*, princess. I'm grateful for what you gave me tonight."

The hint of a frown mars her perfect lips, and I see a spot where her red lipstick has smudged near the corner of her mouth. I carefully wipe it away and bend down to kiss it; when I lift my head, she's still frowning, a troubled line between her brows.

"Tell me, princess."

"I feel like you didn't get what you needed," she says a little sadly. "You acted like the perfect submissive, and I couldn't even act like a passable domme."

"You were marvelous," I assure her, kissing her again and then helping her sit up. "The only reason I enjoyed it was because of you, and I learned under the best dominant you can imagine, so that's high praise."

"You're the best dominant I can imagine," she says, her frown relaxing a little.

I laugh, standing up and gathering my clothes. I hand

her a monogrammed handkerchief so she can clean herself, and then I do the same. "I'm flattered, but even I'm a little scared of Mark. He's the kind of person who would chase you if you ran, if that gives you an idea."

"Did he chase you?" she asks.

"I never ran."

"Of course not."

I start getting dressed again, both amused and warmed by the way Greer's eyes drink in the lines of my body as I do, the way they darken slightly in disappointment as more and more of me disappears beneath the tuxedo. Even so, it could only be a tithe of the ache I feel when she pulls her dress down over her well-used pussy. My desire for her is bottomless; I could spend the rest of my life in this room with her. "Also, there was no reason to run. He was a teacher, my mentor for six months. Anything he did to me was part of a lesson and never a true scene. But I often watched him perform scenes with true submissives, and I've never seen someone so compassionate and so cruel at the same time."

The last time I saw Mark was last autumn, and he was in a scene with a slender young thing named Isolde, kissing her shoulder blades after welting them up with a weighty-looking flogger. I'd just gotten word that he would be collaring her next weekend. I wouldn't attend, but I did arrange for flowers and a hand-tooled leather leash with their names on it to be sent.

"I haven't forgotten my original point, though," Greer says, her hair and dress put back to rights. She walks over to me and helps me button up my shirt. "Did you get what you needed?"

I think about the false sense of happiness I felt, about waking up from that happiness and realizing Greer was still unsatisfied. I think about right sacrifices. I think about the man I am, the man I will always be.

I won't lay down this crown until I know the world will be a better place for it.

I run my hands up Greer's arms and then catch her hands in my own. "I saw what I needed to see."

"Which is?"

"The right thing to do."

We emerge back into the gala, perhaps a little rumpled and flushed, but it's all too easy to blame that on the champagne and the crowded ballroom. Luckily, I'm required to step out of events frequently enough that no one seems suspicious that I disappeared for any reason other than a matter of state, and we were only in that gallery for an hour anyway.

It was worth the risk. Everything inside of me feels cleaner, better, less bruised. As if I've finally stopped bleeding. As if I can breathe again. And when Belvedere comes to my side and discreetly indicates that the long-awaited call from Berlin has come, I take the phone and think, for the first time in twenty-four hours, that I might do more than survive this.

I might be able to make the world a safer place for it. I might be able to win my prince back to my side.

I might once again be a king worth kneeling to.

CHAPTER 9
ASH

THEN

WHEN I WAS TWENTY-TWO, I MET A PRINCE. HE SEEMED TO be the exact opposite of everything I was—loud where I was quiet, smiling where I frowned, careless where I was careful. Embry joined the army because Vivienne Moore wanted her son to craft the perfect politician's résumé. I joined because it seemed like the place to continue my never-ending quest for honor, because becoming an officer in the army had a certain cachet in my neighborhood, because I wanted to somehow cosmically return the favor for my college scholarship, because the structure and rigid hierarchy of military life appealed to me.

Most importantly, I joined because I knew Carpathia was the most dangerous place in the world at the time, and I felt needed there in a way I can't describe. It was like a barometric pressure that made my bones and teeth ache when I tried to resist it. I knew that I was supposed to be there in the same way I knew that God was real or that I was bisexual. It was a fact, even if it couldn't be seen.

And after all that, then I see this lieutenant refuse to break up a fight? When we were there on the brink of war and responsible for safekeeping innocents nearby? No. I wasn't an angry person, but I was a disciplined one, and the one thing I couldn't tolerate in other people was a lack of it.

I only meant to shake some sense into him, to tell him clearly and unmistakably that he wouldn't get away with that shit while I was around, but then he turned, and I saw his face for the first time.

And it was over.

Done.

One look at those winter-blue eyes and those delicate lips and I was finished. One glance at his lean, long body, and I was falling. Every part of me responded with heat and flush and wrenching want, like a hook had been fastened somewhere in my chest and was now giving an almighty tug, and the only thing to ease the ache would be to get closer, closer, closer.

I'd never seen a boy so beautiful. Haughty as he was, overindulged and so obviously dissolute, he was the loveliest person I'd ever seen.

I still pinned him against the wall, though. And it was when I had him against the wall with my forearm on his throat and my body trapping his that he sealed his fate. As I was choking him, he looked at me with his whole world in his eyes.

To say I became preoccupied with my haughty co-officer is an understatement. He became something of a meditation for me—at night, I fell asleep mentally sketching the lines of his face; during the day, my focus settled on him as he worked.

His body so slender and tempting as he did calisthenics, the sweat glistening on his throat as he ran. His easy smile and his careless, lavish charm. He had the face of a Regency novel hero, but his personality belonged somewhere in the twenties or thirties. Sebastian Flyte at Oxford. Gatsby in his mansion. An American expat in Paris merrily burning all his money on liquor and food and women…or maybe men. He made jokes sometimes, sly references that had the other men in his unit howling with laughter or shoving his shoulder in embarrassment, but it was impossible to tell from afar how much truth lay in his jokes and nudges and how much of it was just Embry performing some persona that I didn't quite understand.

But oh, how I wanted it to be true. Even though we hadn't talked since I'd thrown him against a wall, even though I could tell by his pointed avoidance of me that he was still pissed, I wanted him to like boys too. At college it had seemed so easy, so open—that common language of smiles and touches to signal availability and interest. But here everything was murkier, submerged beneath the masculine gloss of military life, hidden in subtexts inside subtexts.

There *had* been that look when I'd pinned him against the wall, so fleeting I might have imagined it…

Then came that day in the woods when I beat him at our drill, roundly annihilating his team and then having the pleasure of shooting him with the paint round myself. I'd been the one to see his eyes flare with pain as the bullet made contact, the one to see his eyes flare with something else when I put my boot on his wrist. I couldn't help but smile then because it felt righter than anything ever had before; this one small thing was the closest I'd ever come to being truly myself with a person I was falling in love with. I didn't just want to put my boot on someone's wrist—I wanted him to *want* my boot on his wrist. And I didn't only want to stand over him and feel the tread of my boot pressing into his skin; I wanted to kiss the tread marks when I was finished. I wanted to feel his almost-curly hair beneath my fingers as I thanked him for letting me hurt him, and then I wanted to press my hand to his chest and feel the beat of his heart while I persuaded his lips apart and tasted his mouth.

I wanted to take him to bed.

The thought scared me as much as it excited me. I'd spent the last seven years very intentionally not bringing anyone into my bed because I wanted to be myself fully in that moment, and here was this decadent princeling of a boy whom I barely knew and taking him to bed was all I could think about.

But then the moment faded, and he said, "You'd have to hurt me much worse than this if you want to hear me beg." And it didn't sound like a dare; it didn't sound like the words of a man who wanted me to make him beg. It sounded very much like he hated me.

It thrummed through me, this hatred of his, unchaining my sense of honor, my dedication to consent. I couldn't take this soldier back to my room and cinch his wrists with my belt; I couldn't ask him to let me inside his body when he clearly felt that I was…that I was what? Some kind of bully? A heartless rival?

Realizing that's how he saw me stung. And maybe that's why I reacted the way I did to meeting his sister in the halls of our barracks later that day. Even now, I can't tell you whether it was purely hurt or a need to be close to Embry *somehow*—even if that was through Morgan—or some mixture of the two, but I decided right then and there that I was willing to take the sister if the brother wouldn't have me. It was a bitter decision, made in a bitter moment, and even now I think it hurt me more than it hurt him. And of course, the consequences of that decision have unfolded into a shameful chaos of tragic scale.

All because I thought this blue-eyed boy didn't want my boot on his wrist. For that one transgression, I sired a thousand more.

"Do you want to fuck my stepbrother?"

The question came sudden and blunt, too fast for me to school my reaction. Morgan took one look at me and said, "Ah."

It was our first night in Prague, and Embry, much to my disappointment, had vanished after we checked into our hotel. I knew he didn't want me, but it didn't stop me from wanting him, even if it was just to watch him smoke cigarettes and quote Coleridge and Keats and Eliot and other boarding school poets until the fog swarmed the city and the streets were silent except for the sound of his voice. I craved him like I suppose addicts crave things; it was blood deep, restless, dangerous. I'd literally never felt that way about another human before, and had I once believed I was aromantic? Now I knew I was the opposite of aromantic; I was all romance, I was all gnawing emotion and pained longing and staring at cobbled streets hoping he would appear.

But he wouldn't appear. Morgan told me that he was already fucking his way through New Town and drinking the top shelves in every club dry. It was just us and might be just us for the entire week. God, how I panged at the thought.

"Don't worry," she said. "I won't tell anyone."

"He hates me," I said, taking a stab at an offhanded tone and failing. "So it doesn't matter."

Morgan just smiled at that, a secretive smile that seemed almost feline in nature.

"And I don't even know if he likes men."

"Oh," she said with a coy look, "Embry likes everyone."

"And anyway," I said, taking a long drink of the Czech pilsner in front of me and then realizing as I set it down that I was a little drunk, "I haven't actually ever fucked anyone. So me wanting to fuck him doesn't mean much."

Her green eyes widened. I'd surprised her. "You're a virgin?"

"Embry would laugh for hours if he knew," I said, half-wryly, half-unhappily.

She shook her head. "I don't understand, and you're going to have to explain this to me—how does a person go to war a virgin?"

I fiddled with the beer bottle on the table, spinning it in slow circles. "I...I have a way that I want to be with people. I'm not ashamed of it, but I refuse to be that way with someone unless they want it. And I won't sleep with someone until I *can* be that way because I believe it's immoral to share something like that if I can't do it honestly—if I have to close my eyes and pretend in order to finish."

I kept my words purposefully vague—mostly out of respect for the fact that Morgan and I barely knew each other and it was hardly appropriate for me to force my sexual baggage on her—but also because I didn't have the language to describe it all yet and I didn't know exactly how to convey what I meant. And I didn't think she'd be interested in my rehashing the plot of *Labyrinth* to explain it to her.

But even so, she understood immediately what I meant. I know now it was because she'd already spent years flirting with kink, but at the time it seemed almost eerie how quickly she grasped my meaning. "Does this have anything to do with you touching Embry's bruise on the train?"

I kept my eyes on the bottle as I admitted the truth. "Yes."

"Were you hard when you did it?"

I didn't answer.

She sat back, that satisfied-cat smile on her face again. "Maxen Colchester. Baby dominant."

"Baby what?"

"There are words for what you like," she said. "There are words for what you are. And there's a whole world of people who like it."

I looked at her. At her long, bare legs, at her elegant throat and long black hair. Her violently green eyes and full mouth. She was beautiful, and even if she didn't make me sore with wanting like Embry did, I was still attracted to her. "And are you one of the people who like it?" I asked carefully.

Her smile deepened. "I am."

"I see."

She leaned forward, her smile turning into something more serious. "Can I show you something tonight?"

"What do you want to show me?"

"How it could be. And if you like how it could be, I'll show you more."

I didn't have a response right away. Everything I'd ever believed about sex and desire had revolved around it being organic, genuine, and deep, and this was undoubtedly transactional and arranged. There'd be no emotional intimacy to underscore our joining, and that had always been important to me.

And then, with a bitter taste in my mouth, I remembered that Embry was out in Prague somewhere at this very moment, enjoying any number of transactional intimacies. I remembered his face as I asked him if he hated me on the train.

Yes, he'd answered.

What did it feel like to want someone who hated you? It felt like hell.

"Show me," I told Morgan.

Cat's smile. A long arch of her back as she stretched her arms. I watched the fabric of her dress pull tight around her small tits and ride up the smooth skin of her legs. It had been a long time since I'd seen a woman in civilian clothes, and I had to admit I'd missed the sight. The curves, the inviting hollows of a woman's body: the space between breasts, the luscious cleft of an ass, the hidden, wet place between the thighs. My body responded exactly as you'd imagine.

I tried not to think of how Embry looked strolling to our hotel in the fog, his coat highlighting the breadth of his shoulders and his eyelashes dark on his cheeks as he lit a cigarette. I tried not to think of how it would feel to see his thighs instead, dusted with hair and sculpted with lean muscle, how it would feel to see his nipples harden under my stare rather than Morgan's.

"So first," she said, after she finished stretching, "say you wanted to take my hand across the table. As if we were on a date."

I extended my hand, enfolding hers within my own. "Like this?"

"Yes. Now hold my wrist instead."

I slid my hand from hers to cover her wrist, and the moment I circled the delicate joint there with my fingers, something changed inside my mind. It shoved roughly into place, like a carpentry joint.

"Oh," I said.

"Yeah," she said.

I gave it a small squeeze—not hard enough to bruise, just hard enough to test the give of her skin—and the tiny flinch she gave at the unexpected pressure was better than any kiss. Then she laughed. "You're a quick learner. Let's keep going."

And we did, as we moved from restaurant to bar to hotel. I ordered for her at the bar; when we crossed the street and I instinctively put my hand at the small of her back, she guided it to the back of her neck instead. When

I kissed her for the first time in an alley beside the bar, she said, *bite me, bite me*, and I did, and I felt like the entire world was spinning around my feet. My cock throbbed and leaked all over itself as my teeth dug into the warm flesh of her neck, the heat in my blood was making me fevered and delirious as she panted and mewled as I bit. And then she guided my hands under her skirt, and said, "See? See how wet you make me?"

I groaned into her neck, my fingers covered with evidence of how much she liked it. She *wanted* it, *wanted* me, all of me. All the parts of me I'd kept hidden out of decency and fear for so long.

"Can I show you the rest now?" she asked breathlessly.

"Yes, God." The thought of replacing my fingers with my cock into that wet, hot place had me nearly wild. "Do I need a condom?"

"I'm on the pill," she said, "and I'm clean. And we both know you're clean."

"I'm sorry if I hurt you," I told her, my hand already on my belt.

She gave a full-throated laugh at that. "No, you're not."

I laughed back because she was right, and the freedom of it felt vast and immense. That I could have someone like this and that they could want it—like the roll of a blue sky before the nose of an airplane. Limitless and thrilling.

Morgan was tall for a woman, so I could sling her leg over my arm to open her up to me. It was dark and all I could see was the place between her legs where she got darker, but it was enough to make me groan again. With fumbling eagerness, I found her wet slit with my penis, using the tip to slip and rub and explore until we were both trembling. The pressure of the air on my skin was too much, like the atmosphere had thickened, like gravity had tripled, and it was that same heavy feeling I felt when I pulled the sword from the stone at the carnival, that same feeling in my bones that this was important somehow, that this would mark an indelible moment in my life. This was a thing that could not be undone.

At the time, I took it as confirmation rather than as a warning, and for that mistake, I have paid dearly, but all of that was ahead of me then. I only knew the slick invitation of her body, the novelty of not having to stop. The joy of hearing someone ask for *more* and *harder* and *everything, give me everything*. So I did—I gave her everything. For the first time in my life, I pushed inside another person's body and took my pleasure there.

I have asked myself numberless times since if some part of me knew or suspected. It's been almost two years since Jenny's funeral—that cheerless day when I both put my wife in the ground and learned about the incest I'd committed in ignorance—and so I've had plenty of time to go over the events in Prague time and again. Surely I must have noticed? Surely there must have been *something*, an inkling, an unconscious familiarity, some signal from her DNA to mine that we shared a mother?

But there wasn't.

Perhaps if I'd been older, I would have been wiser. I would have made familial connections; I would have sensed that something other than mutual attraction connected us. Or perhaps if I hadn't been a virgin, if I'd been well seasoned and worldly, I would have been able to slow down and think about it. Maybe I wouldn't have slept with her at all.

But I wasn't older and I wasn't worldly. I was young and eager and fervid. I was like an animal in rut, and once I'd felt what it was like to fuck someone, I was mindlessly keen to do it again. And again. And again. Morgan had laughed at me that week, at my appetite, which only grew as it was fed, and at my impatient willingness to do anything she wanted, so long as it meant I could fuck her again.

There was more than fucking that week too. She showed me how to spank her, how to hold her over my lap and alternate swats with teasing rubs to her clit. She showed me how to tie someone to a bed frame, how to push my cock into an open throat, how to paddle an ass with a hairbrush. She showed me how to make a woman come as I rode her, how to fuck sitting and how to fuck standing and how to fuck lying down in a bed.

There was one moment when I had her standing in front of the bathroom mirror with her hands braced on the sink, when I was fucking her from behind and staring at the slide of my erection in and out of her vagina. She looked up at the mirror and I did too, and we both stared at our reflection, which was striking not only in its carnality, but in the way we matched. Black hair, green eyes. Full lips and high cheekbones and noses slightly Roman at the bridge.

"We look good together," she said.

Perhaps that was the moment I should have noticed. The moment I should have asked myself if there was any chance in the world that things were not as they appeared. But then Morgan said, "You know you can spank me while you're inside me," and the moment burst like a soap bubble, making room for my palm on her bare ass and the gasping orgasm that followed.

We only saw Embry once that week, the night he taught me how to dance, but he was on my mind constantly. Even as I fucked Morgan, even as I spanked her and bit her, my thoughts bent toward him. Was he on the other side of the wall right now, fucking someone he'd picked up at a club? Was it a boy or a girl? If it was a boy, did he pretend they were me?

Did he think about our little waltz as often as I did? Was he humming Strauss as he got dressed, was he touching his own shoulder to remember the feeling of my hand there? I was almost driven to madness with the lack of him, with the lack of hope for our future, and Morgan offered relief. With her body, with her attention. She offered me a glimpse of myself that I'd never had before, and for that I will always be thankful. Even knowing what I do now, I can't ever erase that gratitude. She gave of herself generously, unselfishly, while she must have known the entire time that I would never feel for her the way I felt for her brother.

Glein happened, the first and most disastrous test of my leadership skills. The war picked up; I barely saw the spoiled prince I'd fallen in love with, and I got the distinct impression he was avoiding me. But the moments when we did see each other, the times I was able to talk to him and joke with him and touch him under the pretext of playful fraternity, there sometimes seemed a glint of thaw in those haughty blue eyes. It sometimes seemed as if he was looking at me when he thought I wouldn't notice, that he closed his eyes just a beat too long when I touched him. That he caught his breath whenever I said his name.

It gave me hope. Hope that he didn't hate me. Hope that he felt even a sliver of what I felt, hope that he had the same glass splinter in his heart as I did, shimmering and deep.

The day before he left, I'd only meant to tell him that I'd miss him. That I hoped he'd stay in touch, that we'd see each other again. But then, somehow, I'd admitted the terrible truth.

Yes. I wish you belonged to me.

I wished he were mine to keep safe, mine to discipline, mine to cherish and to fuck, and finally saying it out loud to him had knocked something loose. My common sense, I suppose, or my sense of propriety. And that's how I ended up on top of him, and if I had ever doubted that he wanted me, all my doubts were erased in that moment. He opened his mouth for me, arched his back in mindless response, rubbed his hard dick along the length of mine. He kissed me back with a fervor that matched my own. And when I told him, a little shyly, that I'd never felt this way about anyone before, what I meant was that that I used to think I was missing the part of my soul that could fall in love with another soul. But now I knew differently. For the first time in my life, I knew what it was to be consumed with someone else. He was my Patroclus and if he ever left me, my world would darken until it crawled with shadows and blighted every promise of spring.

He did leave me.

And the shadows crawled.

CHAPTER 10
GREER

NOW

"YOU'RE NOT SUPPOSED TO BE HERE."

My cousin stands in the doorway of my Georgetown office, polished and glossy as always, a dress of robin's-egg blue highlighting her slender figure and the small swell of Embry's unborn child. The sight is like a slow stab in my own belly, going deeper and deeper every minute she's in front of me.

"You're not supposed to be here," I say again. "I would have thought that my refusing to answer your calls made that quite clear."

Abilene just smiles and walks into the office, finding a chair and sitting down on the other side of my desk. "You did make it clear, but this is important. And if you really didn't want me around, you would have told your Secret Service agents, but they seem to still think I'm an approved visitor."

"I could call them," I warn her, sliding my phone close to me. "Right now. I don't care that you're pregnant."

"Yes, but you won't call."

I hesitate as I reach for my phone, not sure what game she's playing. Of course, up until my kidnapping in May, I had no idea that she was playing any games at all. I'd trusted her. My cousin, my best friend. She'd sold me to Melwas all because I'd had the audacity to marry the man she was obsessed with, and even my abduction hadn't been enough—she'd blackmailed Embry into an engagement, and she held the threat of going public about Lyr over all our heads.

It's for Lyr's sake, and Ash's, that I relent.

"Okay," I say. "I won't. Tell me what you came here for."

Abilene pulls a creamy stock envelope out from her purse and puts it on the table. "I wanted to make sure your invitation didn't get lost in the mail."

Oh fuck you, I want to say to her. Instead I just say, "I'm afraid I won't be able to make it."

"What a shame," Abilene says mildly. "I really wanted you to be my matron of honor."

I keep my voice as steady and cool as hers while I say, "Abilene, that will never happen. You must know this."

She shrugs. "It would make for an excellent story after Embry announces his campaign, you know. If you and Maxen were at the wedding."

I study her for a moment. I've always been good at reading people, and I've had more practice with Abilene than almost any other person, but something's changed inside her that makes her difficult to understand or predict. She's a satellite with an unstable orbit, destined to swing wide and crash into another moon. "What do you want from all of this?" I ask. "For me to be miserable? For me to know that Embry strayed? For me to get kidnapped again?"

The edges of her mouth curl up in a mocking smile, but when I speak next, the smile disappears.

"You want Ash to love you?" I ask.

She blinks and glances away, and for a split second, I see the girl I used to know. The girl I grew up with. Headstrong and selfish, but not evil. Not *this*. And it's in seeing this that I realize I'm right. All of this is about me taking Ash away from her. Embry is a casualty of proximity, just a means to hurt me. All she's wanted since high school is Ash, and there's a part of her that realizes she'll never have him now, not after what she's done. I hope that knowledge is agony.

I'd been taught in my youth how to identify these weak spots and how to press on them, but I don't do that now. I don't want to press on them because I don't know what will happen. I don't know her limits anymore, I don't know the rotten ice edges of her spite, I don't know what words or looks or gestures might send me plummeting into dark, freezing water. I don't know that she won't walk out of here and decide to announce Lyr's existence in front of the clock tower outside.

So I change tactics, and instead I say, "It was terrible, you know. Being taken by Melwas."

She looks back to me, the vulnerability fading fast in her face. "Good," she says. "I wanted it to be."

"Are you upset that I escaped?"

"I'm upset that you lived," she says in a bland tone of voice, as though we're talking about our work schedules or the weather. "That wasn't supposed to be the case."

"Sorry to disappoint you," I respond, unable to keep the bitterness out of my voice. "Sorry for wanting to be alive."

She shakes her head. "You still don't get it, do you? This is just all some fairy tale to you, and it always has been, ever since we were kids. Perfect, sad Greer, all alone in her tower, and she gets rescued and wooed by not one but *two* men. Don't you see how stupidly unfair that is? How ridiculous it was when you were already Grandpa's favorite? When you already had the perfect childhood?"

"My parents died, Abi," I say, leaning forward in my seat. "I was orphaned. I hardly had the perfect childhood, and if I was Grandpa's favorite, it was because he had no choice but to take me in."

"You had *everything*," she says angrily. "And Maxen Colchester was the one thing in the world I ever really wanted, and you took him away from me."

"I'm sorry that I didn't take your teenage crush into consideration when I fell in love."

"It wasn't a crush. Maxen was the goal for me, always," she insists. "Every congressman I fucked, every lobbyist I dated, it was all to get me closer to him. I knew more about him than he knew about himself, *that's* how much I loved and wanted him. It was hard; it took me years to discover all his secrets, but I did it." She lifts her chin as if expecting some kind of trophy for this.

"Congratulations," I say. "It's helped quite a lot with your blackmailing him."

"I never meant to blackmail *him*," she says, as if this distinction matters now. "In fact, I never meant to blackmail anybody. When I found the letter in Grandpa Leo's desk, all I felt was excited."

I hate that even now, despite everything, I'm curious. "What letter?"

Her smile returns—she's happy to know something I don't—but it's not mocking this time either. She genuinely lights up as she tells me, and I realize it's because she's proud. She's proud of herself for putting it all together. "I was staying with Grandpa at his penthouse, years ago. He was out doing something—you remember how he was never home—and I was bored, so I started looking through his desk."

"You went through his desk?" I don't know why after all she's done that this feels like such a transgression, but it does. Grandpa Leo's desk had been sacrosanct, inviolable, a shrine of politics and business that we'd never been allowed near. Even as small children, we'd been swept up in his arms anytime we got close to the desk and deposited elsewhere. He always claimed the ecosystem of reports and memos and letters was too delicate to be disturbed.

"Greer, the reason he didn't want anyone inside his desk is because he had the most incredible things in there. Dossiers on almost every politician you can imagine. Ledgers with money trails that went to all sorts of interesting places. And letters. Letters from so many people…including Penley Luther."

Something fits together in my mind, and I start to see. "Luther confessed the affair to Grandpa Leo?"

Abilene nods. "He was in agony with guilt during his last days," she says. "He knew he was dying and knew he'd failed this child, failed his precious, dead Imogen. But even though he felt all this guilt, he still couldn't bring himself to find Maxen. See his son for himself. He still worried about what the press would say."

God. I'd grown up hearing Luther's name invoked like some sort of ritual blessing on a politician or a new bill, hearing him talked about as if he were an uncanonized saint. And to learn that this hero was actually so weak is unsettling. My heart twists for Ash and for the long-dead Imogen, who died in order that Ash could live. Two people Penley Luther failed in the most unforgivable ways possible.

Abilene correctly reads my expression. "Exactly. Reprehensible. And I have to imagine that Grandpa told him exactly that—that he had a duty to this son and that he wouldn't die in peace unless he'd found some way to make amends. Luther's version of making amends was to set aside some money for 'Imogen Leffey's youngest child,' and it was a laughably small amount given the size of his estate."

"So that's how you learned Luther had a secret child with

Imogen Leffey. But how did you learn that child was Maxen Colchester?"

She smiles like a teacher might smile, as if I've asked exactly the right question. "Because Grandpa was named the executor of his will. He knew that Imogen's youngest child was also Luther's, and after Luther's death, he hired a law firm that employed a young Merlin Rhys to find this child. He knew who Maxen was all along. He knew before almost anyone else."

I sit back in my chair. "Grandpa never uttered a word about any of it..." I say, mostly to myself. I think of all the times we talked leading up to my wedding, of the time we saw Ash in Chicago. Never once had he breathed a word about Ash being Luther's son.

"Luther swore him to secrecy, and I'd imagine Grandpa felt invested in protecting his legacy."

"And you knew this years ago?"

"Yes," she says. "A year or so after Chicago."

"You never told me." Until this last year, Abilene had confided everything in me. I'm shocked that she kept something so huge to herself.

"I liked being the only one to know," she admits, glancing down at her lap. "It felt special, to know something that important, that secret. And so exciting—I could just see the story when it blew up. *Handsome War Hero Actually the Son of Revered Leader*... I mean, it has this epic feeling, you know? Like something out of a soap opera."

"Or Thomas Malory," I murmur. "But then how did you find out about Lyr? Surely Grandpa couldn't have known about that."

"He didn't," Abilene agrees. "That came later, only a couple of years ago. I finally decided to tell Morgan Leffey, and there was something about her when I told her the truth. Like, something about her face. She just looked so sick, sick and sad and *scared.* It was not at all what I expected. That she might want to exploit it for political gain, yes, that she might be angry at Penley Luther or at her mother or even me, certainly. But it was none of that. It was like she'd just seen a dead body or something equally horrifying."

I trace the wooden edge of my desk with a fingertip, that hateful invitation still within sight. I can't believe I'm sitting here talking with her, letting her explain herself, letting her preen over all her victories. But I still don't reach for my phone.

Instead, I ask, "So that tipped you off that she must have had a secret child of her own?"

Abilene doesn't miss the skeptical edge in my tone, but it doesn't seem to bother her. "That's what tipped me off that *something* was strange about her and Maxen. I mean, sure, they'd been political rivals during his campaign and they must have crossed paths a few times because of Embry, but even then, that didn't explain the existential horror I saw. I tried to ask her about it, get her to talk about Maxen, but she showed me out of her office after that and refused to speak with me again." A look of anger crosses Abilene's face. "Like I was some kind of crazy constituent and not Leo Galloway's granddaughter. Like I should be ashamed of myself when I was the reason she ever learned something so important in the first place!"

I'm impatient to get back to the story. "But if she didn't tell you, then how did you find out?"

"Ah." She looks pleased with herself. "It was actually quite easy once I decided to start tracing timelines back. I started with her, used a cute guy in her father's lobbying firm to dig up old records, old expenses. And guess who'd taken two visits to Ukraine at the same time Maxen was stationed there?"

"Morgan." I know this part of the story already, about

how Morgan and Ash had met, fucked, and then she'd returned and almost died at Glein. "But the baby?"

"About five months after her second trip to the Ukraine, all her expenses stopped, came to an abrupt halt. Except for a fifteen-thousand-dollar fee paid to a Manhattan law firm."

"The same one Merlin worked for?" I guess.

"The very same. Merlin arranged everything for Lyr through them—the guardianship transfers, the burying of hospital records, everything—even I couldn't get to the truth from there. I had to fly out to Seattle and actually bribe an administrative assistant to get into the old records to see for myself. Found the nurse who'd been in the delivery room. I didn't think she'd remember anything, but it was worth asking her, and guess what? She did remember something unusual: the mother had wanted to name the baby Maxen after his father, and then she changed her mind after a family friend suggested the name Lyr. Uncommon names, the nurse thought at the time, and the birth stuck with her."

"God," I say. Even knowing the truth on my own, listening to the story unfold still holds a sordid kind of shock.

"From there, it was pretty easy to track Lyr down and see him for myself. And once you see him, there's no doubt."

She moves her own phone onto my desk, sliding past a screen and pulling up a picture of a dark-haired youth. When she spins the phone around so I can have a better look, I have to catch my breath.

It's Ash—he looks just like Ash.

Younger, of course, and there are a few differences here and there. Lyr has longer hair, tousled and messy and curled at the ends in a way that surely makes his classmates swoon, and his features are slightly more angular than Ash's, more otherworldly beautiful than the classically masculine strength his father has. But otherwise I could be looking at a teenaged photo of my husband. The black hair, the full lips with their sharp upper peaks, the eyes as green as old bottle glass.

I understood before, what it meant for Ash to have a son. I understood what it meant for us and for Morgan and the boy himself, and everybody caught in the tragic web around him. I understood that Ash had fathered a child with a woman I am jealous of, and I understood that we had not yet had a child of our own. I understood that my jealousy of Morgan would grow a thousandfold, that she could do by accident what I so wanted to do on purpose.

But seeing this boy, so handsome and tall like his father, shakes some new kind of understanding into me, which is the same knowledge but deeper and heavier and more terrible, and it's crushing my chest and balling my throat.

Ash has a child.

Embry will have a child.

I am not the mother of either of those children.

And in this moment, it doesn't matter that Ash never loved Morgan or that Embry might actually despise Abilene because they will still always be bound to these women in a way that can't be expunged or blanked out. They will share a connection that I have no part of, that I have nothing to do with, and I will forever be exiled from these pieces of them. There are now parts of the men I love that will never belong wholly to me. There are places inside them that are forever stamped with another woman's name, and even if I have children of my own, I will always, always have to share that title of *mother of my children* with someone else.

"Handsome, isn't he?" Abilene says. Too late I realize that I've been staring at Lyr's picture for too long, and although I'm normally quite good at mastering my expression, there's no doubt Abilene saw a glimpse of the tumult inside my mind.

"He is," I comment, pushing the phone back to her. "He looks like his father."

"You can see why I knew for sure after I saw the boy," Abilene says, taking her phone and giving the picture a fond glance. "And for a long time, I was happy with just knowing. It didn't taint Maxen for me at all, you see, and I hated the idea that people would take this and turn it into some tawdry V. C. Andrews–style story."

"But you don't hate that idea anymore? You're okay with ruining his life and Lyr's life and Morgan's?"

Her eyes flash. "I would never ruin his life."

I'm suddenly furious again, and I try to hide it by standing up and walking over to the window so she can't see my face. "Then what is it you think you're doing now?"

"He needs to know that I'll love him no matter what," she says confidently. "Then he'll see. When everyone else has left him, when everyone else has abandoned him, I'll be there. And I won't care what he's done with Morgan; I won't care that they had a son. I'll be the only one to forgive him for everything. So you see, it's not ruining his life at all. It's bringing him to the one who loves him the most."

I turn to look at her, to say something about how delusional she sounds, but before I can speak, I'm transfixed by the look on her face. I've never seen anything like it—her lips tilted up in a dreamy smile and her eyes bright with some uncomfortable fire and her cheeks flushed red with excitement. There's a small tug in the back of my mind, a tug as old as humanity itself, a quiet alarm that says *take care, there's danger, danger from this person*. It's the first time that I've truly realized that Abilene is not operating purely out of malice or cold manipulation. There is a fever inside of her, something deep inside of her mind, and whether it was always there or whether it's only newly developed, I don't think it matters. It's tilted her thinking, sent her sliding down paths no human should go down.

She's beyond being reasoned with. It doesn't matter what logic I throw at her, what facts I tell her; she will believe this fantasy about Ash above all else. That they're somehow meant for each other. That his love for me is some kind of aberrant mistake that he'd realize if only he could see. And she seems oblivious to the fact that the more she tortures him in the hope that it will drive him to her, the more she pushes him away.

And with a chill that I feel deep under my skin and in my bones, I realize that she could do more than try to kill me by proxy. She really could harm me—and more importantly, she could harm Ash or Embry. She could harm that child nestled inside of her. I no longer believe that there's anything she wouldn't do in her wild pursuit of Ash, anything she wouldn't do in order to punish me for getting to him first.

"And Embry?" I say, trying to betray none of these thoughts, trying to pretend that this conversation hasn't revealed the slithers and creeps of her mind. "He's really just a way to punish me? To isolate Ash?"

Abilene tilts her head in something like pity. "You really do love them both, don't you?"

There's no point in lying about it, and I don't want to. "Yes," I say. "I really do love them both."

She stands up and tucks her clutch under her arm, sweeping her hair off her shoulder with a smooth shrug. She looks like an ad for high-end maternity clothes, or maybe a socialite caught in a semi-casual but still glossed-to-perfection moment. "Then I suppose you have your answer. And while you're pining after Embry, and Ash is missing his best friend, I'll be there to comfort him. Me."

She doesn't know about Ash and Embry, I realize. That's one secret she couldn't uncover, and thank God. If she knew that Ash loved Embry as well as me…it would go badly for him. Maybe Embry's safe for now, at least as safe as anyone can be around Abilene.

So I don't threaten her as she makes to leave; I don't say anything provoking. I say what I think she wants to hear so that she'll leave and go home appeased for the time being, and then I'll have space to think. Space to fix this.

"You succeeded, you know. Hurting me. Melwas aside, knowing that Embry slept with you—even if it was because you were blackmailing him—cut me deeper than almost anything else you've done." I'm being truthful, and the honesty seems to call to her.

She turns back from the door, and her face is softer, less disquieting than before. She looks genuinely remorseful about something. "Greer, I—well, I think you should know. That night with Embry…" She absentmindedly touches her belly as she searches for the words. "I wanted to get pregnant. I planned it that way, and if I hadn't gotten pregnant that month, I would have tried and tried again. If I couldn't have Ash's baby, then this seemed like the next best thing." She looks down at her stomach with a smile and then back up to me. "I had help from a doctor because I knew there were a great many things I could make Embry do, but that wasn't one of them. Embry didn't know it was me. He was barely even conscious."

I stand there, stunned and sick, my thoughts racing. "You raped him."

"If you like," Abilene says, lifting a shoulder. "I thought I did it rather kindly, as things go. It's not like I pretended to be you in the dark. It's not like he has to remember the feeling of betraying you."

I simply stare. I'm past words, past real thoughts even; my mind is somewhere vacant, someplace where horrors dwell.

"I thought that might comfort you," Abilene says magnanimously, as if she's granted me a great gift and hasn't just admitted to rape. And then she leaves, not bothering to close the door behind her.

I don't know how long I stand by my desk, how long it takes to reel in these dark fishes of thought, how long it takes for this to forge into action, into a plan. But it's close to dark when I have the answers I need.

I have to call Embry.

I have to stop Abilene.

CHAPTER 11
EMBRY

NOW, SIX WEEKS LATER

ELIOT SAID APRIL IS THE CRUELEST MONTH, BUT I CAN THINK of many crueler ones. January, when the holidays are over and the cold is hard enough to break your teeth on. November, when the skies go gray like they've forgotten how to be blue. March, with its muddy thaw and tree branches stark and skeletal.

But no month is crueler than October. Because October is the month I marry someone I don't love for reasons I'm not sure I entirely believe in. October is the month when I take more steps that can't be untaken, weave more webs that can't be unwoven. But what choice do I have? What choice have I ever had? There's only ever been the choice between doing nothing and doing something, and goddammit, I'd rather choose something than nothing. I've chosen to do nothing long enough.

It's a cold night tonight, and so quiet that I can hear the ash burning on my cigarette. So still that even the smoke refuses to move, hanging around me like a toxic fog.

I shouldn't smoke, I know. It was a habit I kicked after the war. It's just that I'm at war again, and this time with the man I love, and the first casualty is going to be my integrity. Twelve hours from now I'll stand in a church and make vows I don't intend to honor, make promises I could never keep, paint myself another face with lies and hollow words, just like Hamlet accuses Ophelia of doing.

Those that are married already, all but one shall live. The rest shall keep as they are.

I remember reading *Hamlet* aloud to Ash in Berlin, during some vacation we stole together during the war. My head in his lap, my bare feet hanging off the bed, acting out the voices and making him laugh at Polonius and sigh at Ophelia. Hamlet himself Ash could never understand, could never grasp why someone wouldn't do what needed to be done right away.

"That's why they don't write tragedies about people like you," I'd said, twisting up to look at him. "It's too boring when the hero isn't morally complicated."

Ash looked amused. "Define morally complicated."

"You know. Fatal flaw and all that. Hamlet's passivity. Macbeth's ambition. Oedipus's pride."

"Oedipus was trying to do the right thing by leaving Corinth," Ash said. "Doesn't that count?"

I glared at him. "Don't be stupid. His leaving Corinth set the entire prophecy in motion. He thought he could defy the gods! You don't think that deserves a tragic end?"

He laughed then, the bare muscles of his stomach jerking against my face. I turned and kissed them, one by one, until I reached his navel, which I licked until he growled. And predictably enough, I ended up with his cock in my mouth and his hands heavy on my head, and after he came deep down my throat, he permitted me to lie on top of him and find release by sliding my cock against his muscular thighs.

Even with that pathetic amount of friction, I still spent my load in a matter of seconds. Which then I had to clean up in the most humiliating way possible, of course.

I loved it.

But after all of that, and a quick shower and room service on top of it, it was clear Ash's mind was still on the earlier topic, and when my head was back in his lap and his fingers were running through my hair, he asked, "So are there tragedies about people who don't deserve it?"

"I said *morally complicated*, not evil. Most of the tragic heroes don't really deserve the magnitude of what happens to them."

"But if you try to do everything right," Ash said slowly, "and try your hardest to be honorable always? Do those people get to avoid the tragic ends?"

I thought for a moment, mentally flipping through college textbooks and deciding. "No, I think it's usually destined, no matter how good or brave the person is. Beowulf didn't have a fatal flaw and he got bitten by a dragon. King Arthur for the most part is a just and fair king, but a single sin committed in his youth ends up being his undoing."

"What was his sin?" Ash asked, fingers still running through my hair.

I closed my eyes, the sensation so pleasant and soothing that I worried I might drift off to sleep. "He slept with his sister."

"It's a good thing I only slept with your sister, then."

"Fuck you," I mumbled.

He laughed again and somehow ended up crawling over top of me, kissing my face and throat and chest, and that was the last we talked about fatal flaws and King Arthur.

And now here we are, in a tragedy of our own. Except we probably do deserve it.

I finish my cigarette and flick it onto the low patio where

I'm standing. Behind me are bifold doors and rows of heat lamps and the silent bustle of the rehearsal dinner contained by glass. *My* rehearsal dinner, because I'm the groom, because tomorrow I'm getting married to the woman who sexually assaulted me and arranged for Greer's abduction.

I pull the silver cigarette case out of my suit jacket and light up another one. I'm not ready to go back inside just yet.

"You don't have to do this" comes a voice at my elbow. I turn to see my stepsister standing next to me in a sleek strapless gown, as if she's incapable of feeling the cold. Which she might be. I always suspected she was part reptile.

But she's a loyal reptile, even as she's reaching for my case and pulling out a cigarette for herself. I offer her the lighter and she lights the cigarette and snaps the lighter shut with an efficient, elegant click.

"You don't have to do this," she repeats, gazing steadily at me over the glow of the cigarette. "It's not too late."

"Morgan, she holds all of our futures in her hands right now. If I do this, I can protect you and Lyr and Ash. Not to mention that I can keep my image for the campaign clean."

Morgan sighs, giving the ash on her cigarette a delicate flick. "I don't know if we can campaign with her at all, not with how dangerous she is. Maybe we should take our chances with her going public."

She blows a pretty stream of smoke over her shoulder, using it as an excuse to glance behind her. Seeing that we are mostly alone, she says, "What she did to you was unforgivable, and how do you know it won't happen again? Are you planning only on drinking from sealed bottles inside your own house?"

"I can protect myself, Morgan—"

Her eyes flare a bright green, so like Ash's that I have to look away. "Is this a male ego thing?" she demands quietly. "Because what she did to you does not make you weak, and it's not weakness to try to protect yourself in the future."

"I know that—"

"I don't think you do," she insists. "Look, the statute of limitations in DC is fifteen years. There's plenty of time to—"

"Absolutely not."

"If we can get Dr. Ninian to testify," she continues over me, "or even just bring evidence against her, then we can get Abilene convicted."

"And then what happens to my image? What happens to my child if she's in prison?"

"Is it definitely your child?"

I study my cigarette for a moment before I take a long drag. God, how I had hoped, how I had prayed when I hadn't bent my head to heaven for years—*please don't let the child be mine*, I'd begged. Let it be anyone's, fucking Melwas's even, just please not mine. But I couldn't ignore the one thing Abilene truly wanted, which was to feel close to Ash. I'm the closest she can get, the truest imitation, and it was stupid of me to have hoped for anything different. Of course it's my child. Nothing else would have satisfied her, save for conceiving a child of Ash's, and thank God that's out of her reach. For now.

"Two different doctors of my choosing have independently run the tests. I'm as certain as I can humanly be." And then I soften for a minute. "It's a boy."

Morgan examines me. "You'd get him, you know, if she was in prison. He'd still be yours."

"Yes. But I'm not going to win an election with the mother of my child in prison. It's just not how it works."

"Do you want him? The baby, I mean?"

I suppose she's asking because she more than anyone knows how easy it is to cover up a child's parentage, but it's all far too late for that. And besides, "I do want him, Morgan. None of this is his fault, and I've always wanted children. And maybe this is as close as I'll ever come to having a child with Greer, having one with her cousin."

Morgan shakes her head as she puts her cigarette to her lips. "I hope for your sake that he takes after you."

"I'll love him no matter whom he takes after," I say, and then add, surprised to find that it's true, "I think I already love him."

"Then you'll have to protect him from his mother after he's born," my stepsister says. "Abilene will use him as a tool, especially if she realizes that you love him. How are you going to live like that, Embry? Cut off from the people you actually love and trying to protect your son from his own mother?"

I look down at my hand, my jaw working as I have to admit, "I don't know. I just know that this is the best move I've got with the pieces I have."

"Abilene frightens me," Morgan says after a minute. "More than I can say."

"Me too."

"What happens next?"

I finish my cigarette and grind out the embers on the patio with my gleaming Fendi dress shoe. "What happens next is I win that election. I keep Greer safe. And then I'll know all of this has been worth it."

The next morning is busy for everyone but me. Abilene, being an event planner, has planned a spectacle that would shame the royal family, something far from the elegant and restrained affair Greer insisted Abilene plan for her. No, this wedding is showcasing money and power—something both our families have in abundance—and the attention to detail is, I have to admit, masterful.

Too bad it's all for a farce.

When Ash and Greer married, it was one of the worst and best days of my life. The heady combination of heartbreak and fucking before the ceremony had me whirling, the fevered hour I spent with the bride, the hour afterward with the groom as he kissed and bit me. It had been almost a full year since Ash and I had fooled around, excluding our kiss under the mistletoe, and it had been six years since I'd touched Greer like that. My body threatened to explode with it all, and as Ash wrestled me up against the wall in the small church dressing room, my body *did* explode.

Ash, stop, stop, I'm going to—

Yes, you are, little prince. I want you to. My dress shoes had slid against the carpet in between his legs, his mouth had been everywhere, licking every last trace of his bride off my face, and his hips had been angry and forceful against mine, his massive cock impressively thick and hard even through all the layers of our tuxedos. And it was in this grinding tangle of tuxedo-clad limbs and hot mouths that I came, right there in my pants.

Ash had been delighted, keeping me pinned against the wall with his teeth and powerful hips, panting through my every moan and shudder as if it were him who was coming and not me.

I want your cock to belong to me again, he'd growled then. *I don't want to miss a single orgasm of yours ever.*

I'd been dizzy, flooded with too many hormones to think clearly. *Ash, you're getting married.*

Weddings are promises, he'd said cryptically, and then ordered me to clean myself up. And so I'd stood through his wedding ceremony and endured his wedding reception, certain that day had been my last taste of paradise, and I was forever banished from the garden. Little did I know that the garden had been waiting for me all along, and that night when they let me inside their honeymoon suite, when we vowed together with words and flesh that we'd be married in this more elemental, important way, I realized that all along Ash had planned on this, on finally anchoring us to him in a way that fit our world best. As always, he'd found the most generous and vulnerable way to care for the people he loved.

And here I am, about to burn all of that down.

It is funny, I think as I pull the tuxedo out of the cleaner's bag and start dressing, that even though I know I'm butchering everything we hoped and wished for that night, I'm still resentful that I'm alone before my wedding. Ash should be here. Even if it were to scowl at me, growl at me, mark me until I bled, I'd take it, because I'm so lonely without him and Greer, and I'm scared of what I'm doing today.

This is for Greer. This is for everyone, I remind myself. I have very good reasons for doing this.

Just.

It hurts.

As I'm sitting down to pull on my shoes, the door opens without a knock, and I don't bother looking up. Out of all the women in my life, Greer is the only one who would knock, which means that it's either my mother or my sister or my future wife, and therefore someone I'm not really in the mood to see.

"Embry," Vivienne Moore says, and I sigh and look up at my mother.

"Yes?"

Vivienne Moore clicks over the marble floor to sit at a dressing table nearby, perfect as always in a beaded dress of silver, her rich brown hair pulled back into a severe knot. Gray threads artistically through the rich brown, and the fine wrinkles near her eyes only make her look more stately and graceful. There are no smile lines around her mouth of course, because Governor Vivienne Moore only smiles for cameras and donors.

"Mother, I'm supposed to come seat you. That's how it works."

My mother glances up at the clock hanging on the wall. "We have fifteen minutes. I wanted to speak to you privately before we went out."

I finish knotting my shoelaces and stand up. "If you're here to talk me out of this, don't bother. Morgan already tried."

"I wouldn't be so foolish," my mother says calmly. "This is the only way to clean up the mess you've made and the best chance you have at protecting your future. But I need to know a few things first."

"There's nothing to know—"

Vivienne Moore holds up a hand and I fall silent. "Please. Firstly, I need to know that you'll send that baby to me the moment you feel he's unsafe. Yes, I see you bristling at that, and no, I'm not insulting your ability to protect your son. I'm reaffirming it—if that baby is in any danger at all, the safest place is across the country, with his grandmother. Understood?"

She's right, as defensive as I feel about it. I give her a curt nod.

"Second, I need to know this purely for my own curiosity. That video of you and Greer Galloway Colchester...was it real?"

I flush, hating that I'm thirty-six and my mother makes me feel like a teenager. "Mother, that's private."

She stares at me with blue eyes that match my own. "I suppose that's my answer, then. It was easy enough to see that you were in love with her, but whether the consummation actually happened, I couldn't perceive. The third question, however—the one I've asked myself for years—is the most important one. Are you in love with Maxen Colchester?"

"Mother."

"Both at the same time?"

"*Mother.*"

She lifts a shoulder. "It's not unheard of, and I've encountered stranger things. But how on earth do you plan on running against a man you love?"

I lean against the window frame, looking out onto the pretty churchyard outside. "Because it's the right thing to do."

"I don't approve," she says, standing. "This is all far too disheveled for my liking. Sloppy. I can't be certain that any of us will come out unscathed."

She extends an arm and I thread it through my elbow. "Still," she says as we leave the dressing room, "you have all the help and power at my disposal. We'll see you through this, Embry. Somehow."

I don't pay attention to most of the things said during my wedding ceremony. None of it is important, none of it means anything. It's a stark act done out of a need to survive, and I treat it as such. Like killing hostiles during the war or smearing a perfectly nice political opponent. I don't enjoy it, I find it distasteful and repulsive even, but the choices had been taken away a long time ago. It's this or a future I have no control over, and I'm done with that.

I will control what happens next.

The only part of the ceremony that rouses me from my stupor is Morgan's voice from the lectern as she gives a reading from Ephesians, one of those readings that's at almost every wedding. "For this reason," she is saying in her deliberate, cool voice, "a man will leave his father and his mother and be united to his wife, and the two will become one flesh. This is a profound mystery—"

Her voices fades in my mind, and for some reason I am

thinking of my own voice quoting soft in a Berlin hotel, *This was sometime a paradox, but now the time gives it proof. I did love you once.*

Fingers in my hair, a firm stomach against my cheek. *He still loves Ophelia.*

How do you know?

Because he's cruel to her. The fingers had tightened in my hair to prove his point. *The strongest love comes with pain.*

Two soldier boys in love. The princess they both wanted. How close we were to our happily ever after, how near it seemed. And now…

I recite vows that mean nothing, and I don't bother to pretend they mean anything. My face is blank as I say the old words, my voice is toneless as I look into Abilene's eyes and promise to care for her in sickness and in health. She is both sickness and health all at once. She looks the perfect flush and bloom of radiant motherhood now—at five months pregnant, her slender form perfectly showcases the plumping nest of our child, her skin glows, her hair shines, her lovely face tips into a beatific smile—but her eyes betray the truth. They flash between lifeless and all too lively, between heartlessness and an emotional wildness that unnerves me.

There's none of that wildness today, not for me. I'm beginning to think that I bore her, that the deep pool of her hatred is kept in reserve for Greer, her animated obsession kept in reserve for Ash, and all I'll get from her now is the lazy satisfaction that she won a crucial battle.

Not for the first time in the last two months, I consider the irony of leaving Ash so I could keep Greer safe, all while I'm marrying the greatest threat to her safety I could possibly imagine. But that only stiffens my resolve to control this, to keep Abilene close. If she's close, then I can keep an eye on her. I can stop her from hurting Greer again.

A Sanctus is sung, we kneel, we take communion, we

stand and finally the kiss. I hear the shutter of several cameras as my lips touch hers. Her skin is warm to the touch, her lips soft with whatever lipstick she's painted on, and her breath is pleasant, scented with some kind of mint. I have no physical reason to hate every instant of the contact, and yet I do. I pull away too fast, and I see the irritation flick over her face before she schools her expression back into a happy smile. I might pay for this later.

The rest of the day is as detestable as the ceremony, but I manage to achieve an anesthetic sense of distance about it all, a dull dispassion that more or less keeps me sober and pliable as the photographers take their pictures at the church and we head for the reception venue (a large flat boat on the Potomac, filled with too much champagne and too many people I'd rather not see).

Abilene is far from perturbed by my detachment. If anything, she seems amused by it, perhaps marking it as some sort of victory. I don't care. I don't care what she thinks or what anyone else thinks or whispers about. All I want is for this beastly day to be over.

It's only once, as we're doing the first dance, that I see her mask slip a bit. She slides her hand around the back of my neck to pull me closer.

"I saw you booked another room for yourself at the Four Seasons."

"Don't worry," I reply. "I'll be discreet about our sleeping arrangements."

"You know there's no need, right?" She looks up at me with eyes the color of fading light between trees, an ominous, lifeless blue. "I'm already pregnant with your child, Embry. Greer is lost to you. Why not take pleasure where you can? You certainly didn't seem to mind fucking other people a year ago."

It's true. When Greer and Ash were falling in love for the second time, I'd kept my bed warm with an almost grim relentlessness. But it brought me no real relief then, and I know it won't bring me any relief now, because it's not what I really need. What I need is mythological and painful and holy, an ecstatic mix of lust and grief and eternity that only Ash and Greer can give me, and if I can't have that, then there's nothing for me in the impersonal fucks I used to have. I would feel no better after than I had before, and I might feel worse, the cheap transaction tawdry and pale when contrasted with my sweaty, golden memories of Ash and Greer.

"No, Abilene. You've won enough. You won't win that as well."

She sighs. "Fine. Have it your way for now; just remember I have an entire honeymoon to change your mind."

God, that sounds unbearable. I'm technically unemployed at the moment, but I wonder if I can find a plausible reason to cut our trip short. Create enough photo ops to slake the press's thirst for gossip about the First Lady's cousin and me, and then vanish back home and spend my days looking at my mother's lake instead of my new wife.

The reception mercifully ends, and we take a limousine back to the Four Seasons, Abilene scrolling through her phone for social media mentions of our wedding, seeming satisfied with what she finds. I stare out the window the entire way, promising myself a bottle of gin when I get back to my hotel room. I won't even bother with a glass.

Abilene's assistant has already checked us in, and some lackey of Vivienne's has furnished me with the key to my solo room. We make a production of getting into the elevator together, but part ways after a couple of floors.

"Are you sure?" Abilene says as the doors open and I am about to step out.

I look back at her. She's not purring or cooing or preening or anything as obvious as that. She's asking in the same tone of voice she might ask a business partner or colleague. Almost indifferently. It's only that weird twilit hue in her eyes that reminds me that her motives and feelings will always, always be too slippery for me to grasp. Assuming indifference on her part carries its own danger.

So I keep my voice polite when I say, "Yes, I'm sure. Sleep well," and step off the elevator. It's only after I hear the gentle lumber of the doors closing and the *ding* of the elevator leaving this floor that I can breathe for the first time since I woke up this morning.

At least until I turn a corner and see Ryan Belvedere leaning against my doorframe, his thumbs flying over his phone screen. I'm so starved for Ash and Greer that even just seeing his personal assistant has my breath stitching under my ribs.

"I'm flattered, but it's not really customary for the groom to fuck someone from his old job on the wedding night."

Belvedere looks up with a smile at my joke, his floppy, dark hair brushing the top rims of his glasses. He impatiently shakes the hair out of his face. "Congratulations, Mr. Moore."

"How many congratulations do you think are in order, given that you're standing outside of my private room?"

"Fair point. I'm sorry I couldn't come to the ceremony, by the way."

"You have a demanding boss."

He nods. "He sent me here."

Hope lifts in my chest, refuses to settle its wings. "He did?"

"Yes. He'd like me to take you to your wedding present."

Now hope is stirring somewhere else—somewhere lower and deeper. I have experienced the kinds of wedding presents Ash likes to give.

"And where are we going?"

Belvedere smiles and tilts his head toward the service stairs, where I presume a discreet car is waiting. "To the White House."

CHAPTER 12
EMBRY

NOW

THE WHITE HOUSE IS QUIET AS BELVEDERE AND I WALK UP the stairs to the Residence; it goes even quieter as Belvedere tactfully melts away before I reach the living room.

Strauss is playing, softly enough that I can hear Greer's laughter floating above it, along with the unmistakable clink of ice cubes in a silver bucket. There's a low husk of male laughter that has my chest going hot and tight, and when I reach the threshold of the living room, I don't walk in. I just lean against the doorframe and watch the charming scene inside.

Greer and Ash are dancing.

She's wearing a simple white top and a caramel-colored skirt that shows off her long legs, her feet bare and her white-gold hair tugged to the side in a messy braid. He's in a white button-down and black slacks, also barefoot, his shirt rolled up to expose his sculpted forearms. I don't know why, but there's something so fascinating to me about the way his forearms narrow into his wrists, the way his wrists widen into those large, rough hands. Perhaps it was all those years at war, his hands in half-finger tactical gloves and hidden from sight. Maybe it's just the masculine perfection of it all—the muscle, the bones, the hair. The dormant power.

I watch as those hands run over Greer's arms, as they move back to a proper waltz position—one extended, the other at her waist. And as they dance, I watch the light catch in Greer's hair, which is every shade of gold from white to honeyed to dark—just as it always gets in the fall. I remember the way it looked spread across my pillow in a Chicago hotel, how it gleamed in the moonlight when I rescued her from Melwas, and my breath catches.

Both of them. Beautiful, beautiful, beautiful.

In only a few seconds of observing, it becomes apparent why they were laughing. Ash keeps throwing off the swiveling box of the waltz steps, his movements as clumsy and stiff as a wind-up soldier's. He never could find the music, never could let go of his mind long enough for his body to move on instinct. And I have to wince a teacher's wince when I watch him attempt the dance, his feet crowding Greer's delicate ones, his deliciously narrow hips moving barely at all.

I suppose all those dancing lessons during the war were in vain, I think. But then I remember the feel of him under my hands, the tinny echo of a CD player against stark mountain trees, how often he'd end up yanking my body flush against his and kissing me with ferocious, possessive kisses. *Screw the dancing*, he'd mumble, and within minutes there would be teeth and sweat and fingertips digging into muscle. I think I still have scars on my knees from all those impromptu mountain fucks; God knows I can still recall the blushing shame of asking the quartermaster for yet another uniform repair kit to patch the knees in my pants, and I have hardly ever blushed with shame in my life.

For a minute I allow myself to forget today, forget the

last two months. The wedding, the blackmail, the green hurt in Ash's eyes when I told him I was leaving him. I allow myself to believe that I'm just coming up to my wife and my husband after a long day at the office, that this sweet waltzing laughter is what I come home to every night, that when they catch sight of me, I will be rewarded with kisses both firm and soft.

In my little fantasy, I don't have to wonder why Ash brought me here. In my fantasy, he brought me here because he misses me.

He brought me here because he loves me.

Greer finally catches sight of me as they turn, and her delighted smile lights a bittersweet flame in my chest. I give her a tentative smile back, my heart racing, and then I slide my gaze over to Ash.

A slow, warm smile spreads across his face. "Embry," he says. "You came."

I answer simply, "You asked me to come."

His smile twists up ruefully. "If only it were that easy all the time."

Before I can respond and spoil the moment, he bends down and murmurs something to his wife. It sounds like, "Go greet our guest."

Her eyes flick up to his, as if silently asking a question, and then he nods, letting go and watching her cross the space between him and me.

And I'm entranced. It's hard not to be entranced with Greer—there's something about the way she carries herself, about the careful reserve of that exquisite face. Like no matter how you open her up and turn her pages, you'll never know all of her. You'll never read every secret; there will always be something out of reach and held apart. You could spend your entire life trying to learn every glow and shadow of her heart and mind and still never finish.

It's been two months since her grandfather's funeral, two months since I've been in the same room with her, and I'd forgotten. Forgotten the power of her moonlight eyes and sunshine hair. Forgotten how she makes my bones ache and my blood hot just by looking at me. All those shameful nights since Abilene drugged me, alone in my bed with nothing but memories and internet searches, jerking off to pictures of Greer—it's a punch to the chest to be confronted with the real woman again and not the ghost.

I stay completely still as she approaches, blood thundering everywhere and making me hot and full in the part that has missed Greer and Ash most. I'm not sure what to say or what to do or even why I'm here, but I do know that I want it. Whatever it is. Abuse, recrimination, punishment—if they want to spend the next hour yelling at me, it would be the sweetest symphony, and if they want to beat me, it would feel like a thousand beloved caresses. I'm starving for them.

Greer stops just in front of me. Slowly, she puts her hand flat against my chest, right over my heart. I realize I'm still in my tuxedo, my unknotted bow tie hanging rakishly around my neck. I feel ashamed of it, ashamed of my wedding clothes, ashamed to be here in such a visible reminder of what separates us.

But Greer moves closer and rises up on her tiptoes and buries her nose in my neck. Smelling me.

The raw carnality of it has me fighting back a groan, a fight I lose when I look up and see Ash watching us with glittering eyes, his arms folded across his impressive chest and his erection pushing against the front of his pants.

And then Greer's lips are against my throat, my jaw, as I stand completely still, not sure what I'm allowed to touch. What I'm allowed to enjoy. I dip my gaze to the woman kissing my jaw and then lift it back to Ash.

Can I?

"Say please," he says.

"Please," I breathe without the slightest hesitation.

Ash gives me a nod, and that's enough permission for me. I yank my queen against my body, one arm banded around her waist, the other behind her neck, and I press my hungry mouth to hers for the first time in what feels like forever.

"God, you taste amazing," I mumble against her mouth. "Fuck."

In response, she slides her arms around my neck and pulls herself up, wrapping her lean legs around my waist, and it's instinct that has me catching her under the thighs to support her.

It's curiosity that sends my hands sliding up her legs to her ass.

No panties.

Shit.

Shit.

My hands are as hungry as my mouth, and they're currently filled with the delicious flesh of her bottom, and I am squeezing and plumping under her skirt as my lips finally slot against her own in a way that coaxes them to part. And then I'm truly tasting her mouth—sweet champagne and the clean taste of her, just *her*—in the first real kiss I've had since…since when? Since that night in Ash's office? When he'd crushed his body into mine, guided my hand to where he wanted it?

And how long since the three of us? It must have been Camp David, after I brought Greer home and before I flew to Seattle. Almost five months.

Five months. And I am so fucking tied in knots over just a kiss from Greer. How am I going to survive the rest of my life without her? Without him?

I kiss her for a long time. Long enough for a full waltz to play, long enough for my muscles to remind me that

I'm carrying her weight on my arms, long enough for me to refamiliarize myself with the swells and swerves of her mouth—the tiny vaults between teeth and tongue, the silky arches of lips, the heat, the taste, *the taste*. She moans against me, squirms against me, the center of her heat right against my stomach, and I hate every fiber of the fabric that separates my skin from hers.

"And what about me?" Ash finally asks. "Do I get a greeting as well?"

Greer unhooks her legs and slides down, squeezing my hand as she steps off to the side. The look she shoots me is encouragement and lust and everything I don't deserve, and somehow I've ended up in some upside-down world where it doesn't matter. I'm here and they're here, and that's all there is.

I meet eyes with Ash, still standing across the room, still obviously and deliciously erect. I see the corner of his mouth twitch, just a flash of that hidden dimple, and then he lifts his chin the tiniest bit. The meaning is clear: he won't come to me. I have to go to him.

I shouldn't. I shouldn't for more than one reason: I'm not the man who kneels for him anymore; I told him to his face that his authority no longer held moral value for me. I shouldn't because I know better than I did years ago, and I know now that the bedroom games we play always have power in real life.

I shouldn't go to him. But I do.

I walk to him, the waltz music swirling gently around us and the thick carpet crushing audibly under my shoes, and when I get to him, I stop when I'm just out of reach.

"How would you like to be greeted?" I ask, not sure what I want the answer to be—not sure of anything, actually, except that I never want to leave. I want tonight to play on a loop for the rest of my life; I want to live inside it forever.

"Oh," Ash responds, "I think a kiss would do quite nicely."

My heart lifts, I step forward, and I'm caught immediately by a hand at my shoulder. "Not my mouth," Ash says. "That will take some earning."

I stare at him, not comprehending at first, half expecting him to push me down to my knees and make me unbuckle his belt. But he doesn't do either of those things, and out of the bottom of my eye, I see the movement of his foot.

I eye it doubtfully. "You're joking," I say.

"Hardly."

I look back up to him and see his hidden dimple flash. "It's just for fun, little prince," he says quietly. "I won't interpret your kiss as anything other than what it is."

"Good," I say. "Because this changes nothing."

"Nothing," agrees Ash.

And I get to my knees and I bend down and I kiss his foot. The skin is warm and clean, and underneath the slight pressure of my lips, I feel the slender rods of bone and plump give of veins and rigid ropes of tendons. How can a mere foot radiate so much power? So much perfect strength? And yet it does, it does, and I could kiss his foot for so much longer than a few seconds—and I have in the past—but he pulls his foot away from me.

"Thank you, I enjoyed that," he says, walking over to the bar cart by the window. I stay where I'm at on my knees, touching my lips, not ready to give up the feeling of his skin against them.

"Do you want a drink?" he asks. "We put some champagne on ice for you, although Greer's already taken care of the first bottle."

"Champagne sounds nice," I say distantly, my mind still replaying the feeling of my lips on his feet. One day, I need to figure out why the fuck I love that feeling so much.

Greer floats past me to help Ash at the bar, and I stand and lean against the back of a nearby sofa, trying to regain some measure of control over my feelings.

"Have a seat," Ash says over his shoulder. "We'll be right over with your champagne."

So I sit and watch the cutely domestic tableau of Ash opening the bottle and Greer hunting under the cart for three flutes. She jumps ever so slightly when the bottle pops, and Ash laughs at her, and then she sticks her tongue out at him, and his eyes darken into a shade I know all too well. "Careful, little princess," he murmurs. "Or you'll get yourself into trouble."

Judging by the smile she can't hide, even with her eyes cast demurely down, trouble is exactly what Greer wants. And I know the feeling.

Soon, the two of them are joining me in the sitting area, Ash handing me a flute of champagne and Greer settling on the sofa at a right angle to mine—I could reach out and touch her arm if I wanted. Ash stays standing in front of me.

"We should toast," he suggests. "What to?"

"Not my wedding," I say, and then realizing how much that revealed, I feel the tops of my ears warm with embarrassment. "Please," I add. "Anything else."

"Let's toast to tonight, then. The three of us together."

"To tonight," Greer says, leaning forward with an extended glass.

"Tonight," I echo. And our glasses clink together with a bright, happy sound that I don't deserve.

Ash and I drain our glasses and Greer sips hers and sets it aside. Then Ash settles on the sofa across from me, stretching an arm along the back and crossing a long leg over the other.

"I missed you," he says straightforwardly. "I'm glad you came."

"Me too," I admit. "It was a long day. And it's been a long couple of months."

"Abilene and the baby are well?" he asks.

"Yes."

Beside me, I feel Greer flinch. She called me about six weeks ago, after Abilene had showed up at her office uninvited and done what Abilene does best—disturb people. Greer had warned me that she thought Abilene was unstable (no surprise there) and also to haltingly apologize for assuming I'd betrayed her. We'd come to a painful understanding about it, painful because the truth no longer had the power to make a difference. There would still be a baby. I would still run against Ash. And she'd confessed then how much she wished she were pregnant too, how jealous she felt of Abilene for stealing that privilege away from her, and the worst, basest parts of me wanted to beg her to meet me, lay with me, give me as many chances as it would take to plant a child in her. Prove to her that it had always, always been her I imagined carrying my child, ever since that night in Chicago.

I didn't beg her to do that, of course. Yes, Ash had made it clear that Greer and I were free to see each other, but I think both of us knew then—and still know—that seeing each other without him would eventually sow a harvest too bitter to reap.

And there was already enough bitterness in bloom.

I explained to her why I had to run against Ash, exactly how I believed he couldn't keep her safe, and what I would do in his place if I had the power to do it. And nothing was more terrible than the silence on the other end as I talked, than her expressionless *I see* when I finished.

What are you thinking? I'd asked, hating how insecure I sounded.

Her voice had been careful when she answered. *Are you asking for my approval?*

I had been, I had realized with a touch of shame…and with a touch of indignation. Why shouldn't I? It was for her, after all. *Yes, Greer. I need to know that you know why I'm doing this.*

Embry, I love you completely, and I always will. But I'm never leaving Ash's side, and I think you were wrong to.

What else could be said after that? I told her I loved her, and then we ended the call.

We haven't spoken since.

What the hell. Tonight is make-believe anyway, an unreal fantasy, *just for fun*, as Ash said, and so there's no reason for me not to reach over and wrap Greer's slender fingers in my own. I don't say anything as I do it, but when I meet her eyes, she gives me a faint smile.

"I know," she says without me having to say anything. "I wish knowing made it easier…but I know."

"It's a boy, right?" Ash asks. "Any names yet?"

I keep my eyes on Greer as I answer, trying to gauge if this topic upsets her, but she seems calm enough.

"Abilene wants something old-fashioned," I say. "Percival or Alistair or Chauncey or something like that. I've been trying to talk her into something more sensible, like, you know, John. Or Jacob. But she wants something that sounds chivalrous, I guess."

"I've always liked the name Galahad," Greer suggests. "He's the knight who finds the Holy Grail. More chivalrous than Lancelot or Percival or even Arthur himself."

"Or how about George?" I counter. "Or Gary? Those start with G too."

She laughs, squeezing my hand. "It would be an unusual name, I admit, but you can't have higher aspirations for your child than wanting him to see the face of God on earth."

She's right, and I'm not religious like Ash and Greer, so I don't need my son to chase after any grail, holy or otherwise. But I do want the entire world for him, and everything in it, and I want to raise him to deserve it.

It occurs to me that I have a privilege Ash never had: the right to know my son from birth. Even though I haven't met him, even though his mother scares the shit out of me, I feel a raw twist of pain in my stomach at even the hypothetical idea of missing a moment of his life.

How much Ash must feel that with Lyr.

"You're right," I answer Greer as I look back to Ash, who's staring thoughtfully at his hands. "Morgan tells me she's still considering your request to meet Lyr," I say to him.

He nods. "I'd like very much to meet him," he replies. "And I'll respect Morgan's wishes—though if Abilene goes public with what she knows, I think it will be less traumatic for him if he's already learned the truth."

"I'll do what I can to keep her quiet," I promise. "For you and for Morgan and for Lyr." I think of the solemn-eyed boy who used to love games of chase, of the smart, bored teenager he is now. "He deserves better."

"I appreciate that," Ash says, then smiles. "I'm sorry. I didn't bring you here to talk about the upsetting things between us. Would you like another drink?"

"Yes, please."

He gets to his feet and scoops my flute from the side table, and while he's refilling it with champagne, Greer threads her fingers through mine.

"I've missed you," she says, looking down at where our hands braid together. "I don't know how I got so used to having what we had, when we had it for such a short amount of time, but I did. And I got used to having you here, with us, even before the wedding." Her throat works, a delicate, silent swallow. "Every day. Every day I miss you."

What can I say to that? To her naked, vulnerable pain? So much of it is my fault, and the guilt is like slick oil all over me because I never wanted to hurt her. I want to keep her safe, I want to make sure no one can hurt her ever again, and yet all of that feels too abstract to explain right now. Too pitiful.

But why? Shouldn't I just tell her these things? Maybe face-to-face, she'd understand, not like over the phone. If I could look into her eyes and just *explain*...but what if it didn't change her mind? What if she still thought I was wrong?

"I miss you every day as well," I say instead, like a coward. "I've missed every single part of you."

"I think I can guess which parts," she laughs.

"I mean it," I insist. I slide off the sofa to kneel by her feet and press her hand to my lips. "I haven't—well, you know I haven't with Abilene, and not with anyone else either, but that's not what I mean when I say I miss you. It's not just the fucking that I ache for. It's your voice, your gaze, your touch. Even your highlighters and Post-its scattered everywhere. I'm miserable without you."

But I can endure it because I know I'll make you safe.

"I'm sorry for all of it," I finish. "But I love you, and that will always be the end of our story."

She drops her eyes, her eyelashes brushing against her cheeks. "For me too, Embry" is all she says. I kiss the back of her hand again and then press my forehead to it. There's not a river wide enough or deep enough to contain everything I feel for this woman.

Ash returns with my drink, and I reluctantly push myself away from Greer and go back to my seat. Ash hands the champagne to me over the back of the couch, and as I take it from him, I swear I feel a fingertip ghost across the back of my neck. But when I turn, he's gone, already folding that powerful body back to a seated position on the sofa across from me. And somehow I know from the way those aventurine eyes look at me that he heard my conversation with Greer. That he correctly interpreted my supplication at her feet.

And that the night is about to change.

"Where's my hospitality?" he asks in a voice that is dark and playful and mockingly polite all at once. "I've offered you a drink, but surely there's more that my weary traveler needs?"

"I'm fine," I say automatically, watching as he snaps his fingers. In an instant, Greer is kneeling demurely by his feet.

"Are you sure?" he asks with a raised eyebrow once she's settled. "Something to eat, maybe? I can easily call down to the kitchen and have them bring something up." His hand drops to idly stroke Greer's head and neck. My eyes follow his fingers, jealousy curling smoky swirls inside my mind. I'm jealous of both of them—of Ash for touching Greer and of Greer for being touched by Ash. It's a knot that I can never fully untangle, a riddle I can't unpuzzle; I can only hope to survive it with my soul intact.

"No, I'm not hungry," I finally answer. Though I think of Greer's heat against my stomach as her heels dug into my back earlier tonight, and I want to add *at least, I'm not hungry for food.*

Ash is toying with her braid now, brushing the tail of it along her jaw, giving it a sharp tug whenever she shivers at the touch. "More comfortable clothes? A shower maybe?"

Both sound amazing, actually, stripping and washing away this terrible day, but I don't have the right to make myself at home here anymore, not even for pretend.

Ash seems to anticipate the shake of my head and tilts his own head with a slow, satisfied smile. "Then I know what. Greer, our guest needs something from you. Go make him feel comfortable."

There's no hesitation in her voice when she answers, "Yes, sir," and no reluctance or shyness when she rises gracefully from her knees to walk over to me. My mouth goes dry as she gets closer, as she gives me a lip-biting smile and then turns to face away from me. With sleek movements and a flirty flounce of her skirt, she's on her hands and knees on the coffee table in front of me, and it takes me a moment to process what I'm seeing. The clean, pink soles of her feet, the toned swells of her calves. The soft skin of her thighs, the hem of her skirt just barely covering the naked pussy underneath. My skin is erupting into a thousand, thousand needy goose bumps; my cock is swelling fast and hungry against my tuxedo pants.

I can't breathe.

Ash stands up, looking at me from across the slender flat of Greer's back. He once again rubs her head in idle affection, and she pushes her face against his thigh like a purring cat.

"Go on, Embry," he says calmly. "I want to be a good host."

I'm still sitting, still several steps behind whatever's happening right now, and he seems to sense it. Giving Greer's hair a final caress, he walks over to me and extends his hand. I stare at it a moment, not sure what I'm agreeing to if I take it. But when have I ever not taken his hand when it was offered? I press my palm to his and grip tightly, and then he's helping me to my feet.

He runs a finger along the hem of Greer's skirt, nudging it up ever so slightly and then letting it drop back down, over and over again. Our hands are still clasped tight, but neither of us lets go.

How good it feels simply to hold his hand. How electrifying to stand here with him behind the woman we both love.

"It was Greer's idea," he says, in a voice still full of the play dark and the mock polite. "And I rather like it. Don't you?"

"I—" My mouth is so dry that it takes more than one attempt to get the words out. "I still don't know what the idea is."

His finger runs along her hem again, lifting it higher this time, and even standing above her as we are, there's a tease of folded flesh and a narrow glimpse of pink. And I'm hard for it, so fucking hard. I haven't felt anything other than my own hand for so long—no soft and slick cunts, no clever and wet tongues, no masculine fists full of Vaseline and cruelty. Not even the hair-rough thrusts against a lover's thighs, like I used to have once upon a time.

"Well," Ash explains, again with that cool, polite voice, as if he's explaining something ordinary and mundane. "I wanted you to come here tonight after your wedding, and when I told Greer, she reminded me of certain ancient customs regarding hospitality."

With an expert flick, he flips the hem of her skirt up and over, so that the heart shape of her ass is completely exposed. As is the welcoming split between her legs.

I'm back to not being able to breathe.

Ash lets go of my hand, the air unpleasantly cool and vacant against my fingers after he does, and then he smooths his hands over his wife's bottom.

"She tells me that in biblical times, the custom began with a man leading the guest to a private tent. The man's wife or sister or daughter was inside, waiting." Ash's fingers dent her skin ever so slightly and he pulls her cheeks apart, opening up her cunt for my inspection. She's already wet, and the sight of it is like a punch to the chest.

"Then the woman would rub the guest's feet and legs with butter. I did say no to that, you understand. Some of the rugs in here are antiques."

One of his thumbs rubs across Greer's inviting slit, smearing her arousal across the outer labia. "But after that part, the guest had the right to relieve his needs with the woman the host had provided."

He lets go of her ass and her wetness is again hidden. He gives her flank a fond slap and straightens. "It sounded..." He trails off as if searching for the right word, and then he shakes his head with a smile as he fails to find it. "Well, I wanted it, is all. I just wanted it."

He makes it sound as if offering up his wife is a favor to him and not to me, a pleasure he wants *for him*, and all I can do is stare. At this woman, who I want above all women, at this man, who I want above all men.

"Ash, Greer, I can't say yes to this. We…we're not—"

Even now, it hurts too much to say aloud what we're not, so I say instead, "This isn't something we can do anymore."

"Things are different now," Ash acknowledges, "which is why Greer suggested giving this to you as a guest right and not as something that belongs to you already. Even though"—he closes his eyes for a minute—"even though it does belong to you. My wife's body and my body. My wife's heart and my heart. Still belong to you."

The back of my eyelids burn and I blink fast, trying to keep the tears back, trying to keep the pain fisting in my throat from choking me.

Greer goes up on her knees and turns, so she can slide her arms around my waist and pull herself tight to me. "I know all the reasons why we shouldn't do this," she says quietly, her face tilted up to mine. "Which is why it's easier if it's a game, you see. I don't expect anything to be different when you leave here later. I don't expect you to change anything. Ash and I—we knew you had a separate room at the Four Seasons. Ash wanted to see you, and I wanted to touch you, and together we wanted to give you this as a…well, the word *gift* sounds high-handed, considering how selfish it is, but a *night,* then. A night when we could play and pretend and make the hurt feel good, at least for a few hours."

My lips are already in her hair, and I'm holding her so tightly she might break from it, but I don't care.

"Are you sure?" I ask. "Both of you? God knows I want it, but I don't deserve it. I don't deserve to be treated like a guest."

"Embry, we'd treat you like a prince if you'd let us," Greer says against my chest. "Please, please. Just for tonight. Just for pretend."

And then, as the coup de grace, she takes my hand and guides it under her skirt, where she is wet and willing, and from the way she rocks against my hand, I can tell it won't be long after I'm inside her that she'll be tightening and coming on my dick.

I pulse in response to the thought.

"Okay," I say. "I trust—" The word is too revealing, and I interrupt myself. "I mean, I understand. I want my guest right. Please."

Ash takes a deep breath, and at first I think it's to settle his nerves, but then I realize from his straining erection and his blown-pupil eyes that it's because he's struggling for control. And Ash at the edge of his control is beyond dangerous, beyond arousing, dosing up my blood with all sorts of fevered hormones.

Greer rearranges herself back on the table, flipping over her own skirt with a saucy look, and then facing forward, once again Ash's perfect submissive, still and obedient.

"May I?" Ash asks, his hands dropping to run along the waistband of my tuxedo pants. His fingers scald my skin through the fabric, and my voice is shaky when I answer, "Yes, you may."

And then I realize his hands are shaky like my voice, trembling as they slowly work open the front of my pants, exposing the silk jersey of my boxer briefs and the dark wet spot made by my leaking, neglected cock.

My former king handles me with infinite care, pulling my boxers down far enough to reveal the fat head of my cock with its wet slit, then the thick, veined shaft. I'm so hard that I actually bob right into his hand once I'm freed, and the feeling is like nothing else. I moan. Then his other hand cradles my balls, cupping them with the perfect amount of pressure, and my eyes flutter closed.

"Feel good?" Ash asks.

"Yes," I manage, my voice as tight as my sac, which has drawn up high to my body, ready to release at any moment.

"How long has it been since you've fucked someone?" Ash asks, his voice as tempered and mild as a doctor's, like this is a checkup, like this is a routine procedure.

"Camp David," I say hazily. A wide, warm fingertip is probing the delicate flesh behind my balls, and I can't remember any moment before this, can't remember any words that aren't about skin and touch and heat.

"That's a long time for a man to go without," Ash says, and I can't tell if there's reproach or sympathy in his words. He gives me a loose and lazy stroke, looking pleased as I nearly buckle from the feeling. "I think you really need this, Embry. Let us make you more comfortable."

"Yes." I don't know which part of it I'm saying yes to, but it doesn't matter. Yes to all of it. Yes to everything. Yes until I die or until morning comes, whichever happens first.

Ash's hands leave my penis, which is the worst feeling in the world, but then he puts them back on Greer's ass and pulls her cheeks apart to show me the best sight in the world. "She's got an amazing cunt," he says conversationally, as if I really am a guest, as if I really don't know for myself exactly how Greer feels underneath me. Impaled, squirming, wet.

"Would you like to sample for yourself? Have a taste?" Ash asks, again in that polite, gracious voice like he's merely inviting me to taste a prized scotch or enjoy the city view out of a certain window.

I nod, and then his hand is on the back of my neck, and it is the most natural thing in the world to let him push me to my knees, to have him guide my mouth to his wife's pussy. It's indecent, I recognize that, obscene and maybe even sinful, but it is the way the three of us were made, and in this moment, I'm ready to forsake everything else I believe just to have this forever.

I can feel Ash's breathing change the moment my lips touch the peach-like split between Greer's legs, and I can feel his hand tighten against my neck, his fingers splaying across the back of my head and pushing me harder into her. Greer lets out a low whimper as I open my mouth and kiss her with an eager tongue, determined to re-explore and reconquer every soft fold, every wet secret. My hands go to her thighs, one of them tangling with one of Ash's, our fingers sliding through each other's and gripping tightly, holding on to each other as he holds my face to his woman's cunt.

Greer is all delicious give and tension, her pussy soft and opening to my mouth and her lissome legs and arms shuddering tight as I eat her. And beside me, Ash is volcanic, about to rupture with heat, his entire body as hard and sharp as obsidian glass. I wish he would rupture; I wish he would explode. I want him naked and demanding and greedy. I want him lost to himself, his control gone, his eyes gone with lust, his desperation incinerating everything that's not the three of us. I want to provoke him past the edge of his restraint and then lap up all the misery he wants to unleash on me, breathe in all his violent delights and drink up all his violent ends.

But before I can figure out how to make this happen, he's pulling me away from Greer, hauling me back up to my feet by the back of my jacket. "That's enough tasting," he says, his cool voice at odds with his storming eyes and his body wound tight and trembling. He comes around to stand behind me, one of his large hands wrapping around my shaft once again, his other hand sliding past my waist to hold tight to Greer's hip.

I stare down, fascinated at the pornographic sight of

him fisting me and now slowly rubbing my tip against the private softness of his wife. The feeling of his fingers tight on my erection and Greer's slick entrance at my head is pulling every bit of heat, every drop of blood, down to this one part of me, and then his hips behind nudge me forward and before I can really absorb what's happening, he's guiding me inside Greer, his hand giving me one last squeeze before he lets go and I'm fully enveloped.

In front of me, Greer gasps, and I can feel her toes wiggling against my legs as she struggles to adjust. I know the feeling—my own toes are curling in my dress shoes and my chin is in my chest as I struggle to take deep breaths and not lose it right away. But I'm fighting against more than the months-long dry spell, more than the cinch of a woman around my member. I'm fighting against the press of Greer's thighs against my own and the adorable scrunches of her toes, the dip and curve of her slender waist under her skirt, and the golden light of the room making her white-gold hair glow like an angel's halo. I'm fighting against Ash next to me, his voice husky and burning when he asks, "Does she feel good?"

"Fuck yes she does," I breathe. I pull out the tiniest amount, push back in, not trusting myself to do more yet, barely trusting myself to even look at her or Ash.

Ash steps back, sitting with graceful strength on the sofa behind him and keeping his gaze on us the entire time. He leans an elbow on the arm of the sofa and props his head against two fingers and his thumb in the pose of a man casually observing something interesting. His tented slacks and flashing eyes tell a different story, however, and I have no doubt that my favorite version of Ash, beastly and wild, will be uncaged before long.

It's a thrilling thought, and I have to work even harder to keep myself in check. With my eyes still on Ash, I finally start moving inside Greer, letting her inner walls kiss along my full length for the first time in so very long. I want to savor it…and I also don't. I want to fuck her sweaty and fast until she's gasping in between moans and squeezing around me in climax.

Savor. I don't know when I'll get to do this again. If I ever will.

I look down to Greer and run appreciative hands over her ass and hips and thighs, trying to imprint every single second of this, every inch of her, onto my memory. The night my king let me fuck his queen in front of him.

"There's no need to go slowly," says Ash, reading my thoughts as always. "This is for you."

It is for me—but also for him and for Greer too, and I wonder if as much as I want to see Ash completely wild, they want to see me the same way. Do they fantasize about me being feral and mindless with lust? Does Greer ever get wet thinking about how rough and reckless I was with her in Carpathia? Does Ash miss the times he had me panting like a dog, shameless and pulsing with need?

I finally manage to find my voice. "Do you like watching this?" I ask. "Watching me fuck your wife?"

It's not meant to be insulting or goading, and it doesn't come out that way. It comes out like I mean it: *Is this how you wanted it? Are we pleasing you? Let us please you.*

Ash smiles against his fingers. "Oh yes. I enjoy watching this very much."

Greer in front of me is voiceless, presumably as part of the choreography she mapped out for our night, but she wriggles and bucks back against me, and I remind myself of the game. I'm a guest and Ash is my host, and Greer is the prized scotch he's letting me taste. His most cherished possession opened up for me and made available for my use, for my guest right.

It's easy to sink into the fantasy now, easy to fuck into this gorgeous woman while her husband watches. Easy to let all those lonely days and bitter nights go, fuck them gone, fuck them right out of existence. There's just Greer in front of me, her obedience fracturing along predictable lines as she glances over her shoulder to watch me and to watch her husband watch us, every part of this torrid scenario lighting her up. There's just Ash, his stupidly handsome face still cradled against his fingers, his perfect jaw tense, and his other hand slowly balling and flexing beside his thigh, as if he's struggling not to touch something. Himself, maybe, or us. And right now it doesn't matter because there's only an *us*. No matter the configuration, no matter how we tessellate limbs and join bodies, it's all as a three. As an *us*. Even from three feet away, Ash is fucking Greer as surely as I am, and even from three feet away, I know he can feel every thrust and slide as if he were doing it himself. And I wonder, in the delirious corners of my mind, if he's thinking about what it would be like to be Greer right now, bent over and shivering with sweat along his back as I moved behind him in a rumpled tuxedo.

Fuck.

"You should play with her clit," says Ash from the couch. "When she comes on your cock, it's quite something."

It is quite something. I know that from experience; in fact, I was the first person to feel that something ever, but it doesn't matter right now, because that's not the game. The game is that I'm taking my guest right, and beyond the game, if tonight is my last night with Greer, I need for her to come hard; I need her body sore and hungry with the memory of me.

I slide a hand over her ass, following the curve to the supple line of her thigh, following that to where thigh meets body. The moment my fingers strum across her clit, her back arches up and she's making this noise of hers that's somewhere between a moan and a kitten's mewl. Every time I hear it, I have to grit my teeth to stop myself from coming right then and there.

And you know what? If I were really a guest and this really were my right, I'd be able to fuck her any way I wanted, and right now I want more of her. All of her. I slide an arm high up on her waist, just below her breasts, and I wind her braid around my hand, and I pull her upright, using both until her back is flush to my chest.

My hands are greedy, fondling her breasts over her shirt with rough plumps, moving with pressing fingertips over her waist and hips and shoulders and collarbone. Everywhere, I want to touch her everywhere, and it's not long before her shirt feels like the worst thing that's ever happened to me, a curse, a punishment, and I yank it off her body with impatient tugs. Then I'm dragging down the cups of her bra, rolling and plucking at her nipples, which earns a low noise of approval from Ash.

It earns me lots of squirms and gasps from Greer, and I need to see her, I need to see her face, so I pull us both down on a sofa, rearranging her so that she straddles me. I strip off her bra and skirt, so that all of her is available for my mouth and eyes and hands, and as I drink her in, she starts moving on top of me, lithe and undulating movements that have us both straining and sweating in a matter of moments. I lean forward and suck on the tips of her breasts while she cradles the back of my head; she wraps a hand around my throat to keep me still; eventually I lock her wrists behind her back, forcing her tits to jut forward and her hips to tilt toward mine. At some point, Ash comes to sit next to us, murmuring the most filthy things in my ear:

I can tell you need to come. I see how much it's killing you to hold back.

Isn't she sexy? Isn't she beautiful? Doesn't she feel good?

Don't you want to come inside her? I'd let you, you know, I'd let you come as much as you needed to.

He takes over holding her wrists behind her back, which means I have a hand free to toy with her firm little clit, all full and needy for attention. It only takes a minute or two with my thumb, and the blush creeping up her stomach and down her chest ignites into a real, frenzied heat. And it only takes another minute for that heat to combust into a pure flaming delight that leaves her gasping and shuddering on top of me, and Ash says in my ear *give it to her* and I do, I give it all to her. I fuck up into her with three hard thrusts, and with a strangled cry and with a painful shudder deep inside my body, I throb and pulse and spill five months' worth of waiting into the woman I love.

CHAPTER 13
EMBRY

NOW

I MIGHT BE DEAD.

There's a moment when my vision dims and my hearing muffles and all I'm aware of is the sweet weight of a person I love slumped against me and there's nothing, not even a heartbeat, between us. For a handful of breathless, mindless moments, there is only her.

And then I breathe and come back to life. There is me. There is Ash next to us, wearing a look that I've learned from long experience means the best kind of danger.

"How does that shower sound now?" he asks.

It sounds like heaven. I tell him so. And together we help shift a boneless, happy Greer off my lap and into the shamelessly lavish presidential shower (part of a renovation done by Ash's predecessor; the ascetic Maxen Ashley Colchester would shower in a plastic box and never think to complain).

Once we have an orgasm-drunk Greer settled under a warm spray of water, we step out and start undressing, me leaving my tuxedo in careless piles and him neatly flattening and folding each article of his clothing, even his socks. His boxer briefs are the last to go, and when he catches me staring at the firm curves of his ass and the heavy pole of his erection, he laughs. It's a rare laugh from him, one that's all happy memories and teasing eyes, and it hooks and yanks at my heart.

"How many times, Embry?" he asks, his hidden dimple peeking out. "Surely you're bored of me by now."

"If you're asking how many times I would have to watch you undress to get bored," I say softly, "you already know there's no number high enough."

His laughter fades, his dimple disappearing but his lips still curling into a bewitching smile. "All these years...I think I know every crook and edge of you. And then you go and say things like that, and it's like I'm falling in love for the first time all over again."

I close my eyes. I have to; I can't look at him and hear him say words like that at the same time or I'll dissolve. "Ash..."

"Tonight's just pretend, little prince. Remember?"

I open my eyes. "I know better than that," I say in a tight voice. "Everything with you has been real from the start. From the moment you pinned me against that wall, everything was real."

His eyes flame a bright, brilliant green, and it's a miracle that I'm not on my knees right now; it's a miracle that I'm not running my tongue along every curve of his throat and chest. "If it's real," he says, taking a step toward me, "what then?"

"If it's real," I say, and I can't believe I'm saying it even as I utter the words, "then it's just for tonight."

Stupid. I'm so fucking stupid. *Just for tonight* is as much of a lie as *pretend.*

The way I love Ash and Greer is not the kind of love that

fades into a dusty memory; it's not the kind of love that can be fenced in and patrolled. And tonight will feed it, nurse it, make a strong thing even stronger, and how we aren't all going to be crushed to death by this, I don't know.

"If it's just for tonight," says Ash quietly, "then I want you to say it to me."

I pass a hand over my face. How, after he watched me fuck his wife, while I'm literally naked, can he make me feel more vulnerable than I already am? How? But he has and he is, and it's the fucking truth and I want to say it to him, and if we lived a different life, a life when two soldier boys could fall in love and get married and buy a horse farm, then I would tell him so often he'd beg me to stop.

"I love you," I say.

He lets out a breath like he's been struck. "And I love you."

"Achilles."

"Patroclus."

And then he kisses me, hot and fervent, slamming me up against the outside wall of the shower.

"Have I earned your mouth, then?" I mumble against his lips, my fingers running greedy arcs over the notched ridges of his stomach and the planes of his chest, and I'm surprised I get away with it for so long before he captures my hands and pins them above my head. His hips press hard into mine—his erection rubbing raw against my own—and then he releases me.

"In the shower," he says sternly. "You have a princess to take care of."

My cock gives an extra throb as I turn and see Greer watching us with unabashed lust in her eyes. One hand is pressed against the glass and her other hand is pressed between her legs. Behind me, I hear Ash make a pleased noise.

"And I," he adds, "have a princess to punish for touching herself without permission."

Ash makes good on his promise to punish Greer, and for several steamy minutes, he and I take turns with her mouth, using her just forcefully enough to make her feel Ash's discipline, still careful enough to keep her safe, since the steam makes it harder for her to catch her breath. Afterward, Ash uses the tiled bench in the shower to pull her over his lap and spank her ass for good measure, and then he gently fingers her to a screaming orgasm as a reward. I watch and kiss her and pet her, hard as a fucking rock through it all, just like he is.

And then there's the actual washing, with the kinds of awkward jostle and mundane clicks of bottles and reaching around for washcloths and shivering waiting for the spray that manages to feel just as intimate as any other part of it. We wash each other, we soap and we rub and we rinse, and I try to burn every second of it into my brain. The way Greer's hands feel running down the corrugations of my torso, the suds dripping off the point of Ash's elbow as he reaches up to wipe the water off his face, the glisten of water in Greer's navel as she arches back to rinse her hair. The way it feels for the three of us to press slippery and sudsy together, every slide and press a new revelation of skin. Every brush a brush against something I love: Ash's biceps, the dimples above Greer's ass, the edible curve of her neck into her shoulder, the dark trail of hair leading from Ash's stomach to his cock.

At the end of it, Greer raises up on her tiptoes to whisper something to Ash, her eyes on me glinting with mischief as she talks into his ear.

Ash nods as he listens, his eyes down and his lips twitching in a small smile. "Of course," he tells her when she finishes talking. "You have my permission."

With that, Greer turns to me with a face that can only be described as naughty. "Embry," she starts. "You left before—we never had a chance to do something together. And I want to do it tonight."

"And what's that?" I ask hoarsely, pretty sure I already know.

She slides her arms around my neck, the slippery press of her tits against my chest unbelievably distracting. "I want you to fuck my ass," she says, looking up at me. My cock gives a hot surge against her belly the moment she says the words, and she laughs. "I guess I won't have to beg you."

"Never that," I tell her, dipping my face low to capture her mouth in a long kiss while my hands slide down to her pert little ass and start exploring. There's the crease where her ass curves into her thighs, there's the yummy place where both thigh and ass meet pussy, and then there's the dark seam between her cheeks. Hot, thin skin and the indecently enticing circlet of her asshole, tight and waiting.

"She's gotten very good at it," Ash says from next to us. Between his lean hips, his cock throbs heavy and dark, and I'm very aware that neither of us have come since we've entered the shower. He hasn't come at all tonight, and it shows in the veined, rigid jolts of his organ. He can control his voice and his face, but his needy erection speaks volumes.

It also tells me that he's waiting for something, saving himself for the right moment, and as much as that should fill me with caution, it fills me with joy. I hope whatever he's waiting for is filthy beyond all bounds; I hope it breaks me.

"Have you?" I ask against Greer's mouth. "Gotten good at it?"

In response, she turns in my arms so that my erection is cradled at the cleft of her ass. "Why don't you see for yourself?" she asks, and I will, I am, I am definitely going to do that, at least I am once I can take my eyes off the way my cock looks like this, framed by the heart shape of her bottom, bracketed by the dimples above her ass.

Ash hands me a bottle of conditioner, and when our hands meet around the bottle, I have a bolt of dizzying déjà vu.

"Just like old times," my old lover comments, and it is, it really is. That almost-year between Jenny's death and Greer was a whirlwind of fucking and making out and furtive orgasms in dark corners and even more fucking. Days in the Oval Office bathroom, nights in this same shower. Even more nights at Lyonesse, Mark's club, with Morgan and Ash, as Ash learned how to whip and tie and clamp and torture.

He learned on me.

On my body.

But those choreographed scenes were nothing like the frantic, fumbling embraces in private, seven years of pent-up lust burning through us like a forest fire, and there were times when I came undone and found that calm mercy under his brutal hands and knew for sure that I would never come back together. He spent that year splitting me wide open, the final blow coming when he proposed a second time and cleaved me right in two. Split like firewood, tossed onto an altar of guilt and lust and politics.

I died saying no to him a second time.

I push the memory of his second proposal and my refusal out of my mind. His flinch at my answer, the raw hurt in his eyes. And instead, I focus on the memories that came before all that. Those nights in the shower, the clean fragrance of conditioner because we were always too impatient to go get the real stuff, the quiet peace that always came when he mastered me. The awe in his voice when I came for him.

I nudge open the cap to the conditioner and drizzle a liberal amount onto my cock and hands, and then I toss the bottle back to Ash.

"Hands on the glass," I tell Greer, "and feet apart."

She obeys immediately, presenting Ash and me with a view of that scrumptious ass and blushing pussy and the tiny little hole I'm about to fuck. Ash and I both groan at the sight, and Ash's hands are flexing by his thighs again, as if he's restraining himself from grabbing his cock—or grabbing us. The latter is more likely, and the instant fantasy of him wrestling to fuck both of us at the same time sends a dart of heat into the deepest parts of me, parts that only Ash and Greer have ever been able to reach. Pure filth and pure spiritual connection fused into singularity right at the base of my spine.

I don't waste another minute—I can't, actually, my dick is so hard that the skin is shiny and tight—and I give myself a couple measured strokes to spread the makeshift lube from base to tip. And then I step close to her, close enough for our feet to touch, and I slide a slick finger between her cheeks until I find the firm rim of her anus.

"Ash," I say.

"Yes?"

I look over at him as I continue to circle Greer's hole with my fingertip, trying to find the right words. So much of what happens between the three of us is unspoken, navigated spontaneously and in the moment, but there are always certain roles we magnetize to. Greer, the compliant. Ash, the master. Me, the mood ring of a lover, shifting and changing depending on the day, the hour, the minute. Out in the living room, we all fell into those roles quite nicely, but in here I'm not sure. Am I allowed to direct the scene? Is he still in charge?

I don't need to find the words though because Ash senses what I'm trying to say. "This is your show, little prince," he says. Then his gaze falls onto the place where I'm knuckle deep into his wife and his eyes darken. "Although I might not be able to stop myself from playing too."

"God, I hope you don't stop yourself," I say. "And in that case, will you unbraid her hair? I want it free."

Ash rumbles his approval at my request—he has such

a terminal thing for her hair—and leans down to kiss her temple before he starts unplaiting her wet braid. She smiles up at him.

"I'm happy right now," she murmurs to her husband, and he looks like he could float away with knowledge that she's content, taking such a deep and genuine satisfaction in her happiness that I almost feel embarrassed to witness it. The purity of his love for her.

Except then I realize I feel it for the both of them as well, this kind of lift in my chest at their smiles, this answering contentment to their own. This feeling like any bruise, gash, or fracture is worth just a moment of their joy.

"I'm happy that you're happy," he says, kissing her hairline again. "And our little prince is going to make you feel very good. Are you ready for that?"

"I am." Another dreamy murmur.

I hope I'm ready for it. With Ash and Greer, sometimes it feels like I've been ready my entire life, and other times it feels like I'm facing down a tidal wave I didn't know was coming. And I never know which it will be.

As Ash carefully tugs the hair band from her hair and slides it over her wrist, I begin expanding my invasion of her hole, pressing against the inner wall closest to her pussy, finger-fucking her ass until I hear a luxurious *mmmm* come out of her mouth. Then I add a second finger, watching her every ripple and seize, watching her blurry reflection in the glass. Ass play isn't for everyone, but Ash is right—Greer's good at it. A far cry from the anal virgin whom I had to cajole into relaxing and opening, this woman is pushing back onto my fingers and making more of her siren-like moans of pleasure...and clearly enjoying every second of my assault.

So I add a third finger, stilling my movements and letting her leisurely fuck my hand with hypnotic rolls of her ass. All while Ash is gently unbraiding her hair, taking care not to pull on the tangled strands, smoothing them between his fingertips until they glimmer wet gold and wavy down her back.

He's so tender with her, so scrupulously avoiding causing her pain, even in something as trivial as untangling hair, and I understand it on a cellular level. It's because he loves her. It's because the only pain she should ever have to feel is the pain he chooses to give her. The play of his large hands on the silky tresses is sexy and elemental, and it's everything physical and spiritual about Ash and Greer that I love.

I can watch him play with her hair forever, I think. Until the sun swallows the earth and the wind itself turns into fire.

"Up on the balls of your feet," I tell her, sliding my fingers out of her ass and fisting my cock. I'm so fucking turned on by watching Ash untangle her hair that even my own hand is about to make me go off. I don't even know how I'll last in the tight squeeze of her dirtiest place for longer than two strokes. Shit, even one stroke.

Greer pushes up onto her tiptoes, her calves bunching into sleek little rounds, her thighs tensing. Her hole at the perfect height for me to push into. Ash gives her hair one final adoring stroke, and then he cups the back of her head and angles her face so he can kiss her. His mouth devours hers, strong and sure, and with his nakedness, I can see the effect the kiss has on him. The tight belly, the tense muscles everywhere. The dark, bobbing cock pointing up at the ceiling like a thick weapon. Again plays my fantasy of him wrestling us both to the wet floor or against the clear, cold glass, using his angry cock on both of us.

I give a shudder of unabashed want. Surely he will want to master me tonight? Surely that's what's burning such a hot, filthy fire behind those pretty green eyes of his? Surely that's who he's saving all that cum for? For me?

And will I let him master me? Despite all that's between

us and all that's happened and all that will happen in a November two years from now?

Of course I will.

Ash breaks off the kiss, looking satisfied at Greer's hazy expression, and steps back, and I realize it's so he can see me better. So he can see how I'm rubbing the head of my cock where my fingers were just a moment ago.

"Reach back," Ash says to Greer. "Spread your cheeks for him. He wants to see the hole he's going to fuck."

Greer complies, struggling a little for balance but finding her equilibrium after a second, and then Ash and I are rewarded with the obscene exposure of her most private parts. Already visible before, now they are on display, stretched and revealed so that nothing is hidden. Nothing.

Ash and I both stare down at where my fat crown nudges into her—teasing little presses that have her whimpering and that show what a big thing I'm about to put into a very small place—and with her spread like this, I can easily breach the first ring of her, in and out, in and out in short, almost-nothing shoves. Just enough to start swallowing my crown, just enough to make her gasp. I might come from this, from fucking her with only the tip of me. Hell, I could come just from staring down at my head teasing at her pretty pleated asshole.

I can't wait another instant, I decide. I widen my stance, put a steadying hand around her hip, and I start wedging my cock into her. She makes a noise, signaling that pleasure-pain I've been on the receiving end of so many times, and I run a calming hand over her flank, chafe her ass in reassuring circles.

"It's okay, baby," I soothe. "I'm here. I'm here."

Goose bumps cover her skin as I slide deeper inside, and fuck, it feels so fucking good. It's tight and slick and hot, like a fist, and the *sight* of it, the thick rod disappearing into her ass as she keeps herself spread open for me—it's almost punishing how hot it is. I have to breathe through my nose as I keep pushing in, feeding inch after thick inch into her greedy body.

And then it's there, I'm all the way there, and I am still breathing through my nose, because I'm going to come any minute, I just know I am, and I'm not ready to give this up yet. The sight of Greer shivering and her sides moving in short, exhilarated breaths and her wet hair like molten gold down her back. The feeling of her channel so slick and so smooth, clenching so very hard on my dick, like it wants to milk the orgasm right out of my body. The stroke and squeeze of her, singing heat and pressure up every nerve ending in my cock.

"You can put your hands back on the glass," I tell her in a ragged voice. "You'll want your balance for this."

"Okay," she whispers, doing as I say and putting her hands on the shower wall. I lean forward and drop a kiss onto a bare shoulder, and then I start fucking her ass for real. Slow strokes at first, until I regain my control. In and then a breath. Out and then a breath. Every thrust measured and cautious until I can adjust to the hot friction of her. Until I can be sure she's ready for more.

Soon, she's bucking back against my hips, seeking out more of me, and I answer in kind, kicking her feet together to make her tighter and then sawing into her with heavy, regular strokes. Ash is practically glowing with lust now, a hot sun of need pacing restlessly around us as I fuck his wife, radiating heat and power and edgy desire.

"Go at her hard," he says one minute, and then the next, "Now give her the deep ones. Slow ones. Spank her when you do it."

He's taking charge again, and I don't even think he realizes it—but I *do* realize it and I still accede because I love it when he's like this. His power is his love, his command is his affection. And as much as I enjoy wrestling for freedom, as much as I savor the looser dynamic between Greer and me, *this* is what we all need. This is what we all want. Our king, making his little prince and his little princess kneel at his feet.

I become his proxy, his words directing me. Fast, slow, deep. Hands on her tits, hands on her weeping, needy cunt. Spank to the ass, yank to the hair. His words like a burned melody floating through it all, and Greer comes again, clenching hard around my dick and her cries reverberating off the glass.

And it's when she comes down from her climax and looks up at him with wide, liquid eyes, blond hair streaked across her face and tits, that Ash growls wordlessly and surges toward us, all brawn and feral need. And it's actually scary, actually thrilling, to have such a tall, broad-shouldered man move at you like *that*, and my heart is pounding, and the next minute I'm slammed against the wall, still inside Greer, and both Greer and I are caged in by his arms. I realize he's shoved us here because it's close to the bench, and at the same moment I register this, Greer's leg is raised and opened and propped up on the edge of it, and Ash's hard cock is pushing and nosing up against the base of mine. And with a cry from Greer that I'll be thinking of every night for the rest of my life, he pushes roughly into her wet, empty cunt.

It's insane. It's actually insane, the feeling of his giant cock through the thin wall that separates us. I can feel him moving, and it's so tight like this, so much tighter than I thought anything could ever be—and his balls rub shamelessly against mine as he fucks up into her, and holy shit, how do I even describe the sensation of his balls against mine under the furnace of Greer's body? It's hot and coarse and such a good feeling I could die from it, and we angle our hips to seek out more, to feel more of the press of each other as we alternate hard pumps into our queen.

Greer is coming apart between us, her hands scrabbling against Ash's chest as she unleashes an orgasm that has us both groaning from the flutters around our cocks, and she is nothing but gold hair and soft, wet skin, and floating, helpless cries, and we end up supporting her between the two of us as her orgasm shreds away her ability to stand and she slumps, her head lolling back against my shoulder. We still work into her, two throbbing cocks, fucking in tandem.

"I'm going to come again," she whimpers with something almost like grief. "I can't do it, I can't—"

I capture her mouth in a searing kiss, sweeping my tongue across hers, and it's her mouth so sweet and hungry against mine and her latest orgasm—a rolling thing that has her sobbing brokenly against my lips and bucking weakly in our arms—that delivers the killing blow. With Ash's penis stroking against mine through the thin membrane of Greer's walls and with her tight, slick ass—I come.

I rumble a low moan of agonized pleasure as I crest the point of no return and the muffled stroke of Ash's cock sends me over the edge. And then the first contraction jerks delicious muscles deep in my groin. Another jerk rips a groan from my lips as I start pouring and spilling deep into Greer, hot spurts that fill her with wet heat, and I can feel the jetting throbs all the way in my thighs, all the way up in my stomach. On and on I pulse, the weight of a satisfied woman heavy against my chest, both of us caged in by her husband's arms. I look at him as I'm still coming, and if I hadn't already come, I would now. His face is a mask of raw, undisguised need—dark eyes, parted lips, jaw set.

And yet, somehow, as I finish my orgasm and slide with a sensitized groan from her ass, he manages to pull out of her pussy at the same time. Without coming. And if I thought he was hard before, it's nothing like now. Every part of him sings of violent, filthy, frightening need—his cock, his posture, his face—and I can't even imagine the tightness in his belly right now, the ache of his full balls.

But his eyes soften when he looks at Greer. I know it's not that he's got some complex about going easy on her—I've seen him fuck her mercilessly, beat her until she's sobbing—but it's that he's got a plan for tonight, and part of that plan was getting Greer like this. His eyes are softening because he's made her boneless with pleasure and joy, and that gentles the beast somewhat.

"Let's rinse one more time," he says, "and then we'll dry off."

"You haven't come yet," Greer murmurs, eyes all pupil-wide and cheeks flushed. She's deep in subspace or endorphin space or some kind of space, and maybe it's the power of knowing I got her that way or maybe it's the simple joy of seeing a lover fucked into sheer bliss, but it's fucking seductive as hell. I can see why Ash is so addicted to being a *sir* if this is what he gets out of it.

"Don't worry," he says to our queen. "The night isn't over yet."

CHAPTER 14
EMBRY

NOW

A FEW MINUTES LATER, CLEAN AND DRIED WITH SOFT, FLUFFY towels, Ash wraps a fresh towel around Greer and scoops her easily into his arms. I expect that I'll follow them into the bedroom, and I'm looking forward to the view—Ash's tight ass and the muscled slopes of his back, the delicate lines of Greer's lower legs and pointed toes as they hang over Ash's arm…maybe even the silver glow of her eyes peering at me from around her husband's shoulder.

But instead, Ash turns to me. "Would you like to do the honors?"

Greer is still in her glassy-eyed sex coma, giving me a drowsy smile from where her head is nestled against Ash's chest, and I can't resist. I step forward and take her into my arms, my chest going tight as she lets out a contented sigh and rests her head against me just like she had with Ash. She feels made to be in my arms—or my arms feel made to carry her—and there's a tiny wail of grief inside my mind as

I consider that I might never get to carry her like this again. That I could have had this every night, and now I never will.

I'm still grappling internally with this as we go into the bedroom (I did get that view of Ash's perfect ass after all) and I lay Greer carefully on the bed.

She rolls to her side, eyes gazing all pearl gray and languid up at us. "You're hard again," she murmurs, running a finger up my thigh and down my fresh erection to prove her point.

I *am* hard again. I can't help it; I honestly can't. It's her and it's him, and I love them, and my love for them has always come bound up in sex. That is to say, the way I love them is through my body and my soul, it's with all parts of myself, every single part of Embry Moore. But I have the decency to be embarrassed about it. It's not like I've gone without tonight, and even with the excuse of my celibacy, it's still a little ridiculous. Like feasting all night at a banquet and then hearing your stomach rumble with hunger in front of your host.

And after five orgasms and two hours of vigorous play, it's obvious that Greer is spent and sore. It feels selfish to want more. Graceless and greedy. But she doesn't seem to think so, letting her legs fall open as she continues to tickle light fingers along my hard length.

"Greer, sweetheart." I catch her hand, catch her eyes with my own. "You don't have to do that. You've already done enough for me tonight. I can just jack it off real quick." Or I could lie and tell her that it'll go down on its own after a while, but I know that's not true. Not with Ash still hard and full next to me. Not with Greer so heavy-limbed and well-used, spread across the bed in easy invitation.

"No." She pouts, a little crease in her brow. "I want you to come inside me again. Please."

My cock gives a little jump at her words. "I'd love that, but I don't want to hurt you."

"You won't hurt me," she promises, spreading her legs even more. Her pussy is flushed and swollen and wet, tempting beyond belief—not the least because it's flushed and wet from *me*. I've already come inside her tonight, and then I remember that Ash fucked her in the shower with my spend still in her pussy, and my semen must have been streaking and sliding all over his cock along with her arousal and his own, and I have to catch my breath. Holy shit, holy shit, holy shit. The messes the three of us make together.

And then there's another hand on my cock—male, rough, big. There's no *may I?* this time, no pretense, no game. There's just his hand on me, where his hand belongs, and then I look up and my heart drops to his feet. Where it belongs.

His face is that raw mix of tender violence, and in the ambient lamplight scattering in from the corners of the room, I remember why it took me so long to figure out his eyes. They're both dark and light, pale jade and vivid emerald and a thick lake green, and they change, they deepen and lighten, they glint and go smoky, like leaves tossed green and thick on a fire.

His lips part as our eyes meet, and I'm haunted by the memory of his mouth on my body. Those lips that are so firm and pretty shaped and full that whenever he looks serious or sad or even angry, they turn down into a beautiful, masculine pout—and he has no idea.

He glances down at where he holds me, and I get a glimpse of white, even teeth as he licks his lower lip in an unthinking, automatic response. And then he squeezes me, as if he's testing for himself how hard I am for him, and he licks that lower lip again, and I make a noise in the back of my throat.

"What is it?" he asks, looking up and sending a lock of raven-colored hair tumbling over his forehead.

"You're too handsome," I accuse him. "It's upsetting."

"Mmm," he hums, still fondling me and stepping closer as he does. His naked toes touch the side of my foot, his cock only bare inches away from my hip, and I can practically feel the heat coming off it. "I think you'll find that I'm far more upset about you."

"Upset means 'hard,' right?" I whisper as his hand dips low to cradle my testicles. In front of us, Greer is still spilled over the covers in endorphin-doped pleasure, a sinuous ribbon of satisfied woman. She continues running idle fingers around my nakedness, watching Ash and me with that lechery in her eyes I find so adorable (and also so fucking hot).

"Upset means hard," confirms Ash, his hand now cupping me with a possessive urgency. "Very, very hard."

He shifts closer, his mouth close to my ear and his hand leaving my sac so he can put a firm palm against my dick. "Do you know what else?" he asks in a low voice, and it's difficult to think right now with him pressing me so cruelly, pinning my cock between his hard hand and my hard stomach. I've oozed enough pre-cum that it smears across my stomach as my crown brushes against the skin, and feeling the wet evidence of my arousal is somehow just as overwhelming as having my cock pinioned like this.

"What?" I finally manage to breathe out.

Ash runs a finger around my navel, smearing it through the wet mess of pre-cum I'm leaving on my stomach. It's humiliating, and Ash seems to think so too, saying in an amused voice, "I didn't realize all you needed was an indifferent palm and your own stomach. I think I've wasted a lot of effort over the years."

My hips are moving shamelessly against his touch now, and I don't bother fighting off the indignity of it. I like the indignity, crave it; I'll starve without it—even if I've always struggled to admit that to myself when I'm in my right mind.

So instead I say gaspingly, "Your palm isn't indifferent, you fucking liar."

He laughs and grinds the heel of his hand harder against me for that, as a punishment for my sass. Or maybe it's a reward. Sometimes, Ash makes it hard to tell.

"What I was going to say, before you so charmingly made a mess of yourself," murmurs Ash, "is that I think I know why you're still not satisfied after two rounds with your queen."

"And why is that?"

"Because," he says, his lips moving across my jaw and ear and neck as he talks, "I haven't fucked you yet."

He's right.

"You're wrong," I say.

"Oh, I am definitely not wrong," he croons, and I feel his other hand run down my spine. My cock jolts without his permission and I can feel his smile all the way through my toes. "Poor Embry. Poor, poor Embry with no one to fuck him. With no one to make him feel good."

His hand slides over my ass, and habit makes me widen my legs. "Poor Embry not being able to make *me* feel good," he says in that low croon still, a fingertip pressing against my ass. "Because you love making me feel good, don't you? Letting me use that ass whenever I need it?"

His finger breaches my hole, and the sharp flare of invasion goes straight to my dick, straight to that place low in my pelvis. Every single sensation feels like it's spiraling out from the place where he fingers me, and I buck back against his hand, trying to drive him deeper inside.

"Look at you," mocks Ash. "Grinding against me like a needy whore. Are you that hard up for it? Are you that desperate to be fucked?"

"You're not playing fair," I groan. Ash has his hands on both the front and the back of me, Greer's fingers are flitting everywhere private and prurient, and I'm about to tumble face-first onto this bed because I don't know if I can support my own weight anymore.

"Why would I play fair?" Ash asks, his finger pushing in to the knuckle. It's going in dry, so it burns, but I welcome the burn and the sting. The biting proof that the man I love is inside me.

"I don't know," I mumble, my head hanging down and my eyes nearly closed with lust. "I don't like it when you play fair anyway."

"Tell me you want it," Ash demands, all the crooning and mockery gone. He's all sir now, all the soldier who once fucked me while I was bleeding and high on morphine just because he wanted to. Well, because I told him to.

Okay, begged him.

And when I walked in here tonight, I didn't plan on ending up at this moment, even though I'd secretly hoped for it. Panged shamefully at the idea that I'd be wrestled into submission by my ex-lover.

It's embarrassing and foolish, but I can't shake this prickly belief that it's unmanly somehow. Not unmanly because of the penetration, you see, but because I'm supposed to be resisting him and publicly challenging his authority...and then a few hours alone with him and all the challenge has left me, driven out by stark craving and this stupid, fateful love for him that I'll never be able to shake.

"I want it," I admit in a defeated voice. "I need it. Please, Ash, please—"

"Want what, little prince? Need what?" His hands leave me and he walks over to an end table by the bed, and I know he'll want me to be specific, to beg specifically. He always does.

"I want you to fuck me," I mumble, watching the fascinating contradiction of his Bible trembling on the end table while he digs in the drawer for lube.

"I'm sorry, what was that? I couldn't hear."

"I said I want you to *fuck me*," I growl loudly. Then I mutter, "Asshole," under my breath.

That earns me a dark look. "Don't make trouble for yourself," he warns, tossing the lube on the bed and closing the drawer.

Jesus. When have I ever done anything else?

Ash smooths Greer's damp hair away from her forehead. "We need you one more time, my queen. Then you can rest."

She nods, turning her head up to kiss his hand. "Do I have to come? I don't know if I can."

Only with Ash is being given permission *not* to come just as much a mercy as the opposite. He gives a small shake of his head. "You don't have to come. Now spread your legs and welcome Embry home."

With a happy smile and a catlike stretch, she unribbons herself, moving to the center of the bed and opening her legs in the world's oldest invitation, and both Ash and I simply stare for a moment.

Glimmers of gold hair spilling over the pillow. A taut stomach with a little well of a belly button. Tits the perfect size for palming and cupping, the nipples furled tight and the undersides dotted with love bites. Even the most mundane parts of her—her knees and her toes and the hollows of her armpits—are perfect. This is the same woman who climbed onto a Chicago Ferris wheel with a complete stranger, who fucked that same stranger in a heady fit of pain and rejection, who can speak three different dead languages and quote medieval poetry from memory, who has coolly stared down journalists accusing her of adultery and left the entire room rattled with her cold dignity. She is all things at once: hot and cold, closed and open. Polished elegance and raw carnality.

My Greer.

"I love her," I tell him.

"I know" is Ash's response. "Go show her."

So I crawl onto the bed to join her, relishing the way her eyes sweep down my body as I do and also relishing just the act of it. Such a small thing to join someone on a bed, to dent the mattress with hands and knees as you crawl, to have them regarding you with anticipation and lust and familiarity. And yet it feels huge now because I don't have this in my new life; there's no prowling toward a waiting lover, no slide of skin on blankets as you move and they arch up to greet you. I commit every tiny, ordinary detail to memory as I gently lower my body over Greer's. The practical little scoots we make on the blanket to line up our bodies. The moment our chests and stomachs touch. The brush of her thighs on the outside of mine. The pleasurable chore of parting the silky fall of her hair so I can brace a hand beside her head.

"I love you," I tell her, searching her eyes. I want her to see, I want her to *know*, and I want her to know it now and forever. Every part of my soul burns for her and always will.

"I love you too," she murmurs, looking so soft and pliant that I lean down and kiss her. Her lips part for me on a sigh, and she tastes like sex and the lingering sweet of champagne, and I lick at all of it, drink all of it in. Below the cradle of her hips, my cock leaks vulgar tears onto the bare skin of her pussy, and it's she who reaches down and takes me in hand. She who guides my tip right to her center. She who wraps her legs around my waist and tries to bring me closer.

"Give it to me," she pleads quietly. "Please. One more time."

"One more time," I say, and pierce her deep and full with my cock.

God, her pussy. Flushed and hot from her busy night, still wet inside from when I took my guest right earlier and spent inside her. The best combination of slippery and tight, and it has my stomach clenching to feel my dick inside. Has my hand fisting in the pillow underneath her and my thighs trembling with restraint.

She arches and wiggles underneath me, her stomach once again pressing flat against mine and driving me mad. I unleash a wicked flurry of thrusts out of sheer reaction, my weight driving her into the bed, my hips moving hard and fast.

"Ohhh," she breathes, staring up at me. "Oh God."

I do it again. I hug her tight to my chest and burrow my face in her neck, and then I pump into her over and over and over, static crowding at the edges of my vision, my mouth open and kissing against her neck and shoulder. Her hand catches mine, and I slow my thrusts as I feel her fingers run across the new metal of my wedding band.

I freeze, lifting my head and staring down at her as she turns her head to see the glint of it in the dark.

"Greer…"

"It's not real," she whispers. And then she puts my hand with its traitorous ring flat against her chest, so I can feel the gentle slope of her breast and the hammer of her heart. "This," she says, looking up at me and holding my hand against her heart, "this is what's real. Us. What we have."

I close my eyes a moment because it's too much, her grace and her forgiveness and her understanding. Her generosity. I'm not worthy of it, and it eats me up inside that I can never be. Maybe…maybe if I win against Ash, and maybe if I can finally smother the Carpathian flames once and for all and guarantee that she'll be safe from Melwas always—maybe then I'll earn it. Maybe then I'll deserve this gift she's giving me.

I open my eyes after I can breathe normally and then I give her a long, ardent kiss. I claim her lips and tongue and teeth, tracing them with my tongue and stealing her breath and replacing it with mine. I fuck into her with slow, deep rolls that have her whimpering against my mouth. And all the while, my hateful wedding ring rests warm and solid between us, and after several minutes of kissing and unhurried coupling, it doesn't feel so evil on my finger anymore. It's nothing more than a hammered ring of inert metal, a *thing*, and it can never compare to the hammered ring our hearts make. To the fragile band that encircles the three of us and anchors us to one another.

This is real.

In my haste to fuck the queen, I'd forgotten about the king prowling around the room—and also that king's bottle of lube resting next to where my hips move against his wife's. It looks so innocuous there, smallish and white, and I remember how some of the most depraved and debauched nights of my life have begun with similar, innocent-looking bottles. And then of course, there were the even more depraved nights—vicious and violating—when we made do without the real stuff. Olive oil or conditioner or aloe vera—or just spit and a prayer. Some of the best nights of my life.

I look up, expecting to see Ash ready to crawl on the bed behind me, but instead I find him kneeling on the floor beside us, his arms on the bed and his head pillowed on his arms. He's watching me and Greer, and his *face*.

His face.

I've never wondered before what it would look like for someone to have their whole world in their eyes, never even thought to wonder. But Ash right now, kneeling and gazing at Greer and me—

His whole world is in his eyes.

And it's incredible to see.

Holy, almost. Sacred.

That kind of awe and vulnerability and bloody, heart-beating love—it's like being offered something on an altar, and realizing the person offering it thinks you're a god. Ash is staring at us like he could forgo food and water and air as long as he had us, and suddenly my chest is cracking wide-open and my heart is falling out and there was never any other way for me to end up than caught between them. With her arching underneath me and Ash beside me, I almost feel like I am a god, like I could conquer the entire world, and I dare anyone not to fall in love with her, not to kneel to him; I dare anyone to resist the undertow of Maxen Colchester and Greer Galloway.

Anyone.

Greer reaches over for Ash, and he takes her hand and rubs her fingers against his stubbled jaw as he watches us move in sweaty, lazy intimacy. "Join us," she says to him.

"In a minute," he answers. "I want to look at you both."

"Looking can't be as much fun as fucking," Greer points out with a little pout that would make any other man weep with lust.

"You underestimate what I'm looking at," Ash says, unmoved, still rubbing her fingers against his face.

I know better than anyone the crude appetites he keeps behind all that honor and Catholic morality, and I know how to get him on the bed with us. I purposefully move Greer's leg to the side and angle her hips so that he can see the stretch of her cunt around my erection, the indolent thresh of my hips against hers. The wet gleam of her on my cock as I pull out and slowly plunge back in.

Ash goes completely still, his hand frozen with Greer's fingers against his jaw, his eyes darker than I've ever seen them. And with the low light of the room outlining the rigid muscles of his shoulders and arms, the tense set of his jaw, and the hunger and thirst expressed by that brutal mouth—I have a moment when I wonder if it was actually wise to provoke him. To stir the beast from his watchful pose. My stomach tightens in both fear and excitement.

With a growl, Ash stands up and puts a knee on the bed. *Everything* is brutal and beautiful about him right now, not just his mouth—it's his vicious body and merciless cock and the way he prowls and crawls toward us, like no predator I've even dreamed of.

And then one sadistic hand is in my hair and his male organ is filling my mouth, invading it, no care or time for me to move my tongue and teeth to accommodate him. Just a rough shove in until he hits the back of my throat, and I know he must have felt the unprepared score of my teeth, the plush resistance of my tongue and the unwelcoming squeeze of my closed throat, but it only seems to inflame him further, a low groan of pleasure coming from somewhere deep in his chest as he pulls out and shoves back in again, ruthless and seeking and finally, finally it's him, the dark master from my best and most delicious nightmares.

"Take it," he says. "Open your goddamn throat and take it."

I try, I do, but he's too big, moving too fast, using me too hard, and there's the distracting glance of Greer's fingertips tracing my lips where they suck her husband's cock, and it's all too much for me to give, which seems to be fine by Ash because he forces his way down my throat with a harsh noise anyway. I choke around him and he tightens his hand in my hair.

"That's it," he murmurs, pushing in even deeper, until my nose is pressed against the close-trimmed hair stretching down from his navel. "That's it. All the way. All the way."

And then he is all the way in and I'm trying to suck air through my nose as water streams from my eyes and the cruel hand leaves my hair to cradle my face.

"You're so fucking handsome like this," he says to me. He pulls out, leaving me sputtering for air, and then he bends down and seals his mouth over mine. Greer whimpers underneath us, her hands going to trace our chests and arms, her eyes big and silver and glued to the sight of us kissing.

Ash pulls back, his mouth wet, his cock wet, and his expression satisfied. "I've been looking forward to that all night."

I'm too busy gasping for air to say *me too*, but he reads it in my face anyway and gives me a darkly knowing smirk. And then he's crawling behind me, hair-rough legs moving against my own, his presence like a sun on my back, hot and life giving.

"Keep fucking," he orders, giving my ass a smack, and so I look back down to Greer and start moving again.

She gives me a smile that I can't describe, except to say that it conveys that hammered ring of love between the three of us and also the common bond that she and I share—which is the communion of being loved by a man like Ash. In her smile I see the understanding and amused sympathy and lust and jealousy that I feel when I watch her and Ash together, and I'm reminded forcefully of why I love her so much. We're beaten from the same metal, she and I, cut from the same fucked-up cloth, and the ways that we love each other will always, always be tangled up in the ways we love Ash and the ways he loves us back.

Love you, she mouths as I trace the shape of her smile with a finger.

Love you too, I mouth back, angling my hips to catch her clit on the next thrust forward. *Love you forever.*

Her eyes glow up at me with renewed heat as I continue working against her most precious spots, as I dip my head to suck at the furled nipples grazing against my chest.

Behind me, I hear the click and flip of the lube bottle, and then two cold and slippery fingers probe impatiently between my legs. I still my hips, my breath shuddering in and out as the fingers find my hole and tease at the rim, circling once before pushing inside, both at once. I hiss at the pressure, at the sharp flare of pain, and that earns me another slap on the flank from the man behind me.

And then the fingers are gone, replaced by the hot crown of his cock. And it's so blunt and so round pressing in against me, and I've forgotten how fucking big he is, because there's a difference between *big* in your mouth and *big* in your ass, and it's been a long time since I've had him inside me, and oh God, what am I doing? What game do I think I'm playing? It's not one I can win, even if it's just for tonight, and if he fucks me right now, I'm going to walk out of here tomorrow morning without my heart, I'm going to walk out of here having given him everything when I had vowed not to give him anything.

I panic. "Wait," I blurt out. "Wait!"

Ash waits.

"I—" I'm breathing so hard that I can feel my sides heaving, and I can't gather my thoughts and my words and everything is just a messy storm of terror and lust. "This doesn't change anything, okay? This isn't a symbol or a surrender or a—"

"I know," Ash says.

"I mean, it is kind of a surrender because that's what I want it to be, but that's what I'm choosing, okay? And I'm only choosing for tonight, and it's not like a real surrender anyway, it's just sex, and just because I want it doesn't mean I want anything else—"

"Embry," says Ash. "I know."

"And this doesn't mean I'm yours again, it doesn't mean that I'm choosing anything different outside of this bedroom, it doesn't mean anything at all, it doesn't change how—"

"Embry, shut up," Ash says and shoves his cock up my ass.

Holy fucking God.

The invasion is so brutal that it steals my breath and blinds my vision. It's raw and piercing and animalistic, and I'm speared on Ash's cock like a fish on a gaff, my heartbeat dropping down to my cock, which is still throbbing inside Greer.

"Is he inside you right now?" she asks with indecent curiosity.

"I—fuck—yes," I wheeze. Behind me, Ash's cock is unpitying and cruel, stretching me and searching out my deepest depths, and shit shit *shit,* I'm so fucking hard I can feel it in my teeth. I'd forgotten, but how could I ever forget? That having Ash inside of me, merciless and lewd, is the most alive, the most turned on, the most *myself* I can ever be? Ash leans forward, pressing me deeper into Greer, and instructs, "When I fuck, you fuck, got it?"

I nod hazily, not surprised to feel sweat already misting along my skin, and then Ash starts, a deep thrust that makes me grunt and push into Greer. The dual sensations of being filled and filling someone else have me dizzy, have me giddy and out of my mind with endorphins and lust and I want to fuck and fuck and fuck forever.

One of Ash's hands roams over my tight stomach, the fingers strumming along the tensed furrows of my abdomen, the hard planes of my chest. And then he's cupping my throat to arch me back to him.

"You think I don't know," he growls in my ear, "that this changes nothing? You think I don't know, every time I look at you, that you aren't mine anymore?"

I pant in response because his fucking is still merciless, wedging into me with deliciously thorough strokes I can feel down to my toes. And because every thrust has me thrusting into Greer, and she is writhing like a madwoman underneath me, pulling on my hair and reaching up to squeeze my biceps and reaching behind me to touch her husband.

"God, if I could fuck you back to me," grunts Ash. "If I could fuck you hard enough to make you stay with me forever, I'd do it, you know I would do it."

Fuck if it doesn't feel like he's already trying, and I don't know if I can even attempt an answer, because all my words are gone. Just gone. Between Ash's cock and Greer's pussy, my body is threatening to dissolve into nothing, into pure bliss, into an orgasm so massive and titanic that I don't know that I'll survive it.

"You like me fucking you through him?" Ash asks his wife. "You like knowing my cock is inside him while his is inside you?"

"Yes," she moans. Her hands drop to my hips and reach around to palm my ass cheeks. And then she pulls them wide apart, just like we made her do to herself in the shower tonight, and I'm stretched open, visible and exposed and on display. Ash stills his hips for a moment and I just know he's staring down at where his wife holds me open for him, and Greer is staring at him staring at me, and all of a sudden, I'm completely and entirely peeled open. Everything is pulped and raw and bleeding out of my soul, because they are all of me, and fucking them is the ritual that makes it manifest, and it's as if Ash realizes the same thing at the same moment, because he becomes unglued. Feral. He shoves me down onto Greer and follows me, his stomach against my back and his hips driving his dick in and in and in, deeper, deeper, deeper, and I can feel his entire body working for the sole purpose of fucking the life right out of me. His feet sliding for traction on the bed, his knees pushing my thighs and Greer's thighs wider apart. His hands fisting at covers and hair and flesh. He is in rut now, an animal bent only on mating, mindless with the sheer need to come inside someone, and he's grunting and I'm barely breathing and Greer is giving delighted, grinning squeaks as my cock pummels into her from the force of Ash's strokes.

This. This is what he was saving his orgasm for. This moment when the three of us are thoughtless, reflexive beasts, joined so elementally that there's no separating us. We are one, we are one, and my body burns and sings with the truth. With Ash's kingship over me, with the secret fire he is forging at the base of my spine, and with the holy devotion we both have for the electric and otherworldly woman underneath us, who's now murmuring words both goading and coaxing.

Fuck him, Ash, fuck the cum right out of him

I want to see your face when you come inside him, I want you to fill him up

Oh I can feel it when you fuck him, it feels so fucking good

Despite her earlier request not to orgasm, Greer is the first to snap, her mouth parting in an O of surprise and her body going so tight around my cock that she squeezes my climax from *almost there* to *there there there*, and then Ash gives a final toe-curling thrust against my prostate and I hear him mutter to himself, *that's it, fuck yes, that's it*, and I'm falling, detonating with a two-ton bomb at the bottom and erupting with what feels like all the cum my body has ever held, spurting into Greer so hard and thick that I can feel it against my shaft and leaking out around my balls. Behind me Ash says, "Shit, Embry, I'm going to—" and then his hips shudder and jerk as his cock throbs palpably and fills me with heat. He lets out a strangled groan.

"Little prince" is all he says as he empties himself into me and I empty myself into Greer and Greer still quavers out her pleasure underneath it all, and the moment whirls on for an eternity, seething pressure and wet friction and pounding hearts. And the rhythmic contractions of our joining for an impossible moment sync and align, and I would swear to every god I can name that we are actually coming together, that we are actually sharing the same orgasm, and that we are shivering through each and every wave together, joined as we should be, bound as we should be, together, together, as one flesh.

Man and man and wife.

It's four in the morning, and a soft October chill fogs the corners of the windowpanes. Outside, the sky is an inky gloom backlit by the tired blare of the city lights, and the wind is tugging at every crack in the building, blowing brittle leaves noisily by.

Inside, however, is warm and the kind of cozy dark that makes a man want to sleep forever, but I'm not asleep because I don't want to miss a single second of this. I want all of it etched onto the metal of my mind, indelible and permanent.

After our intense scene, Ash spent a long, intimate hour with aftercare. He cleaned us with warm rags, he gave us cold water, he rubbed our legs and backs and kissed along every inch of Greer and me as we lay tangled and spent underneath him. And after he finished tending to every bruise and sticky spot, after he finished murmuring words of pride and affection to us—that we made him so proud, that we made him so happy, that we were so precious to him—he also stretched out on the bed next to me. And without preamble, Greer poured herself into the narrow space between us, threw a leg over my hip, hugged Ash's hand to her heart, and fell immediately asleep, her rosebud mouth slightly parted and her hair—freshly brushed by Ash—gleaming on the pillow.

But I stayed awake to watch her, and Ash did too, and now we're staring at each other over Greer's head. He moves his hand from her chest and runs it over the muscles of my bicep and shoulder. And then he takes my hand. Not to bite or bind, not to use on his cock. He takes it to hold it, and that simple touch undoes me, breaks open whatever little armor I have left.

"Tonight," I say.

"Tonight," he agrees.

I think of being between the two of them, of being so in love and blown open that I forgot who I was. I think of holding Greer and kneeling before Ash, and I think of the long days ahead with none of that. With a cold bed and a lonely heart, shut off from the only two people I ever want to love, and tonight was a painful blessing, with every high underscored by the bitterest low.

"It was cruel to give it to me."

"Maybe."

"And kind."

His thumb rubs at the back of my hand. "Yes."

"Because you love me."

His eyes look like captured shadows in the dark. "Because I love you."

His fingers move to the band of metal around my ring finger, rotating the ring and caressing the skin around it.

I don't know how it makes me feel to have his fingers on that ring. Not when that ring should have been his. It always should have been his, and I can't even imagine how he feels right now, touching something that should belong to him.

I swallow. "Why did you invite me over, Ash?"

"You said it yourself," Ash replies, still playing with the flat gold band. "To be cruel and to be kind. Because I love you."

"But why tonight?"

Ash sighs, releasing the ring and threading his fingers through mine. "You can guess."

"You were jealous. My wedding night should have been yours."

"Yes."

"And?"

He props his head up on his other hand, staring at me.

"And what, Embry? What more do you want me to admit? Of course, I was fucking jealous. Of course any wedding night of yours should have been mine too."

He stops, his jaw setting and his throat working and his eyes glassing with unshed emotion, and then he regains control. Blinks. Breathes. "But my jealousy isn't important, and I can't change the past, so instead I wanted to give you something. No bridegroom should be alone on his wedding night. Especially not my little prince."

My throat tightens and I can't speak and all I can do is raise Ash's hand to my mouth and kiss it. Let him feel the tears slipping down my face. Because no matter how jealous he was, no matter how possessive and bitter and sadistic, I know that ultimately he always intended tonight as a gift. He knew tonight would be one of the loneliest nights of my life, when for most people it's one of the happiest, and he wanted to make it better for me. He wanted to help me shoulder the burden for as long as he could, and I know without a doubt that he would take it all from me if I asked. If I told him I couldn't bear it alone, I couldn't live with all these hooks tethered in my soul, he would lay down his heart and his life to make me happy.

In fact, I am certain he would do it even as I ran a campaign against him. He would let me into his arms at night even as I fought him during the day; he would love me and keep me even if I refused to stop running against him. All I have to do is ask, and it's done. Forgiveness would be mine, and I'd have a place at his feet and in his bed once again.

But…I can't. The thought is as bitter as it is true; I can't deny it even as it slices a fresh gash across my already scarred heart. I can't do it because it wouldn't be fair to Ash. For me to demand his care and love with one hand while I fight him with the other, for me to solicit his protection and adoration while I smear and malign him when we're apart. To make him love me as I try to steal everything from him.

Even I'm not that selfish.

He rubs his hand across my tear-wet cheek, along the early morning stubble roughing the edge of my jaw, and then brings his hand back to his face. I wonder what he's doing and then I see the part of his lips and the slide of his tongue. He's tasting my tears. Something I've seen him do a hundred times, and yet every time is as sexy and sweet and terrible as the last.

I can't help it, I let out a groan as I watch the dart of his tongue and the press of his mouth. "You make me crazy," I whisper, and I mean it in every good way and every bad way and every way in between.

He pauses, his hand still at his mouth and his eyes glittering in the dark. And then I see his throat working again, a clench and swallow against some powerful emotion. Somehow I know, I just do, what he's going to say.

"Embry," he starts.

"Don't," I say. "Don't ask. Please."

"Why?" he asks in agony. "Why can't I even have the asking?"

I could lie. I know I could, just as I know that he would recognize it for what it was immediately—and just as I know he would let me lie to grant me whatever shreds of dignity I wanted to grasp at.

But I won't lie. Morning is almost here, and the truth is edging at the horizon with the sun, ready to shine a pale, weary light on us anyway.

"Because," I say, fighting back more tears. "If you ask, then I won't be able to say no."

He rubs at his face with his hand, spending a long time with his fingertips against his eyes. "All you've ever done is say no when I ask you things. I don't see why now is any different."

His bitterness stings. "I suppose I deserve that," I say.

"I'm sorry," he says, his voice tired. He drops his hand from his face and looks at me. "I want you, and I want to have you and to keep you, and for fifteen years, I've been trying. And I can't tell what's the best way to love you, whether it's trying to catch you or to let you go."

"I'll always want to be yours," I say. It should be embarrassing, it should feel weak to admit it, but it doesn't. Not here in the dark with our tears and our sweet Greer warm between us. "Always. But…" I trail off.

"But you can't allow yourself that," he finishes for me.

"It's how things have to be, Ash. You know why."

"I suppose."

And we go quiet. The air is unsettled, painful, and just when I start thinking it's time for me to leave, Ash gets off the bed and comes around to my side, crawling under the covers behind me and wrapping his big body around my own. His knees tuck behind mine and his arm snugs in across my waist, and his groin presses against my ass. He nuzzles his face against the back of my neck.

"You have to kiss me goodbye when you leave," he murmurs.

"Yes, Achilles."

And despite the oncoming dawn, I fall asleep in his arms, knowing that when I wake up and kiss him goodbye, it will be for real and probably for always.

And it will kill me.

The Crown

Chapter 15
Ash

NOW, TWO YEARS LATER

"Mr. President," Belvedere says, coming up behind me.

I turn from the journalist interviewing me to nod at him. "Ten more minutes?"

He gives us a wincing look and glances down at his watch. "You've only got five, sir. I'm so sorry," he apologizes to the journalist. "We'll of course be happy to set up a call to pad out anything else you need for the piece."

The journalist—a short and jowly bulldog from *Time* magazine—sighs at Belvedere's words but doesn't push back. When the bulldog glances down at his notes, I wink at Belvedere, who gives me a little smile back. He's my keeper—he keeps me, and most importantly, he keeps my time. He plays the bad guy whenever it's time to bustle me away from eager crowds and curious reporters, and he's got the "apologetic but firm" performance down pat.

I finish my five minutes with the reporter—it's for one of those campaign profiles they will inevitably cover with a close-up shot of my face, shadowed and serious—and then Belvedere whisks me back to my office on Air Force One, expertly fending off some milling members of the press corps who are not pleased their usual time with me has been cut short because of the *Time* feature, and shepherding me past my personal photographer, who has been begging for more candid shots on the plane.

We end up in my office, alone, and Belvedere hands me a folder while he steps outside to order me a cold can of sparkling water and my usual lunch of grilled chicken and kale. It's too easy to eat like shit on the campaign trail—the travel and the dashing from one place to the next—and most of my staffers have succumbed to the seductive ease of room service and greasy delivery. I refuse, as much as I refuse to curtail my morning workouts or my evenings alone with Greer, and in any case, Belvedere takes a strange delight in finding me healthy food no matter where we're at, a trait I exploit relentlessly.

I'm flipping through the folder as he walks back in with my lunch and his own—a cup of oatmeal and a smoothie. I start eating as he talks.

"It's the latest notes from Uri and Trieste for the debate Thursday. They've also asked if you want to prep one more time against someone pretending to be Mr. Moore, or if you also want to prep against someone doing Harrison Fasse."

Fasse is the Democratic candidate facing Embry and me, and a clever young man, if sometimes hot-blooded and stubborn. But while he's a good candidate overall, Embry and I are polling too close to each other for Fasse to be my main focus.

Embry has to be my main focus.

My fork pauses ever so slightly above my plate, and then I resume eating. You'd think after all this time that I'd be able to think of Embry without that reflexive flinch, without that cold puncture of pain in my chest, but no. Not even after all the practice I've had over the last seventeen years of having my heart broken by him. It never stops hurting.

"We don't need to practice against Fasse," I tell Belvedere. "We'll have Uri do Embry again."

Belvedere makes a note. "Tomorrow evening, then. We could also do a practice run the day after, on the day of the debate itself?"

I finish eating and go back to the folder, skimming over the notes. This debate is focused mainly on energy and the economy—two places where my administration has excelled—and also two places where Embry and I hold only mildly different beliefs. Most of Merlin and Trieste's debate strategy is focused on clarifying those differences and illustrating how I've already implemented my ideas. As debates go, it shouldn't be truly difficult.

The most difficult thing will be Embry himself…and the two years hanging between us.

Two years. Two years since he left my bed on a chilly October morning and never looked back, and he hasn't so much as texted me since then, not even after the campaign began in earnest. Not a word, spoken or written, not an accidental meeting of eyes in a crowded room, because of course he's taken great pains not to share any kind of room with me.

"That won't be necessary," I say. "I'm solid on the issues and on Embry's position. The only difficult thing about the debate will be *seeing* him, and nothing can prepare me for that except for him."

Belvedere nods, but I don't miss the slight catch of his lower lip on his teeth. The mention of Embry's name has an effect on him too.

Three times in the last two years, I've sent Belvedere to him, just like I did on the night of his wedding to Abilene, and three times Belvedere has returned alone. I sent Belvedere to him a fourth time, with different instructions, and was rewarded with my aide coming back rumpled and flushed, and newly freckled with bites and sucks.

He was my body man in a literal sense that night, a gift to Embry, since my little prince wouldn't come to me. I knew from my occasional conversations with Morgan that Embry has been strictly chaste since our last night together—refusing even to relieve his needs with a mistress or a lover, and as much as I wished he would come to me, I couldn't bear the thought of him being lonely. Of his body starving for the simple touch of a bed partner. And Belvedere was willing, eager, squirming, and hard when I asked him to do this thing for me, and so I sent him, and when he returned several hours later, well-used and glowing, I made him tell Greer and me every sordid detail.

It was wrong of me, I suppose, for a host of reasons. Firstly, even though I'd introduced Belvedere to Lyonesse a year before and he was training formally as a submissive, he wasn't *my* submissive, and there was the small complication that I think he wanted to be. That, in addition to the yearning looks I'd seen him give Embry, meant there were enough emotional snags between us to make it a cruel thing to ask. And a cruel thing to give Embry because I knew he wouldn't be able to refuse. It's one thing to hold a lover at a distance; it's another thing when that lover comes to you already dripping with temptation. Even if that lover is using the mouth and hands and body of someone else.

It's a testament to Belvedere's faithfulness that our strange night never changed anything. I still treated him as fondly and respectfully as I ever had, and he never betrayed a hint of longing or frustration that none of the events had repeated themselves. I've asked him more than once about it, checking in with him to see if he's grown to resent that night—or me. It's a form of aftercare, of course, and also I do genuinely care. I wouldn't have asked him if I wasn't certain the task would have excited him, and he gave me clear and eager consent that night—but still. It's not an everyday thing, fucking your boss's old lover…and even less everyday to deliver the kind of gifts Embry and I exchange. But my instincts about Belvedere were right, and we've only ever been richer for the experience.

"So you'll touch down in Portland in an hour, and then we'll do our meeting with the fishing and game lobby right after, which means we'll have to move fast to get you to the rally after that—" Belvedere, who was in the middle of sliding a fresh piece of paper across the desk, pauses as his phone buzzes on the table…at the same time as mine also buzzes.

There's a knock on the door, and Greer steps into the office, closing it behind her. Even after two years of marriage, my blood still heats at the sight of her, my chest still goes tight with intense love and possession. Right now, she's that adorably bookish and clever version of Greer that I love more than almost any other: her hair's up in a messy bun, stabbed through with a pencil, and she's barefoot with a highlighter still in hand. She'd taken the semester off from Georgetown to campaign with me more easily, but she's in the final rounds of edits on her book, and she's spent every free moment working on the manuscript.

But it's not western concepts of kingship or power in the Dark Ages that's driven her inside my office now.

"Angel?" I ask as she leans against the door.

"Ash," she says quietly. "Have you seen it yet?"

I glance down to see the call I just missed from Merlin and several unread text messages. I scroll down quickly as I hear Belvedere swear under his breath.

I catch a few words:

Lyr.
Public statement.
Press.
This is bad, Maxen, really bad.
"She did it," says Greer. "Abilene went public about Lyr."

In some ways, I should be grateful that it took Abilene so long to unleash the truth. It didn't haunt my last two years in office, and with that freedom, I managed to get almost everything on my ambitious list done. Merlin told me it wasn't possible, practically dared me, in fact, but here I am two years later, triumphant. Even if I lose this election, there will be no undoing that much work. This country is safer, smarter, and richer—and that would not be true if the scandal about Lyr had been hanging over my head.

In other ways, I'm not grateful at all. For this to happen two days before the first debate is not ideal timing, which is surely what Abilene intended. Wholesale destruction and distraction.

But mostly, I'm worried for Lyr. Despite the election, Morgan still hasn't given me permission to meet my son; she still hasn't told him the truth. I've begged and cajoled, reasoned and pleaded, but she's been adamant that she doesn't want him to know. And I recognize that it's not only about me—if I confess my paternity to him, she'll be forced to explain her maternity, and there's no doubt that it will sting very much for him to learn that his mother gave him up as an infant, even if she remained nominally in his life as a cousin.

What that means now, however, is that Lyr is learning it all from the news instead of from us, publicly instead of privately, which was just as I feared.

Fuck.

I do the fishing talk; I do the rally. The reporters are relentless, and I can see the questions on the faces of the people I meet with. Is it true? Is it real? Can I really be Penley Luther's son *and* the brother of Morgan Leffey *and* the father of some incestuous love child?

Merlin tells me on the phone to say nothing, as does Trieste, so I say nothing about Lyr or Morgan. I stick to the topics at hand. Belvedere hustles me through my events, and then I'm sitting next to Greer on Air Force One, clenching a warm glass of scotch in my hand as the plane streaks through the dark to Seattle.

Seattle because I'm not waiting anymore. Because I deserve to look my son in the eye and explain everything.

Not for the first time, I think of Embry and his son. Even with as little as I watch the news, there's been no escaping the photographs of the little boy, the video clips of them playing together in the leaves or running after the family dog. And there's every order of jealous hurt inside me as I think of Embry as a father—mostly because I'd dreamed for so many years of us being fathers together, and now here we are, each with sons we love but didn't plan for. How much I want all those moments I missed with Lyr and how much I want all the moments I missed watching Embry become a parent. I missed his eyes as he held his child for the first time, I missed the awe and the wild happiness and the exhaustion and the worry.

There's now a part of Embry entirely separate from me, a part of him that was born alongside his son, and perhaps it stings so much because that part of me never had a chance to be born at all. I not only missed Embry becoming a father, but I missed it myself as well.

"Sir." Belvedere comes up, looking apologetic. "It's Berlin. Should I say it's a bad time?"

Berlin. Shit.

All I want to do is drink and run my fingers through my wife's hair. All I want is to have just an hour to think about what's waiting for me in Seattle, to think about what I'm going to say to my son when I have the chance.

But I never say no to a call from Berlin. The calls are rare enough as they are, and the week after next will be the keystone in the plan we've built over the last two and a half years. And I've built it too fucking carefully and slowly to let something like a personal crisis tear through it now.

I hold out my hand for the phone.

"Hello?" I greet.

"*Guten Abend*," goes the voice on the other end. And then we get to work.

"I wish you would have given me more time," Morgan says tersely, tightening the belt on her trench coat as she, Greer, and I walk up the stairs of Vivienne Moore's intimidating lake house. It's near midnight, and the house gleams pale and otherworldly in the gloom, the lake behind it shimmering with secrets. "It's a school night, and he needs his sleep."

"Do you really think he's sleeping?" I ask her, my voice just as short as hers. "Tonight? After what people have been saying about him online and on the news all day?"

"You don't know a fucking thing about him," she hisses in response, "and you have no right to tell me what you think he's doing or why you think he's doing it."

Next to me, Greer stiffens in anger, but before she can defend me, the door is opening and Vivienne Moore, governor of the state of Washington and the mother of two of my ex-lovers, is standing in the doorway. "He's in the library," she says, giving me a regal nod. "Nimue is in there with him. They're waiting for you."

I let out a shaky breath, and Morgan does the same, and

even though this election stretches between us, along with years of fighting and bitterness, when we look at each other, all I can see is the green-eyed girl who once asked me to hold her wrist instead of her hand. The dark-haired woman who dragged me to Lyonesse after Jenny's death and forced me to find myself again.

Her earlier rancor has slipped into nervousness, and she offers me an unsteady smile. "Well?"

"Yeah," I say with an answering unsteady smile, and then we all go inside.

Vivienne leads us through the impressive house to the library, and there Greer stops and gives me a reassuring kiss. "I'll be just out here," she says softly, her hand gentle and warm against my jaw. "If you need me."

I search her face.

"Are you sure you don't want to come in with us?" I ask, secretly hoping she'll say yes, even though I know it would probably be less overwhelming for Lyr to have fewer people in the room. But I selfishly want my angel in there, I selfishly want her in there for *me*, to comfort and hold *me*. But we had talked about it on the plane here from Portland, after I'd made the decision that I was seeing Lyr tonight at all costs. It had been Greer's idea to give Morgan and me privacy with our son, and it was a good one.

Just. I want her with me is all.

"Are you sure that *you're* okay?" I ask so that only she can hear. "This happened too fast for—"

"I'm fine," she says firmly. "I love you and I'm fine, and after tonight we will have plenty of time to talk. Or work through it in other ways." The mischievous emphasis she puts on *other ways* almost distracts me from how her hand drops to press against her belly, which is flat, taut, and empty, and has been for two years, despite much effort on our part.

I put my hand over hers, press both into her belly.

"Whose pain is it?" I ask quietly.

She lets out a long breath, her body relaxing ever so slightly. "Yours, Mr. President."

"Good girl," I say. "I'll be back, and then you will give me your pain as you're supposed to."

Her eyes flare with heat, and I hope for the moment her ache will be less. I hope it won't scratch at her to think of me in a room with my son…my son who is not her son.

Morgan opens the door to the library, and together we walk inside, and even with my nerves, I notice the subdued wealth of the room. Two-storied and lined with books and fireplaces and massive, hulking chairs, and I can so easily see my Embry here as a boy, as a spoiled teenager. Reading with his legs slung carelessly over the arms of the chairs, sneaking in boys and girls to fool around with by the fire. Staring out the yawning windows and out onto the lake, cocooned in whatever rippling, dark thoughts make up Embry's mind.

But then of course, Embry wasn't the only little boy to have grown up wandering these halls. There was Lyr, all the while thinking Nimue was his mother and Vivienne his aunt and Morgan his cousin. And his father a ghost somewhere, a deadbeat, a spineless waste of air.

It's hard to feel like he would have been wrong about that, as I walk to meet him for the first time in sixteen years, as I walk to meet him after my silence has destroyed his life.

It isn't difficult to find him in the room, even as full of dancing fire shadows and nooks as it is. It's as if my heart is magnetized to him now, on alert, and once I catch sight of him sitting in a window seat, his head bent over a book and his profile etched by the contrast between his pale skin and the charcoal night outside, I wonder how I never saw it. All the times I saw pictures of him in passing, that massive Moore family portrait that Embry had in his vice president's office, random social media posts from Embry at the lake house, lounging with his family. Lyr had just been one of Embry's clan, just another wealthy scion that would eventually attend an expensive college, wear expensive clothes, and go on to rule the world.

But how could I not have seen it then? The black hair? The high cheeks? The nose with its slightly Roman bridge, the full mouth, the dark slashes of eyebrows over bright green eyes? He's made so much like me he's uncanny to look at, uncomfortable even, a reflection with the shadows and angles just different enough to make you think you've imagined any difference at all. Morgan is in him too: in his features, which are slightly more refined and elegant than mine—clear and angel-like—and in his hands, which are slender and delicate as he closes his book and looks up at us.

His eyes meet my own, slide over to Morgan's. He doesn't speak, although I can almost hear all the words pressing against the inside of his lips, all the questions he's swallowing back down into his throat. But his expression isn't hostile, and when he speaks, his voice is as calm as it is guarded. "Hello."

"Hello," I say back. Morgan just nods her greeting.

Nimue stands up from a sofa nearby, willow thin and as tall as me. She's only a few years older than I am, but she looks much younger, her eyes bright and her skin clear and her hair dark and tumbling over her shoulders. A crystal glints at her neck, and when she walks, she moves like a dancer—limber, lean, musical even in silence. I understand now why Merlin loves her.

"I'm going to give you privacy," she says. She gives Lyr a small smile, one he doesn't return, and I realize that this has been hard on Nimue too. Lyr must feel like everyone has been lying to him, everyone he's ever cared about, and he's not wrong.

He has been lied to.

Morgan and I take the chairs clustered around the window seat, and for a moment I think Lyr is going to stay up there, and I wouldn't blame him. The window seat probably feels like the safest space in the room, and he's sixteen—I can't fault a teenage desire for seclusion. For a position that would feel strong and familiar.

But he climbs gracefully out of the window seat and finds a chair next to me, with a stoic and reserved bravery that I respect very much. It makes me proud to see how handsome he is, how strong and healthy, how sober and composed he appears. It makes me proud to see him face this so bravely, even as I wish he didn't have to.

Morgan speaks first, her voice faltering. "I suppose you might have some questions for us."

Lyr nods, his face still careful. "I do."

I look at Morgan at the same moment she looks at me, as if we're deciding who should speak first, and the moment is almost laughable in its parody of a real family. Two parents sitting down with their teenage son, having a family meeting. It would be funny if it weren't so fucking sordid and terrible.

I go first. "I didn't know my biological parents," I say, still trying to find the right place to start. "I know now that Penley Luther had an affair with Imogen Leffey, and that she died giving birth to me. I know now that Penley Luther was too embarrassed or selfish to try to find me. But growing up, I only knew that I hadn't been wanted, that I'd been cast off. It made me too bitter to ever try learning anything about my past."

"And I knew that there had been a baby boy, a half brother," Morgan adds. "But I never knew his name, and I thought if I ever found him, it would be through years and years of searching. I didn't think—I couldn't have expected that I'd meet him like I met Maxen."

Lyr listens, his face betraying nothing. "And then after I was conceived?" he asks.

"I failed your mother," I say, to spare Morgan having to tell the story herself. "At a place called Glein. There was a battle, and she almost died. You almost died with her that day."

"I didn't tell your father about you," Morgan says, lifting her head to face Lyr. "And you can hate me for that if you'd like. I was angry because I felt like...oh, I don't even know anymore. Like it would be fair if I kept him from you because he almost let the two of us burn alive. I thought I hated him for that." She glances at me. "I lied to myself about it for a very long time. But I guess I'm old enough to understand now there are things outside any one person's control, and a battle is almost certainly one of those things."

I don't know why, but I reach out to squeeze her hand. My sister and ex-lover and current political enemy...and mother of our son. Jesus Christ. I'm surprised lightning hasn't struck us all down.

She allows me to squeeze her hand and gives us both a thin smile. "I was young, and you know Vivienne—she was adamant that I wasn't ready to be a mother, and even now, I think she might have been right. But it was purely my fault and mine alone that Maxen didn't know. I accept responsibility for that."

Lyr watches our hands meet and then part. "But you have known since before now?" he asks me. "Since before I knew?"

I want to hang my head, but I don't. I deserve this and I'll look him in the eye and endure whatever pain or anger spills out of him as I tell the truth. It's the fucking least I can do. "I learned the truth two years ago. Abilene—your cousin Embry's wife—was the one to discover the real story through her grandfather's personal effects. She used you to blackmail Embry into dating her, and Embry did it, to keep you and Morgan safe. But he did eventually tell me."

"Maxen wanted to tell you. Wanted to meet with you." Morgan takes a deep breath, and I wish I could tell her right now how much I appreciate her honesty. "He wanted it right away. The moment he learned, he called me and asked to meet you. And I said no."

Lyr flinches. It's the first real sign of emotion he's shown all evening. "Why?" he whispers.

"Because—" Morgan presses her lips together and looks up at the ceiling, and I see that she's close to tears. "Because all I ever wanted was for you to grow up free from knowing the truth about your birth. Because I love you and I didn't want to hurt you. And I know all of that wishing and wanting seems so abstract as to be meaningless right now, and I know at your age all you can see is the unequivocal truth and the too many ways that you've been failed. That's natural, to see the failures of the adults around you and call their reasons weak. Perhaps they are weak, but—and I know you might also scoff at this—when you have a child in your life, it's like everything flips upside down and turns inside out, and reasons that seemed weak or dishonest before are suddenly so powerful. I'm not saying they were right," she finishes, tears openly brimming at her eyes now, "but they were powerful. I love you, and I wanted to protect you from the sins your father and I had committed."

Lyr doesn't answer, but he looks down at his feet, processing what Morgan has said.

And again, that spike of pride. I like that he thinks before he speaks, that he'd rather listen than talk. It's exactly how I'd want my son to be if I'd raised him myself.

"We failed you, Lyr," I say. "And maybe we still are. We didn't tell you the truth and we didn't protect you from Abilene and we are both ashamed. I hope you can forgive us, but you have every right not to."

"Both of you did lie...for a long time. And so did Aunt

Vivienne and my mother—I mean, Nimue." A slight hitch in the word *mother*, as he remembers how that word is now complicated for him. "And Embry. And I wish you hadn't. I wish you hadn't lied. I wish—" And my heart breaks watching his face fracture into feelings he can't control. "I wish I'd never been born."

The fire crackles behind us, and outside the moon glimmers on the lake for a watery moment before it disappears back behind the clouds. And Lyr's words are worse than any screed, any insult, anything else that could have been flung my way. I had been prepared for his anger, but I had never thought to prepare myself for this—that he would transmute his anger into something so painful for a parent to hear.

"I've thanked God for you every day since I learned the truth," I tell him softly. "Yes, it's unusual—all of it is unusual—but that doesn't make it bad. It doesn't make you bad."

He rubs his thumb across his forehead in a gesture so like my own that my heart twists. "But now everyone thinks I'm bad. That I have…I don't know, that I have webbed toes or something." He moves his hand away from his face to gesture vaguely, and the movement is so aristocratic, so disdainful, and he goes from looking like me to being all Morgan. "Inbred. That's what they were saying online. That I'm inbred."

I can feel Morgan glance at me, and I know exactly what she's thinking because I'm thinking the same thing. That I don't know how to fix this for him, that I brought him into this world and now I've exposed him to every kind of judgment and insult simply by creating him. It's a gross feeling to have failed my child so utterly, and I mean *gross* in both ways—viscerally disgusting and also large, huge, occupying the center of my chest and my major muscle groups. My shame has never been thicker, never been so viscous inside my mouth and heavy in my lungs.

"Egyptian pharaohs married their sisters for centuries," Morgan says. "And they didn't have webbed toes. Same with the Incas and Hawaiian royalty. Taboos are social constructs that vary from culture to culture and are created to reinforce selective behaviors—you should know that from watching Nimue do her sociology work. Just because your parentage is considered taboo doesn't mean you are defective as a human or worth less than anyone else. You are worth everything to me."

The naked emotion in her voice is plain to hear, and Lyr looks down at the carpet again, as if trying not to cry.

"And I've seen your toes," she says, clearing her throat and trying to sound composed once more. "They're fine. You're fine. You're a straight-A student, completely healthy, completely normal. You get to choose what this means about you and how this defines you, and I don't care if you hate me forever, as long as you promise never ever to hate yourself."

He peers up at both of us through his long eyelashes, eyes green and wet. "I don't know what I can promise right now," he says after a minute, his voice both vulnerable and guarded all at once. "But I suppose I can promise to try."

"Thank you," Morgan replies thickly, carefully wiping the tears away from her eyes so she doesn't smudge her mascara. "That would be enough."

"Will I—I mean…" He chews on the inside of his lip a moment. "Are you going to try to be my parents now? Am I going to see you again, President Colchester?"

I grimace a little at the title. "Call me whatever you like, Lyr, but please don't call me that."

"So I should call you dad?" I hear the defensive note in his voice, the bitterness threatening to break through its trammels.

"I would never ask that of you, as much as it would make me happy. But you can call me Maxen, if you'd like, or Ash. Ash is what the people closest to me use."

"Ash," he says slowly. "I think I can do that."

"And I'll be around as much as you want me. I'll talk about you as much as you'll let me. You can move into the White House tomorrow with me as far as I'm concerned. I'm not ashamed of you, Lyr."

My words stir up something potent and artlessly emotional in him; he finally does start crying.

"I'm here as much or as little as you want me," I finish. "I'm yours as much or as little as you want me. We've taken so many choices from you, but this is one you get back."

He swallows, still crying, and stands up, and I know exactly what he wants. I stand up too, and for the first time in his life, I pull my son into my arms and hug him. For every milestone and year I missed, for every other person's arms he's felt holding and carrying him, for every empty, bitter moment he felt today when he learned the truth and had to endure it alone.

I hug him. I close my eyes, press my face into his already strong and heavy shoulder, and I thank God for this unexpected grace. This undeserved mercy.

Thank you.

Thank you.

Thank you.

CHAPTER 16
ASH

THEN

BELVEDERE TELLS ME THAT THINGS HAVE CHANGED SINCE I was his age, but well into being a young man, I'd encountered this insidious idea that bisexuality was a phase, a transient place. A stage of ghost queerness. And after a few years, you would realize that you were truly gay or truly straight, and then you would end your experiments and move on to a real life and a real identity, whatever that meant. The idea that you could truly remain bisexual into mature adulthood seemed only academically possible—even David Bowie settled down and married Iman, after all, and if David fucking Bowie could tame his sexuality, then clearly anyone could—or at least so the subliminal messaging seemed to say.

If you were gay, then be gay; if you were straight, then be straight. Anything in between was denial and make-believe.

Of course, that's all nonsense. But there was enough of that old thinking to leak into my brain, and so I found myself in an uncharacteristic stage of unrest after Embry left

Carpathia. Embry was the first person I had ever loved, and surely that meant something crucial about me? Maybe bisexuality *had* just been a stepping stone and I was a gay man after all, one who'd muddled to the realization after years of sampling and research. Perhaps all that clarity I'd felt as a bisexual teenager had simply been the naive certainty of youth, because I knew, as I watched Embry leave the barracks in the gray light of dawn, that I would love him until the day I died. And because he was the first, I assumed that he would be the only, and I rearranged my soul to accommodate this new belief. I wasn't bisexual. I could only ever love Embry Moore.

And it felt true for a long time.

Until London.

Until Greer.

I dragged around a broken heart for three years. I carried it like a wounded soldier, limping and bloody, to a destination that looked close but felt far. I nursed it, fed it even, though I had no real reason. Embry and I had shared…well, what exactly? A dance once? A kiss in the woods? How was that enough to make me feel this way? And how was he the one I could fall in love with when so many others had tried, and arguably he'd given me little more than disdain, mixed signals, and a waltz?

Nevertheless, it was enough and he was the one, and for three years, I tended my love for him like a garden. I searched for him online whenever I could, asked mutual friends about him constantly. I even went back to my pre-Morgan practice of pseudo-abstinence. I fucked no one, because no one was Embry except Embry and he didn't want me. And the aftermath of the shameful mess I'd made of Morgan's emotions was a powerful reminder—fucking belonged with feelings.

Maybe it didn't have to be love but at the very least affection and respect.

But after three years with no word from Embry—with rumors of his sexual exploits reaching me even overseas—something had grown brittle inside my control and then that something finally snapped. It wasn't that I stopped loving him—never that—it was just that I was twenty-six and I hadn't even kissed anyone since him. I'd been fucking my own fist for so long, turning away interested men and women out of a principle that grew more and more abstract every day, and I was lonely.

Or maybe lonely isn't the right word. It was more like I was anemic or starved for something or stuck in the darkness so long that my body cried out for the sun at a cellular level. I had known what it was to unleash myself with Morgan. I had kissed the man I loved with the knowledge that he would let me do whatever I wanted. I had felt intimate, aching power, and there was no *un*feeling it after the fact, no way to forget.

And the longer I went without it, the more listless and unhappy I became. That and the insomnia—this blood- and mud-filled fog of memory that replaced my sleep—were twin millstones around my neck, dragging me to the ground.

There was a month gap between a posting in Krakow and yet another deployment to Carpathia, and it felt pointless to go home. I missed my mother and I missed Kay, but at least in Europe there were always new things to do and see, and if I went home to Kansas City, I knew I'd just succumb to the dull misery that seemed to follow me wherever I went. It was better to stay busy.

And then Merlin found me, pulling up in a sleek black car as I waited at the bus stop closest to the Krakow base. He rolled down the window. "Shouldn't they be driving you to the airport?"

I gave him a genuine smile. He had become a real

presence in my life over the last few years, writing and visiting frequently, and often with incredibly valuable advice and wisdom. I thought of him as something like a mentor, but also as a friend. "I told them I'd take the bus into the city," I said. "I wanted to see Krakow some more before I left. And it's good to see you."

He nodded. "It's good to see you too." He tilted his head at me, giving me an appraising look. "How would you like to go to London with me?"

Which is how I ended up in England.

Merlin took me to meetings and dinners and parties, introducing me variously as his assistant or as a family friend or as a military liaison—whichever excuse held the most weight at the time—and for the first time in my life, I saw how war worked on the top end of things. I saw how people in expensive suits at expensive restaurants made decisions for tired, freezing soldiers thousands of miles away, I saw the almost careless tabulation of mortalities and morbidities as an impersonal inventory instead of the bleeding, screaming things they actually were. I saw the incremental and subtle currents of diplomacy, how one slight at a dinner or one misstep in a memo had powerful ramifications for the men and women actually fighting the war.

It bothered me.

Merlin could see it bothering me, and he let me unspool all of my tangled feelings about it when we were alone, encouraging me to find the reasons *underneath* the reasons I could articulate, and that was the real beginning, that month in London. The first time I was forced to confront the intersection of politics and war, and to want both of those things to be better. The first time I began to search for the strands of international and domestic power and decipher where the answer lay in the web of it all.

I didn't know it was the beginning of anything then,

obviously. All I knew was that I'd spent the last four years of my life with bullets and mud, and the last three without the man I'd fallen in love with, and even London, teeming with bustle and energy as it did, couldn't do anything to transmute my restlessness into anything productive or good. All I had was a blunted ache of loneliness and zero hope for the future of this war as I watched the arcane and stupidly blithe rotations of Merlin's sphere.

And one night, it was just too much. The war, Merlin's world, the familiar ache of wanting Embry. I sat drinking at a gin bar down the street from Merlin's flat where I was staying, and I decided that I was going to drink until I couldn't find my way out the door. I was going to drink until both Embry and the war didn't exist any longer.

At least, I was going to until a man sat down next to me at the bar. It was a rather impersonal, trendy kind of place—in one of those perpetually-building-overpriced-flats parts of London and obviously had been opened to cater to the young City types who lived around the neighborhood. And the man was dressed to fit the scenery, as all the City types were when they went out at night (as if needing to sartorially prove that they were so busy working late and making money that they didn't have time to change into "going out" clothes).

Or maybe he really was just working late and wanted to cool off with some gin before he went up to whatever glass-balconied tower he lived in. Either way, he was handsome and brimming with the sleek confidence of a man in his twenties already making lots of money, and the way his suit pulled at his arms and back when he turned to look at me was quite arresting.

He smiled. He had skin a burnished shade of golden brown, near-black eyes, and meticulously tended scruff.

"All right?" he said by way of greeting.

"Yeah."

His eyes sparkled with interest. "Are you American?"

I nodded.

"Here on holiday?"

"Sort of." I looked down at my glass of pricey pear-infused gin. "I'm in the army. Between assignments right now."

"Oh, a military man," he said, and I didn't miss the way his eyes traced over the button-down shirt and flat-fronted slacks I wore, lingered on the places where the slacks hugged my thighs. "First time to England?"

"First time I've stayed for any length of time."

"Seeing the sights?"

I gave him the same lingering look he'd just given me and was rewarded with him biting his lip. "You could say that," I finally replied. "Can I buy you a drink?"

He leaned forward, bracing some long-toed, hand-tooled shoe on the bottom of my barstool. "I've got an even better idea. How about I make us both drinks at my place?"

I glanced back down to my gin, making up my mind about something. Because what the fuck did it matter if this man bolted from me when I told the truth? I was in a different country, and it's not like I'd ever see him again, and he wasn't Embry, so it would never matter.

"I'd like that," I said carefully. "The thing is I—well. I like to be in charge. Is that something you can be comfortable with?"

He grinned again, teeth white against his dark scruff. "You're new to this, yeah?"

It didn't make me feel defensive, but I wanted to clarify. "New to what?"

"Pulling men at bars."

"I've been in the army," I pointed out. "I'm certainly new to doing it like this."

He laughed. "Yeah, all right. Well, I'm flattered to be

your first English pull, and for what it's worth, I definitely can be comfortable with you being in charge. In fact..." He reached out and clasped my upper arm. To the people around us, it might have looked like a fraternal clap on the shoulder, but I could feel the teasing way he squeezed at my muscles. "In fact, Mr. Army, there's nothing I think I want more than for you to be in charge right now."

That brittle thing inside me snapped. I dropped some coins on the bar and stood.

"Lead the way."

He led the way. His place was just around the corner, and it was indeed the glass-balconied status flat I'd assumed, and he did indeed want me in charge. He went to a sleek bar niche to make those drinks, but when I crowded in behind him, my hands teasing at the lapels of his suit jacket, he leaned back against me with a moan that I liked very much. Almost as much as I liked how pliant his body became, and the way he ground his ass into my hips.

We kissed, and then we drank, and then we properly made out, toeing off shoes and pulling at shirt buttons and hair, falling onto his bed, and then I unknotted his tie and slid it from around his neck.

"I'd like to bind your wrists," I told him. "But I'll keep it loose enough that you can free yourself, since you don't know me."

"You are the politest, Mr. Army. Do it," he said, holding out his wrists for me, and so I did it. And then I found his cock with my palm, rubbing it and rolling the heel of my hand along the underside until he was writhing underneath me.

I unbuttoned his pants. "Okay?"

"Okay," he said back. And then I freed his cock and took him in my mouth.

It was old and it was new at the same time. It was not the

first cock I'd sucked, but it was the first time I'd had the man tied up, the first time I'd been driving the scene rather than simply taking part in an urgent tug-of-war. Not to mention how long it had been since I'd had any sexual contact at all.

I worked his pants all the way off, then I began stroking him below his testicles, along the fleshy line leading to his entrance.

"Okay?" I asked.

"Okay," he moaned.

And then with a finger inside him, bound by his own tie, he came in my mouth, panting and long. And when I pulled up, he was smiling dazedly at me. "There's lube and condoms in the drawer. I, ah"—and his skin was too warmly brown for me to see a blush, but I imagined his cheeks would feel hot against my fingers if I touched them right now—"ah, I don't mind staying tied up for the next part. So you know."

I was hard. I was hard, and this was a willing man, all pretty and full-lipped, already tied up for me.

And yet.

He wasn't Embry.

It had been three years, and still I could not do this. I couldn't bring myself to do it—and yes, by that time, I was beginning to understand that my constructions around honor and penetrative sex were problematic—but the understanding wasn't enough in that moment. In that moment, all I could think of was how much I'd wanted my first time fucking a man to be with Embry, and it didn't matter how submissive or handsome or available this stranger was; he was no Embry. And I couldn't give that first to a stranger. The idea of firsts *at all* is flawed, I know, but it was too late for me. They were important and they are important to me still, and so I untied the pretty stranger's hands without moving to the drawer.

"I think I'm good, but thanks," I told him. "And thank you for letting me…you know. Take charge."

He gave me a sad smile. "All right?"

"Yeah."

And I went back to Merlin's with an aching cock and a miserable heart.

What was wrong with me? I'd found a hot, respectable guy, and—more than being handsome and normal and willing—he'd wanted *that* part of me. So why had it felt so wrong? I had done everything the way I thought an emotionally healthy gay man would do it, but then when I'd gotten to the most crucial moment, I'd still felt something missing.

Which meant it had to be more than the kinky and the queer that I was searching for. But then what?

I didn't know.

And I still didn't know the next morning when I woke up from a fractured, nightmare-filled sleep, cock rigid and annoyed that I'd wasted last night. I stroked off thinking of Embry as I always did, showered and dressed, and then found Merlin reading a paper on his own glassed-in balcony, so like the stranger's from last night. Merlin gave me a look I didn't understand, a look that seemed full of reluctant worry, a look I dismissed, because Merlin had zero reason to worry over me.

He folded his paper down. Somewhere along the nearby Thames there was the crash and boom of a construction site.

"There's a party I want you to go to tonight," he said. "Wear your uniform."

All that night, I couldn't shake the feeling that something was wrong. Or maybe wrong isn't the word I mean, but that something was *different*. Something was heavy in the air, and it wasn't the silver moon or that strange brand of wet summer coolness that crowded against the windows of the cab. I chalked it up to the night before and my aborted attempt at meeting someone new. I chalked it up to frustration over politics and heartache over a boy I kissed once.

It wasn't until much, much later that I realized it was the same feeling I'd had when I'd fucked Morgan and when I'd put my boot on Embry's wrist. The same feeling I'd had when I pulled the sword from the stone. A feeling like something deep inside of me was alchemically changing, a feeling like this moment marked some sort of fresh stroke on my canvas that could never be painted over.

No, at the time I just assumed it was smothered libido and impatience with Merlin's scene. An assumption that was reinforced inside the party itself, which was full of the requisite political types, all being as obtuse and oblivious to the real effects of their actions as ever, and even though I knew Merlin had brought me here to make introductions and schmooze, I couldn't bear it. I couldn't bear another second with these people. I was stifled by their ignorance and pointlessness and callous disregard for actual human life, and it was so easy to find an empty room that led to an empty patio and just breathe for a moment. Just stare at the fresh, silver moon and wonder what Embry was doing at this very moment.

Staring at the same moon, thinking of me?

Ha, went a bitter voice in my mind. *Right.*

Feminine laughter stirred me from my thoughts, and then a male voice that was singsongy with persuasion and—ah yes, an Italian accent—and I heard the two of them crowd into the room I'd just walked through, the unmistakable sounds of kissing and fondling echoing out onto the small patio where I was now trapped, hedged in by a stone railing and a pretty garden.

Ah, fuck.

I edged my head around the corner, just to verify that I couldn't sneak past them, and alas, yes. The library was too cluttered with furniture to make any path other than the main one, which was currently occupied by one of the diplomats I'd been attempting to escape and a girl who looked young enough to be his daughter. She was very pretty, though—sleek red hair and long limbs set off by a bright blue dress—and she certainly didn't seem to mind the diplomat's attention, so I suppose I couldn't fault him for anything other than inconvenience.

With a sigh, I turned back to the patio and resigned myself to staring at the moon some more. Maybe when these two finished, Merlin would be ready to go—or at least, be neutral to my leaving early. There was no point in me being here. There was hardly any point to anything, except the war, which seemed to be the last place in my life where I could matter to anyone or anything. Too bad the war was also the reason I couldn't sleep.

I'd finally managed to lose my thoughts in the moonlight once more when I heard the library door open and hesitant footsteps. Someone else had come into the library, walking in on the kissing couple. But I only had a minute to feel relieved that I wasn't the one in the awkward position of intruding on the couple before I heard a high-pitched yell.

"Who the fuck do you think you are?"

And then I realized I was in the significantly more awkward position of eavesdropping on what sounded like an incredibly vicious and passionate argument between two young women. The man, it seemed to my ears, had fled the scene, and God, I couldn't blame him. I stared at the well-groomed garden outside the patio railing, trying to will a Narnia-like door into existence.

It didn't work. And the fight went on and on, and I couldn't stopper my ears to it, as much as I wished I could.

"You can't fix it," the loudest voice said scathingly. "Just stay away—"

"I'm not going to do that. I *can't* do that—"

"Just leave me alone!" And then the sound of glass fracturing, a musical rain that startled me more than any gunshot. What was wrong with that girl? Who broke a glass at a fucking party?

I heard the second quieter girl whisper something, and then there was the brisk staccato of high heels and a slammed door. Someone had left the room, or both of them, and either way, I felt a compulsion to go clean up the mess they had left. It was the right thing to do, and while I might have done so many wrong things in Carpathia that I couldn't sleep without sweating through my sheets, I still tried to be a good man. One who did the right things…like cleaning up a broken glass at a party.

Except when I rounded the corner into the room, I saw that someone else had beaten me to it.

I saw two things first, and those two things nearly brought me to my knees.

The first was a spill of hair over her shoulder, a cascade of platinum white silk, which was like nothing I'd ever seen. It promised thickness and softness and light; I had half a mind that if I touched it, I'd be struck dead. It seemed like the kind of hair mortals weren't allowed to possess, which meant that she had to be some kind of demigoddess. When she moved to reach for a shard of glass, the warm light of the room moved through her hair like water—or maybe it was her hair that was like water, gold and white, rippling and fluid.

The second thing: she was kneeling.

In a pool of broken glass.

It was like a fantasy I'd never known enough about myself to have, but once I saw it, I knew nothing could ever be the same. I was being rewritten, reshaped, or something better—like I was being reshaped to find out that it had been my true shape all along. Some door inside me swung open, some key slid easily into an old lock, and the air sang with heavy fate.

This beautiful creature, on her knees. Suffering for someone she loved. Pain and strength in every line of her body, in every duck of her head and stretch of her hand as she plucked splinters of glass one by one off the parquet.

And I was drowning in it. I didn't know her face, I didn't know her name, but in an instant, it felt like I knew her. It felt like she slid into the empty places inside me.

Embry was the only other time I'd felt that, and I had to take in a breath as I realized what that meant. My cock—slowly stiffening in response to the sight of this person kneeling—was hardening for a woman. My chest was tight for a woman. My mind was abuzz with ideas about every way I could make this woman my own, my little one, for always.

There was no time to sift through the implications of this, and even if there had been, I wouldn't have needed to anyway. The speed at which I rearranged my beliefs about myself matched the speed in which I found myself fascinated by this girl. Matched the speed at which I made a decision.

I stepped into the room.

"You'll hurt yourself if you're not careful," I said.

CHAPTER 17
EMBRY

NOW

"DON'T, DAH-DEE," GALAHAD SCOLDS, TAKING THE WOODEN apple out of my hand and putting it back inside the suitcase lying open on the floor. "There," he says, satisfied. "There, Dah-dee." At less than two years old, his baby accent makes the *th* in *there* sound like a *d. Dere. Dere, Dah-dee.* It makes my heart break with how fucking cute it is.

He makes my heart break with how fucking cute he is. Every day. Every minute. Since that first time I held him in the hospital, wrapped up like one of those Glo Worm toys from my childhood, just a sleepy burrito of soft cheeks and dark hair peeking out from a hospital hat. If I thought I couldn't live without Ash and Greer, I'd been wrong, but it was only because of Galahad, the son whose name Greer ultimately chose. From the moment I first saw him, so sweet and curious, I knew he was the Grail knight my queen had described, the kind of child that would grow up to see the face of God, and I didn't care how ridiculous the name sounded.

It felt right that he should be named by Greer. Necessary. (Abilene didn't know that, of course; she assumed I'd picked the name myself, and I didn't bother to correct her.)

"But if I bring the apple, then you won't have it here to play with while I'm gone," I explain. "Are you sure you want Daddy to take it?"

Galahad nods with baby conviction and then turns to leave the bedroom. He stops after a step and points back to the suitcase. "There, Dah-dee," he says sternly. The meaning is clear: *keep that fucking apple where I put it.*

And then, because he's so cute toddling off with his little deck shoes and his little diaper butt under his corduroys, I run over and scoop him up, pretending to eat his belly while he laughs and laughs.

"I'm going to be late," Abilene says, coming out of the bathroom behind me, still fastening an earring into her lobe. "Are you sure you don't want to take a later flight and join me?"

I pause the *nom*ing noises I'm making against Galahad's tummy and lift my head. "I'd rather be roasted alive," I say cheerfully, and then resume tickling my son until he's shrieking with delight.

Abilene rolls her eyes. If I had held any distant hope that she might reveal a secret maternal gene after Galahad's birth, I'd been sorely mistaken—she's just as Abilene as ever, although she's surprisingly self-aware where our child is concerned. While she can't muster the kind of parental affection that comes so easily to me, she's never been anything but safe, organized, and determined about his life. She hired the best care when he was an infant—the most sought-after nanny in the district, a woman named Enid who I cannot pay enough money for being as warm and clever as she is—and aside from her incurable coldness, she's never endangered him, never emotionally poisoned him, never even raised her voice around him.

It's absolutely the least that should be asked of any parent, but yet I'm still grateful. Between Enid and me, I can harbor the faint hope that he might escape his childhood unscathed.

"It would be a good opportunity to schmooze the RNC donors," Abilene is saying as she finishes with the earring and moves back to her room on the other side of our shared bathroom. "A last infusion of cash can't hurt anything."

"We already have too much cash," I say, setting Galahad on his feet and watching him tear out of the door to find Enid. "And I told you, I'd like to spend the night before the debate preparing."

I hear her make a scoffing noise in her room.

I walk through the bathroom to her doorway, stopping at the threshold and crossing my arms. I don't come into her room as a rule, and she mostly stays out of mine, and her acceptance of my boundaries has been one of the reasons I've stayed sane over the last two years, even if she does try to push me on them every now and again.

"By the way," I say mildly, "I hope you go straight to hell for that press statement you released yesterday."

She looks up at me with a mock-innocent expression. "I'm sure I don't know what you mean."

"It doesn't matter that you fed the *Times* that story anonymously. Morgan and I know—and I'm certain Ash and Greer do too—that it was you. I just got off the phone with Morgan, and she's furious."

"Morgan will get over it, and so will you," Abilene dismisses. "It will hurt Ash's campaign far worse than ours."

"I'm not concerned about the *campaign*," I say incredulously. "I'm concerned about my fucking sister. My nephew. You've just single-handedly ruined their lives, and you don't even care?"

"It was time," she says, all nonchalant. "And they'll get over it."

"Fuck you."

"I've been asking you to for a long time. Are you finally changing your mind?"

I stare at her for a moment, and she stares right back, no regret or shame anywhere on her face. I don't even know why I looked for it.

"I know what you're thinking," she tells me. "Right now you're thinking about how good it would feel to announce that you're going to divorce me. To take Galahad and storm out of here."

"It would feel very good," I agree. I can almost taste the relief now, the sweet freedom, and I've daydreamed of divorcing her so often that I have an entire Rolodex filled with different fantasy scenarios. Leaving her in public or leaving her under the cover of night; having her served with divorce papers or tossing the papers myself onto her dinner plate. You name it, I've lived it inside my mind with unhealthy relish.

Abilene tilts her head at me in a way that's uncomfortably sympathetic. "But you're also thinking about all the reasons why you can't do that. You can't win this campaign in the middle of a divorce, and you know that I wouldn't make it quiet or easy for you. I'd make it so messy and public that you'd not only lose the election, you'd never hold office again. There's no end to the lies I could tell in divorce court, Embry. Drugs and drinking… prostitutes. *Teenage* prostitutes. That you also gave drugs to. And paid to have abortions. It wouldn't be as hard to fake as you'd think."

"Jesus, Abilene."

She shrugs as she turns back to her mirror and ruffles her fingers through her hair. It shakes in perfect copper waves over her shoulders. "Still want that divorce?"

I don't answer her, and I don't bother telling her goodbye.

I get my suitcase, cuddle Galahad for as long as he'll let me, and tell Enid to text me if she needs anything.

Then I catch my flight to New York.

My aide—a young white woman named Dinah—checks us into our hotel, makes sure I have all my notes, and then we go our separate ways. Her up to her room and me up to mine, and it's as I'm holding the hotel key against the door's RFID pad that I notice there's someone else in the hallway.

I don't recognize the face, but I'd recognize that stance and suit and earpiece combination anywhere: he's Secret Service. Which means…

I open my door and all the air is caught in my chest, trapped and sharp and urgent.

Greer is here.

Greer is here in my room, standing at the window and looking at the Manhattan skyline, and I can't breathe, can't even think. She turns to face me with a smile, the city lights twinkling behind her as if they love her as much as I do, as if they want to touch her as much as I do.

"This is kind of familiar," she teases. "You walking into a hotel room, me standing at the window."

And like that, all the heat and urgency in my chest arrows to my groin. Because it is familiar, and the last time this happened, she ended up sitting on my face in her wedding gown, and I ended up making a mess of the inside of my tux as her husband licked the taste of her off my lips. And she's even wearing a white dress now, a short sweater dress with long sleeves and boots up past her knees, making her legs look a million miles long, and shit. I need them around my waist, wrapped around my head, I need that sweater dress bunched up between our stomachs, yanked up to her neck so I can bite at her breasts.

But I stay where I am, slowly setting my suitcase against the wall and letting the door close behind me. "Why are you here?" I ask, struggling to keep my voice neutral, struggling to keep the two years of loneliness and longing hidden.

"Ash sent me," she says, and of course he did, and I don't know why that fills me with equal parts excitement and disappointment. Excitement because if Ash sent her, if she came here when he asked, that means there's only one way tonight will end.

But then why isn't he here too? Why not come himself? Why not the three of us?

"He's spending the night in Seattle," Greer says softly, reading my face. "Lyr asked him to stay, and Ash would do anything for that boy."

My pain deflates a little, replaced by the sharper pain of loving that man so fucking much. Of course he would want to be with Lyr right now; of course he'd be sacrificing anything he could for his son.

Greer bites her lip as she watches me process this. "It's been two years," she says in a quiet voice. "If you want me to leave, say the word."

"And if I don't want you to leave?" My blood is thrumming hot through my body, and my cock pushes against my zipper like it's trying to split the metal teeth apart.

Greer releases her lip from her teeth with a small lick and big smile. "Then my safe word is Maxen."

And I'm on her. It takes me several long strides to eat up the distance between us, but I'm there, I'm against her, I'm slamming her against the wall and sealing my mouth over hers.

"I can't wait," I mumble against her lips.

"Then don't," she says, and I spin her and push her back on the bed, and I don't even give her time to move up to the pillows; I don't give her time to catch her breath. I curve my body right over hers and fumble with my zipper between us, and the back of my hand touches bare wet skin as I do.

"You're not wearing anything under that dress," I growl, pausing work on my zipper to shove her dress up and see for myself. "You needed to be fucked that badly?"

She's arching now, trying to roll her hips against me, but I pin her to the bed with a hard hand on her hip and just *look*. Just look at the sleek rift between her legs, the tiny parabola of her mound silhouetted against the chunky knit fabric of her dress, the bevels and curves where her cunt meets her thigh, where her thigh meets her ass. The tiny pink rosebud of her ass and the plump little berry of her clit peeking out between her lips. And she's wet already, so wet that it's on the outside of her, and all of her private skin is so flushed and so needy.

"Embry," she moans. "Put it inside me. Please. I can't wait any longer."

Fuck, I can't either. "It's going to be fast, sweetheart," I mutter apologetically, bracing my hand on the bed, my other hand digging my cock out of my pants. It's going to be pointlessly fast, but I'm too ashamed to tell her that. Embry Moore, once known up and down the West Coast for his godlike prowess in bed, is going to come after a single thrust…if that. It's been more than a year since I've had anything other than my hand and a silicone toy I bought in a fit of frustration while my eyes burned with stupid tears and my room was illuminated by the blue glow of my laptop screen. I've only had that one night with Belvedere to disrupt my celibacy, which means I'm practically a fucking monk now, and in the face of a willing, spread-open woman, I don't even know how to make myself last. My balls are already drawn up so fucking tight, ready to pump her full.

I push the head of my cock against her and suck in a

breath. Even Greer's slick heat at my tip feels like too much, far too much.

"Can I go in bare?" I manage to say through gritted teeth, and the little minx laughs at my desperation, her fingers wrapping around my tie and tugging playfully.

But then she gets serious as sin. "Make me messy," she says in that haughty little voice she uses sometimes, her queen voice. "I want all the cum you've been saving for me. I've been thinking about it all day, how it would feel to be full of you. Dripping with you."

Shit yes. None of the *I just want to feel all of you* stuff that lovers sometimes say about going bare, none of the pretense of delicacy. Just the raw, crude biology of it, the physical release and natural purpose of it.

The angle is fucked, with her legs still half off the bed and my upper thighs still cinched with my flat-fronted suit pants, but I don't even care. I yank her hips to mine, breach her wet split with the first inch of me, and then give her the other seven in a rough, grunting shove. She's so wet that it takes almost nothing to push inside, and I press a forbidding hand to her lower belly to keep her still as I reach underneath us and tug down on my balls to stop the orgasm already strangling every muscle and vein and pipe of me.

Despite my hand hard on her belly, she's still arching, the raw contact after two years so fucking incredible, and she's saying, "God, I missed you, I missed you, I missed you," as I finally let go of myself and pull out to the tip.

"I missed you more," I breathe as I push inside, and holy fuck, there are stars crowding the edges of my sight, actual fucking stars—supernovas and white dwarfs and goddamn pulsars shooting beams of pure energy across my field of vision—and then I'm fully inside her, hunched over her like a fucking teenager, tangled in my clothes, marveling at the press of my balls against her ass like it's the eighth wonder of the world.

Every muscle in my body is clenched so hard that I might snap in two, but I'd rather snap in two than miss this, than rush this gift that I didn't expect but that I need so, so badly. I love her, I love her—

"I love you," I mumble, kissing her roughly on the mouth, biting at her jaw. "I love you."

"Embry," she murmurs, "there's going to be more. I'll be here all night. Use me quick, and then I'll use you slow, but don't hold back. You don't ever get to hold back with me."

My hands grab everywhere even as my hips and dick are so still that I could be a photograph, a sculpture. The slightest twitch will throw me over the edge, and I don't want it yet, except I do want it; I want it to last forever at the same time that I want to blow all this pent-up pressure inside her and show her exactly how chaste I've been. Exactly how much I've missed her.

I have to touch every part of her, press and squeeze every inch that has only known her husband's touch over the last two years. Her slender waist, her pert breasts, even her fucking shoulders I have to clutch and rough up and clasp.

Her *shoulders*.

And then my hands are on her head, threading through her hair as I cradle her face and kiss her, kiss her, kiss her. And it's not even her sweet pussy that sends me over the edge, it's the slide of her tongue silky and wet against my own, just so fucking intimate and naked.

"I'm gonna come," I grunt into her mouth.

She kisses me back even harder in answer, and then fuck it, it's coming, my first real orgasm since I fucked a presidential aide a year ago, and it's a hard, angry throb jabbing deep into my balls and then I'm groaning low in my throat as I spill into Greer's warm cunt. It feels like it's being yanked out of me, tugged, *forced* even, and my forehead rolls against hers as the entire lower half of my body is caught in a merciless, vicious storm. I come, and I come, and I'm almost embarrassed to feel how much is leaking out around us, but she's not embarrassed at all, she's reaching down to smear her fingers around where we're joined, and it's too much to take on top of everything else. I collapse fully on top of her, finishing out the painfully sweet emptying with our stomachs and chests pressed hard together and my hips pumping as worthlessly as any green boy's.

Finally, after what feels like hours, I'm done and drained. I grab Greer's hand where it wanders in bawdy curiosity between us, and then I feed it back into her mouth and make her lick off the mess. Her eyes glow like molten silver when I do it, and it spikes heat through me all over again.

"You like that, dirty girl?" I ask breathlessly.

She nods, cum-covered fingers in her mouth, her eyes so wide and innocent and fuck me—

"You're fucking filthy," I tell her, pulling out and then dropping to my knees in front of the bed without bothering to pull up my pants. I take her ass in my hands and raise her up to my mouth, feeling the leather kiss of her booted calves slide against my shoulders. I give her one long, dirty lick from her ass to her clit, tasting the mix of the two of us—bitter and sweet—and it's so damn fitting that we should taste this way together. Bittersweet, messy and mingled, just like our lives and just like our love.

Her thighs squeeze tight around my head, and I can feel the heels of her boots on my back as I kiss and suckle at her, as I lick and dart my tongue and taste everything, all of it, all of her and me, and it's not long before her hands are fisting at the hotel bedcover, her wedding ring winking in the light of the bedside lamp as she writhes and squeals. I can't stop staring at it, at the gold and diamond flash of it as she chases her orgasm, and then at my own ring as I wrap my arm over the top of her thigh and press on her pubic bone to keep her still. Twin glints of dull gold, visible stamps of other people's ownership. She is somebody else's wife and I am somebody else's husband, and God, that thought shouldn't be so fucking wrong and thrilling that I'm getting hard all over again.

But it is.

And I am.

Her hand tangles through my hair and holds me hard to her cunt, and with my tongue and teeth working like I'd never get to eat a woman again, she comes so fucking hard that her thighs tremble and shake against my cheeks and her boots gouge and scrape at me, and I know I'll have bruises and ruptured blood vessels dusted across my back in decoration.

The thought is like a cold drink on a hot day. A relief. Thank God, let her mark me, let her mark me, let there be proof that tonight is real.

Please.

Slowly, the flutters and contractions subside against my mouth and the hand in my hair loosens. I lift my face from between her legs, loving how I can feel her wet on my lips and chin, and even my cheeks, and she whimpers at the sight, her booted feet falling to the floor with twin, carpeted thumps.

"Holy shit," she pants. "Holy fuck."

"Yeah."

She gives a breathless laugh, and then I'm on top of her again, hauling her up to the pillows and yanking her tight into my chest, our legs tangled and our clothes tangled and her hair tangled all around us.

"God, I missed you," I say, my lips against her head and my words coming out muffled and faint. "So fucking much."

"I know," she sighs, her arms sliding around my waist. Her face is buried in my chest and it feels so perfect, all of it so perfect, that I wonder how I've been alive so long without it. I wonder what the fuck kind of love this is that it can survive two years of starvation and then still devour me alive the first chance it gets.

Greer must be thinking the same thing because she says, "I kept thinking that maybe I had started to invent how you made me feel, like I was embellishing it in my memory, but…" She tilts her head and looks up at me with a smile that could make stone sing. "It's just like it was in Chicago, just like it was on my wedding night and in Carpathia. I'll always be that girl falling too hard for her knight in shining armor."

"Shit yes, you will be," I growl, bending my head to kiss her. "I'll fucking make sure of it."

We fuck again in the shower, and this time—God and his saints be praised—I last long enough to make her come first and to be able to look at myself in the mirror after. And then I fuck her against the window, watching the city lights kiss at her still-wet skin, and then she uses me like she promised she would, shoving me into an armchair and riding me until we both glisten with sweat and we can barely breathe. She comes as my toes dig into the carpet, as her fingers scratch at the arms of the chair, and then I hold her hips over mine and fuck up into her until she screams with another climax and I empty whatever I have left into her.

Which necessitates a final shower—no sex this time, just the gentle wash and touch of contented lovers—and then we slide in between the sheets, tucked in close in the dark.

"I'm glad Ash sent you," I say, my arms tight around her and my chin on the top of her head. "I can't—it… I'm just glad, is all. Grateful."

Greer draws idle circles on my back. "How long has it been? Since you've been with anyone?"

"Belvedere," I confess, and I feel her surprise.

It makes me a little…well, maybe *resentful* isn't the right word, but weary. That anything other than rank promiscuity on my part is counted as a shock. "Is that so surprising?" I ask her, unable to smother all the irritation I feel at her response.

She moves to look up at me. "It's painful," she says quietly. "To think of you alone so much. I knew you wouldn't sleep with Abilene, but I thought…had hoped…that you weren't lonely."

I sigh, my defensiveness settling back into my bones and going quiet. "The old me wouldn't have stayed lonely. And at first, with the campaign and with Galahad—it just seemed like the smart thing for the time being. Lie low, keep my pants zipped. I didn't need another skeleton in my closet when election time came around."

"And then?"

I trace the arches of her eyebrows, the line of her nose. "And then, there were times when I could have fucked someone subtly, safely, and I found I couldn't. Not even just that I didn't want to, but that I actually *couldn't.* My body would turn cold at the very thought, and eventually I realized that you and Ash had ruined me for anyone else. Once we became a three, I didn't—I can't be anything else with anyone else. The night Belvedere came to me was the only time I was able to take someone to bed because it felt like I was taking you and Ash to bed."

"Did you have to pretend it was Ash?" she asks.

"No," I say, shaking my head. "It's hard to describe… like the whole time I was fucking him, I wasn't pretending it was anyone other than Ryan Belvedere, but that was because I didn't need to. Because it had been you and Ash acting through Ryan, so fucking him was like fucking you." I pause, remembering that night. Sweaty and rough and long. "Did Ryan tell you about it later?"

"He did," Greer answers with a smile. "Ash was so eager

to mount me after Belvedere described it for us that he didn't even wait for the door to close."

My tired cock gives an instinctive jolt against her thigh as I imagine it.

"Ash fucked me on the floor until I screamed. Then he spanked my ass and fucked me again. We were thinking of you and Belvedere the whole time."

I groan. "My dick hurts too much to fuck again but I'm hard."

"I can help," Greer says sweetly, and in an instant she's climbing over me, settling her wet cunt over my face as she sucks my sore erection into her mouth. And I'm back to zero stamina again, but luckily she is too, and after a few pulling sucks, I'm jetting down her throat as she's fluttering against my tongue.

And then she's snuggling back into my arms like nothing happened, nuzzling against my chest. If I were a big cat, I'd be purring right now. Warm and sex-sleepy, with my mate all warm and sex-sleepy herself against me.

"Embry," she says as I start to drift off. "There's something you should know. About Abilene."

That kills my purr instantly. "What is it?"

I can't see Greer's face because it's still cradled against my chest, but I sense her hesitation. "A while ago, I met with Dr. Ninian."

Dr. Ninian. The White House doctor who helped Abilene drug me the night Galahad was conceived. Ash had fired her discreetly, although he'd wanted to do much worse, but he'd stopped at termination because I asked him to. Because I couldn't have something like that hanging over my head during the campaign.

"She's agreed to go to the police after I threatened to on her behalf. But I'd been stalling, because I didn't want to drag it out into the open during the election."

"But then Abilene went public about Lyr," I guess.

"Abilene has to be stopped, Embry. And even if you refuse to press charges, the tampering with medical records and collusion to commit a crime might be sufficient to send her away. At the very least humiliate her enough that people stop trusting her."

"It doesn't matter," I tell Greer. "If she goes to jail, if she's humiliated and friendless—she will always be dangerous. Isn't it safer to keep her satisfied for now?"

"I'm not asking your opinion on this," Greer replies. "I'm just warning you that it's coming. Maybe in the next couple of weeks. I don't want to hurt your campaign, but I don't have a choice—I don't know what she'll do next, and sometimes I worry that she might do something extreme. Hurt someone like she tried to hurt me through Melwas."

My arms tighten around her. "I won't let that happen. I have her watched, Greer. I have every possible communication line tapped and observed. She can't hurt anyone while I'm still around."

Greer doesn't answer, and I know it's because she doesn't believe me, and I'm trying to think of something else to say to reassure her—and also to dissuade her from any scheme of going to the police—when she speaks again. "I saw the protestors outside the hotel tonight."

I roll to my back and groan up at the ceiling. "I know."

"Embry, please be careful. Those Carpathian extremists—they're dangerous."

It was Carpathian extremists who murdered her parents when she was a child; she has every right to be nervous about them. And I wish I could say something to reassure her, but what can I say? I intentionally adopted an aggressive anti-Carpathian platform. It's what I believe in; it's what I am running on, even though I knew it would make enemies both abroad and at home. The protestors here at home are not a real bother; they're the usual protesting types, holding up signs about warmongering and the military-industrial complex and xenophobia and whatever else. It's the Carpathian extremists that perhaps I should worry about.

I mean, I don't actually worry. For one, my Secret Service protection starts tomorrow, and for another, it's a long stretch from online threats to real danger. I spent several years with their bullets and bombs and ruined towns full of trip-wire explosives. I'm not worried about a few assholes venting on Twitter.

"Please, Embry," she says, her fingers running along my hairline, following the topography of my temples and ears and cheeks. "You're not invincible."

"I know I'm not."

She makes a noise. "I forgot. It's not that you think you won't get hurt; it's that you don't *care* if you get hurt."

"Now you sound like Ash."

I hear her temper flare in her words. "Because I have the audacity to care about you? The audacity to want you alive?"

"You'd be the only one," I mumble, not because it's true but because she's pushing buttons I don't want pushed and so it's easier to hide behind self-loathing.

"Oh, shut up," she says, and she's annoyed, but I hear amusement in her words too. "You can't pout your way out of being loved. Not with me or Ash...or Galahad."

I soften at the mention of my son's name. At the sound of his name on Greer's lips. With an urgency that's just as heartbreaking as it is selfish, I want them to meet. I want to see her holding him, reading to him, giggling with him. I want to see if he makes her light up the way he makes me light up. I want to see if she's just as blown away by his sweet and shy curiosity as I am.

"Have you...will you ever forgive me for him?" I ask, my mouth dry. Suddenly I need to know, need to know right away. "Will you ever be able to forgive him for his mother?"

"There's nothing to forgive," she says, and her voice is all clarity, all warm honesty and earnest truth. She guides my hand to her stomach, which is flat and narrow. "I wish—I mean, there aren't enough wishes in the world for how much I want to have a child with you and Ash, but I do wish for it. I've lit about every candle in St. Thomas Becket, I've prayed to every patron saint of women and childbirth and children. I can't say I still don't feel a stab of jealousy when I think of him, because I do. I do feel that, but I also feel like I want to love him and there's nothing that will ever make me stop loving you. And whatever Abilene's done, she's still my cousin, which means Galahad is my family too."

"We'll find a way for you to meet," I promise. "You need to know him. And I—well. *I* need you to know him."

"I'd like that," she says. "And Ash…Ash should meet him."

My eyelids burn and I blink fast. "Yes."

"Do you remember that first time after you brought me back to Camp David? The three of us?"

"Yes, of course."

"There was this moment when you told me you loved me, do you remember? You said it so only I could hear."

My mind is still thinking of Ash's strong arms carrying my son, and it takes me a minute to process what she's saying, but then when I do, guilty heat warms my face. I remember that moment well, and I'm not proud of it. "Yes, I did."

"Why?"

I chew on my lip, searching for the right words. The honest ones. "I wanted you to know that I loved *you*, that I wasn't loving or fucking you through my love for Ash… and I wanted you to know because I was jealous of him. Of how you looked at him that day. Even though I'd just brought you home, it seemed like child's play compared to how well he took care of you after. Like he was doing the real rescuing. And Ash is so—he's so *everything*—he's like water and he fills up every space—and I had this moment where I wanted just this one thing for myself. Loving you." I inhale. "And I know that Ash and I have years and years of history, that it would be easy to think that what I felt for him was more than what I felt for you, but you needed to know that it wasn't true. There was a part of me that was only just for you. That still is."

She lets out a breath, nodding. "I know," she replies. "I mean, that's what I thought you might say."

"Why are you asking about this?"

She takes a long time to answer, and when she does, her voice is soft. "Because sometimes I wonder if we would have lasted as a three, even if you hadn't left. We love each other so much, but we're all so tangled up and snarled together, how could it have ever worked?"

"Ash," I say. "It would have worked because of Ash—and because of us. I believe that, Greer. I really do. That no matter how jealous we were, how broken and how messy, we would have made it."

"And if we had made it, what then?"

"I would have been in your bed every night," I say with a smile. "And there every morning to feed you coffee and pet you awake. And eventually after all the politics were done, we'd find a nice place out in the country and fill it with babies and grow old together."

"Babies," she smiles. "That sounds nice."

"Maybe I got you pregnant tonight." I barely dare to say it, but I'm too caught up in what our lives could have been like to stop myself. "Maybe it's happening right now."

"Oh, Embry," she says, rolling on top of me. Her hair is everywhere, sweet smelling and soft. "I hope so. I hope so with all my heart."

And we don't say much after that, letting the hopeful thump of our hearts and the slow swells of our breath carry us to someplace dark and peaceful. Someplace where the woman I love can hold my son, where her belly is full of a child we made together. Ash is there too, and the four of us are happy and laughing and expansive and safe, and in this place, there's only us and our love and the family we grow together.

There's no Carpathia.

No Abilene.

No election and no debate.

There's no balling dread that I might take the stage against Ash and fall to my knees before he ever says a word.

There's no tentative, prickling excitement that I might take the stage against him and hold my own, that I might *win*, that I might find myself stronger and smarter, at least for that one crucial hour.

There's no fear that I'll wake up to an empty bed, with only the bootheel-shaped bruises on my back and the lingering smell of fresh shampoo to remind me that it wasn't a dream.

No fear that tomorrow will find me alone.

And defeated.

CHAPTER 18
EMBRY

NOW

TOMORROW FINDS ME ALONE.

Tomorrow finds me defeated.

I'm not surprised when I wake up alone, although that doesn't make it sting any less. But I am surprised when Ash not only wins the debate, he *trounces* me. He destroys me.

Guts me and hangs up my head and my heart for the world to see.

He is the king, after all, and I have no one to blame but myself for forgetting.

I only remember flashes from the debate itself. The backstage at Hofstra University, crowded and jostling with people re-taping audio cords and adjusting camera settings and arguing about Wi-Fi. Searching for Ash as someone touched up my camera makeup. Searching for Greer. Seeing only strangers and lights. Going over my notes on my phone as Vivienne Moore texted me an unending stream of advice.

> Look into the camera. Speak clearly. Don't let him anger you.
> Don't fuck it up.

I remember stepping onto the stage first, waving and smiling at the intimate crowd. And then turning. And seeing him.

In person.

Up close.

Green eyes. Full, sharply peaked lips. Black hair shot through with strands of silver—so far apart that you think you've imagined them in the light. A suit cut so perfectly to his tall and masculine proportions that the tailor probably wept and came at the same time he cut it. A presence like a saint or a conqueror or a demigod, a presence that expands like heat from the wide shoulders and narrow hips and ruthlessly handsome face.

I remember shaking hands, his hand huge in mine, and rough and strong, and how were we shaking hands like strangers? We didn't even shake hands when we first met, unless you'd call a forearm in your throat a handshake. And our eyes meeting, and I always forget I'm just that little bit taller, but somehow it doesn't matter with Ash; I feel like I'm standing at the feet of Zeus and peering up in supplication. It's that *presence*, and I'm helpless in the face of it, or I always have been, and then Ash cups my elbow and leans into my ear.

"I love you, little prince" is all he says.

No insults.

No threats.

After I've spent the last year doing everything I can to

undermine his power, to woo politicians and donors to my side, relentlessly stating and restating every single way I think he's a bad leader, publicly forswearing our every bond and oath, trumpeting about his weaknesses—after all of that, all he wants to say to me is *I love you*?

Oh my God. I'm fucked. I'm done. I had prepared to debate in the face of his hatred, but I am nothing in the face of his love.

Nothing.

I pull back and look into those bottle-glass eyes. "Achilles," I manage in a whisper before the audience erupts in polite applause and the moderator exhorts us to take our podiums. His heart cracks open in his eyes when I say it.

I crack open too. Open and apart. Into nothing.

I remember taking notes as he and Harrison Fasse talked. I remember scribbling down points and errors, and also just drawing nonsense lines because I needed someplace to look that wasn't my king's face, something to concentrate on that wasn't his charred, melodic voice. It didn't work though because how could I not hear him? How could I not see him?

I remember making most of my points fairly well. I'm good at talking; I'm good at smiling. I'm persuasive. I'm from a liberal state with a Democrat for a mother and I'm also a decorated military vet, the perfect swirl of blue and red—not to mention young and handsome and smart. I'm an ideal candidate, as moderate and inoffensive as you can get. If I were running against any other person than Ash, this wouldn't be a contest.

But it is Ash.

And he is the king.

To every question, he has a better answer. To every point, he has a better counterpoint. And it's not only his eloquence, although that's part of it, but it's that clarity and honesty that spills through him like light, that radiates from him in a shine of equanimity and strength. It's irresistible even to me, and I know the audience feels it, basks in it, takes it and holds it close because it's the feeling of knowing someone *good* is in charge. Someone good is here and trying to make things better, and they will do all the hard work and fighting for you, and all you have to do is believe them and trust them.

The terrible thing is that I know he doesn't mean to do this, but without trying to, he paints a picture of me as overeager and inexperienced, unseasoned in a way that makes me feel clumsy, like a boy trying on his father's suit.

And finally I remember Ash delivering the killing blow.

"Mr. Moore was my brother in arms, my running mate, and my dear friend. I still have nothing but respect and affection for him. But I will tell you that he swore to stay by my side through my first term, and he left to follow his ambition. Can you trust that he won't do the same to you? That he won't swear to serve you and then follow his ambition elsewhere?"

The room is thick with tense silence, and the moderator turns to me. "Mr. Moore, a rebuttal?"

I remember stammering something out about my conscience and Carpathia—a topic this debate hadn't even touched—and how I was called to run out of service for my country, the same service I'd given of myself during the war.

And even caught by surprise, even being flattened by the king, I know I gave my answer well and with enough charm that I wouldn't walk off this stage worse off than when I walked on. But I knew that I'd lost. That he'd painted my leaving him in the worst way, and that the damning part of it all was that he wasn't entirely wrong. That the truth in his words would find purchase in so many undecided voters. And actually, fuck the undecided voters.

The worst thing is that it found purchase in *me*.

I remember walking off the stage and Dinah handing me a fresh bottle of water. I remember craning my neck to see where Ash went. I remember Morgan stepping forward and saying, "What the fuck was that?"

I remember Belvedere waiting patiently behind her and Dinah until he could slip in close, and then pressing a hotel key card into my palm.

"If you're available, President Colchester would like you to come to his room tonight."

And I remember thinking *fuck him, fuck him* as I pocketed the key card and asked Dinah to arrange my ride to his hotel.

My phone won't stop on the way back to Manhattan. After the *Post* news alert declaring Ash the winner, and after the sixty-seventh text from Vivienne Moore, I throw it onto the seat next to me and press my fingertips into my eyes, ignoring the Secret Service agent sitting in the row behind me.

Humiliation runs through me like hot tar, it's sticking in my throat, it's muffling all noise and searing away any taste that's not the taste of shame.

I lost.

I did my best and I lost.

Ash won.

Hempstead passes by, then Queens, and finally we are over the East River, heading to Ash's hotel. I watch the concrete and steel morass of the city flit by with the weary distaste of a native Seattleite, and the hot tar feeling grows stronger and stronger the closer I get to the man who just outmaneuvered me on national television. The man who smashed me into splinters like a ship against sharp rocks. How ironic that *this* is so agonizing, so dishonoring somehow, when I've let him beat me with any manner of whips and paddles, fuck me into unconsciousness, taunt me into hardness, jeer me into ejaculating, use my soul and my heart as brutally as he likes to use my body.

But I'd rather be whipped. I'd rather be fucked raw and bleeding, I'd rather be tied up and led around by the cock than be suited and made up and so carefully prepared and then to still be so easily outperformed. And I was *good*, I know I was. I know that if it had just been Harrison Fasse and me on that stage, I would have walked off the handy winner.

But Ash will always be better.

Fuck him, fuck him.

How can he love me and still crush me? What kind of love is that?

It's his own kind of love, I think bitterly. His love is so like his cruel Catholic god's—the god who punishes you for your sins at the same time he bleeds to forgive them. Eternally tender and coldly just. A contradiction I used to cherish and now I despise because it has made me despise myself.

My SUV pulls up to the back of the hotel, I tell my driver to get a room for the night and make himself comfortable, and then my agent and I are walking through the service entrance and to the elevator. The key burns a hole in my pocket, a plastic rectangle that might as well be my thirty pieces of silver. But who am I betraying?

Ash?

Myself?

Neither?

Both?

My Secret Service agent—a hard-faced white woman named Leonella—says nothing to me in the elevator on the way up, for which I'm profoundly grateful. Even the smallest question, the shortest remark, would have poured another barrel of hot tar over me, and my skin is blistered and peeling with shame as it is. I'm sick and shaking with it when we make it to the top floor and the doors open. Ash's agents are expecting me.

They are familiar. I know their faces, their names, their children's names.

They know that I'm the opponent here to visit the incumbent—the incumbent that I quit on, the incumbent that just thrashed me on television—and I'm here to visit him by myself. And sex might be the least awkward reason that I could be here, and I find myself avoiding their gazes as I press the key card against the door and let myself inside his room.

The first thing I notice is that Greer isn't here. Her absence is distinct, touchable almost, like she's left a hole in the very room, a reverse imprint of herself.

The second thing I notice is that Ash is a fucking god, and I hate myself for wanting him, yearning for him, even as I'm a defeated worm curling over the toe of his shoe. He's by the window, a glass of scotch dangling carelessly from his fingertips, although it's not careless with him, nothing is, and I know he has a firm grip on it, as he does on everything. His jacket is off, his tie loosened, his sleeves rolled up, and his expression as he turns away from the window is furious and hungry.

"Took you long enough," he says.

"I came straight here."

"I'm not talking about tonight."

I don't have an answer to that, and he knows it. He sets the scotch down and prowls toward me. Everything inside me is screaming to take a step back or to fly at him—to run or to attack.

I don't do either of these things, but I feel the closed door behind me like an iron barrier, I feel cuffed and collared just by standing in front of him, and I *hate* that I still love it, that I miss it, that I want it. I hate myself. I hate him. I hate the lamps around the room that make him glow with an almost angelic radiance. I hate how good he looks with his tie loose and the city lights behind him. I hate how his green eyes burn for me as hotly as they burned in that Carpathian forest when he put his boot on my wrist.

"Why did you bring me here?" I ask, as if I don't know. As if I'm not deliberately provoking him.

"Why do you think?"

"To fuck me."

"You really think," he says dangerously, coming close to me, "that you deserve to be fucked right now?"

"You would have been there with Greer last night," I point out. "Why not, if not to fuck me?"

"If I'd been there with Greer last night, you wouldn't have been able to sit down today, and your cock would still be hard. You don't know what I would have done if I were there, but I guarantee you that you would be a lot less impudent tonight."

I almost laugh. We just spent an hour and a half sparring over the most important issues facing our world today, and he whips out the word *impudent*? If I hadn't felt unmanned before, I certainly feel unmanned now—my best efforts and all the Republican Party's best money, and it's just childish impudence to him? He might as well call me a brat.

"I can't decide whether I want to hit you or kiss you," I tell him honestly.

He steps closer. His shoes touch my shoes, and for a terrible moment, I remember every time that's ever happened, the intimate knock of leather against leather. In the army and during his first campaign. At his wedding to Jenny, when he asked for help with his boutonnière, and my toes bumped against his as I fiddled with the stupid flower pin and he stared at my mouth and I pretended not to notice.

"Funny," he breathes, "I was just thinking the same thing."

"You won," I spit. "How can you possibly be thinking the same thing?"

"I won?" he demands. "Really? You call listening to you slander me for a year *winning*? Fighting you tonight—that's winning for me?"

"You used to like fighting me," I say sulkily. I know I'm being deliberately shitty, but I can't stop myself; I can't force myself past it, can't stop it. It's been two years since we've seen each other and all we've done tonight is argue publicly and now privately, and it's stupid. It's so fucking stupid because all I wished for last night was for us to be alone and happy, and now all I want to do is choke him. Or be choked by him.

His nostrils flare, his jaw tightens.

My skin prickles with alarm, but I keep my chin lifted, my eyes narrowed. "And now you've won fair and square, in front of everyone, without even rumpling your suit. Surely that's enough?"

I shouldn't have said it, I realize that now, because the word *enough* is a bit of a trigger word between us, a word that dredges up memories of closets and cages and boundaries, the word I used a long time ago to tell him he was good enough to fuck but not to marry, and it was a lie, of course it was, but I sold it so fucking well.

The first time I used that word with him, he slapped me right across the face. This time, it's worse.

He does nothing.

"Go ahead," I dare him. "Slap me. Wrestle me. Fuck me. You won, so that's what you get to do, right?"

"So that's how you want it to be," he says in a cold, slow voice.

"I don't want it 'to be' any way, Mr. President," I say with something between a smile and a snarl. "I'm just being *impudent*."

"You," he says grimly, "are asking for trouble."

"And that's a problem?"

"You don't have a safe word."

"I remember."

His hand slams hard at the wall next to my head; I can't help but flinch. "Give me a fucking safe word, Embry," he growls. "Right the fuck now."

"We've never needed one before."

"I," he says, finally taking that last step forward, and oh fuck, he's hard, and his whole body is hot and so deliciously firm, and then his nose runs along my jaw and his lips are at my ear, "have never needed a safe word with you before."

"And why is that?"

I feel him inhale, smelling my skin; his cock swells even harder against my hip. My own cock is a fucking lost cause, hard enough to pop like a fucking jack-in-the-box, leaking all over the inside of my pants.

"Because I've never needed you to be able to stop me before."

I choke on the air I'm breathing. It's terror and lust and possession. And a tiny voice that tells me not to give him a safe word because if I don't give it to him, then I know he won't touch me. Even in his wrath, he is too loving (once again like his Catholic god), and if I tell him no, he will listen, and even if I don't say no, if I say nothing, he will take a step back, he will draw in a breath, he will fist his hands in his hair and tell me in a choked voice to leave. If I don't give him a safe word, I could crawl in front of him naked, I could present any hole, my weeping cock, and he'd be stone.

And I hate him for being so safe. For being so good. I hate that he will still take care of me in the same moment that he wants to rip me limb from limb. I want him to destroy me, even if it's just one more thing to hate him for.

"You give me one," I say. "Give me a safe word and it's mine."

His eyes flare. "You're supposed to choose."

It's my last petulant stand. "No."

"*No*? Unoriginal, I suppose, but workable."

"You know that's not what I—"

But it's too late, his hand is fisted at the neck of my shirt and I'm being shoved down to my knees, and I expect his other hand to fall to his zipper, I expect my mouth to get fucked, I expect anything other than the door opening with an electronic whirr and click and Greer walking in, looking nothing like the autumn princess of last night and every bit a queen. Black cigarette pants hug her hips and ass, and she's wearing a matching black shirt with suit-like lapels and a neckline so low that I can see the inner slopes of her breasts. Sandaled heels showcase her delicate Barbie-like feet, her blond hair waves silkily over one shoulder, lipstick the color of sin stains her lips.

For a ridiculous minute, Ash and I are frozen, just staring at her. Ridiculous not because she shouldn't be stared at, but because I'm on my knees, because Ash's hand is at my neck, because both of us are flushed and dilated with angry hunger. She sets her black clutch purse on a nearby table and steps toward us, her face keen with carnal delight.

"What are my boys doing without me?" she asks.

I can't speak. Adrenaline and God knows what other hormones are surging through me, along with all the shame and rage from earlier. Ash speaks for us.

"I won," he explains simply. "So I get to do what I want with him."

"Oh," she says, the apples of her cheeks going rosy with interest. "Are you going to fuck him?"

"He doesn't deserve to be fucked."

"You could fuck his mouth."

"He doesn't deserve that either."

I try to clear my throat—not in an *I'm right here*

noise—but in actual nerves, in actual discomfort, because I'm scared and angry and horny and I actually don't know which feeling is which any longer. They've all blended together, mashed and pulped into the same thing.

It's as if the noise reminds Ash that I'm still here, still kneeling at his feet with his hand gripping the back of my neck. He looks down at me.

"I think I know," he says softly. "I know exactly what to do with you."

"Go fuck yourself," I say.

"That, my little prince, has never, ever been the plan." And then he's dragging me toward the bed like a dog, too low for me to stand, too fast for me to crawl, and I know I'll have bruises on my knees, I can hear rips in the fabric of my suit, and for a minute, I think about just standing up and saying it.

No.

No, I'm not playing this game with you tonight. No, I'm not your pet, your boy, your plaything. I'm not your lover. I'm not your prince. I'm your enemy and you said you loved me tonight and then you drowned me in your power, you held me under until I was clawing at my own throat and the blood vessels exploded in my eyes and all I could taste was you.

It would be so easy to say it. So easy to stop.

So why am I not stopping it? Why am I letting him throw me on the bed? Crawl over me? Yank off my jacket and tie and shoes as if they've offended him somehow?

It was less terrible when I didn't have a safe word, when I didn't have any agency in my own humiliation. When I could fight back knowing that Ash would win, pretending I didn't have a choice. But now, I have the easiest word of all—*no*—and the mere existence of the word is driven into me like a nail, like a spear into my heart and I'm leaking blood and water around it. It can't kill me because I'm already dead—or at least my self-respect is, because I could stop this, but I won't.

I won't, I won't.

I'm disgusted with myself.

I'm stripped bare, and the moment my cock springs free from my boxer briefs, Ash gives it a punishing slap, making me cry out and arch. My cock responds in the most embarrassing way, bobbing and leaking merrily, my balls drawing up tight to my body as if they're ready to spill their load at any moment.

He slaps it again, and his answering erection is so massive right now. He gives it a thoughtless, impatient shift to readjust it, too busy making me feel bad to make himself feel good.

Another slap. There's pre-cum on my belly again, my toes are digging into the covers, and Greer is slowly undressing by the side of the bed, her eyes glued to the sight of my punished cock.

"Why are you doing this?" I ask on a groan.

"Because maybe you've forgotten after two years apart," he says, "but you belong to me."

Another slap. My erection is mottled in shades of red, and I'm shivering with the sudden endorphin rush from the pain.

"You could say no," he says. "Right now. Tell me that you don't want me to touch you. To speak to you. To look at you."

I close my eyes. "Fuck you," I whisper.

"That's not your safe word." Another slap, this time lighter but right against my testicles. I grunt in pain. "Do you need help remembering it? It starts with *n* and ends with *o.* Say *no* to me, Embry. Say it right now. You've never had trouble saying it to me before."

"I hate you."

"I love you and I'm going to make you cry tonight if you don't say no to me." My nipples are twisted with angry speed, I'm rolled over and spanked so hard on the ass that I feel it reverberating through my hair follicles, spanked on that tender spot where my thighs meet my butt, spanked so hard that I know he must have ruptured blood vessels in his palm.

I grunt into the covers, my body rigid. It hurts like fuck, but he can beat me till I scream and I still won't cry for him. Not tonight, not ever again.

"Goddammit, Embry, just say it," he seethes. His palm is like a hail of fire behind me; Moses himself has never seen fire like the kind Ash is burning into my ass, and he doesn't stop. He won't stop until he wrenches that safe word from me, but he won't get it—or my tears. He doesn't get to parade victory in every corner of my soul tonight. No fucking way.

"I hate you," I mumble again into the sheets, and then there's the cool, slim fingers of Greer's hand on my neck, running through my hair. I feel her curling over me, her hair soft and whispering against my skin, and I'm distantly aware that she's naked too, and that she's murmuring gentle things into my ear as Ash lays blows on my ass like I've never had before. *It's okay* and *you're so brave, so good to him to let him do this* and *you're so handsome right now, I'm so wet over you, Embry, so wet.*

"Say it," Ash growls though gritted teeth. "Fucking say it."

"You can't make me safe out," I gasp. "And you can't make me cry."

"And you can't make a liar out of me. You'll cry."

"You already lied," I say petulantly into the bed. "You said you loved me before the debate."

The spankings stop; the bed dips as he climbs over me,

and the fabric of his trousers on my bare, spanked ass is so cruelly abrading. "I do love you," he murmurs into my ear.

"Liar."

"Do you really think that I can't be angry and in love at the same time?"

"What do you want from me?"

He unknots his tie and it drops ominously next to my face. I feel him unbutton and shrug off his shirt. I feel him unzip his pants and tug them down his hips, and then he's flipping me over and straddling me. I moan as he leans forward and our naked cocks knock together, which makes him smile wickedly.

"What I just said," he breathes, leaning down to run his nose along my jaw again. "For you to know that no matter how far you run, no matter how hard you fight, no matter how much you think you hate me, you will always belong to me." He bites my earlobe, straightens up, and then rubs his cock along the abused length of mine.

"*Shit,*" I gasp. "Holy shit."

He does it again, hot velvet skin on hot velvet skin, and all the tender spots on my cock are singing, weeping, thrilling with ecstasy. Pain and pleasure sizzle up my spine. My skin sparks into the very air.

"Greer," he says, his hands bracing by my head, and holy shit, he's moving his entire body over mine, moving over me like a man fucking another man below him, but he's not fucking; he's teasing. Cock against cock, heat against heat, hard against hard. Shit, it shouldn't feel so good, but it does, it does.

Greer is perched in nude perfection next to me, her legs kicked out to the side and bent a little in an adolescent display of indolence that shouldn't be as sexy as it is. Her hard nipples peek through the tumbled veil of hair over her breasts, and her hands are fisted in the blankets.

"Yes?" she answers Ash.

"Hand me my tie."

She does, holding one end of it while he pushes off my body and I groan with the loss. And then he's measuring, studying, the length of silk and my penis and my testicles—no tailor or architect was ever as serious or as focused as Ash right now with this fucking tie—and then I feel the cool silk rubbing against my balls, my inner thighs, my frenulum. I writhe and whine.

"You know what I'm going to do with this, Embry. Tell me not to."

"Go to hell," I pant, bucking my hips against the touch of the tie. It's too much, too soft, and it feels too good and it's so demeaning, and oh Jesus, I'm going to come if that tie slips against my skin one more time…

But it never comes. Instead he makes good on his word and begins binding up my erection and my balls, and a heartless cinch around my sac means the orgasm building behind my dick is mercilessly yanked away. And then more cinches and Ash says, in a voice so gruff with wonder and excitement that I almost do manage to come despite my bound cock, "Look at you. Look at you."

I look. I look at my cock so fucking swollen and dusky red and sad. I look at Ash hovering over me, pants yanked down to his hips, his own dick so rigid and thick that it points straight up to the ceiling, his chest moving in deep, excited breaths. I look at Greer next to us, wearing nothing but red lipstick and flushed cheeks.

"Ash," I beg. "Don't leave me like this. Please."

"That's getting closer to your safe word, but yet you're still missing the mark. It's *no*, remember? You say, *no, Ash, don't tie up my cock and tease me*. And if you don't say that, then you say *yes, sir*."

"Or else what?"

"Or else," he says with an evil look, reaching for Greer, "you don't get to taste Greer's cunt."

I drop my head back with a growl. "That's cheating."

Ash raises Greer to her knees, not answering me. Instead, he asks her, "What's your safe word, precious?"

"Maxen," she replies promptly.

"And do you have any objection to torturing Embry with me?"

She sends a coy smile down at me and my cock throbs. I growl again.

"I want nothing more."

"I'm glad to hear it." He helps her move over me, and in a moment's work, she's got her knees astride my head and her hands on the headboard, and her pussy unfurls like a flower in bloom right above my face. On instinct, I lift my head to suckle at her, but I'm stopped by Ash's hand cupping her, his fingers now firmly between my mouth and her wet skin.

More growling.

"Say it. Say *yes, sir*, and that cunt is yours to eat."

"Embry," Greer pleads, my name dripping with honey as it leaves her lips. "Please eat me. Please." And it's the sweet sound of her helpless need and the little wiggle of her hips—as if she's trying to press against Ash's hand and get closer to my mouth at the same time—that undoes me.

Ash has me and he knows it, and he was right earlier: I do belong to him and I want to belong to him, and I love him just as much as I hate him, and I only hate him because he's better than me, because he's the third side of our triangular heart, because I can't live without him.

Monster.

"Yes, sir," I say. And then I'm broken forever.

Ash makes a low, satisfied noise at the verbal signal of my inner destruction and pulls his hand away from Greer's pussy. Faster than a spark flying from a fire, my hands are digging at her hips and tugging that beautiful cunt to my mouth. I give her a long, dirty lick, just like I did last night, and then I trace every crease of her with my tongue, I dart tasting licks into her vagina, I suck her clit between my teeth and work it like it's my job. I hold nothing back, not even when she is riding my face and all I can breathe is her.

"That's it," Ash says approvingly. "I know you've missed our princess, and one night wasn't enough, was it?"

And then he is astride my chest, his hands resting large and demanding over mine on Greer's hips, and there's almost no warning when he wedges his cock at her entrance and pushes inside his wife. Greer cries out from being filled, and Ash lets out a vicious exhale as my tongue traces along his shaft, as I gently suck on his sac.

"Yeah," he mutters. "Yeah."

That's how we move, with me flat on my back, cock bound and leaking, and Ash and Greer astride me, my mouth searching to service them both.

"Lick me, Embry," Greer begs in a whisper. "Lick me, lick me. Make me come, oh please, oh please—"

She comes on Ash's cock and my tongue at the same time, all while I'm mindlessly writhing against the air myself, my ass and thighs and cock one continuous clench and ache, and then as she comes down, she looks over her shoulder to Ash, whose eyes are gazing down at where he and his wife join, at where I'm running the flat of my tongue along the underside of his cock every time he pulls out.

"You said he didn't deserve his mouth getting fucked," she says, voice still honeyed with arousal. "But maybe he's done enough to earn your cum."

Ash's hand drops underneath Greer's ass to cup the back of my neck. "Would you like that?"

Where's the shame in admitting it now?

He's won.

He's won, he's won.

In response I open my mouth, tongue over my bottom teeth, my cock threatening to split open merely at the idea of being used like this.

"*Fuck*," Ash groans, unraveled by the sight of my mouth waiting for his cock, and he lets loose into Greer with a flurry of hard, brutish thrusts, and from down here, I can see how powerful he really is, how sculpted those thighs and how tight that stomach, how wide and hard his cock. I can see the intimate, practical biology: the stretch of her cunt around his erection, the sway of his balls, the wet glisten of aroused skin.

"Open wide, little prince," Ash grunts, and then he pulls of out Greer's tight pussy and into my open mouth, shoving down into my throat and erupting with a groan that I can feel everywhere in my body, the kind of groan I'll remember for the rest of my life. Primal and male and triumphant.

Hot semen pours down my throat, and he's coming so hard I can actually feel the pulse and throb of his organ as my lips stretch around him and I can feel the contractions that clench all the inner workings of this cock I love so much.

"Oh, you have such a pretty mouth," he growls, his thumb running along the corner of my lips to gather up a pearl of leaked cum, and then he licks it off his thumb as he keeps pumping his hips and fucking through the last spurts of his orgasm. "So fucking pretty. I want to fuck it every day."

He leaves my mouth with a faint *pop* noise, but he doesn't move. Instead, he uses his fingers to guide his cock back into my mouth and to rub it around my lips.

"Greer," he says. "I know what you want, and you can have it. And as for you," he says, fingers pressing down on the top of his cock to push it between my lips again. "Clean me off."

Greer is scampering down to my cock like a happy little bunny, and then she's moving, and oh, fuck, oh fuck, she's on top of me, she's touching me, she's sinking down onto my aching, abused penis and taking it inside her body. I can't help but to arch and buck and whimper around Ash's cock, and he loves it, his eyes are glowing with heat and amusement—and goddammit, even with love—and Greer rides me hard and fast, her fingers at her clit, and her wetness everywhere, ruining Ash's tie, but who cares, who fucking cares—

"Suck it," Ash says darkly, shoving his cock into my throat again, and then it's as I'm choking on his cock and Greer is shaking in a fresh orgasm that I come, and it's the worst and best thing ever to happen, so fucking painful and so fucking brilliant that I'm sure I lose consciousness, just as I'm sure that Ash keeps fucking my mouth for the half second that I fade out, and then he pulls out as Greer and I both shudder to stillness and completion. And with a massive hand around that brutal organ, he jerks off hard and angry, fists a hand in my hair, and marks my face with his cum.

The shower is silent.

What is there to say?

But even with the stain of the election, we can't stop touching, can't stop wanting, and in silence Greer sets her foot up on the shower bench and reaches for me, and in silence, Ash and I share her. He takes her ass, I take her cunt, and she takes both of us, both our devotions and both our hearts. These two people I love so much that I'm dead with it, and a disconsolate voice inside my head wonders if it would have been better if we'd never met at all. If I'd never had to feel surrender and union and real marriage of souls—because then I wouldn't have to feel its absence or live inside the hollow of what might have been.

Once more is not enough—when is it ever?—so then there's twice more, three times more, the final time a joining of such excruciating sweetness that when the three of us meet mouths to kiss and to taste and to simply breathe together, I do cry.

Ash wins.

I cry and Ash tastes my tears and Greer nuzzles into me with her own face tear-soaked, and he tastes her tears too. And it's a strange thing to orgasm as tears drip down your face, but it's beautiful too. To climax in joy is such a common, ordinary thing—but to come in anguish, in torment and in sorrow, what a rare jewel indeed. Faceted and flashing. Unforgettable.

Just like two years ago, we cradle Greer between us, and I fall asleep with the gentle swell of her chest against mine, the cool kiss of her hair twined through my fingers, the steady, metronomic sound of Ash's breathing. And like last night, I fall asleep dreaming of a different place, a different life. It's us and Galahad and all the other children we can grow, and a puppy maybe, why not a puppy?—and every betrayal, every tragic misunderstanding and missed opportunity is gone forever. There's only what should have been from the beginning, which is this love the three of us have found like a city in the desert, strange and holy. Empty and waiting just for us.

My sleep is light and troubled, and when I surface to Ash's voice, it almost feels like I haven't been asleep at all, save for the lingering memories of a place that doesn't exist and children that haven't been born, and an easy joy that could never, ever be mine. Greer wakes too, but like a cat stirring when someone leaves the room. She stretches, yawns with an apathetic glance around her, and then falls right back asleep.

I don't.

Ash is at the other end of the suite, speaking German

in a low voice, and I only catch a few words in my hazy state. *Berlin* is one, *gipfelkonferenz* is another—a word my high school German skills weakly translate to a summit or meeting—and then *nächste Woche*. Next week.

Next week, Germany, some kind of meeting or conference? I filter through my brain, flipping through my internal database of schedules and events, because surely I'd know if Ash was going to Germany next week, surely that would have been on my radar?

I hear Ash ask in German how the person is doing, if their cold has cleared up, if they need any help with anything, and I'm surprised more by his tone than by his late-night diplomatic call. If this were truly just business, then I know exactly the voice he'd use. Strong, clear, and kind in the way that weather is said to be kind, not because of its unpredictability, but because of its distance. It's so easy to earn Ash's respect, his good nature, his earnest collaboration—but his genuine affection and warmth? You might as well try to cup a sea reflection of the moon in your hands. You'd feel foolish for even hoping.

But right now, on the phone in the dark, speaking German and making plans, his voice is gentle and concerned. Not how he is with his prince and princess, but how I remember him being with the victims in the war. *Vy v bezpetsi, vy v bezpetsi,* you are safe, you are safe.

Who the fuck does he know in Germany who deserves that kind of voice?

He ends his call and stands for a long time at the window, looking out at the city spread below. I know what he sees. It's a model train world of overnight janitors and ambling cabs and trashmen coming for the trash mountains that sprout on New York sidewalks after midnight. Small and twee and twinkling from so high up, and also so big and so busy as to inject even the most extroverted person with a dose of pure, existential loneliness.

"You don't have to pretend to be asleep," says Ash after a while. "I wouldn't mind the company."

I get up, and I'm past caring that I'm naked, past caring that my body bears every bruise and slap and suck of my defeat tonight, and I go to stand next to him.

He looks at me. "I don't suppose if I asked you to kneel, that you would?"

I study his profile in the multihued city lights, the silver threads in his hair and the fine lines hidden around the edges of his mouth and eyes. It's a joke that the presidency ages the men and women who bear that burden, but it doesn't feel like a joke to me right now. Not when I can recall that virile young man from the mountains, not when I remember that for the last two years I've only added to his burdens. "Do you need me to?"

"Just for a moment."

I kneel. And I feel him relax the moment my knees touch the carpet, the moment my head bows, as if he's remembered how to breathe simply by watching me humble myself. He runs a fond hand over my hair, once, twice, letting it stay heavy and benevolent at the crown of my head on the third time over, and we stay like that for a long time. Hotel carpet pressing into my knees, Manhattan glowing lambent and drowsy outside.

And after the silence has become comfortable and close, he whispers, "Look up at me."

I look up at him.

In this light, he is half-real, shadowed and masculine and powerful, like the deer-horned god my aunt Nimue is so fond of, and I can't be sure he's *not* that, not some kind of pagan infusion of greening life force into the body of an energetic and potent man. It's a silly notion, beyond silly, and I would tell anyone as much in the daylight when there were miles between Ash and me—but right now, at his feet and in the gloaming city dark, the notion doesn't seem silly at all, and I have the strangest sensation of knowing this moment already, of this exact same feeling, like déjà vu, except I can't pinpoint where the déjà vu comes from. I just know that it's real, that somehow I've lived this same scene before, kneeling in a cloud of my own betrayal before a weary king and thinking *he is part god, he is more than just a man, and if he is just a man, then he is the best man ever to have lived.*

Ash looks down at me looking up at him, and his entire face seems to melt in relief at whatever he sees. He breaks into a smile so heartbreakingly beautiful that I can't bear it.

He murmurs something so quietly that I can barely hear it, but hear it I do.

"Still the whole world" is what he says.

And together we fall through this moment, a king and a prince and the whole world, until we land with abrupt pain in the light of day and I sneak out of his room, bruised and shamed, and back to a campaign only a few steps behind his.

No man can keep the whole world forever, after all. Which is why it's better to burn it down before it slips away.

CHAPTER 19
ASH

THEN

ON A COOL SUMMER NIGHT IN LONDON, I LET MY HEART drop to the floor. I let it roll in broken glass. I let every tiny shard and splinter pierce into me because the piercing was like a form of worship, a religious experience. For one hour, I felt with this flaxen-haired princess what I thought I could only ever feel with Embry, and it meant so many things, for me and for her, for the man I thought I was and for the king I wanted to be.

For the first time in my adult life, I fully appreciated and understood the complicated and wonderful way I felt desire, the knots and loops of a heart braided this way and that over time; because while maybe I was born into queerness, I'd also shaped it myself, I'd also thrown it and spun it and fired it into what it was now. And every sojourn into sexuality, every dead-end trail or sheer drop, every path that widened into a road or climbed summits, every step had been my own and my choice, and at the age of twenty-six, I could finally look at that with clear eyes and a clear heart. Which is not to challenge the idea that sexuality can be connate, or at least partially so, and not to dismiss those who've had their choices taken from them. It's only to say that in my own life, I've had the privilege of being an active participant in my own desire, and it took falling in love twice for me to see this and fully apprehend what it meant. To see where this bled into my need for power and for control and for unbridled devotion and surrender.

And this new truth ultimately evolved into the knowledge that this girl fit me, fed the most elemental and hidden parts of me, made me feel alive again in a way that I thought I'd been forever denied in Embry's absence. It was opening my eyes after a long sleep, seeing the sun chink through the clouds after weeks of rain, and it felt like even more than that. Like for the first time, I could see myself as clearly as I'd always hoped to, and I could see everyone else that way too.

Greer did that for me.

When I was a child, I talked like a child, I thought like a child, I reasoned like a child. When I became a man, I set aside childish ways. For now we see through a glass, darkly; but then we shall see face-to-face.

The moment I saw her kneeling, the moment I licked the blood from her fingertip, the moment we kissed, I no longer saw through a dark glass, through mirrors and reflections. I saw face-to-face. I became a man.

Nevertheless. Greer was sixteen. I was twenty-six. I had kissed and pressed my aching cock against a sixteen-year-old girl.

That was wrong. That was not moral. I left the party obsessed with her and also hoping I never saw her again because the temptation of her was too fucking much.

Anything, she'd said. *I'll let you do anything to me.*

Jesus Christ.

If I saw her again, I'd take more than her first kiss; I'd take her first everything. I'd cuff her ankle and chain her to my bed like a pet; I would play with her hair and worship every corner and turn of her body. I'd marry her and build houses with her and walk beaches with her, and then I'd carry her in my arms to the darkest places I knew and open every part of her to me and myself to her until my heart beat in her chest and her heart beat in mine.

I knew I shouldn't see her again. It was safer for her, better for her, certainly until she was fully grown, but maybe it was true that I'd always want too much from her young, open heart and so it was wiser for me to stay away indefinitely.

And as it was, the war flared up again. Krakow was bombed, and I went back to Carpathia, and then—God, how knotted and raveled my loyalties were about to become—Embry came back to me. Right after I'd fallen in love with someone else, however hopelessly, he came back and if I'd had any doubts about the nature of my desires after London, they were wiped away the moment he kissed my boot.

God, I still loved him. I loved him so much that it tore me open, and I wanted to tear him open, and Greer too, and I wanted to share everything, everything, everything, and how could I be one person and still feel so much, want so *much*, and was this how love was for everyone? Was it being queer? Kinky? Or was it just me and this new three-cornered heart I'd grown, and now that I'd grown it, had my craving and my lust simply swelled to fill the space?

Could I have ever loved just one person?

Was this a new problem? Or simply something I'd never needed to know about myself until now?

And I wasn't supposed to love Embry; he made that painfully clear when he returned to Carpathia. He didn't want my love, he didn't want any future I could give him, but oh, if he would've said the word, if he would've pressed his lips to my bare chest and murmured, *I changed my mind, love me, love me,* then I would have loved him with all the corners of my heart—I would have. And maybe there would have always been a pang for the teenage girl who wrote me her darkest and brightest thoughts, but I would have ignored it for him, shoved it so deep and so far down that it would gather dirt and moss and vines.

But that's not how it happened. I loved him anyway, but I tried to hide it—for his sake and for mine—because it hurt too much to love so nakedly when I knew it was unwanted. And I kept thinking of Greer, of her large gray eyes and her hair like light. How prettily she bled and how sweet her blood had tasted on my lips, how she wanted to kneel, and how she wanted to be dragged into the darkness and bared there. It never diminished, my burning for her. I read and reread her emails; I printed them out as if I were sixteen and not twenty-six; I carried them around for years as a kind of amulet of protection and personal pornography all in one.

I heard the questions hidden in the subtext of her very last email to me, the unwritten underneath the written.

Do you get hard when you think of me?

Do you come?

Do you want my name on your lips as you do?

Yes, yes, yes. Yes, even the sight of her name on my laptop got me hard, the serifed boat of the capital G, the pretty rill of the following r's and e's. Yes, I came. I came so much for her and she'd never know, never even realize there was a soldier across the continent who worshipped the memory of her with his fingers and his palm. Yes, I said her name, out loud when I was alone, silently if others were nearby.

It didn't escape my notice that the only two times I'd fallen in love were in laughably limited situations—Embry after a mock battle and a waltzing lesson, Greer after a single kiss—but I didn't care. For the first time since my days as a cocksure teenager, I knew what I wanted and what I felt, and I accepted it. Perhaps the only thing I couldn't accept was *not* loving who I loved, which was how I found my walls weakening around my little prince. How our vicious fucks slowly transformed into power exchanges so intimate and breathless that we were both left shaking afterward. During our little trips together—away from the public eye and the army, where we could be two anonymous lovers in a Europe that didn't care—gradually I began to slip. Taking his hand as we walked through a Florentine piazza, standing behind him as we waited in line for gelato and resting my chin on his shoulder. Ordering for him at restaurants, kissing him whenever I felt like it, staring at him instead of the paintings and sculptures and buildings we'd come all this way to see.

And he let me.

He let me, and he squeezed my hand when I took his; he leaned back into me when I stood behind him. When he caught me staring, he'd wink and murmur something dirty enough to have me hauling him by the arm to the nearest alley or bathroom and making a mess of him.

Slowly, I realized he loved me too. He loved me like I loved him, and when I looked in his eyes, I saw everything I felt. I saw a future we both wanted and he wouldn't let himself have, and I was foolish enough to think I could persuade him to want it, to take it, if only I proved how deeply I wanted it too. I thought maybe he was simply frightened of moving forward, or maybe he was worried I didn't understand the social implications of loving another man, or maybe it was a mixture of both.

I waited a long time. I prayed about it, thought about it, studied his every word and sigh and smile, and when the opportunity for promotion came up, I knew I had to act. I had to show him that I didn't want a job over him; I didn't want *anything* over him, not a rank or a place or a piece of paper in city hall, nothing. I only wanted to love him as my own soul for as long as I lived and for him to let me. That was all. *Please, please,* and with my gun pushed to my back and my knee in the cool Carpathian soil and a small velvet box in my hand, I asked him, let me be the one, let me stay with you. Let me and I will.

And Embry said no, like it was absurd that I'd even asked.

"There's a small project I'm starting," Merlin said one afternoon almost a year later. We were in Chicago, where he was living at the time; I was on a short leave of duty and he'd invited me to stay with him for a few days. We were currently on the balcony of his sleek Gold Coast condo with a bottle of good London gin and the remains of our dinner.

"What is it?" I asked, idly swirling my glass and listening to the noise of water and waves below.

"I want to start a new political party in America, and I want it to win the presidency within the next ten years. Five would be ideal."

"That's not a small project, Merlin," I said, amused. "That's an impossible one."

"I'm not finished," he said, completely serious. "I want you to lead it."

I laughed. "Merlin," I said. "I'm flattered, but aside from the fact that I already have a job, I'm not a politician. I have no political background and no interest in acquiring one."

"I'm not asking you to be a politician," he said mildly. "I'm asking you to change things for the better."

"Merlin—"

"When this war ends, America will be at a crossroads, and we need the right person to steer her to a real and stable peace. Who better than the hero of the war himself?"

The word made me uncomfortable. "I'm not a hero."

"It's just a word, Maxen. It's a word that means that you're brave and ethical and good. And that's the kind of person we need in the White House."

Everything in me was reluctant and defensive. I didn't want to be a politician. I never had. That kind of pen and paper power always seemed so ordinary to me, so clichéd. Not to mention self-seeking and hollow. Hadn't I just spent the last few years despising every politician who puppeteered wars from the safety of their carpeted offices? Hadn't I been disgusted at their lack of consistency and drive?

No. Everything about who I was and who I wanted to be rejected the idea…

…everything except this tiny, infinitesimal sliver that buried itself into my denial and resistance. *What if?* the sliver seemed to ask. *What if?*

Merlin seemed to sense that little voice, and said, "If you can make a difference in the world, you should."

I stared down into my gin, thinking.

"Don't answer me yet. In fact, don't even answer me soon. I want you certain."

What if?

What if?

But I couldn't ask myself any what-ifs without thinking of the what-ifs that really haunted me. What if Embry had said yes? What if I found Greer Galloway and she remembered a soldier from four years ago and she still meant everything that she'd written to me? What was the point of considering Merlin's wild scheme when the only two things I really wanted were so far away from me?

I looked up to find Merlin watching my face.

"There's someone I'd like you to meet tomorrow," he said.

I had no interest in meeting any new men or women.

I'd fuck my fist to memories until I died; I'd spend my nights with an aching chest and thoughts that pinged wildly from longing to gratitude that I'd at least known love on my terms—and that was how I preferred my life. But I also didn't have the energy to fight Merlin on this tonight. I'd meet this person for his sake, feel as I always felt about people who weren't Embry or Greer, and then apologetically explain to Merlin that we didn't hit it off, I was so sorry, he or she was a lovely boy or girl.

Except the next day when I met Jenny, I did feel something. It wasn't dark or brutal or strange; it wasn't transformative or heady or fateful. I didn't feel as if a veil between heaven and me had lifted, like I was somehow closer to understanding God for loving this person—like I had with Greer and Embry.

It was familiar though, in a way that was newly fresh too. Jenny talked and smiled like normal people talked and smiled; she flirted subtly and gracefully, with no subtext of hunger or despair. It made me feel normal to flirt back in the same manner, it made me feel whole again after the void Embry had ripped through me.

Will God ever forgive me for loving her because it was easy? Loving her asked nothing of me but denial, and denial felt like a relief after all the vulnerability I'd given Embry, all the honesty and the hope. A relief after kneeling on a mountain and having my heart broken. I could pretend to be a normal man. I could pretend to want what everyone else wanted.

And had I said I was happy with memories and my fist earlier? Then I lied, because I wasn't happy. I was the furthest thing from it, and here with this kind, smart, thoroughly vanilla woman, I saw a chance.

More than a chance at my own happiness, I saw that I could make *her* happy, and the only cost would be my suffering. But after I had to let Greer go, after Embry refused me and we were both miserable, being able to make someone happy with the mere act of loving them how they wished to be loved felt like a gift.

When she asked me if I'd like to grab a drink later that night, I agreed, and when we kissed later in the sparkling dark of a street corner, I let her press her lips to mine without fisting her hair, without biting, without growling or grabbing. And if it felt muted and subdued and quiet compared to the dizzying heights I'd known before, then it was reassuring. Heights only meant a fall, when you really thought about it, and it was safer to love this way.

Gently.

Without cruelty. Without raw, open need.

It would be easy, in retrospect, to believe that my love for Jenny was less real or valid than what I had with Greer and Embry. It would be tempting to say that I only *thought* I loved her or that it was a constant, painful struggle to care for her without *caring* for her as a dominant would, with firm discipline and tender affection. I did love her and I did desire her, and it was only hard sometimes. Like a barometric headache that came and went, the occasional reminder that I would always be who I was. Embry made it difficult, unknowingly on his part. Being so close, being so *him*, and there'd be these moments when our thighs might touch on the couch as we watched TV or our fingers might graze as we reached for something, and it would rise up in me, the loving of him and the particular ways I wanted to love him until he wept with it.

But still, despite him, despite the torment of that day in Chicago when I saw Greer—when the force of loving her punched a hole straight through me once again—despite it all, I did love Jenny. I loved her with all but one part of me. I stayed faithful, I served her happiness with all my energy, and her death was the harshest hell I'd ever known. And when she died, not only did she leave me when I needed her gentle, sweet love the most, but she took the part of me that could have been capable of that kind of love again.

When Jenny died, she succeeded where war and rejection had failed, and I was truly, utterly destroyed.

CHAPTER 20
ASH

NOW

"YOU'RE SO CLOSE," MERLIN SAYS. "SURELY THAT'S WORTH taking some pride in?"

I look over at my old friend. We are in the back room of a Kiev restaurant, waiting for two Carpathians to join us in a meeting I shouldn't be having and neither should they, and Merlin seems as remote and as composed as ever. I, on the other hand, am weary as shit and I'm sure I look like it. It's as if everything over the last three years has finally come to bear against me, all these emotional debts have now come due, and I can't pay them. The cumulative weariness of the office and the campaign and Greer's loneliness and Embry's betrayal and my faraway son…and and and.

There will never be an end to the ands. Once upon a time, all I wanted was a horse farm with the soldier boy I loved—now I'm in an Escher staircase of crisis and exhaustion.

"I'll take pride when it's finished," I say, rubbing my thumb along my forehead. "I'm still not sure I trust that it's real."

"You've built this carefully over three years," Merlin assures me. "Of course it's real."

Careful is another word for *secret*, and while Merlin has never been uncomfortable with secrets, I certainly have. Perhaps it's the soldier in me, but all the plotting and late-night phone calls and even this trip, which we hid from the press and everyone else for as long as possible, makes me tired and doubtful. I wanted to avoid war at all costs, but subterfuge doesn't sit well with me, and all this sneaking around is beginning to feel like a fairly high cost indeed. Especially if we fail.

The door to the private dining room opens and in steps a man I've never seen before, short and balding and eminently bland, and then behind him comes the delicate doll figure of Lenka Kocur, Melwas Kocur's wife. She is the person who will destroy Melwas. Not me, not Embry. This will be her victory and hers alone.

I stand and take her hands, kissing her on the cheek. She flushes warm and smiles at me. "Hello, President Colchester," she says in Ukrainian. "May I introduce Denys Shevchenko?"

I release Lenka and give Shevchenko a handshake. His grip is firm and dry, and his face when he meets mine is honest, creased with the faintest edge of concern. And he absolutely should be concerned. I've brought him and Lenka here to discuss treason, after all, and if he wasn't nervous, if he didn't grasp the gravity of what this meeting could reap for him, then I'd think less of him.

"Let's sit," I say, also in Ukrainian. "Mr. Shevchenko, I assume Mrs. Kocur has informed you why we are here today?"

He nods.

"And what are your thoughts?"

"On Melwas? On this plan?" He sighs, and he looks like

any middle-aged man sighing over something thorny and difficult. Both his ordinariness and his sighs make me trust him more. When Lenka told me about him, I'd immediately seen the wisdom in the choice. Shevchenko is the current Carpathian minister of state, with a long résumé of work for the Ukrainian government before the war and also within various intergovernmental agencies in Europe. He's a bureaucrat, a genuine diplomat, and however boring he would look giving national addresses, he's sedate and mild of temper and he knows how to run a country.

"Both," I say.

"Melwas is a monster," he says with a shrug. "And this plan could be madness, but I think it is necessary madness. Carpathia will not survive under his rule, and the people know it. And especially once they learn the truth, I think they will be very eager to be rid of him."

"And you have the support of your parliament? What about the military?"

"They are with me," Shevchenko says with cautious confidence. "They are ready to move as soon as the information goes public."

"And they will support you as interim president?"

At this, Shevchenko gives me a reluctant, sad smile. I recognize my own reluctance in that smile, the same hesitation I showed Merlin when he asked me to lead his new party. "For better or worse, I suppose," he says. "I still believe it should be someone else, someone with more, ah, charisma." There's a self-aware tilt to his lips. "I know I'm not the picture of a leader."

Lenka shakes her head, puts her hand over his. "Melwas was the picture of a leader, Denys, and look where that got us. We need someone with the heart of a leader now."

I stare at them both for a long minute, then glance over to Merlin, who is sitting back in his chair with his legs crossed and his head propped on his hand, his expression seeming to say, *Well?*

I take a breath. Perhaps it had been a formality, insisting on meeting Shevchenko in person, but I'm glad I did, because I trust him.

"You have my support," I say. "And my country's, provided you act fast. There's a possibility I won't be in office within a few months, and I can't speak for what will happen then. But you do this now and I will do everything in my power to help."

Lenka breathes a sigh of relief. "Tonight, then. We will do it tonight."

I turn to her. "And you will be safe?"

She nods. "Melwas believes I'm visiting family now, but I've already arranged for asylum here until he's imprisoned and it's safe to return."

"You are very brave, Lenka," I tell her. "This is a courageous thing to do."

Her eyes shine as she says, "I never would have been brave enough to start without that ballroom dance so long ago. Thank you for being patient with me, and for your friendship."

"Always."

And then it's arranged and done, the overthrow of my greatest enemy. And it happened in suits and heels over an expensive dinner, and while it's everything I've always hated about politics, I know we've done the right thing by moving slowly and quietly.

We've avoided a war, after all.

Almost three years ago, I asked Lenka Kocur to dance with me in Geneva, and while it was the first time I'd ever met her, it wasn't the first time she'd met me.

“Bassas School,” she said quietly as we moved across the dance floor. “Do you remember it?”

Of course I remembered it. The insurgents had stormed into Bassas in order to block off a key road, shooting anyone who tried to stop them and lighting almost everything on fire to block our vision. Most of the town had managed to shelter in the high school, and there had been a bitter argument between me and my superior—he’d wanted to secure the entire perimeter before evacuating the school; I’d wanted to secure a safe passage out and start evacuating right away. In the end, I’d pretended not to hear his last radioed order and evacuated the building without securing an entire ring around it, and a good thing too, because the building went up in flames not moments after we got the last people out. I could have been court-martialed, but instead I was proclaimed a hero. Proof that PR makes all the difference in the end, although I only allowed myself a single short moment of cynicism afterward. It was enough to have done the right thing, and if I had been punished for it, I would have accepted it gladly, knowing that people were alive and safe because of what I’d done.

“I was one of the people trapped inside,” she continued. “You saved my life that day.”

“It was nothing,” I said, a little embarrassed. “We were just trying to help.”

“It was something to me,” she said. “The revolution—it was supposed to make our lives better. In Bassas, that’s what we wanted. But the revolution didn’t happen the way we thought it would—the young people who joined, it was like they forgot where they came from, and they’d torch their own family’s farm if they thought their family was anti-Carpathian.”

“I know, Mrs. Kocur.”

Her face turned bitter and sad. “It feels like there’s no

justice for what happened—we have a new country, yes, but it's half-empty and most of it is still in ruins, and there's still so much pain. No one ever had to pay for that pain. They became rich, they became leaders."

"Like your husband."

She looked up at me. "Like my husband."

"If you don't mind me asking," I said, trying to be gentle. "Why are you married to him?"

"I had no choice," she said, blinking back some terrible memory. "They came through Bassas a second time, killed my father and my brother. That's how Melwas saw me, crying over their bodies, and he told me that he'd kill my mother too if I didn't come with him. At first I was nothing more than a camp follower, a mistress that he loaned out whenever he pleased; then he had this idea that he couldn't be a president if he wasn't married. I suppose I was the convenient choice."

"I'm sorry," I said, and I was. "Can I help?"

"Well," she said carefully, "I think you might be able to. Do you remember Glein?"

My throat tightened on reflex; I swallowed against it. "Yes."

"There was footage of that night. A rebel following Melwas had recorded their incursion into the village, wanting to document a glorious victory for the cause. Instead he caught Melwas and his fellow soldiers sending the village's children out to die on that boat."

I stared down at her. "There's proof?"

She stared back at me. "Clear proof."

"And you have it?"

She nodded.

"What would happen if you released it?"

At that, she sighed. "I don't know yet. And I don't know what would happen after it was released—what if someone worse than my husband came to power? What if our country sank into chaos again?"

"You'd have to be careful," I said, even though my thoughts weren't being careful at all. My thoughts were spinning, racing. If Melwas could be exposed as a murderer, if he could be imprisoned or impeached, if someone new and safe could replace him…

So many problems, solved.

But it would have to be done with so much caution, and no one could ever, ever know I had a hand in it.

"Will you help me?" she asked.

"I'll help you," I said immediately. Because there was caution and then there was passivity, and I refused to be passive. "When can we talk next?"

"Not for a while," she admitted. "But I go to Berlin to visit family in several months. There I can find a place to call where I won't be overheard."

"You call me from Berlin when you can, and I promise I will pick up the phone."

She smiled, the first real smile I'd ever seen on her face. "Thank you," she said. "Thank you."

It took me almost three years to bring down Melwas, and it's happening right now as I drink my scotch and read through my debate notes on a plane thousands of miles away. It's anticlimactic…and that's how it should be. That's how I wanted it. Democracy is anticlimactic, and so is peace. Peace is working and working and working, and knowing that if you do your job right, most people won't know you've done a job at all.

"It's why I chose you," Merlin says out of nowhere, nursing his own drink.

"What?"

"It wasn't just that you were smart and looked good in a suit, Maxen. I wanted you for this job because I knew that you would do something like this. Pour time and energy into something that stayed hidden. You don't do things for the glory; you do them because they are the right things to do, and that, above all, is what makes a good leader. And a good person."

"That's kind of you to say. Thank you."

He makes a *tsk*ing noise. "You're allowed to feel proud, you know. Happy. Take joy, even just for a moment, in what you've done."

Proud.

I'm too tired to feel proud; I'm too tired to feel smug—although I'd be lying if I said there wasn't a small part of me that *wanted* to muster up smugness, that wanted to revel in the satisfaction of having resolved this without war, without violence, and without Embry. He had doubted me and I had succeeded.

It should feel good.

But the satisfaction isn't there, and neither is the pride. There's only fatigue and the faint worry that somehow this might make things more dangerous for Embry in the long run. The Carpathian extremists have been hating and threatening him with relentless energy over the last two months, and if Melwas is taken down, if the country is put into the hands of a bureaucrat and it's clear that the extremists won't get the war they so crave…what then?

No, I can't think about this right now. That by saving my country and theirs from war, I've put Embry in danger.

Except now it's all I can think about.

I press my fingers into my eyes for a moment, trying to think of the most coherent way to explain to Merlin how far away from *proud* I feel. "I have a debate in twelve hours, and I haven't slept in over twenty-four. The press is dragging my name and my son's and my sister's through the mud as we speak, and we can't get anyone to focus on the issues because they're so obsessed with the incest I committed sixteen years ago. I don't know right now what will happen to Lenka or Carpathia or Melwas. I don't know if I can take joy in any of it yet, or if it doesn't matter because it's onto the next thing. I want to do the most good for the most people, but right now I'm tired and heart-sore and it feels never ending. The things to do are never ending and all my losses feel never ending. I'm at a deficit."

"Losses. You mean Lyr? Embry?"

I rub my face and drop my hands. "Yes."

"Lyr will perhaps always be a shadow on your heart, but as for Embry—it was worth his anger to solve the Melwas problem this way."

I want to raise my voice, I want to scream, but I'm too tired, too broken. "Maybe," I say, just to end the conversation.

There's a long pause, a silence in which I want to lay my head on my desk and close my eyes. I settle for staring at the ripples in my scotch, drinking the ripples down. Merlin does the same.

"Maxen, I need to tell you something," he says after several minutes of this. His tone of voice has changed from his usual cool sharpness into something different. He almost sounds *uncertain*, and that above all makes me go still.

"I—" He gives a small laugh. "I'm not sure where to begin, but I don't know that it matters. Either way it will be impossible to believe. But I think believe you must, if we are to go forward—"

Belvedere chooses that minute to open the door to my office. Merlin and I both turn.

"Sir, I thought I'd tell you that the news has just broken about Melwas. The Glein footage is everywhere, and Carpathians are starting to gather in protest in the streets. It looks like some people are already calling for his removal."

Merlin stands. "We can finish this another time. Ryan, make sure that our president gets some sleep after he's briefed. He needs it."

I don't get any sleep.

The insomnia is too familiar a bedfellow to surprise me, but I do find myself annoyed with it. I try the bed on the plane with no luck, and then after we land in Denver, my hotel. It's the morning of the debate now, and I draw the curtains against the sunshine and take off my clothes. I close my eyes and meditate like a sixteen-year-old princess suggested to me years ago. I hate that she's not here now, that she's doing some campaign event in California for me, because fuck the campaign. I want her with me, in my arms, tracing sleepy circles on my chest.

I breathe. I try to clear my mind.

Melwas is handled.

I've already won one debate; I'm well prepared for this one.

I can sleep, I can sleep, I deserve to sleep, I need to sleep, there's no reason I can't—

If only Greer were here. If only, if only, if only—

I doze off for a weak hour, my consciousness in and out, and there is a dream, a dream about a boat, a boat that will take me someplace I need to go. The sound of water laps through my dreams, and there's the flash of sunlight off a sword as it's thrown into a deep, still lake—

My eyelids flutter open and I'm breathing hard. I can still smell the fog and the grass, and the strange tang of blood…

It was just a dream, Ash, I tell myself. I flip over onto my stomach and try meditation again.

Hours of this go by. Racing thoughts, irritation, breathing. Until I realize that I'm nudging close to two days without sleep now, and I need to get up and shower and dress because it's time for the debate.

I wish I could say that I perk up as I reach the University of Denver, that my mind somehow shakes off the murk and the gripping haze of exhaustion. I wish I could say that even though I don't perk up, I still manage to stand beside Embry and deliver a ringing offense and defense of the night's topics.

I wish I could say that I win.

But I don't.

Instead, I fumble for answers that normally I know well. I struggle to keep up with Embry's charming, smiling arguments, and I can't seem to gather my thoughts together. They drift away like leaves on a lake; they slip through my fingers like water. I sound as I feel—tired and confused—and the debate seems to last weeks. It's my entire life, these bright lights and the handsome, sweet form of the man I love growing even handsomer and sweeter as he fills with strength and confidence, as he realizes he's winning. I see him glance at me once or twice, that confidence tempered with concern, as if it worries him that I'm not doing well, and I'm so grateful for those glances that I almost forgive him for winning and myself for losing.

When it's over and I walk off the stage, everyone is silent. Belvedere and Merlin and Trieste. They don't say anything as we make for the car, and I don't say anything, and there's nothing to say really. I lost. I'm fried from my trip to Kiev and this campaign and Lyr and everything, and it got to me. I deserved to lose.

A young woman runs up to me, and I recognize her as Embry's personal assistant, Dinah. "Mr. President!"

We stop and I hold up a hand to stop Luc, who's just stepped forward to block her path. She's out of breath, like she's sprinted all the way to me, and her hand is slightly damp as she presses a rectangular plastic card into my palm.

"The Four Seasons," she says, glancing over to where Merlin and Trieste stare at her and looking a little intimidated by them. "He said he'd be there tomorrow too."

And with a flush, she turns and leaves.

"Well, you definitely won't get any sleep now," says Merlin.

Chapter 21
Embry

NOW

I ALMOST EXPECT HIM NOT TO COME. IN FACT, I'M *CERTAIN* HE won't come; I don't know that I would, in his shoes, and given what's on the news at this very moment…

Complicated, shameful fury overwhelms me once again, just like it did after the debate when I sent Dinah after him. No, he has to come, he has to.

I'm pacing and tugging at my tie when I hear the electronic clunk of the hotel door and turn to see Ash walking in.

He looks like shit.

No, he looks good enough to eat.

No, it's both.

He wears his insomnia like fucking Heathcliff and his torment like Edward Rochester. The smudges under his eyes only set off how green and brilliant they are, the tired press of his mouth just begs the person looking at it to make him smile, make him laugh.

His hair is in the kind of Stygian tousle that would make Charlotte Brontë cream her Victorian panties, and his sweater clings to the hard planes and curves of his chest and stomach and arms. His tailored slacks hang off his hips like they worship his body.

Same, pants. Same.

And that desperate exhaustion surrounding him—it's heady, it's intoxicating. He looks wrecked and reckless, beaten and dangerous. Everywhere on me I feel goose bumps, a wisp of fear ghosting over my skin, telling me, showing me, warning me.

I ignore the warning.

"I won," I say after the door closes and he faces me. "So I get to do what I want with you."

"Is that right?" he says. It's the first nondebate thing he's said to me all night.

"Yes," I respond. "That's right."

"And what do you want to do with me?"

As if I hadn't had the last two weeks to think about it. As if I haven't had the last sixteen years. "You're going to kneel in front of me and suck my cock," I say.

A faint smile tilts his lips, the first smile I've seen from him all night. "If you want it, you're going to have to take it."

"Is that a dare?"

He lifts his chin, already roughening up with delicious stubble, and I take a step forward. And another. And another, until I have him caged in against the wall. "It's the truth," he says.

I use my extra half inch on him now, forcing him to look ever so slightly upward. "Do you think I won't take it?"

His eyebrow arches the tiniest bit, that small smile still on his perfect lips. "Here's what I think, little prince. Here's what I *know*—and you know it too. You don't need to call me sir to submit to me, and I don't need you to kneel to know that you're my possession. You may not wear a collar, but we both know the minute I snap my fingers, you're mine. And you can fight me all you want because it doesn't change shit between us."

His words are scalding the air between us, and I'm so fucking hard right now, hard and furious. Furious that I won, but that I only won by caveat. Furious that he's right about me and about him.

"Tonight's not about that," I growl, and it's too late—a touch of defensiveness enters my voice and he hears it.

His smile deepens but his eyes grow harder. My awareness of danger grows and grows. "You think tonight is about you getting to dominate me at long last," he says, leaning forward so he can breathe into my ear. "But you're wrong. You think what we have is about titles or words? About sex positions? You think I can't dominate you while you're fucking me? Then you don't know the first thing about it. I'm telling you I could have your cock in my ass and a gag in my mouth and I could still own you."

He pulls back, satisfied. "So by all means, Embry, vent your anger on me. Wrestle me, hit me, kick me, tie me up, and fuck me raw. And when you come, you tell me who belongs to whom."

I can't answer him, I *won't,* because I hate him so much for being right, for being weak enough tonight for me to win, for being strong enough always that winning is as unbearable as losing. I collar his throat with my hand and crash my mouth into his in a bruising kiss that steals our breath and closes the distance between our hips. As our tongues and lips and teeth fight, our hips do the same, pressing and grinding and sliding, all male, all rough, muscles and thighs and trapped cocks.

"I wish she were here," he says against my lips. "She'd love to see you like this. And see me like this, maybe."

I kiss him even harder in response, imagining Greer with her curious little hands and her wet little cunt, and I know he's thinking the same, and we're both all the more desperate for it, for her. We want her and she's not here, and we *need* her—any combination of twos has always been unstable, volatile; we always need to be a three, and somehow I know that the reason tonight won't end well is because Greer isn't here. Without her we are nothing but flames and pyroclastic debris, ready to level cities.

I tighten my grip on his throat, and oh, it feels so good: that big, strong neck under my fingers, the hard lift of his Adam's apple knobbing against the heel of my palm.

"The sides of my neck," he murmurs.

"What?"

He reaches up and uses both hands to center mine, so that my thumb is on one side of his neck and my fingers are on the other. There's something so erotic about him showing me how to choke him, so intimate, that I feel almost close to tears looking at his two hands cradling mine around his throat, showing me where to push in.

I do push in at his guidance, biting at his lips and jaw as I do, and within a handful of seconds, I see his eyes begin to flutter, his lips begin to part. I ease up on his neck, watch his eyes brighten and focus once more, watch his tongue dart onto his lower lip, as if waiting for mine to join his. Then I press in again as I kiss him, feeling his mouth go soft against mine. His hands drop to fist my shirt and loosen and tighten and loosen and tighten in tandem to my playing with his consciousness.

I watch him grow flushed, dizzy, drunk looking, swaying on his feet, and it's so fucking beautiful to have a king like this. Compliant and warm and trusting—and the amount of vulnerability he's showing me is shocking and terrifying and wonderful.

Is this how it feels to him? Like a gift? Like a secret?

I could watch my hand on his throat forever, watch his handsome face go soft and urgent at turns, but I want more, I need more. One final time I squeeze, until his eyes almost close for real, and then I let go and kick his feet out from under him.

He falls to his knees with a surprised grunt, and before he can recover, my hands are at my zipper and I'm fishing out my dick, shoving it past his full, bowed lips. His lips are the only part of him that's soft and yielding, the only part of him that looks more ready to love than to rule.

The moment my head touches his lips, I exhale with a ragged grunt, and then when my cock slides past his teeth, I'm undone. I'm beyond being able to draw in another breath. The sight of it—oh God, how many nights have I come in my hand just imagining it—and now here it is, my big strong bull on his knees, lake-green eyes staring up at me through eyelashes like dark fans.

I pull out for a moment, just so I don't come right away.

"You'd like it better if you held me," he offers, raising his hands, and I get the picture right away. I cross his wrists together and pin them above his head, a position that makes me lean forward and makes it all the easier to push into his mouth.

And suddenly I'm so angry again, I'm so ashamed and furious. How dare he *help* me, how dare he peer up at me with that pretend docility that his heated gaze declares a sham? How dare he lose? How dare he be him when all I can be is me?

I thrust into his mouth with a coarse movement that sends me to the back of his throat, and I'm rewarded with the sound of his choking a little. "So even the great Maxen Colchester has a gag reflex," I mutter, which earns me a reproachful glare from below.

"Well, now you know how the rest of us feel," I counter in a surly tone, shoving into him again to make him gag, but to my shock, he opens his mouth like a pro, and suddenly my tip is being squeezed by the tight heat of his throat. He swallows around me, a constriction unlike anything I ever could have dreamed of, and I cry out, rocking against him, seeking out more and more and more.

I try to soak in every moment of my angrily face-fucking the president—the feel of his crossed wrists straining the grip of my hand and the occasional scratch of stubble along my rod or against my balls when I'm all the way down his throat. His watering eyes and tousled, highwayman hair. The noises he makes—crude, wet, mechanical even—the glisten of his lips around my erection.

I let him have every angry thought, every angry flare and flash that has haunted me over the years, every time I've wanted to hurt him or hurt myself or hurt both of us just so that I wouldn't have to feel so fucking much anymore. And I give him every feeling now, even awe in the midst of all this anger, awe that I have a king on his knees and my cock down his throat, and every part of it feels magical somehow, even the accidental catch of his teeth on my skin or his convulsive shudder when I hit his throat at the wrong angle.

"I'm going to come," I rasp, looking down at him. "I'm going to pour it all down your throat."

He merely nods, as if I've said something mildly interesting. Nods with his eyes streaming the tears of the deep-throated and his lips stretched wide around me. And then I do something I've wanted to do for sixteen years, and I fuck him as hard as he's ever fucked me, I fuck him, wanting him to feel as I feel—torn apart with him, shredded by him.

Nothing without him.

It comes all in a rush, and I grunt, "Fuck, fuck, yes, all the way down, fuck, *fuck*—" and I can feel the contractions and clenches in my belly, in my thighs, I can feel tingles sparking up to my fingers and down through my toes, and I can feel Ash struggling to swallow everything I'm jetting into him, and I look down and he's looking up at me and then I realize somehow our hands have shifted in my fury or maybe it was as I came, but I'm no longer holding his wrists.

He's holding mine.

I stare at our hands as I drain into his mouth, and then I pull away and stagger backward, bracing myself on a nearby table.

He stands up slowly, wiping his mouth with the back of his hand in a gesture that has me getting hard all over again.

"See?" he says.

"Fuck you."

"Such a mouth." Coming from him like this, it's both a quip and a compliment. *Such a mouth.* I know he's thinking of fucking it right now.

"It doesn't mean anything."

"If you say so."

He reaches down to tug his hard cock into a better position, and I have an idea—a wicked idea. "I'll let you between my thighs," I say, with a sharp smile.

I expect him to say no, I expect him to flare with anger at my insulting offer, but instead he tugs his sweater off his body right away, kicks off his shoes.

I'm speechless as always at the sight of his bare chest, his furrowed abs arrowing down to his groin, and then when his slacks are off and there's those boxer briefs clinging to the muscles of his thighs and the curve of his ass—

And then the briefs are off and I'm swallowing hard. His cock is brutal looking, a dark near-red, with pre-cum beaded at the tip, and he's so hard from sucking me off, and that thought is so fucking arousing. That I had this effect on such a powerful man simply by taking my pleasure in his mouth.

I peel off my own clothes, trying not to revel so much in the hungry way his eyes trace over my naked body, and then I move to the bed and he follows. I take the position that he's used when I've fucked his thighs and lay flat on my back. It had always felt so patronizing on his part, the way he'd lay after he got off, supine and pretending to be bored. It had always made me feel like the needy youth, the eager boy climbing onto his experienced lover and spilling after only a couple thrusts.

But now, as I'm lying back and watching Ash prowl over my body, I realize that somehow the roles have flipped again. I should be the patronizing one, I should be the one delivering bored generosity—but as he lays his massive body over mine, skin to skin, the power thrumming between us is thrumming the way it always does.

He doesn't stay against me for long, though. He moves down my body, licking at the flat discs of my nipples until they pucker tight, and licking down my stomach until my cock starts jolting back to life. And then he moves past my cock altogether and to my thighs, where he spends a long time kissing and nibbling there.

To get them wet.

He lies back over my body again, reaching between us to slide his cock between my wet thighs, and then he braces himself up on his hands so that he can look down at the sight. I look too and then groan.

It's so fucking dirty to watch that needy cock moving between my legs, my own cock now hard and leaking and whining for the party. Then Ash lowers himself so that we are pressed together *everywhere*, his face in my neck and our chests against each other's—oh God, and his hard abs against my cock, and I can feel the hair of his stomach rough against my erection and I don't care, I love it all the more for the bit of roughness.

Ash pumps his hips like a man fucking in truth, his breath loud in my ear and as my eyes rove over the tantalizing stretch of his back and ass and legs. My skin goes haywire over the feel of his cock pressing and sliding against me, and then he catches my earlobe between his teeth.

"I'm going to come," he whispers.

"Yes," I whisper back, and as embarrassing as it is, I won't be far behind him. "On my stomach," I say on impulse, remembering the first time I did this with him. "On my stomach."

With an animal groan, he's up and straddling my hips, big hand tugging rough and fast on his cock and then without warning, he reaches for mine too. I gasp and arch, and then fuck fuck fuck—

I spurt all over my own chest and face as he does the same, and he gives a muttered curse as he shoots all over me—my stomach and chest and face and even in my hair, and our eyes are meeting, and I understand. I do. I just commanded everything about this moment, and yet somehow he's looming over me while I'm covered in his pleasure.

Except it's not even that. It's not the postures or the visible traces of orgasm that tell me he was right—it's how I feel, how he looks at me now and how I know I'm looking at him. I will always belong to him, and it was silly to think that conquering his body changed that for even a second. He let me conquer him because it was his pleasure to do so, but if at any moment he had gripped my jaw in his hands and told me he was going to master me right then and there, I would have let him. I would have fought, as I always fight, because I like the struggle—but I would have wanted him to win.

Ash leans down, kisses my lips. Semen smears between our mouths and I don't know whose it is, and somehow that makes it better. And then he goes to get a washcloth for us, and we clean up in silence, passing the rag back and forth like old times. Once I'm finished, I wrap a sheet around my hips and sit against the headboard.

Ash starts to dress by the window, hiding the cock I worship and the ass I covet. And the more dressed he gets, the more tired and inscrutable he looks again.

"Are you angry with me for winning?" I ask him from the bed.

"No. Are you angry with me for losing?"

"Yes."

That does seem to surprise him. He pulls his sweater on slowly, looking puzzled. "Why?"

"Why? Because you're supposed to be strong. Because I'm not supposed to be able to hurt you. If I fight you and I win, it makes me feel…" I stop because I don't know how to say it. I don't even know if it can be said. "I want to win, *I do*, it's just that it always seemed abstract, something I could want but which would be terrifying to have. And if you can be defeated, then maybe everything else I believe is wrong."

"There are some flaws in your philosophy," he says dryly, sitting down to pull on his shoes.

"And," I say heavily, "I'm angry because I know why you lost."

"Oh, you do?"

"I saw the Melwas thing on the news today."

He stiffens for a moment, his motions slowing, and I know I've hit the mark.

"I knew it was you. That was the Berlin person you were talking to, that was the trip you had planned. And so you sacrificed your energy, your sleep, your debate performance, all for something that you can't tell anybody you did. Goddammit, Ash. It would have been one thing to have beaten you fair and square, but to know that you lost because you were off saving the fucking world beforehand sucks. It's a cruel feeling."

"I didn't do it to be cruel to you," he says, still in that dry tone, as he laces up his second shoe. "I did it to fix things."

"It was stupid," I say. "Ridiculous."

"What do you want from me, Embry?" he asks as he stands up. "To apologize for losing? To apologize for solving the Melwas problem without violence?"

My cheeks heat, and I'm defensive. "You never told me that you had this secret plan—and it took years anyway—and I'm not ashamed of what I've built my campaign on—"

"It doesn't matter," he says, pulling my hotel key card from his pocket and flicking it onto the bed. "It's dealt with now. And check your email. I've had Agent Gareth compile a folder on all of your Carpathian threats, and she will send you a new briefing every morning until further notice. If Melwas is deposed, those threats directed at you might become real faster than you think."

I sigh. "I'm not worried about it, Ash."

"Well, I am," he snaps. "You may not care about what happens to you, but I fucking do. You're *mine*, no matter how far you run, and I'll do everything under heaven to keep you safe."

I stare at him, furious all over again, and he stares back, equally angry. Neither of us says a word, and then he's walking to the door. He leaves with the quiet close of the hotel door and its lock—no door slams for Maxen Colchester. He has too much control for that. And despite the fight, despite the sex beforehand, I fall asleep fixated on one thing.

He didn't kiss me goodbye before he left.

CHAPTER 22
ABILENE

NOW

I HEAR THAT UNHAPPINESS IS GRAY. A NONCOLOR, AN IN-BETWEEN thing, the feeling of flat clouds for weeks in the winter, the smell of tired water. It's a damp, cold street under a damp, cold sky—not wet enough to shine or cold enough to ice over—it's nothing that real or beautiful. Just crumbling pavement and tire-smeared curbs with weeds pushing through the cracks. Just darkness half-heartedly lit by the blear of buzzing streetlights. Just the ruined jut of an aqueduct pressing up into the sky.

Why am I here?

I forget.

A bicyclist whisks by, all primary colors and determination, the kind of person who makes a point to exercise in the cold darkness because he's desperate for the routine or for the self-discipline or for the smugness, and I stare at him as he disappears down the trail. Everything else around me feels still and flat, even the Key Bridge, which at four in the morning is mostly empty of cars.

I climb up on the aqueduct and walk to the edge. Virginia stares back over the Potomac, still sleepy and studded with twinkling night lights, the kind that used to be in my room as a girl. Little dollhouse shore with its little dollhouse buildings and medium-rises, little dollhouse people who are happy happy happy.

Why am I here?

I sit down, not minding the bite of the cold stone through my dress. It's a very pretty dress, white and gold with a black belt, long and a little flouncy. I wore it to Greer and Maxen's engagement party, and Maxen had told me that I looked nice. He had said it in a perfunctory way, maybe, and while his eyes were glued to Greer across the room, but it was easy to tell he really meant it. Maybe if we'd been alone, maybe if Greer hadn't been there, maybe if I would have tried just a little harder to make him see…

Unhappiness is the color of Greer's eyes. Because it's the color Maxen loves.

I put on this dress before I came here. I remember that now. I remembered the earrings but forgot the shoes. I'm still holding my car keys in my hand. Where is Galahad?

Enid. I left him sleeping with Enid. That's right, because even now I can feel the plush sink of the carpet under my feet, hear my dress rustling as I bent over his crib and brushed his hair away from his face. Can hear Enid's snores in the adjoining room.

How I wish I could have loved you more, I thought. *How I wish you were Maxen's.* If only he'd had black hair instead of brown, green eyes instead of blue. Morgan doesn't deserve Lyr, she doesn't deserve to have a son of Maxen's, but I would have. I would have deserved it.

I left the little Embry baby to his baby dreams and went driving alone.

Below me, the Potomac is a cold swish and drift, boring

to watch, boring to hear, not dirty enough to be interesting, not clean enough to be pretty.

I watch my bare toes silhouetted against the dark water. Now *that* is interesting. Romantic maybe. I could see someone in a movie like this—beautiful dress, naked feet, dark river. But the movies are better; it's too chilly to stare for long and the wind won't ruffle my hair like I want. Instead it whips up in weird, sudden bursts, yanking tangles into my hair and blowing it across my eyes into my mouth.

I hate it suddenly. I hate it for ruining my unhappiness—my unhappiness is supposed to be *pretty*, it's supposed to be tragic, it's supposed to be the flower-scented Ophelia and the regal Cleopatra and the noble Lucretia. How fucking dare it be a shitty kind of cold, a shitty kind of windy?

I can't remember why I'm here still. It's like a half-forgotten word, pulled out with snapping fingers and exclamations, or a song that you can remember loving but the melody has vanished somewhere in your mind and all that's left is a single broken bar.

I stand up and walk back the way I came, off the aqueduct and down to the path on the river, thinking of the dress and how much Maxen liked it. I knew he would. I picked it for him; I've done everything for him ever since the first moment I saw his face on the television. Done everything for him since I'd discovered we'd been at the same London party mere weeks before he became a hero.

What if I'd ended up kissing him instead of the diplomat that night? What if he'd seen me first, my shape so tempting in that electric blue dress, what if he'd seen me and kissed me? Slipped me his hotel key? Said nothing but dreamt about me for years and years like I did with him?

Of course he did. It's what happened, I'm sure of it. He saw me and he was captivated, but he knew I was too young and so he waited for me like I was waiting for him, and Greer was only ever a way to get close to me—just as all the politicians and lobbyists I dated were a way to get close to him.

How can I ever tell him how much I loved him? How that love grew and grew when I was still a student at Cadbury and then later in college, as if it grew bigger the longer I lived without meeting him? As if his perfection doubled itself over and over again all those years I went without even knowing what he looked like in person? He was so bright, so perfect, all mine, and every other boy around me seemed like a cheap facsimile, a pointless fake when I had Maxen in my mind.

He had me in his mind too, I know he did.

Maxen.

Can't you see it? I can see it. Can't you feel it? I can. I'd fit you better than any woman; you'd love me like I love you if you only knew me.

Maybe you already love me.

The edge of the river is awful up close, and I watch the orange bob of an empty prescription bottle float by.

A memory floats by with it.

Pill bottles in a bathtub. A wineglass shattering on the floor and my father's voice, so angry, so angry, followed by the splash of water and a hard slap across my mother's face. He'd never hit her before or since, but she'd found the one thing that could break him.

I'd forgotten about the bathtub, the bottles. The times my mother stared at the ceiling with an empty face and an even emptier mind, when I'd crawl up next to her and try to hug her and it would be like hugging a corpse. The jags of crying that would last for days and days and days. It was easy to forget those because who would want to remember? *She's not well today* was the delicate way we talked about my mother.

Not well.

Not well meant days in bed, or flashes of anger so hot

they burned everyone around her, or strange, brittle laughter echoing through the halls. Not well meant it wouldn't be long before I was sent away again, because I upset her in mysterious ways that were never properly explained to me, because I was the opposite of the rest and quiet everyone said she needed to become well.

Am *I* well?

I pick my way closer to the shore and dip a toe in. It's so cold I feel it seeping through my skin and into every bone in my foot. Doubt follows, even colder than the water. I don't want to remember why I'm here now; I know why, but I can't look at it directly. If I look at it, I will go mad. I will go *not well.*

Unhappiness was the color of Greer's eyes as she said Dr. Ninian's name tonight. As she sat in my living room with her Secret Service agent hovering by the door, as she told me that she was going to cut me down at the knees with my own sword.

My hate became such a gentle, floating thing then, enlightened even, because I was proud of her even inside of my hatred. Who else but me remembers that pale shadow of a girl who could barely bring herself to speak above a whisper—and now she is a queen. Now she has learned to be strong and cruel. I suppose she has me to thank for that.

I could have borne Greer. I could have borne Dr. Ninian and any legal battle, any shame; I have fought and conquered much worse.

But then Greer stood up, smoothing her skirt and nodding at the Secret Service agent, who opened the door, and in walked Maxen. In walked Maxen, tall and cold and stern, in all the ways I've ever wanted, because I craved his coldness and his sternness, because I knew they would make his warmth and affection all the more special when he gave them to me…and maybe he was there to give them to me?

Maxen didn't sit. He didn't come close, careful to keep space between us, careful not to touch me. "I understand that you were the one to reveal the truth about my son to the world," he said. His voice made it clear it wasn't a question, and I shivered at the chilled rasp of it. He was angry underneath all that calm, and suddenly I felt a flash of victory. I had made him feel; I had made him feel something about me.

"Yes," I said. "I did it."

"Why, Abilene?"

He said my name. And oh, it had tasted just as good on the shared air between us as I thought it would. That cool, rough stoic's voice. *Abilene, Abilene, Abilene.*

"Because," I said, being very brave, "I love you. And Greer doesn't—not like I do, and you'll see that now."

And then his brow pinched in an expression I didn't recognize…until the horrible, nauseous moment I did recognize it.

Pity.

He pitied me.

I felt the sickening split of my gut from my heart, my heart from my head, like the three of them were separate pinballs of shame, all spinning away from each other. How *dare* he pity me? After how strong I'd proved myself? After how far I'd come?

"You must know that I will never choose you." He paused, his beautiful mouth sharp, and I saw the face of a man who could hurt people effortlessly. "And you should know that you failed. Nothing you've done has even nicked the love I bear for Greer and Embry."

Something about his words itched. "Embry?"

Neither Maxen nor Greer answered, but suddenly I knew. I knew and it sent me spinning in even more directions, bumping aimlessly off the walls and ceilings and floors.

He loved Embry too.

It explained so fucking much. The sordid triangle of the three of them—of course I couldn't compete with that, I couldn't compete with two people, and how had I not seen it before? That all the angst between the three of them was something different, something...tawdry?

"It's finished, Abi," Greer said, stepping into her husband. "You've failed to force Maxen to love you, and whether or not Embry wins the White House, I'm using Dr. Ninian to finish your career and influence—if not your freedom. The games are over."

I looked at Maxen, all the parts of me gathering again in a fever. *He* was everything, without him there was no reason to any of this, and I knew if he left right now, I wouldn't be able to breathe any longer. "I love you," I said in a wavering voice. "Maxen, I'd let you do anything to me, please. Just don't leave."

"Stay away from my family," he said quietly.

And then they left and I spun apart into clacking chaos.

And then I came here. Here where the water is cold and where the current tugs on the hem of my dress. I slip my toes under the water again, stepping all the way down. Rocks and cold mud, just as cold as the water. Then the other foot, until I'm ankle deep in the Potomac.

Why am I here?

Perhaps you've guessed by now. It was Maxen's pity perhaps, or the shame it caused, or those mean, flinty words: *I will never choose you.* He doesn't see all I've done for him, how much I've loved him, and it's no different than my parents, or my grandfather, or all the people who were supposed to love me and let me love them and instead sent me away.

I'll send myself away this time, I think shakily. Half anger, half freedom. It will be me pushing away from the world, and that will send a spear of pain right through everyone and they'll deserve it.

She died because she loved him so, that's what they'll say. *She died of a broken heart.*

I step in up to my knees now, the river sucking more insistently at my dress. From my knees to my thighs, and I'm past goose bumps now. My lips would be blue if I could see them, and I'm shivering so hard my teeth chatter. Up to my hips. My navel. My breasts. My dress is so heavy that my feet still press against the riverbed floor, but the current is pushing, pushing.

Come, come, it seems to say. *This way. We have business this way, you and I.*

The gelid water gnaws at my nerves, but I persist, pushing forward until my hair swirls dark in the dark water and I can't fight the current anymore. My feet dance along the bottom as I struggle for balance and turn back to look at the shore, and for a moment, there's a vision of another life, another Abilene. She forces back against the current and pushes to shore; she strips out of her dress like a selkie from her skin and stumbles gleaming and numb-footed to her car. Maybe she finds a way to love the little blue-eyed toddler and the blue-eyed husband whom she wrung the baby out of. Maybe this other Abilene can forget Maxen. Maybe she makes her way back to her house and starts her life over, a kind of frigid Potomac baptism that births her anew.

But even as I see the vision of the other Abilene, I despise her. I despise her for living without Maxen, for living without the hope of him, and I'm just as cursed as that Lady of Shalott poem Greer teaches.

The curse has come upon me, the Lady of Shalott says when she falls in love, and I am the same. I am cursed. I am *not well* with my love.

I turn away from the shore, and for some reason, all I

can think of is my mother's face below the rippling mirror of her bath, pill bottles bobbing like strange dead fish in the water, the elegant curve of the abandoned wineglass. I had screamed for my father, had struggled with a child's hands to pull her back into the air, had saved her life, and for that, I was sent away yet again, flicked away like a terrible, ugly bug.

There's no one to scream for me now. Whatever my failings, I've spared Galahad that at least.

And I've been flicked away for the last time.

The cold is curling into something else now, and my limbs are heavy and light all at once. The current pulls at my dress the way I wanted Maxen to, with affection and gentle insistence, and I let it, the way I would have let Maxen. I let it pull me down and forward, I part my legs to let the cold water inside me where he should have been. I let it tug on my nipples, nurse from me the way his child would have, if he would have allowed me to have his child. I let the river lick my throat and my lips; I part my mouth so it can stroke against my tongue.

My cold river lover is everywhere, cradling me, caressing me, going into my most private places, and yes, yes, yes, it's what I wanted, to be fully his so that I wouldn't have to be mine anymore, so that I would be wanted, so that there would be love waiting for me at the gates of at least one person's heart. The water is tender with me, companionable.

Eternal.

And I let it kiss my eyelids good night.

CHAPTER 23
ASH

THEN

A YEAR SPANNED THE TIME BETWEEN LOSING ONE WIFE AND finding the next, between Jenny's death and glimpsing a long fall of gold-white hair at Mass and feeling my heart roll worshipfully in broken glass all over again.

That year between wives was the hardest year of my life. Not even war could prepare me for the lingering, bone-deep grief of widowhood, and it certainly couldn't prepare me for enduring that grief so publicly, so openly. Jenny's death was the story of my election, my inauguration, my first one hundred days—all of it revolved around the wife who died young and pretty and in pain—and likewise, it was as if the world salivated over watching my pain. I often felt like a circus oddity in those days, people gathering with avid curiosity to see my red-rimmed eyes, the hurt etched around my mouth. It was as if they could see as I could the ghost of a sweet, happy woman whom I'd failed. I'd given her everything of myself that I could give, and still, I'd failed her. I'd watched the layers of her life peel away like an onion in those last weeks, until at the very last there was only the unselfish, bright soul I'd always seen shining through her amber brown eyes. And the sight of that soul shamed me beyond compare. I had loved her as gently and as thoroughly as I was able, and it still had been so much less than she deserved.

War had prepared me for one thing, however, and that was doing my work even as it felt like my world was ending. I was used to working without much sleep, with multiple crises, while the shock and confusion of a battle still stung my senses. And so I threw myself into the work after Jenny's death too. I ate and drank and breathed my new job, I surrendered sleep to it, mental peace to it, leisure to it. So long as I worked and kept busy, the grief stayed where it belonged, until one day I looked up and it wasn't quite so hideous to endure. I found I could feel sad, simply just sad, and miss her, and it didn't flood me with an inky emptiness like it had before. I could pretend it was time that was healing me, or work, or some combination of the two, but I knew even then it was neither of those things.

It was Embry.

That night a week after Jenny's funeral—the night Morgan took me to Mark's club for the first time and let me flog her—it didn't end at the club. It ended in Embry's bed, with me desperate and him supple and willing, with every one of those seven years apart being mourned with bite marks and kisses over every inch of my beloved's skin. It ended with him begging so beautifully—*more* and *harder* and *make it hurt, make me feel you for days*—and it ended with me knowing that it was wrong to take an old lover into my arms a week after my wife's funeral...and also knowing that I wouldn't stop.

I didn't stop.

Whatever restraint and resentment had been corking the

heat between us finally crumbled into the dark wine of our need, and it spilled everywhere. Stained everything with heat and urgency and a love that I'd never been able to quench, not even after a decade, not even after a war, not even after my wedding to someone else.

Let's go public, I'd murmur to him. *Let's tell everyone.* Because I wanted that, had wanted it before, had never stopped wanting it. It was stupid to deny ourselves a second time around—now when it was legal, now when I was already elected. Who cared? Jenny's death had taught me in the most vicious, sawing way that no one had forever with the people they loved, there were no promises, there was only holding tight to what you had.

I just wanted to be able to hold tight to him in public finally, finally, finally.

But he'd flush and fidget and change the subject, pain thorny and defensive in his eyes, and I decided I wouldn't push him yet. Because I *was* going to marry him, but I could be patient…for a while. Even if it meant sneaking around like our old army days, with secret fucks and private smiles and hidden hearts. Every day and every night, any moment we could steal, any yank of his tie to bring his mouth to mine, any press of a thigh on a shared couch, any nip of an earlobe to tide us over until we were alone, and then when we were alone, nothing remained undiscovered, nothing remained undone.

Save one thing.

"Relax," Mark said.

I nodded and pressed my eyes closed, trying to breathe, trying to stir up my sense of mastery over my own body, but it was difficult while I was flat on my back with my hands cuffed above my head and my knees pulled up to my chest.

I opened my eyes. Took a breath. Grounded myself in my surroundings—opulent, familiar, crowded with every tool for pain and pleasure imaginable. One of the rooms at Lyonesse, Mark's private room in fact. The décor reflected his tastes: luxurious, careful, decadent. Like the court of a king of old.

"Okay," I said. "I think I'm ready."

Mark ran an appreciative hand over my naked body, smirking a little as I tensed. His hand lingered over my flaccid cock, rolling it against my stomach and giving it a teasing squeeze. It gave a half-hearted jolt—Mark was an incredibly handsome man, after all—but both the cold toy pressing against my pucker and the condescending dominance of his touch kept me mostly soft.

He was hard though, and I couldn't help but take a small amount of masculine pride in that. Even if I currently felt no desire and just wanted this lesson over with.

"It's a shame you're not submissive or even a switch," he sighed, giving my testicles a longing little fondle. "You are a very beautiful man. I'd like to fuck you very much. And how many men can say they've gotten to fuck the president?"

"Even if I were submissive, I'm afraid the vice president keeps me too busy to share," I said with a smile.

Mark smiled too, although his expression was still edged with hunger. "One day," he murmured, hand gripping the heavy muscles of my thigh, "I'll have to find a male submissive that reminds me of you. Get it out of my system."

He cradled my testicles once more, pulling them gently upward to keep my hole exposed. "With your own subs, you'll want to dedicate some time throughout the week to anal play," he said, back into teacher mode now. "I like to make my own subs wear plugs for the first part of a scene—or even in public or at home before we play, to heighten anticipation—but be careful not to plug them for more than an hour or two, even if they tell you they can do more. Otherwise you risk injury or ulcers, or compromising sphincter control. Speaking of, I'm going to press in again with the toy, so push back against me as I do."

It was cold and hard and unpleasant, and even as I felt it slide in, I still felt like I was doing something wrong. "I thought it would feel better," I said.

"It's barely inside you," Mark said. "We haven't gotten to the good part yet."

"There's going to be a good part?"

His mouth quirked up at my words, and once again his gaze snagged on my soft penis, on my tense body. "Actually, wait a moment, will you?"

He pulled the toy out, and I heaved a giant sigh of relief as he left the room. For the last seven months, I'd been training at the club, learning how to channel my desires into safe, structured play. Not everyone agreed with Mark's philosophy that a dom should be willing to experience anything they would put a sub through, but I did, and frankly, most of it was fairly easy to endure. Maybe I couldn't find release in pain as a sub could, but I enjoyed the strength and discipline it forced to the surface. Maybe I didn't feel a dizzy sense of freedom while I was bound, but every moment in bondage was worth learning for all the ways I could later tease and torture Embry.

But this—this was the first time I was actively disliking my training, and despite how intensely I tried to peer at why, the answer wouldn't show itself to me.

Was it the domination? Was I that fundamentally incapable of submitting to a man like Mark?

Or was it the penetration? God knew I'd only just started to pick apart the ways I'd internalized messages about masculinity and sex. But when I thought of Embry inside me, there was none of this cold tension, this gritting of teeth. There was only warmth and excitement, and oh fuck, how much it would mean to him, how much it would mean to me, to still have this first between us, a first that wouldn't have to happen with blood and bullets, but with clear, open eyes and assenting hearts and with as much time as we wanted.

The door opened and then Embry walked in with Mark, obviously having come straight from his office, stress-tousled hair, flag pin, and all.

"I called him here earlier," Mark said, "because I thought you might want the extra nudge. But of course, you can tell me to fuck off if you don't want to do this in front of your sub."

Embry had stopped right in front of the door, and as Mark was talking, I watched my lover's face process what he was seeing. Me, stretched out and hands bound, legs parted. Toy, towel, lube.

I could see the minute his mouth went dry.

"No," I said softly. "I want him to stay."

Mark glanced between us and then smiled to himself. "You know, I think this might go better if I leave the two of you alone. Can I trust that you'll carry out his lesson thoroughly?" This last he directed to Embry, who looked at Mark as if Mark had just asked him if blow jobs were any fun at all.

"Uh, yeah," Embry mumbled. "Real thorough."

"He needs to try both toys," Mark said, canting his head toward the table next to the bed. There was the plug he'd been using on me earlier and a full-sized dildo, veined and lifelike.

Embry swallowed. Hard.

"And in a few different positions," Mark added, "although make sure he's still bound for one or two of them, so he can experience it while being restrained."

"Breathe, Embry," I said from the bed, amused.

Embry's voice was choked when he finally managed speech. "Okay. Okay. Yes—restrained. Toys. Positions. I can do that."

"I thought so. See you two later." Mark laughed, and then he left us alone.

Embry drifted over to the side of the bed, pulling absent-mindedly at his tie knot and blinking fast as his eyes moved between my naked thighs and the table of toys. I was having so much fun watching him that I'd almost forgotten to be unhappy about my upcoming lesson.

"Stop dimpling at me," he grumbled. "This is hard enough to handle as it is."

I couldn't stop dimpling at him, though. He was just so fucking cute, stripping off his tie and jacket with shaking hands, his teeth digging into his bottom lip as if he couldn't trust himself even to speak. It was like watching a child glimpse the presents under the tree at Christmas, except a thousand times better because it was a grown, vigorous man who was glowing with uncontrollable excitement.

Embry finally managed to pull off his jacket and tie, and after dropping them in a crumpled and expensive mess on a nearby chair, he rolled up his sleeves and managed his first real breath since he walked in. He put a knee between my spread legs to climb onto the bed, and I never thought I'd enjoy the sight of him crawling toward me fully clothed—especially not while I was naked and bound—but my breath caught regardless. Maybe with Embry it didn't matter what we were doing. Or maybe it was because it all felt like something I was allowing, something I was giving, rather than something he was taking. Either way, my cock was stiffening, going thick. The moment he saw it, he froze.

"Shit," he muttered, closing his eyes. He appeared to be counting to ten. Even from down the bed, I could see the ridge of his own erection shoving hard against his pants.

"Okay," he said after a minute. "Okay."

He finished climbing onto the bed and knelt fully between my legs, close enough that I could feel the fabric over his knees brushing against my inner thighs. He put his hands on the tops of my legs, his thumbs brushing the sensitive skin where my adductor muscles creased into my groin, and my cock stirred, giving a lazy bounce up before coming back to rest on my belly. Embry's head dropped between his shoulders.

"I'm sorry," he mumbled. "This is just a lot to take in."

"Me tied up? Or that you get to use toys on me?"

"Don't forget your stupid dimple, you asshole. Okay. I can do this. Without coming in my pants. I think." He reached for the plug and a little more lube.

"Have you done this before?" I asked, watching him. "The toys, I mean?"

He flushed a little again. "There's not a lot I haven't done, I guess. Yes, I've used toys on someone before."

"Does it always get you this hot?" I asked curiously. I would definitely be filing away this information for later.

He gave a very cosmopolitan shrug, at least as much as he could shrug while expertly swirling a dab of lube around the end of a butt plug. "It's always fun, but"—he leveled a look at me—"you know this is different."

I dropped my head back on the pillow. "I'm glad. It's different for me too."

"Ash, I…"

I looked back up to see him swallowing again, this time from something other than unabashed lust. My own throat tightened, and I wanted all of a sudden to beg him again—no matter how ridiculous it was with me naked and tied up and him with a butt plug in his hand—just to marry me, just to fucking marry me, and to hell with everything else.

"Thank you," he continued. "For trusting me enough to do this. For giving me this."

"Of course."

"No," he said, closing his eyes again. "I mean it. I…don't feel worthy of it." He opened his eyes and it felt like there was no other color in the room. Just blue, blue, blue, and it would be the only color I'd ever be able to see again.

"I want you to have all of me," I said simply. "It doesn't mean that I don't feel like you're still my little prince as we do it; I do. All it means is that I want to allow you everything, I want to share everything, I want nothing left undone between us."

Embry gave me a hopeful look. "Does this mean I've earned it?"

I couldn't help but smile again at his eager expression. "No," I teased, not because no was the real answer, but because I decided right then and there that he'd earn it the minute he said yes to me. The minute he let me marry him, we'd mark that minute with our last first. Him inside me.

My cock surged at the thought, and he laughed. "It turns you on to say no to me?"

"No," I said seriously. "It turns me on to think about when I'll say yes to you."

Embry froze again. "Jesus Christ," he muttered. "You can't say shit like that right now, or it's just going to be embarrassing for me." Then he managed this thing where he peered up at me through his eyelashes somehow, even despite being above me. "So you know what I'll have to do to earn it? What will make you say yes?"

"I do." *It's you saying yes to me, say yes, Embry, be mine, be my husband and I'll make sure you never regret it. I'll make sure you're the happiest man alive, just say yes.*

He kept doing the peering thing, the Jane Austen hero glancing sidelong across the ballroom thing—if an Austen hero had been obsessed with fucking another man in the ass. "Are you going to tell me what it is I have to do?" he asked. "Or will we be in our nineties before I get to top you?"

"First of all, fucking is not the same as topping, which you'll find out when the time comes. Second of all, I've just decided that I'm not going to tell you." I grinned at him. "I think you'll figure it out for yourself fairly quickly, though."

And God, I did think that. I was so certain of it. He'd realize when I proposed how vulnerable I'd been with him always, how willing I was to surrender myself and my pride and my heart and how it had been that way for fourteen years and how it would never change. How I wasn't asking for anything but a yes. Just agree, just agree, and I would turn over everything to him.

Embry narrowed his eyes at me. "You are being coy tonight," he said. "Somehow, even with a butt plug in the equation, you are managing to be coy. This must be some kind of skill they teach at the G7."

"Just do it," I said, spreading my legs farther apart, and the way Embry's gaze hooded as I did that was worth every heartbreak it took to get to this moment.

"Okay," he said, one hand dropping to my inner thigh. A single thumb stroked up my seam and I shuddered, fluid leaking out of my flared, needy tip and onto my stomach. "Breathe out and bear down against it."

"Okay."

The hard tip of the toy pressed against me, cold and alien, and then Embry said quietly, "Look at me."

I looked at him.

Eyes like the sky, lips on the aristocratic side of thin, refined cheekbones and nose, that almost-curly Regency hair that just begged to swoop over his forehead in the most endearing manner. And his expression was everything—rapt, awed, eager, desperate. He wanted this as much as I did, if not more, and that fact transformed everything. It made this for him, about him, and the moment it became about him, it could be about me. Even now I can't articulate precisely what that meant or how it happened, just that his pleasure allowed me to take pleasure. Suddenly, like a switch had been flipped, it began to feel good. The tip probing at the aperture of my body warmed, pushed against the nerve endings in the pleated skin there in all the right ways, and when it finally penetrated me, the feeling was so breathtakingly dirty that I moaned.

"Fuck," Embry breathed, watching my face. "Yes. Holy shit, Ash. Yes."

He moved the plug with expert care—enough strokes not to force the issue and slow enough that there was no pain but fast enough that I was chasing the edge of discomfort the whole time. And the discomfort itself was fascinating, the way it forced openness, the way it forced trust, the way it made me feel a kind of shame I hadn't felt in years.

Then the plug was fully seated and Embry sat back on his heels, his eyes glued to my ass. "How does it feel?" he asked.

I squirmed in response. "Full." As I squirmed, my cock slapped against my stomach, veined and rigid and wet at the head.

Embry groaned. "I don't know if I can watch you wiggle around like this."

"Do you need to touch yourself?"

"Oh God, yes please," he moaned, hand already yanking at his belt, and then I had the double stimulation of his plug in my ass and his beautiful cock on display. He gave it a few rough tugs as he watched me.

"Do you want to try a few positions?" he asked once he'd tamed the urgent edge of his need.

"I suppose we'd better," I managed, even though at this point it was hard to fathom how I could breathe, much less move with this fullness. But move I did, with his helpful thumb keeping the plug seated as I flipped over onto my elbows and knees with my wrists still cuffed.

Embry made a noise behind me, and again I felt a flash of pride. That I could make a man as handsome, as charming, as sought after as him moan simply by presenting my body to him.

"You can touch me," I told him over my shoulder. "In fact, it might help me if you did."

He was on me like he'd been barely holding himself back before. His knees on the inside of my knees, his hands trailing up the sides of my hips, the crown of his unguided cock bumping clumsily into the backs of my thighs.

"Can I do the bigger toy now?" he asked in a whisper.

"Yes."

The plug slid out and then I felt the adept twirl and crook of his finger. "More lube," he explained. "Just a bit more." And then the new toy was there, and I felt a sudden tension ripple through me as I realized how much bigger this felt against my asshole than the plug, and Embry was running a calming hand down my back. "It may feel like pain at first," he told me, "but you just have to keep reminding your body that it's not pain. It's pressure. It's pressure and remind yourself that you want it."

"I want it because you're the one giving it to me," I told him honestly, and he groaned a little.

"*Please* stop saying stuff like that or I'm going to come all over the back of your legs," he said a bit irritably. "Okay, breathe out and push against me and remember that it might take your mind a moment to rewrite the feeling."

He pushed the dildo against me, and I did as he said, and he was right. It *did* hurt a little at first, and I found myself having to force back against the pain, having to breathe into my stomach to move past it. But then I looked over my shoulder at him, at his face as he slowly fucked my ass with this toy, and the pain shimmered into a brighter version of itself. A more interesting version of itself. Until the moment the crown of the silicone cock grazed against a place deep inside and I let out a shattered moan, and Embry exhaled as if he'd been struck.

"Yes, that's it," he said shakily. "That's the feeling you want to hold on to."

"Little prince?"

"Yes?"

"Fuck me with it."

"Christ. No, don't with the dimple now, are you trying to kill me? I'll go slow and then speed up."

And that's exactly what he did, with gentle twists and rocks of his hand. Slow, careful strokes that left me tingling and breathing hard, and then they turned deep and hard and rough, until the silicone was as warm as a real cock, until I was shaking and beaded with sweat. Until my stomach was clenched tighter than any fist, until my cock was harder than it had ever been and I knew when I came that I'd spray this entire bed with an embarrassing load of cum.

"God, Embry," I moaned, rocking back into the toy, which was really an extension of his hand, which was really an extension of him. I could pretend right now, yes I could, and I told him that. "I'm imagining it's you. All you."

"Fuck," Embry croaked, and I could hear his fist behind me beating his cock, the awkward tattoo of a left-handed jack as his right hand kept the dildo fucking my ass. "Are you going to come?"

"Yes, goddamn—" The orgasm was like nothing else, coming from somewhere in my body that I'd only barely known before, and it was Embry giving it to me, and I wanted to give him everything in return, and I looked over my shoulder again. "Uncuff me, I want more, I want—*shit*."

He uncuffed me, fumbling with the buckles long enough that both of us were swearing with dripping cocks by the end of it, and the moment he released me, I raised up to my knees and grabbed his hands. Somehow, despite the slide of the dildo and the tangle of his slacks and the length and width of muscled limbs, we ended up as I needed us to: his chest to my back, my legs folded outside and on top of his so that I almost sat in his lap, and both of his hands clenched tight on my cock, with my hands wrapped around his.

I fucked up into both his fists, each downstroke pushing the base of the dildo against him and back up into me, and so I was being fucked both ways, inside and out, and Embry's face dropped onto my shoulder from behind. "I can't," he mumbled. "You're going to kill me."

"*You're* going to kill me," I gasped, because this orgasm was going to kill me; it was going to rip right through me, and then I gave a final thrust right into his tight double grip and slammed back into his lap, which shoved the dildo back into me hard.

And I ejaculated. Embarrassingly.

It erupted everywhere, huge thick spurts of it, all over Embry's fists and all over Mark's bed and all over my thighs and belly, rope after rope of cum, and Embry swore up a storm the whole time, as if I were personally torturing him by making him watch this, and it spurred me on—it spurred me on to think of his cock hard and aching behind me, of how it would feel to let him inside my ass.

But even in the heat of my clenching spurts, I remembered. He had to earn it.

So finally when my climax slowed, I rolled to my back. "You can come on me," I offered. "You can rub yourself anywhere."

Without hesitation, he rubbed himself everywhere. He bucked against my thighs, he used his cock to trace the place where the dildo still stretched my hole. And then finally he braced himself above me and rubbed his cock on my semen-wet abs and came in a few thrusts, surging a fresh wave of white over my stomach.

And then, like we were boys, we both started giggling. Not *laughing*, but giggling, high-pitched noises that had us both fighting for air and our faces hurting with giant smiles, and Embry collapsing on top of me and our stomachs sliding together in a sticky mess.

A few minutes later when our giggles had settled, I tangled my legs with his and guided his head to my chest. We lay there for a while after that, me stroking his hair, him pressing lazy kisses to my chest, our bodies still glowing with this pseudo-first of ours.

"Imagine," I said gently, "how it will feel when it's your body inside of me. I can't wait."

He looked up at me with the whole world in his eyes, and then he sighed. "You're doing the dimple thing again. It's evil."

A few months later, Embry and I were walking around the edge of Vivienne Moore's lake outside of Seattle. It was morning and chilly, despite only being September, and a low mist hung over the lake and threaded through pine trees. Above us, the same mist came down from the clouds, shrouding the mountains like a pale, gray cloak. It reminded me painfully of the day in that Carpathian valley when I'd proposed.

The lake water lapped quietly at the rocky shore, and Embry made a contented sigh.

"You're happy here," I observed.

"Of course. It's home."

"You know that anywhere you wanted to live, I would live."

He stopped walking then, staring out over the fog-crowned water. "You don't have a choice about where you live. Not for the next seven years."

I stopped next to him and threaded my hand through his. He didn't look over at me, but I felt his body respond to my nearness all the same. "I don't have to run again, you know," I told him. "And I wouldn't, if that's what you wanted."

He made a noise. "And why would I want that?"

"Any reason. All reasons."

He didn't answer.

Despite his silence, a happy, nervous excitement was curling in my belly, and it had been all morning. Ever since we'd woken up and Embry had wanted to go on a walk, and we'd forced the Secret Service agents far enough back for some real privacy. The ring—the same one from all those years ago—burned a hole in my pocket, and I wanted to do it here, now, with his favorite lake at his feet and the fog wrapping us in an otherworldly blanket.

There was a large dry log set off from the shore a little, and I went to go sit on it, tugging Embry's hand to make him join me. And after I sat, planting my feet wide enough to make space between them, I nodded my head at the rocky place I'd left between my shoes. Embry flashed me a hot look, but even with his evident grumpiness, he still settled on his knees in front of me.

"Such attitude," I murmured as he finished kneeling and looked up.

"Maybe one day you'll find someone who actually wants to be a sub," he said in a surly voice.

I laughed a little at that, using the toe of my shoe to prod the hardening cock in Embry's pants. "This looks an awful lot like you like it to me."

He sighed plaintively, but I didn't let him say anything else. I took his face in my hands and kissed him, as soft as the rocks were hard under his knees. I kissed him so softly that he moaned into my mouth, so gently that his anger at being mastered melted away, as it always did. "You forget that I know you," I whispered against his lips. "You want to fight it, but this is where you're happiest. This is where you belong."

A wounded sound came from somewhere in his chest, and then he was nodding against me, emotion thrumming through him, and I allowed him to nuzzle into my neck, my chest, to rub his cheeks against my thighs and my erection. "It is where I'm happiest," he said with his face against my thigh. "God help me."

The nervous excitement leapt at that. Because now was the time, and I knew he wouldn't say no, I knew he wouldn't. How could he when he'd just admitted this was where he was the happiest? When he admitted that this was where he belonged? And surely this last year together had made him as happy as it had made me?

I pulled the ring out of my pocket, and there was a perfect moment—as perfectly golden as that ring—when he hadn't seen it yet. When his face was still against my thigh, all trust and surrender and devotion, when the asking was close enough to thrill at but the words hadn't been said yet, and everything hovered in anticipation and joy.

And yes, there was a small voice that asked me if I was ready to hear no. If I could survive Embry refusing me a second time, and the answer was that I didn't know if I could. But I did know that it was more noble to love openly and honestly than to hide out of fear, I knew that loving takes courage and vulnerability, and if I had to expose my beating heart for Embry to scorn a thousand times to earn his love, then I'd do it; it would be worth it. A million times. A billion.

"Embry," I said softly.

"Yes, Ash?" He looked up at me, and suddenly I felt so young, and he seemed so young too, we were just boys barely crossed over into manhood with all our fresh hopes and desperate love pressing up into everything.

I couldn't help it; I kissed him again. Kissed him while

I was gripped with a feeling so fierce that it made my throat constrict and my eyelids burn. "Please," I mumbled against his lips. "Please."

I pressed the ring into the palm of his hand.

Embry didn't move, and for a single second, as my eyes opened from my kiss to look into his, I saw an expression of dazzling, vivid joy. My own joy surged in response, my heart jumped, my blood spiked, and oh I'd let him fuck me right here on this shore, rocks digging into my back and everything, because he'd said yes, he would marry me, he would be mine.

And then, slowly and with the burning fall of a spark, the moment fizzled into pain.

Embry put the ring back in my hand. He wouldn't look at me. "Don't."

I couldn't make words come out at first; they were still trapped behind the joy, queued behind the happier words and kisses that were supposed to come next, and now I couldn't make any noise at all.

He swallowed. "We can't, Ash. You know we can't."

"Why?" I finally forced out the word.

"Because," Embry sputtered, straightening up and looking at me, "you're the fucking president!"

I stared at him, not sure if he was being serious or not. "I can't be queer and be the president?"

"Exactly," he snapped. "And certainly not like this. If they'd elected you knowing you were bisexual, maybe it would be different—"

I was growing angry now. "Well, I am elected now, so what does it matter who I want to marry? They can't impeach me for not being straight."

"They could probably find a reason to impeach you for fucking your vice president, though. Or something else. They'll find *something*, Ash. It won't just be reelection you're kissing goodbye, it would be this term too."

"They'll have to fight me for it, and I've always won every battle I fought as long as I had you by my side." I caught his chin in my hand, forced him to look at me. He was like a wild animal right now, a spooked horse, skittish and rearing. "Embry. Stop this…this bullshit. You fooled me the first time, but I'm not letting it happen a second time. I *know* you love me, I *know* you want to be with me. Nothing else matters."

Embry bucked against my hand, trying to pull free. "Everything else matters, Ash. God, I so fucking wish it didn't. I wish that we could just vanish from this world and never have to care about anything other than each other, but we *can't*. I promised—" And here he broke off, as if catching himself saying something he shouldn't.

I dropped my hand from his chin. "Promised what, Embry? Promised who?"

And the way he looked at me then, I somehow knew that this was bigger than this private moment by the lake. This was about everything somehow, and if he answered me, then I'd *know*, I'd finally know why I'd spent so long hurting for him.

But his look changed, grew guarded and careful. "I promised myself that I wouldn't sacrifice my career for you," he said, and his eyes screamed lies, but I couldn't turn them over in my mind properly because everything just stung and burned so fucking much. "I promised myself that I wouldn't stop chasing what I wanted, which is my own turn in the White House someday. Maybe you're comfortable being openly bisexual in politics, Ash, but I'm not yet. I'm sorry."

There was nothing to be said to that. The lake spoke for us, gentle and timeless, brushing clear rolls of water across the rocks.

"I don't suppose I can command you to marry me," I said after a while.

Embry wrapped his hand around my fist, the one that still clutched the ring that was supposed to be his. "I wish so many things, Ash, but sometimes I wish nothing more than that we'd never met so I wouldn't have to say no to you."

"Am I so awful?" I asked in a broken voice. "Am I so much worse than anybody else that you can't marry me?"

"God, Ash, no. Fuck."

"I would give up anything for you, Embry. Just say the word. Kink, the presidency, even my life—I'd lay it down at your feet if you would only love me like I love you."

Embry's head dropped onto our joined hands and I felt his tears, warm as the lake was cold. "It's not enough," he mumbled into our hands. "And I made a promise."

"Is this…is this like last time?" I asked, my voice already going tight with pain. "You're going to end it between us now, aren't you?"

"I think it's for the best," he whispered.

"I—"

But now the words really were gone, my throat too balled up and watery to speak.

Embry stood up and brushed the rocks off the knees of his pants. "It's for the best," he repeated, as if trying to convince himself. "It was fun though, yeah?" He gave me a pained smile. "While it lasted?"

I stared up at him, and I knew he could see all of my pain, and I didn't even have the desire to shield him from it. Let him see it, let him see my hurt, and if he won't walk away with my ring, maybe he'll walk away with my pain in his heart and that will be something at least.

"I'll see you at the house," Embry said, shoving his hands in his pockets and then setting off across the shore.

Me, I stayed there for a long time, until the fog was gone and the sun burned hot above, and then I stood up and cocked my arm, ready to throw that hateful ring into the lake where it could never, ever torment me again.

CHAPTER 24
ASH

NOW

"EMBRY, IT'S ASH. I KNOW IT'S LATE...OR EARLY, I GUESS. Greer just told me about Abilene, and I wanted to tell you that if you need anything, I'm here. I love you, little prince."

I end the call and toss the phone on the table in front of me, Abilene's death like a millstone around my neck. Even though I don't regret finally confronting her, I do regret her death. Less for her sake than for Greer's and Embry's, who will have to sift through all the complicated holes her suicide will leave in their lives. For the sake of a little boy named Galahad, who no longer has a mother.

How funny life is, I think, spinning the phone idly on the table with one finger. That both Embry and I should have found ourselves widowed in the crucial moments leading up to an election. And I know exactly the circus it will become. Within an hour or two, the news will be frenzied with it, and Embry will have to give a statement, he will have to perform a grief he might not feel, and it will dog his steps for the rest of the campaign.

At least it means the press will turn their attention away from Lyr.

I stand up and stretch for a moment, looking around my hotel suite, feeling so tired and lonely for a moment that I almost just want to go straight to the airport and fly back home. After speaking with Abilene, Greer and I had both flown out in the dark hours of the morning to separate campaign events, and now I'm in Kansas City having done a rally, a speech, and dinner with my mom, and then spending the remainder of the night restless and alone. When Greer called at four a.m. to say that they'd found Abilene's body in the Potomac, I gave up on sleep. After making sure my wife was okay, I called Embry, and now here I am, awake and alone in my hometown.

I open my hotel door and call for Luc. "I'd like to go for a drive," I say.

"Yes, sir," he says as if there's nothing unusual about me wanting to go somewhere in the freezing predawn cold. "Tell me where and we'll get it ready for you."

So an hour later, I'm bundled in a coat and scarf and walking through the dark, leafy hollows of a nature trail I used to enjoy as a young person. The agents are fanned out around me, but they give me space, and after a while, it almost feels as if I'm alone. Just me and the crisp darkness of early morning, the bright splash of a stream running next to the path.

The water sounds so happy, so lively, so different than the cold Potomac, and I feel a chord of pity for Abilene. She tried to have Greer killed, she assaulted and blackmailed Embry, she exposed my son to the worst kinds of public censure and ridicule—and yet, I do still pity her. She only knew love as a mangled, mechanical thing, she never knew it for the extraordinary gift from God it is, and for all the times my heart has been broken for this gift, at least I can say I've lived with it in abundance.

"I thought you might come here," a voice says from behind me. I turn to see Merlin, lean and at home in the murky woods. Through the branches, the hazy blue light of dawn casts a net of shadows over his face. The shadows move as he walks toward me, and for a moment, I feel as if I've seen this before, as if I've dreamed it. Yes, it would have to be a dream, because when I saw it before, he wasn't wearing a wool coat and a fashionable scarf and even more fashionable glasses. He'd been wearing something else, something ancient, but the net of shadows had been the same, a cold forest that looked much the same as this…and had there been a cave?

How strange.

Just a dream.

"I suppose you've heard about Abilene Corbenic?" Merlin asks, interrupting my thoughts.

"I have."

"A sad thing," he says, and together we start walking down the path again. "A very sad thing."

"She said she loved me," I say. "I feel culpable somehow, although I wouldn't have done anything differently."

"What did you say to her when you saw her the night before last?"

I push a branch out of the way as we walk. "That I wouldn't choose her. I told her to stay away from my family."

"She was dangerous, Maxen, and it was time she knew that her antics weren't working. And you have a duty to the people you love to protect them," he says. "No one is responsible for her death save for herself."

"I wish it had ended differently."

"So do I, but there was no possibility of it. Not this time."

The way he says it sends a sear of déjà vu sizzling through me. "Not this time?" I ask, and then immediately wish I hadn't. Suddenly, I don't want to be in these woods anymore, I don't want to be with Merlin, in this morning. I want to rewind time to last night, or to the last time Embry, Greer, and I were together and then just stay in that moment forever, because somehow I know that this morning is going to change something, and it's going to change it profoundly and terribly.

"Never mind," I say quickly. "Don't explain it."

"Ah," Merlin says carefully. "But it's time for me to explain things."

We've come to a wooden bridge that arches over a wide, shallow stream, and I stop in the middle, leaning against the railing and looking down at the water below. "Is this the secret you told me I had to wait two years to learn?" I ask.

"It is, and it's been two years. It's time."

"This secret of yours, will it change anything?"

"It will change everything."

"And I must know?"

"I can't see any way around it. No good way at least."

The last time Merlin hid secrets, I'd slept with my sister. I'd gotten her with child. And that child had been kept from my knowledge for fourteen years.

Merlin's secrets are not usually good ones.

I chew on my lip, watching the water frill and lace around the rocks jutting above the surface, reaching a decision. It is wrong to be afraid of the unknown—it's cowardly and ignoble. I take one last look at the water, breathe in a last breath free of knowing whatever he's been hiding, and then I turn to face him with all the courage I can muster.

"Okay, then. I am ready to hear it."

Later that night, it would be the stream I remembered the most. The clear song of it, the ordinary, everyday prettiness of water going where it needed to go. It seemed so normal, so *sane*, that it was impossible to reconcile its sweet presence with the things Merlin was saying to me. Surely those things were only said in books or in badly scripted TV shows. They weren't said on a bridge that I'd stood on a thousand times as a boy; they weren't said in some little nature park in Kansas City as the sun rose above the trees and tried valiantly to chase away the near-Halloween chill.

But it isn't later tonight yet, it's right now, on the bridge still, and I'm listening to Merlin tell me a secret. An impossible secret. And right now the water below us barely registers as anything other than noise.

"I knew who I was when I was born," he says, leaning backward against the railing in an uncharacteristically relaxed and unalert pose. His eyes are fixated on something I can't see. "As soon as I became aware of myself, as children do, I became aware that I was someone else. Or had been someone else."

I study him. Throughout our friendship, Merlin has been the definition of pragmatic, grounded, interested in practical details. It's true that Greer has told me he was very cryptic with her once upon a time; I've met Nimue, Embry's aunt and Merlin's former lover, and it's hard to believe that you wouldn't have to be a little spiritual to love someone who wears as many crystals as she does. But with me, Merlin has always been brass tacks. War, politics, information. We've never dealt in the abstract, he and I, and I'm not sure how to react now.

"Like...a past life?" I say. I know my voice is uninflected and open—a skill I've perfected while sitting down to make deals with querulous Democrats and Republicans—but there must still be something in my face that makes Merlin smile.

"Yes, I know how it sounds," he says, amusement

crinkling around his eyes. "And it won't get easier to believe, but I need you to keep listening."

"Of course," I say. "Go on."

Merlin looks back out over the stream. "My grandfather came from a long line of what they used to call cunning folk. He took one look at me after I was born and knew I was born *dyn hysbys*. A wise man. A conjurer."

"A conjurer," I repeat.

He smiles again. "*Wizard* might sound more palatable to you, if you prefer that. At any rate, the Welsh take these things seriously, or at least they did in my village, and I was put into the frequent care of my grandfather so he could teach me how to train my Sight. Make it useful. See what I needed to see."

He sounds completely calm, completely normal, even though he's using words like *wizard* and *sight* as if they are common, everyday things. "Like, for example," he continues, "that it was crucial that the president of the United States find his way to the room of his advisor one night almost forty years ago."

At the mention of Penley Luther, my stomach turns a little; my so-called "father" has that effect on me. "You knew what was going to happen between Penley and Imogen?"

"I mean, I didn't know there would be a child named Maxen Colchester and that he would win a war and become president himself," Merlin says wryly. "But I knew that it had to happen, even as young as I was. That if it didn't, everything would shift sideways and off-balance."

"And then there were more things you knew?"

"Yes," he says. "Yes, there were more. The older I grew, the clearer things became. My grandfather helped me, and I...that other self that was born with me, he remembered things. I know that sounds strange, and all I can do is assure you that it's not, that it's real."

"I see," I respond slowly. "So this is the secret? That you were"—for the sake of our friendship and also from years of politics, I find the kindest way to rephrase what he's said—"able to perceive the future?"

"I know, Maxen, I know. Believe me, if I thought there was a way I could convince you to do what needs to be done without telling you all of this, then this conversation wouldn't be happening. Alas, I can see no other way."

"And what needs to be done, Merlin?"

"Always a man of action." He smiles. "You were last time too. Fascinated by God but disdainful of what you couldn't see."

I'm reluctant to ask, but I think he wants me to. "'Last time.' What does that mean?"

"Surely, Maxen, you've noticed that things about your life are different? Extraordinary and strange? Have you never wondered why?"

"I've never thought myself or my life extraordinary," I say. "It simply is itself. And I simply am myself."

Merlin presses his fingertip to his mouth, gazing at me. "Being a secret child of a world leader? Winning a war? Having a child with your sister? The love between you, Embry, and Greer? All of that seems common and unremarkable to you?"

"Well, anything can sound remarkable if you say it like that."

"No. Not like that. You've never come across anything, any stories that feel strangely familiar? That seem to echo your own life?"

Before I can start to answer in the negative, he follows up with, "You've never felt like the air has gone heavy? Like the world is holding its breath? Like something is singing in your bones?"

I don't respond.

"Like…right now, in fact? Can you feel it right now?"

I can. I can feel it. It feels like gravity, like God, like everything has been crystalized and cut from stained glass into a vivid, magical tableau, something out of a fairy-tale book.

"How do you know about that?" I ask quietly. I haven't ever told anyone about that feeling, *ever*. Not once, not even Embry or Greer, and not because it wasn't real the times I felt it, but because those times had been so important to me, so private, so…I don't even know because there aren't words for it. It had always felt like a secret between God and me, and for someone to just *know* without me telling them…

I look at Merlin with fresh eyes.

"They are the echoes, Maxen. And perhaps they do come from God, as you've always privately believed, but if they do, then God has allowed them as such. Anchors to a life you lived long ago."

"I don't believe in past lives," I say, but my voice sounds strange in the thick air, like it lacks conviction in itself now. Maybe it does.

How did he know about the feelings?

"It's not quite a past life," Merlin says. "It's *a* life. One life. The same."

"I don't understand," I say, my brows pulling together. "The same as what? The same as who?"

"Have you not guessed?" he asks. "Have you never once sifted through Greer's research and wondered?"

I stare at him as something stirs in my mind, like dreams I've only just now remembered. Memories that can't be memories. The low cry of a baby smuggled somewhere secret. A sword flashing in the light.

The sun setting behind an island. A golden circlet set in a wave of flowing hair the color of light.

And all of the faces I've ever marked dear to me, all of the faces that I've found around me, but in places that I know I've never been, in memories that can't be real.

Greer.

Embry.

Morgan.

Kay.

Belvedere.

Vivienne Moore and Luc and Galahad and Gawayne and Nimue and—

"Stop," I say, turning away abruptly and gripping the railing. And I don't know whether I'm speaking to him or to my own thoughts. "Just…a minute. I need a minute."

From the edge of my vision, I see Merlin give me a gracious nod. "Of course."

I stare at my fingers clenched tight around the weathered wood and rusting nails of the railing. I take a breath and try to push away whatever just happened.

It's the power of suggestion, I tell myself. *He's started talking about past lives and now you're imagining the same thing. That's a natural response, right?*

One image keeps rising to the surface though, and I find that I don't want to push it away. Embry, Greer, and me alone under a massive tree, both of my lovers stretched out in the grass looking rumpled and well used, and me with my back to the trunk, looking at a flat-topped hill in the distance. The air smells like apples and sex, and next to my feet, there are two thin circlets of gold and two swords, a careless pile of metal shucked off in our hurry to love each other. Embry is dozing with his arms wrapped around Greer, and Greer is reaching for my hand. Her dress is still pushed up to her thighs and Embry is still shirtless.

"Come take us again," she murmurs. "Before we have to go back."

And I fill my lungs with the smell of summer and love, and I crawl back over to them.

That's it, that's all of the memory—or the echo or the dream—and it has me completely transfixed. I'm still staring down at my hands, thinking of that tree, of that flat-topped hill and the long limbs of my wife and lover when Merlin speaks again.

"Arthur."

And when I look up at him, it's out of instinct, like I'm responding to my name.

"You see it now," he says.

"No—I—this is not *real*, Merlin." I shake my head, trying to clear away all the false memories. "It can't be real. It's literally not possible for it to be real."

"Arthur—"

I flinch. "Don't call me that."

"You're upset."

"I'm not upset," I say in a voice that betrays exactly how upset I am. I clear my throat and start again. "This is absurd. I can't believe we're standing here talking about nonexistent past lives when we should be talking about the campaign or the country or *anything* other than..."

I can't actually bring myself to say the words. They feel childish and silly in my mouth.

"Than the fact that you are the person people call King Arthur?"

I push back from the railing to leave. This is ridiculous. I heard what he had to say, it was nonsense, and now I'm leaving. There's too much to do to entertain this...this fantasy.

"There's one more part, and then you can leave," Merlin says, reading my body language correctly. "One last thing."

No. No more things, I want to shout, but I don't. I only nod at him and tug at my scarf. I'm hot all of a sudden, hot and anxious. "What is it?"

"Embry is going to die."

My hands drop from my scarf, and everything is in slow motion, even the water trilling underneath us. I can't even get the words to make sense together in my head.

Embry.

Die.

Jesus help me.

"The last debate," Merlin adds. "A Carpathian terrorist is going to infiltrate the venue."

I force my mind to catch up, to absorb—I've always been good at reading things on my feet, at assessing a combat field within an instant—but this is different. It's so different because it's *insane.* It's ludicrous to think Merlin can somehow see the future, that he and I and Greer and Embry are all some kind of annual plant that springs up periodically with new flowers but the same roots.

But the moment he said Embry's name, something opened up inside me. Because am I willing to risk being wrong? No matter how foolish, how slight the chances are that Embry could die, am I willing to refuse to listen? No. I'm not. I'll be all kinds of foolish for my little prince.

"I can't see the details," Merlin says apologetically. "I couldn't last time either. I don't think I'm supposed to. It's like there's a veil between it and my Sight, and no matter how I try to part it, it's not meant to open for me." He sighs, looking up at the sky. "It's quite bedeviling, actually."

"Merlin."

"Yes?"

"I need you to start over and explain to me exactly what you know."

"Yes, yes, of course." He looks down to the railing, his gloved hands gesturing across the wood. "You've succeeded in containing the Carpathian threat and Melwas—almost entirely. The outliers are the extremists, and in a normal course of events, they would be no more dangerous than your average political dissident, but after Melwas's deposal, they are angry. Embry is the obvious target because he's been so publicly inflammatory about Carpathia. Kill him, and they might finally get another war, which is what they want more than anything. A war would put Carpathia back in the hands of men like Melwas, stop what the extremists see as a corrupted spiral of European integration."

"We're not going back to war with Carpathia," I say, my jaw tight. Good God, if I've done anything in my painful, flawed life, please let it be that. Please let it be that I brought peace, for however short a time.

Merlin raises an eyebrow. "Even if they killed Embry? Even if you cradled him as he died and his blood soaked through your shirt, and the last thing he whispered to you was your little Greek pet name and—"

I hold up a hand to make him stop, my eyes closing tight. He can't know, he *can't*, how much that image terrifies me, how it used to terrify me, how I spent every day in that fucking Carpathian hellhole terrified that Embry would die and die on my watch.

I take a breath. Listen to the water.

"Not even then," I finally say. "It would kill me, but not even then."

"I thought so," Merlin says, sounding gentle…and a little relieved? As if he hadn't been sure what my answer would be.

"But obviously," I state, "I'm not letting anything happen to that man."

"I know. And you will do your best to stop it—you did last time as well, although last time it wasn't Embry at the end."

"Then who?" But the moment I say it, I see it. A green field under a sky heavy with unspilled rain. Lyr's face as our eyes meet, his jaw set in trembling determination. "Fuck," I mumble, rubbing my thumb across my forehead as if I can rub away the unbidden image.

"You did everything you could. You parlayed, you sued for peace, offered half your kingdom. The lengths you'll go to avoid war are commendable. But you failed, Arthur."

"Don't call me that," I say, distracted, my mind already racing ahead to any and all practical measures to keep Embry safe. I still don't know if I believe any of what Merlin is telling me, but I refuse to dwell in any uncertainty when it comes to my prince's life. "We'll move the debate. Or we'll do it remotely, each of us in a secure location, no audience."

"If he agrees," Merlin reminds me.

"Of course he'll agree," I growl. "If I—"

"If you what? Command him? Force him?"

I glare at Merlin. "If I prove there's a credible threat."

"You won't because there won't be any evidence for it. And you can try to move venues, try to arrange for something more secure, add an army of Secret Service agents, but even if he agrees, it won't be enough."

"You're telling me," I say, my anger growing, "that there's nothing I can do or say to stop this? That I'm supposed to be resigned to the possibility that the man I love will die?"

"I'm not saying that," Merlin says, "but I am saying that you will be given a choice when the time comes."

I look at him. Study those dark eyes, that face still vibrant and handsome even with the faint lines around his eyes and mouth. "This is really it, isn't it?" I ask. "What you're about to say? It's the real thing that I need to know."

Merlin gives me a look full of compassion. "The choice in the moment will be your life or his, Maxen. I'm sorry. I wish I could tell you exactly how it will unfold and why and when and how we could stop it, but I can't see any of that. The only thing I can see with any certainty is the moment itself, the choice: Embry's life or yours."

I sit. I don't care how ridiculous it looks, me sitting on the damp wooden bridge, my coat bunching around my torso as I lean my head back against the railing. I just need to sit for a minute—just sit and *think*.

"If Embry dies, you won't go to war with Carpathia, and all your hard work will stay in place. But if you give your life for his and he becomes the president…then he might very well go to war over your death."

Merlin's right. If Embry was willing to leave me and climb his way to power just to avenge Greer's abduction, then I can't even imagine what he would do in the face of my death at Carpathian hands. And I give a bitter laugh because now I'm faced with the same choice he was two years ago—a person or a nation. One soul or three hundred million.

The king in me knows the right answer.

But the man in me does not.

"Of course…" Merlin says cautiously, "there's always the chance that Embry wouldn't go to war. That he's grown and changed enough over the last two years. That if he knew it was your express wish that he keep the country at peace…"

"I don't believe any of this," I say perfunctorily, because a small part of me is starting to believe. I don't know why, and I shouldn't, because it's clearly preposterous, but despite all that, there's this sliver of recognition inside me that I can't dislodge or pluck out. This feeling at my core that he's right, and no matter how fantastical, how delusional it sounds, that I'm somehow walking steps in this life that I walked fifteen hundred years ago. "I can't believe it."

Merlin sits next to me. "Close your eyes," he says, and I do it, although not before shooting him a look that's half begging him to stop this and half desperate for him to say more.

And I feel Merlin move around me, straddling my legs in a position that feels intimate in a way that isn't sexual, necessarily, but vulnerable. And then he presses his forehead to mine. "Breathe in," he says. "Breathe when I do."

I breathe with him, and then he presses his lips to mine, and it's still not sexual; it's not a kiss. Our mouths are still as we literally share breath, in and out, in and out, and then whatever curtain separates his mind from mine is pulled back, and I see everything. Swords and guns and castles and barracks, and a coolly beautiful queen and an impetuous prince and the White House and a flat-topped hill and Vivienne Moore's lake house, and a bright green tor soaring over a glassy, fog-shrouded lake.

I see it all.

I see myself, and I see all the people I've loved and all the people I've fought, and all the ways that our lives have doubled back in on each other's. I see all the ways we were the first time, all the ways we are now, and the shimmering silver threads that sew us together, twines of fate that restrain and chafe and anchor every heart to the other.

I see the beginning.

And I see the end.

Chapter 25
Ash

THEN

"It would be polite," Merlin said, "to visit another parish in DC. If you're going to make such a point about going to Mass every Sunday."

I leaned back in my chair. We were in the Oval Office, running through damage control about some ill-advised remarks one of our New Party senators had made, and then out of nowhere, Merlin had brought up my church habits. "It's not a point," I said, a little amused. "It's a faith practice. I try to go every time I can."

Merlin waved a disinterested hand. "It's good for business, so I'm not trying to discourage you. But Mass is the same everywhere, right? It doesn't hurt to make another parish feel special for hosting you."

"Okay, I'll have Belvedere make the arrangements," I said, ready to move on to the next thing.

Merlin gave me a small smile, and in that smile, I got the sense that I was missing something important, that Merlin knew something I didn't. "I've already made the arrangements," he said. "Tomorrow you'll be at St. Thomas Becket."

It had been three weeks since Embry had pushed a ring back into my hand, and sometimes I didn't know if I'd survive it. Loving him. Wanting him. Knowing that he didn't love and want me as much or in the same ways, or if he did, that I'd never know why he couldn't bring himself to marry me. It couldn't be the politics; it just couldn't—the man I loved wouldn't pick something so petty and trivial over what we had. It had to be something else, something I couldn't see or perceive.

But knowing there was a hidden corner inside the prince I'd spent fourteen years loving…Jesus, that hurt almost as badly as his rejection. I'd kept nothing from him, *nothing* except my relationship with God and the memory of a girl in London—and even those I'd shared as much as he'd asked for.

So at Mass that day, I wasn't looking for a future wife, for the girl who stared up at Jephthah's Daughter with me. I was looking at my prince. As we prayed, as we knelt. As he parted his lips for the priest and let the priest place a wafer on his tongue. I had to subtly adjust my swelling cock against my leg as I stepped up for my own turn, the sight of that white wafer on his pink tongue too much for my broken, hungry heart to stand.

And so it wasn't until we were both back up in the balcony, watching the rest of the parishioners shuffle through the communion line that I noticed a glimmer of familiar hair in an impossibly complicated shade of gold.

Embry noticed at the same time, his shoulders stiffening over his folded hands and his eyes going bright. Alert.

Below us, the young woman took her communion,

crossed herself, went back to her pew. She wore a sweater and a pleated skirt, not a blush-pink gown, and she was no longer a shy girl burning with desires she didn't understand. She was lonely now. Cold. Pulled in, locked away.

Watching her made me sad and excited all at once. Sad because I'd never wanted to see that curious innocence dampened, but excited because I wanted to be the one to tease it back to the surface. She needed a sir to care for her, to make her feel safe and loved so that she could blossom again. She needed someone to tend to her darkest needs, to transform them into something real and vital; she needed to be spanked and bound and fucked, and also petted and cherished and cuddled close to a sir's heart.

I could see it in every step, every sigh, every careful movement she made as she lifted the risers behind the pews into place or turned the pages in her missal. The same thing I'd seen in that London room years ago as she knelt in a sparkling pool of glass, the same thing I'd seen in Chicago when I fisted my hand in her hair and she said those magic words:

Yes, please.

And when I turned to Embry and saw that he was just as rapt as I was, gazing just as intently at her, his body just as tense and hungry, I should have known. I should have. But at the time, I thought it was only because she was beautiful and singular and so regal in her lonely, quiet prettiness. Who wouldn't stare? Who wouldn't be thinking about her throat under their lips or her hunched shoulders between their knees?

The air was heavy with that fateful God-feeling as I leaned over to Embry. "That's Greer Galloway," I whispered. "I… That's her. That's the email girl."

And Embry's eyes flared with something that looked like pain—and then they went still and dark. "If you'd like," he said slowly, in a low voice that wouldn't carry far under the priest's prayers, "I could find her. See if she'd like to meet with you?"

"Yes," I said, my eyes on her. "Yes."

"It's done."

"She bled for me," I said for no reason in particular, other than I just wanted to say the words out loud. "I mean, it wasn't really for me, it was for her cousin, but I was the one to pull the splinter of glass from her finger." I run my thumb over my own pointer finger, remembering the feeling of the glass tugging free from her skin, the black pools of her pupils, the welling crimson salt that pooled on her fingertip. "I pulled it free and I tasted the blood there. And she let me. God."

I ducked my head to catch my breath. I'd forgotten, of course I had, after a year with Embry, after years of marriage, I'd kept the memory of her like a cherished pearl, a priceless heirloom, but I'd forgotten her power over me in real, vivid life—

"I'll bring her to you," Embry said in a strange voice. "The girl who bled for you."

I had to wait for three days after he met with her. Pure agony. But the moment I heard her slide into the pew behind me, heard the quiet rise and fall of her breathing as she watched me pray, I knew it had been worth it—the wait and everything else that came before. All that I had wanted to do to her after the first time we met—chain her to my bed and carry her every place she ever wanted to go—I still wanted.

And miracle of miracles, she wanted it too.

Even now I don't presume to know God's plans or thoughts, but it was impossible not to see the shape of his hand in my life as I slept a full night's sleep for the first time in too many years to count with her in my arms. It was impossible not to see that Greer fit me, or I fit her, and the way I was around her shaped me into a better person. Perhaps love is a mystery in this way, because the love strung between Embry and me had been mysterious too, only different in the parts of me that it fed. Which almost felt like a betrayal to both Embry and Greer.

I still wanted them both; I still loved them both.

My heart still beat and my bones still ached for them both.

Perhaps it was that first night that truly drove it home, what I'd always suspected but hadn't been able to prove until then—that Greer wanted me in the same ways I wanted her, that our keening urges met and mated at the same place deep inside our souls. She wanted to be dragged to the edge and I wanted to take her there; she wanted to be bruised and I wanted to bruise her; she wanted to crawl and I wanted to watch every slope and dip of her body as she did.

It was different with Embry.

My prince had knelt to me and had felt the uncontrolled sear of my burning needs, but I knew that whatever mechanism drove my prince's submission was a complicated one. Greer knew herself, she saw herself with a clarity and self-knowledge that made me trust her implicitly—she said she wanted all that I was, and because I trusted that she knew herself, I could believe her. I could give it to her.

But to say that Embry didn't know himself like Greer knew herself would be an understatement. Yes, I relished the fight with him, I relished the relief shimmering in his snowdrop eyes when he finally gave in to me and himself and surrendered to what he really needed—and perhaps a part of me even loved him *because* of the fight. But with Greer, our exchange was so deliriously mutual, so deeply consensual and offered freely from each of us…it was a fairy tale. And who among us doesn't want to love like that at least once in our lives? Where nothing is held in reserve, and every moment of pain and pleasure and obedience and power feeds on itself to create a brimming cup of generous spirit?

Is it so strange that I would want to marry both of them? Exchange hearts with both of them?

No, of course not. Maybe not every man would, but I am not every man. I require the whole world, and one person alone never could have given it to me.

It wasn't until the night of the state dinner that I began to see that one person wouldn't have to.

Embry paced restlessly around the room as I sat on the sofa enjoying a glass of Macallan 12. After the third or fourth time he checked his watch, I set down my glass.

"Everything okay?"

He looked up a little guiltily, as if I'd caught him doing something he shouldn't. "Um, yes. Yes, everything's okay. Just keeping an eye on the time. Maybe I should go down without you and Greer, just to start talking and shaking hands."

I rested my head against my fingers as I looked at him. He was strangely chatty tonight, jittery almost. It was unlike him, and only one thing about tonight was unlike any other night.

"Is this about Greer?" I asked softly. "I know it's only been a month since the lake. If it's too much, too soon, I can find another way."

Embry made a strangled sigh. "Are you asking me if it's hurting my feelings that you have a girlfriend after I dumped you? Dammit, Ash."

"What?"

He ran a hand through his hair and picked up my glass where I'd set it down. He took a fast, messy drink and then wiped his mouth with the back of his hand, and I wanted to crowd him against the wall and do things to him that would send the glass tumbling across the floor. "You have to stop worrying about me," he said. "It makes me feel even shittier about what happened between us."

"I'll never stop worrying about you," I told him. "Patroclus."

"Don't. God."

"Tell me if it's her."

"So then what will you do? Break it off to spare me the pain of watching you with someone else? Stay with her but hide your joy from me? I don't want either of those things; they would gut me."

"Then what do you want, Embry?"

"I want…" He put the glass against his forehead, closing his eyes. "I don't even know. It's too tangled up now. You. Her. Me."

Her.

Why would she tangle him up?

I watched him carefully, sensing rather than seeing something revealing itself, a floor of ice between me and him finally thinning and cracking.

"Did she submit?" Embry asked, eyes still closed. "When she was here the other night? Did she submit to you?"

"Yes."

A pause. "Does she do it better than me?"

"That's like asking which ocean is better. You are different in the way you let me love you. She gives. You fight." *And I need both*, I wanted to add, but I didn't.

The only response I got was a mumbled, "Everyone knows the Pacific is the best ocean." The ice got thinner and thinner as Embry opened his eyes and saw me staring at him. His pupils dilated as I ran my tongue along my top teeth.

"Are you jealous of her?" I finally asked.

"No," he said.

I studied my hands for a moment. "Is that the truth?"

Another pause. "No."

I widened my feet, planting my dress shoes farther apart on the carpet so that there would be plenty of room for a grown man to kneel there. "Get on your knees and tell me the truth."

He set down the now-empty glass, his eyes flashing. "No."

I was on him before I even knew I was going to do it, my fist in the shoulder of his tuxedo jacket and my other hand cupping the back of his neck, and it was only a moment's work before he was panting on his knees. I kept hold of him, wary that he might bolt at any moment.

"Now tell me the fucking truth."

He looked up at me with pain and defeat in his face. "Does it matter?"

"Everything about you matters to me. Why shouldn't your jealousy?"

He didn't answer.

I traced the line of his lips, and he shuddered beautifully at my touch. "It's more than jealousy, then. Something else, something you don't want to tell me. What could that be, Embry? What do you want to hide from me?"

His eyelashes swept up in the most mesmerizing arc, twin spots of color pinked his cheeks. And he was so handsome, still so mine, and if I pulled him to my mouth right now, I'd be able to kiss him, I'd be able to kiss the lies and the secrets right out of him.

How? How could I want that so much at the same time I still wanted Greer so much? I felt it but I didn't understand it, and I knew it was as unfair to them as it was necessary to me, and there had to be a way forward that was fair to all of us, healthy for all of us.

Embry was about to answer me, and I leaned even closer because I didn't know that I still hadn't ruled out kissing, and then we heard a woman's voice around the corner, and it was Greer, and as she stepped into the room I kept my eyes on Embry and I saw it.

I saw the truth.

He wasn't just jealous of her—he was jealous of *me*. He wanted her too, and of course this must be shredding him—his ex-lover and a woman he wanted together in front of him. Who wouldn't be upset? And the thoughts came unbidden and hot, the idea of watching him move between her legs, of watching him pet and caress her. Of watching him service her at my command.

My cock went hard so fast I forgot to breathe.

I watched the two of them at the dinner that night, the first time I'd been able to witness them together, and what I saw fascinated me because it wasn't only that Embry was clearly drawn to Greer. It was reciprocal; I could tell by her flushing and laughter that she was just as attracted to him, and of course she was, because he was Embry Moore, handsome and delicious and princely.

What really fascinated me was the current running between them. It was subtle, momentary; like a silver fish darting through dark water, it could only be perceived in glimpses and guesses. But it was there, and it pointed to something more than casual attraction.

I considered this.

Just as I considered Greer's blush as we danced and I explained how Embry had taught me to dance, *we took turns being the man*, and I didn't miss the brief gnaw of hunger in her eyes as she thought about it.

And so I made a choice that night. A choice to see. It was an idea or a hope, but it was still unformed and dangerous—but oh God, it would be more dangerous *not* to do it, not to explore this a little bit. Not to confirm what I suspected to be true.

It was in their faces the moment they saw each other, the moment I walked through that door with Embry. I could feel it between them, and yet it also included me. I didn't feel apart from it, walled off from whatever hunger they had for each other. That's not to say that I wasn't *jealous*—I was that very much—but underneath and over the jealousy was something terrifyingly sacred. Glorious and dirty and fated. I couldn't quite feel my way around the edges of it yet, but I knew it was there, and I knew I yearned for it.

"Are you sure this is what you want?" Embry had asked me, his posture tense and unhappy, trying to look everywhere except at the beautiful woman kneeling on the floor with her wet cunt open to view.

"I know you want her," I leaned in and whispered. "I know she wants you."

Embry let out a pained breath.

"And little prince, I want both of you. I want the two of you to want each other. It gets me hard. And I think the idea of the three of us gets you hard too."

Sure enough, when I pulled back, Embry's face was a vivid painting of lust and defeat, and I knew I had his surrender, I knew I'd won. Won what, I still wasn't sure, but it would either show us heaven or burn us alive, and I couldn't wait to see which it would be.

CHAPTER 26
ASH

NOW

ALL OF MY LIFE, I'VE BEEN LUCKY. IN THE BIG WAYS—WITH my mother and sister and lovers and friends—and in the small ways, down to good grades and laws getting passed and the generally favorable course my life has run. I suppose there are parts of my life one could call less than fortunate—my week with Morgan and the resulting son chief among them—but I've never felt that those things were un*lucky*. They were mistakes, debts of judgment that eventually came collecting, and I earned every ounce of pain or scorn that came with them.

Now, however, I feel truly, actually, *painfully* unlucky.

Stupidly unlucky.

Cruelly unlucky.

Merlin was right on the bridge. I am going to do everything I can to stop this from happening.

I leave the nature park with unfamiliar memories swirling in my mind and still so many doubts, and the first thing

I do is call Trieste, then Belvedere. The debate is a week from today. Embry could be dead a week from today.

I will not allow that to happen.

Trieste tells me that a venue switch would be difficult but not impossible—but it has to be decided by tomorrow for the Secret Service to have enough time to vet the building.

Belvedere tries to patch me through to Embry's phone, but there's no response from him or his campaign manager—which makes sense in the aftermath of Abilene's suicide but is beyond frustrating. I leave him a message, as clear and as explicit as I can make it without sounding nonsensical.

"Embry, I'm sorry to call you again today, but I have information that the debate might be a staging ground for something dangerous. I want to move it to a new venue or figure out something else. Call me back."

I put Trieste and Uri to work on finding a new venue and liaising with the television network hosting the debate to get their cooperation. I ask Gawayne to pull all of the threats made to Embry and cross-reference them with the final debate location in Richmond. I ask for a huge increase in Secret Service agents present at the event.

But strange things start happening. Phone calls get dropped. Emails vanish between servers. The television network balks at a change of venue. No one can get ahold of Embry, and both Kay and Trieste act as if I've lost my mind.

After two days, Embry sends word through his campaign manager that he'll agree to a change of venue so long as it won't interfere with Abilene's funeral arrangements—but then Harrison Fasse kicks up a fuss and starts a media flurry around the venue change, and the outcry forces our hand in revealing the new venue options.

After three days, Gawayne's team turns up nothing, no evidence for any attack happening at the debate at all. Kay and I argue about the message increasing the Secret Service presence sends.

Embry won't return my calls.

We manage to get the venue switched and the extra agents, but everything else has gone to shit, and I'm worried Embry's just as exposed as ever; Merlin asks me about doing the debate remotely, and I call Embry and ask if he'd be willing to do that in a voice message.

No response.

I decide it's better if I'm with him anyway, not sequestered away in some remote location. I want him close, near to me, so I can intervene if need be.

I ask Merlin if I should tell Embry and Greer about it all. The other memories. What Merlin sees in our futures. He doesn't give me a real answer, and I don't have one for myself. Do I tell them this unbelievable story and hope it somehow keeps Embry safe? Or if I tell them, will that make Embry less inclined to believe me about the debate threat?

Do I even really believe the debate threat? Or any of it? Am I fighting for nothing?

Or is this the beginning of the end? A week of stupid mistakes and pointless errors, when everything that could go wrong did go wrong, until the only thing left to offer the universe is my own tiny life?

I don't know.

I don't know anymore.

And the entire week I have the dream, the same dream always—water and fog, a waiting boat. Four waiting queens. In the dream, I know there's someplace to go.

A better place, over the water.

Abilene's funeral is a somber affair. There had been some fretting at her church about the seemliness of a suicide funeral, but as it isn't against church doctrine, and also as I had Kay call them on my behalf, the fuss was quickly stamped out.

The bleak reality, however, is another story.

Galahad in particular is difficult to see in his little suit, holding tight to Embry's hand and asking *There, Mah-mee? There Mah-mee?* every time he glimpses the large portrait of Abilene near the casket at the front. Greer stands slim and regal through it all, her head up and her gaze clear. Only the smudges under her eyes reveal her sleepless nights, only the clench of her hands folded together show how deeply this has ripped through her. I hold her close when I can. I wish I could do the same for Embry. For Galahad. Just gather my prince and his little son into my arms and shield them from anything hard or difficult ever ever ever.

I stare at the casket during the service as I hold my wife's hand and go through the motions of a mourner, and I think of the debate tomorrow. Of the danger I've done everything I can to avert.

There is one last thing to try, and I'll try it tonight.

The truth.

When Greer and I go through the receiving line, Embry looks like a ghost, shaking hands mechanically with the mourners, nodding and presenting a facsimile of a smile when required. But when Greer steps in front of him, a shock passes over his face.

She leans in, kisses a spot that could charitably be called his cheek but is really the corner of his mouth. He closes his eyes, exhaling slowly as she pulls away.

"Tonight," I say quietly. "Where will you be?"

He opens his eyes and stares at me, his lips parted. For a moment I think he's not going to answer, but then he says, "My town house. I'll be alone by midnight."

And I give him my own kiss, not caring who's watching,

only wanting to feel the clean-shaven velvet of his cheek on my lips before I leave.

"We'll be there."

Seven hours later, Embry's neighborhood is dark and silent as our car rolls up to the front of his house. A hard frost has gathered in the cracks and edges of the sidewalks and streets, a veined spread of white under the streetlights.

Before an agent comes around to open Greer's door, I say, "I think you should go in first. Alone."

She turns to me, pretty eyebrows drawn together. "Alone?"

I turn so that I can face her, take her hands, watch her eyes as I speak. All through this last week, I've been thinking about tonight, about the debate tomorrow, and two things grew very clear to me. First, I would not let anyone harm a hair on Embry's head, and second...that means, if Merlin is right, that I must be harmed in turn. It means I will have to lay down my own life for his.

Which means a host of other things I can barely look at, but primarily it means I need to make sure both my prince and my queen are taken care of if all my other contingencies fail and I am asked to die tomorrow. Part of that care starts tonight.

"You and Embry share a connection through Abilene," I tell Greer gently. "There should be time for the two of you to feel this together. To mourn together."

"I don't want to mourn her," Greer says in a tight voice. But her eyes betray her. "She tried to kill me, she hurt both you and Embry."

"Greer," I say, using my Sir Tone so that she'll listen to me. "Mourning isn't about missing someone. It's about reflection. Examining all the places a person affected your life. Mourning isn't for the dead—it's for the living."

She sighs. "Yes, sir." But then she looks over at me. "We need you, though. He and I."

I smile and brush some hair off her forehead. "And you'll have me, sweetheart. I'll be in to see him after you, and then you and I will share the rest of the night together. But I think it's for the best if you two have some time alone."

And I'm selfish and I want to have you each to myself when I say goodbye.

And I'm scared, and if I have you both with me together tonight, I'm worried I won't be brave enough to do what I need to do tomorrow.

Greer gives me a kiss on the cheek—sweet, quick, unburdened by the knowledge of what tomorrow will bring. "Will you wait outside?"

"Yes."

And then the agent opens her door and she walks to the front door of the town house and disappears inside. I watch from the car window as Embry's silhouette moves against the glass front of the window, and then I watch as their shadows meet, as Embry's head drops onto Greer's shoulder, as Greer holds him, as they finally lift their faces for a kiss I can feel all the way out here in the car.

I smile to myself fondly, a little sadly, as I watch them. It is a strange thing to have jealousy nestled so close to generosity and love, but it is a beautiful thing. It is both haunting and divine that I can take joy in seeing them together, that as I watch them kiss I am brimming over with every good and pure feeling, and at the same time feel fear prick like icy pins along the curve of my heart. The two complement each other, love and fear, hot and cold, light and dark. Perhaps the same algorithms that suit me to kink suit me to loving like this, with the pain too close to the pleasure to tell apart.

I watch my lovers' shadows move away from the door, and I imagine what they'll do next. Talk? Slow and awkward, because death makes clumsy speakers of us all? Or will Embry take Greer's hand and press it against his heart, and in turn she'll take his hand and press it against where she needs him? Will he drop to his knees and use his mouth under her dress until she cries out? Will she climb onto his lap and ride him with the hard desperation of the grieving?

Because they are both grieving, even if they hated Abilene. No life leaves this world without a ripple, simply erases itself without a trace. Even if Abilene only left behind scars and smoke, those scars have to be tended to before anyone can move on. Especially Embry, with his little boy. Especially Greer, who used to count Abilene as her closest friend.

I lean my head back in my seat and close my eyes for a moment, imagining the two of them together. Remembering the strange new memories Merlin gave to me. In that other life, it was my favorite thing too, to watch them together. To watch Embry tease laughter out of Greer's mouth, to watch her arguing with him about court politics and crop yields. In that other life, my heart had squeezed just as it does now, with the greatest happiness possible and the greatest jealousy. Because for the two of them I felt an almost God-like love: just that they were *alive*, just that they *existed*, was enough to thrill me with measureless joy. That on top of that, they were also happy and in love with each other gave me peace, and because I loved them like I loved nothing and no one else, their happiness was a greater prize than my own.

But like God, I was also jealous of their love, possessive of their hearts. God, I believe, is jealous of his people in the purest way, but me—well, then and now, I was jealous because I was afraid. A king, a warrior, a strong man, secretly undone by the fear that those closest to him didn't love him.

In that other life, I had figured jealousy as the price of the extraordinary love I felt. Who could love as a three, even for years and years, and not still feel the occasional pang of neglect or shame? That didn't mean I was willing to lose a single moment of their love or loving them, but in this other life, it had meant that I hadn't thought enough of the future. I hadn't taken care of the people I loved because it hurt too much to think of them going on together without me, being happy without me.

But that is going to change. This time, in this life, I embrace the jealousy, I embrace the pain, and I let every thorn and burr dig into my skin, and I relish every second of it, because it reminds me that I'm alive and that I can still do the right thing.

And I know what the right thing is for Greer and Embry.

I call Merlin.

"About tomorrow," I say after he picks up.

"Yes?"

I watch shadows move across the bedroom window on the top floor. "There's one more thing I need your help with."

Two hours later, Greer steps out of the town house with flushed cheeks and messy hair. I open her door, and I can't help it, the moment she's inside, I yank her to me and kiss all the sex right off her lips. I lick into her mouth, hungry for her taste, and I run my fingers up her leg to feel that she's been well-used by Embry.

"God, that turns me on," she gasps into my mouth. "How you touch where Embry's been inside me."

"Mmm," I say, moving my mouth to her neck to nip at it. "It turns me on too."

It does, and it does more than turn me on; it makes me love as God loves—unselfishly, eternally. Their pleasure is my own.

"Thank you," she says. "It was what we needed." And

she lets out a breath that tells me even more than her words, because it's a breath shaky with hormones and grief. They cried and they fucked. I feel like a doctor who's watching a compliant patient heal thanks to his advice.

"He's ready for you," she adds.

I give her throat a final kiss and remove my fingers from her cunt, sliding them in her mouth for her to clean. "Will you go home to wait for me or stay here?"

"I'll go home, I think. But you will be back tonight?"

"Yes, my queen."

Back to say goodbye.

CHAPTER 27
ASH

NOW

EMBRY OPENS THE DOOR FOR ME CLAD IN ONLY SWEAT-pants, a glisten of sweat still stippling his collarbone. The contours of his arms and chest and stomach are on perfect, sweaty display, and I know he worked up that sweat by fucking my wife.

I have to take a deep breath to keep myself in control.

I want to lick that sweat right off him, I want to reach into those sweatpants and grip what's mine by right. I want to shove him to the floor and give him everything he's ever given me, all the anguish and the longing and the happiness, I want to hammer it back into his body until it becomes part of him forever…but that's not why I came here tonight.

I came here for a goodbye. No matter how much I hope telling him the truth will save him, no matter how much I hope that all my diligence this past week has succeeded, I have to be prepared for tomorrow. In another life, I wasn't prepared, I wasn't ready, and when I died, I died leaving a kingdom in ruins.

This time will be different.

"Achilles," Embry says as he closes the door.

"Patroclus."

"Do you want a drink?"

I do, oddly enough, and I tell him so. Together we walk into his study, where he opens up a globe bar and pours us each a healthy glass of scotch. He leans against the edge of his desk and I lean against the doorframe, and I take a minute just to appreciate him. To savor the picture he makes. Those tight, flat muscles along his stomach and chest, the compact swells of his arms.

He's always been like this—lithe and graceful, sculpted in the slender, idealized ways of a Greek statue—the kind of body built to make my heart pound and my cock ache. Where I'm rough with dark hair across my chest, he's almost boyishly smooth, and where I'm curved and clad with muscular power, he is light and lean.

The differences and samenesses between our bodies fascinate me not because we are both men, but because we are both people, because he has a body and I have a body and we love each other with those bodies, and every secret of his body is fascinating to me because *he* is fascinating to me. I want to find every place where we are different and every place where we are the same and compose hymns to them both.

"I can't think straight when you look at me like that," Embry complains, taking a drink.

I smile at him, knowing it will flash the dimple that torments him so, and he groans. To think it might be the last time I hear him fret about my dimple has my stomach clenching in fear and grief.

You can't stand here staring at him forever, I chide myself. *Do what you came here to do. Say your goodbye in case there is no chance for it tomorrow.*

"Have you ever wondered about what you had to do to make me say yes?"

The way his hand freezes in midair, the scotch glass hovering near his lips, tells me he knows exactly what I'm talking about. "Ash…"

"You see, at first, it was simply the delight of denying you, and after our night together in the woods, it was the only thing left to deny. But I never meant to deny you long. I thought, soon enough, there would come a moment that would perfectly mark all the denial and waiting, and we'd both remember it forever. You know how unhealthily obsessed I am with firsts."

Embry doesn't respond, those sooty eyelashes blinking slowly as he takes a drink, as he processes what I'm saying.

"And then that moment never came because I proposed and scared you off. But the second time—the second time, I made a real decision. I thought, *when he says yes to me.* When he says yes to me and there's nothing left between us, then we'll have our last first. That's what I wanted you to do to earn it, Embry. I wanted you to say yes to me."

I take a step forward, and he closes his eyes, looking pained. "Ash."

"What I didn't realize," I say quietly, ignoring him as I take another step forward, "was that you were saying yes to me all along."

The air between us seems to hum and throb, destiny again, fate, except there is no other memory of this. I never did this in my other life. This moment, in both of my lives, is happening for the first time.

"Ash." Embry's voice is strangled.

"Every time you gave me your trust, your obedience, and your surrender. Every time you fought me knowing you would lose, every time you carried me when I couldn't limp along myself, and every breath and kiss you ever shared with me—it was all you saying yes, every moment of it. You've said yes to me so many times I'm surprised I could even hear the word no."

Embry's head is ducked down; he's breathing hard. "Stop," he begs. "Please."

"You were saying yes, Embry, and I wasn't listening. But I'm listening now."

He looks up at me, and I'm close enough to touch him now, so I do. I take his right hand, and from my pocket, I pull out the ring I'd wanted to throw into the lake three years ago but couldn't bring myself to. And I slide the ring on his finger, an older, slightly different twin to the one on his left.

He watches as I do it, his jaw tight, his chest shuddering with every breath, and when I'm finished, I bring the finger wearing my ring to my mouth. "You are just as much mine as Greer is," I tell him. "And I am just as much yours as I am hers. I wish to God it hadn't taken me so long to see that I could have told you this years ago. That I could have given you this years ago."

He watches my lips against his finger with something like agony. "Given me this ring?"

"No. What comes after."

"Our last first?" he asks raggedly.

"Our last first."

And then he's on me, grabbing at my tie and yanking me to his mouth, and we kiss like we used to kiss in the early days—hard and searing and uncertain—and then we're both stumbling out of the study and up the stairs, kissing frantically as we climb, and Embry's hands are so eagerly stripping away my jacket and belt that I have to laugh, and then we're in his bedroom.

"Galahad is with my mother," he says. Then he shakes his head. "Not that it matters—if he were here, I'd just close the door and fuck you anyway. Do you have any idea how fucking much I want this?"

I laugh again because I do have some idea. His erect penis is straining hard against his pants, his chest is flushed a very appealing shade of red, and his fists are clenched at his sides.

He glares at me. "It's not funny."

"It's a little funny."

More glaring. "You're a bastard and an asshole."

"All true," I say, "although I was hoping to hear the word 'asshole' in another context tonight."

His mouth twitches in a way that makes my chest tight. What if this is the last time I get to see that smirk, that smile of secret amusement? "Shit, I can't laugh now," he says. "It will ruin the moment. Take off your clothes."

"Am I your submissive tonight?" I ask as I unknot my tie and unclasp my cuff links.

"No," he says immediately, softly. "No. You will always be my king. That's how I want it."

An uncomfortable warmth chokes at my throat. "Little prince."

He steps forward and takes my cuff links from me, sets them on his dresser and returns to me to help me peel off my shirt. "You asked me two years ago how I wanted it," he says after we've bared my chest. He drops down to untie my shoes, and the sight of him kneeling at my feet and tending to me sends an extra—and unnecessary—jolt of heat to my cock. I've been hard since the moment I saw him, but I'm leaking now. Pulsing and needy.

Embry tugs off one shoe, then moves to my other foot. "For a long time, I thought I'd want to fuck you the way that you fucked me sometimes. I would be the man and you would be the youth, I would be the king and you'd be the knight kneeling in supplication. But after the last debate, I realized"—the other shoe comes off and he moves to my socks—"that's not what I really want. At all."

"What do you want?"

He stands up, taking my hand and then curling it around the back of his neck and pulling our foreheads together. "To serve you."

It's my turn to breathe raggedly now; I can't even remember how to breathe. "You know it's all pretend, Embry. Every bit of it—the kneeling, the bruising, the humiliation. It's a game. Make-believe."

I'm telling the truth.

"Liar," he breathes, stepping in so that our stomachs and chests press and heave together. "I told you before, everything has been real with you from the very start."

And he's telling the truth too.

Maybe that's why so many people don't understand kink, because we're both right. It's real *and* it's make-believe, it's deadly serious and sinfully playful, the truest expression of ourselves and also an elaborate game of pretend. Both, both, both, and to forget either is to forget the reason behind the kink, which is to be intentionally and vulnerably and happily…human.

That's it, that's the heart of it. To be human.

He kisses me again, gently this time, taking care to kiss around the edges of my mouth, to kiss the special spot behind my ear, to rub his cheek against my own. He sighs as my stubble chafes his still-smooth cheek. "The first time I saw you, I knew you were a man who couldn't keep his shave."

"I should shave more."

"And then where would I go for such scratchy kisses? Don't you dare."

He kisses my chest and stomach, and then he carefully unfastens my pants, undressing me as carefully as a valet, folding my clothes and setting them aside as I prefer, instead of just dropping them on the floor. We both make a noise as he peels off my boxer briefs and my erect cock springs free, glistening at the tip, and then he repeats, "I want you to be my king when we do this. Please."

"Do you want me to be in charge?"

He breathes out, and it seems to free him and shame him as he answers, "Yes."

"Hey," I say, taking his hand. "We can change at any time, okay? If you don't want me to have the reins five minutes from now or sixty minutes from now, you just tell me and we'll change. I can be your submissive or we can meet each other as equals. Nothing's permanent tonight."

Even as I say the words, a knife of fear slices a wedge out of my happiness, reminding me that tonight won't last forever and that some things *are* permanent. Death, for example.

I shake away the fear, returning my attention to Embry. "Do you understand?" I ask. "I don't care which way the power flows tonight or if it flows at all. I told you once that I'd be any kind of man for you, and I meant it. I want to share my body with you, whichever way you want it."

Embry stares at me in the near dark. Our only light comes from the open door to the hallway and the streetlights glowing outside the window. "When you say you'll be any kind of man for me," he whispers, "my heart beats so fast. But oh, Ash, I don't want you to be any kind of man for me. I just want you to be the man you already are."

I kiss his sweet forehead, understanding. "Okay, little prince. We'll start now, and just know we can stop at any time."

"It's ridiculous that you need to tell me I can safe out when I'm going to be the one fucking you," he says with a choked laugh. "But it makes sense somehow. You are more dangerous wielding love than you are wielding pain."

It makes sense to me as well, and I suppose it's always

made sense, because it's what I've wanted from the very beginning. People don't look at you with the whole world in their eyes because they fear you—they look at you like that because they love you.

I pull away and walk over to the bed, where I recline against the pillows and make myself comfortable. "Show me your cock," I order him. I don't bother fisting my own—I'll make him suck it in a minute anyway—and instead I turn all of my attention on him, on this last time I'll get to see him go red with humiliation. This last time I'll see him hook his thumbs in his pants and reveal the V of his abdominal muscles, the spread of dark hair at the end of his happy trail, the narrow lines of his hips. The bounce and sway of his full, hard cock.

He's struggling with himself as he kicks his pants away on the floor, and it's another last too, seeing him plunge through every depth of shame at my command.

"That's just exposing your cock," I say lazily, imperially. "*Show* it to me."

He takes a deep breath and then uses a thumb on his staff to push it down, to make it jut perpendicular from his body. And then he takes a step closer, turning so that I can see his body in profile, the hard penis and the tight stomach above it. The glow coming from the window puts a silver burnish on his skin, limns every hair with light. He's all Embry, all perfect.

"Mmm," I say. "I suppose that will do."

The tiniest flicker at the corner of Embry's mouth relieves me—he realizes what game I'm going to play—but then he ducks his head again, and I'm reminded that the game has power, that the game is real.

I spread my legs. "I need to be cleaned," I say, again like a magistrate, bored almost, although I'm anything but bored as I watch the tremors ripple through Embry's body as he approaches me. He climbs onto the bed with shaky limbs, his sides heaving hard as he lowers himself to his stomach and slides his arms under my thighs.

I watch his head dip low to my most secret place.

I feel the hesitant flicker of his tongue across sensitive, creased skin.

It's unbearably carnal to witness, the dark crown of his head between my legs, and I have a moment when I realize this is what Greer sees when we eat her. I've seen a lover bob up and down on my cock, their every flinch and gasping inhale exposed to me, but this—it feels so private somehow, truly intimate, because there's so much I *can't* see—I see only the flutter of his eyes and the wrinkle in his brow as he concentrates so hard on rimming me properly. But I can only *feel* the bump and press of his nose against me, the sides of his cheeks smoothing against my hair-rough thighs—even the point of his chin feels like a new discovery as he turns his head this way and that to lick and nibble.

"We've never done this either," I murmur, sliding my hand through his hair. "So much I've missed out on."

He moans his agreement, and I feel the vibrations against my skin, which makes me moan. It's so wet, so *dirty*, and so loving and servile, and intimate and earthy, and everything I've ever loved about sex all rolled into one. When I look down the length of Embry's body, I see the hollows in his ass cheeks that reveal how hard he's pressing his cock into the mattress right now. I wish I had the time to make him come all over the sheets first, I wish I could see his body trembling with an inadvertent orgasm while he has his tongue inside me, but alas.

Maybe in our next life.

I grab his hair tight and guide his mouth to my cock for a moment, purely so I can see and feel it one last time. The stretch of those refined lips, the flex of that perfectly chiseled jaw. Those dark eyelashes resting on his cheeks. His mouth so hot and wet and good on my skin.

Last time, goes the voice in my head. *Last time.*

I ignore it. "Put your cock inside me," I say, as if I'm ordering him to give me a massage. As if I'm a spoiled king making the most depraved demands of his courtiers. "Make me feel good."

Embry comes off my cock with color high in his cheeks and a gasp. "Yes," he says. "Yes, I will."

He slides off the bed to get to the night stand and opens a shallow drawer. Inside there's a bottle of lube and a silicone toy. No condoms, no baby wipes, nothing that speaks to partners or to the anticipation of partners. Just a lonely life.

That's going to end, I think, and the thought gives me relief. That it's pain I will be able to soothe away, that like a good sir, I'll be able to give Embry aftercare for all these hard years. The best aftercare I'm capable of giving.

Embry is careful but thorough, using his finger to coat me inside and out, his eyes flicking up to mine constantly, gauging my expression. I can see his heartbeat in his cock as he works his way inside, the pulse hammering at the side of his neck, the stunned bite of his lip as he slides his finger all the way to the knuckle and feels the full clench of me around his digit.

"Fuck," he whispers. "You're so hot inside. Burning hot."

"Give me more," I say, keeping my tone imperious, although I'm not fooling anyone with my cock dripping onto my stomach and my hips making slow rolls against Embry's hand. "I want more."

"Yes, sir," he says with a comely flutter of his eyelashes and adds a second finger.

I arch a little at the feeling of fullness, at the protest of the muscles around my entrance, and he puts a calming hand on my stomach, sliding it underneath my erection so that he can press down on my stomach at the same time his fingers hook upward and stroke a spot that has my toes curling.

"Remind yourself that it's not pain," he says, echoing his instructions from that long-ago night in Lyonesse. "And you want it because I'm the one giving it to you."

"I want it because you're the one giving it to me."

The fingers stroke in exploration, in preparation, and right now the kink is so thin and light, like a sheet thrown over furniture, showing the shape of the real thing underneath.

When I say, "Service me with your cock," what I mean is *let's share everything, let's leave nothing else between us.*

And when he removes his fingers and slicks up his erection with a trembling hand and I say, "Such a good, eager boy," what I mean is *I love seeing you shake with love for me because I am always shaking with love for you.*

And when, for the first time in both my lives, he presses his tip against a place I've never shared with anyone and I say, "Make me feel good," we both know I mean *I want to make* you *feel good, I want us to feel good together, I want to see your face as you feel it and as you come for me.*

Embry closes his eyes and pushes in. Just an inch. Just enough to send a frisson of electric pain up my spine.

Another inch. He lets out a moan like he's dying, his eyes still closed.

I inhale sharply at the new invasion, and I can't help but arch again, which makes him open his eyes and look down at me with a dazed expression. It seems to take him a moment to remember where he is or what's happening. He pulls back enough to run his hands up my inner thighs and spread me wider, and then he pushes my knees ever so slightly up. Opening up my center, baring my hole to him.

And then he guides himself back to my anus, his massive cock pressing in past the ring of muscle more easily this time.

"Jesus, you're big," I grunt, and he laughs—which hurts, and I groan, which makes him laugh even more.

I reach up and collar his throat with my hand, pleased to feel how fast and eager his pulse pounds under my fingers. "Serve your king now."

"Yes, sir." And Embry gives a slick thrust, pulls out, and then slides all the way home.

"Fuck," I mumble, my grip on his neck growing tight as my body breaks out into a shivering, happy sweat. It's a feeling so close to pain, so close to pleasure, but it's not quite either yet, something unformed and unshaped, something that is sensation in its rawest form. And it's dirty, it's so fucking dirty, making him fuck me while I choke him, watching his stomach muscles flex and work to push into me and stroke me from the inside out.

"Fuck is right," he pants, closing his eyes again. A drop of sweat rolls along his temple. "Jesus Christ, it's tight. It's better—*God*—better than I ever could have dreamed. Fuck."

"Open your eyes," I order. "Watch my face as you serve me."

He obeys, opening his eyes with what appears to be a struggle, his mouth all parted and his cheeks flushed and his pupils blown wide. And whatever he sees in my own face unravels him.

"Oh God, Ash," he says in a choked voice, his hips still moving in dirty, delicious thrusts. "Oh God."

I can't fucking handle how handsome he is like this. How perfect. I pull him down for a hot kiss, sloppy and urgent, and whatever change in angle that creates sends a bolt of pleasure straight to my core.

"Oh," I breathe. "*Oh.*"

I think I see now why Embry likes this so much. I mean, I've always known in an abstract way that it must feel good, and it felt good when Embry fucked me with that toy at

Lyonesse, but it's nothing like *now,* nothing like having a virile, beautiful man between your legs, nothing like having something hot and vital seeking out your own hot and vital places. And then that man being someone you've loved for so fucking long, that man shivering with how good you're making him feel…

Another slow thrust against my prostate, and my vision sparks along the edges.

"Oh, Embry," I say. "Oh, fuck. Fuck me."

That earns me another urgent kiss, more of those exquisite strokes. And then we fall into each other, the kink sliding away as easily as a sheet, the thing underneath as naked and needy as our bodies in this deep, filthy moment. Embry braces himself on a forearm over me, sliding his other arm under my waist to crush my body tight to his, and then we kiss like we'll never get to kiss again. Each kiss is mirrored by a piercing stroke down below, each stroke is followed by ripples of muscle and flesh, each ripple is followed by pants and moans that we swallow up from each other again and again, hungry for the other's hunger, thirsty for the other's thirst.

And each kiss, each slide and stroke, each brush of thigh against thigh, seems to say *last time, last time.*

The first and last time.

He breaks the kiss so he can gaze down at me, his eyes soft, and the light catches on a few silver hairs near his temple, on the fine crinkles around his eyes, and I think of the spoiled young prince I met almost twenty years ago, how young and eager to fuck and fight we both were. How little we knew of ourselves and the world and love. What bloody, aching messes we made of each other's hearts.

I wouldn't trade away a single second of it. Not for anything.

I reach up and trace the tiny lines around his eyes. "We're not young men anymore," I murmur.

He drops his face so he can whisper the words against my mouth. "You make me feel young."

And there are no more words after that.

He crushes me against him once more, lying flat and full along the length of me, so that I feel every pound of him, every inch. Every stroke comes with the weight of his body, each pound of his heart is echoed by mine. And we make each other feel young, with something we should have done in our youth but are now sharing instead as men in our prime, and it's painful to think of the years we missed of this—and somehow all the more perfect that we waited until we were almost forty to do it. There's a reverence in our touch now, an awe and a gratitude that comes with having lived-in bodies and scarred, wise hearts.

I come first, my cock pinned between our stomachs, and he kisses me the whole time I come, cherishing me, thanking me, and when our mouths part he tells me all the things I've ever told him—*you are so handsome when you come, so pretty like this, you make me feel so good.* And I come like fucking death itself, nearly blacking out with the ecstasy of Embry inside me and above me and around me, each wave of wet pleasure hotter and more airless than the last. Until I am nearly blacked out for real, my vision hissing with sparks and my ears ringing as my cock pumps spurt after spurt of cum onto us both, as my orgasm unspools from a place so fucking deep inside that it doesn't even feel real, it feels like a part of me so old and elemental that it must have existed before time itself.

And then Embry follows me over the edge, and I don't let him kiss me because I want to see every second of it on his face, every flutter of his eyelashes and part of his lips and furrow of his brow as he grunts his release into me, ejaculating so hard and so hot that I can feel the pulse of him in my ass, I can feel the heat of his semen scorching the insides of me.

"I love you," he says.

"I love you," I say back. And neither of us moves for a long time, even as the semen on our bellies cools and goes sticky, even as we go soft, because we want to savor this moment forever, live in it forever and never leave. The final gift.

Our last first.

"Does this mean you've forgiven me?" Embry asks. We've showered—Embry looking so puppy-dog eager that I allowed him to slake his lust inside me again…and then I flipped him around and returned the favor—and now we're in his bed.

There's something hard and small under my back; I reach behind me and pull out one of Galahad's binkies. My chest tightens, so does my throat. I'm never going to have that. Binkies in bed, children wriggling and messy in my house. I missed my chance with Lyr, and tomorrow will be the end, and I'll never know the feeling of a warm little body snoozing against my chest, or the sound of baby giggles or the sight of my wife or my lover cradling a child of my own flesh and blood.

I place the binky on an end table and then turn back to Embry, pulling him into my arms and feeling his cheek against my chest.

Last time, last time.

"What would I have to forgive you for?"

"Saying no to you. Leaving you. Everything."

I kiss the top of his head. "There's nothing to forgive. I know now why you said no. I know why you left. And, Embry, even if I didn't know, even if it still broke me in half knowing you didn't want to marry me, I couldn't have faulted you for needing what you needed. Asking you to marry me—both times—it had implications beyond us simply loving each other. I was asking you to be *publicly* queer. Even now, it isn't always safe, and there's no way I could have promised you that we wouldn't lose our jobs—or worse—over being out together. The only thing I could promise you is that I would have loved you no matter what, stayed by your side no matter what the price."

"I know that." He sighs against my chest. "Which is why I worried you thought I was cowardly because you were willing to do that and you thought I wasn't."

"Safety isn't cowardice, Embry. I was hurt, of course I was hurt, but how could I blame you for taking care of yourself?"

"And now it doesn't matter. Tomorrow will come and we will fight each other, and all these years of back and forth will have been for nothing."

"Not for nothing," I say, running a thumb along his arm. "We got to have tonight."

"And your wedding night."

"And *your* wedding night."

"The forest after Caledonia."

"That night in Rome with the wine bottle."

"The night after the inauguration."

"You couldn't walk for a day afterward, remember?"

He laughs. "It was worth it."

"It's all been worth it, little prince. For me."

He presses his lips to the skin above my heart. "For me too."

Last time, last time.

"If I asked you not to go to the debate tomorrow, would you listen?"

He groans and rolls onto his back. "Is this about that nonexistent Carpathian threat? I saw the files, Ash. There's nothing there."

"Merlin says there's something. I'm terrified there's

something. What if I didn't go—if I pretended to be sick or there was an emergency or a crisis—would you agree to postpone the debate then?"

"It would throw off my entire campaign schedule. I can't."

It's my turn to groan. "Not even for your own safety?"

"I've come too far to fuck this up," he says, propping his head up on his arm to look at me. "I'm sorry, Ash, but I'm not going to throw away my shot at the White House just because Merlin has a bad feeling. You can play hooky from the debate all you like. I am going to be there."

"Is making war on Carpathia that important to you still? They're done, Melwas is gone. Greer is safe."

Embry looks down at my chest, biting his lip in thought, and when he raises his eyes back to mine, what I see there gives me some hope. "You might be right about Carpathia," he says softly. "And war. Putting Abilene in the ground today reminded me that even if you're burying an enemy, it doesn't feel good. And seeing Galahad ask for her..." He breathes out. "I don't know if I have a taste for making orphans," he says, attempting a joke.

I stay serious. "Do you really mean that?"

Can I trust you with this country?

He nods. "Yeah. Yeah, I think I mean that."

"But you still want to win."

He gives a one-shouldered shrug that manages to look elegant even though he's propped up on one elbow. "Even if I didn't, it feels too late to turn back now."

"I'm worried it's too late for a lot of things."

It's like everything is arrayed against me at once, everything has gone wrong, and the one person who could fix it all just by listening *won't.*

Is this what fate feels like from the inside? All those tragic heroes Embry told me about in Berlin, is this how they felt as their lives converged in inevitable ruin around them?

Embry leans down to kiss me. "It's not too late for us to love each other."

And I almost tell him. It's what I came here to do after all—to tell him the truth. I almost spill out every last unbelievable detail about this other life, which may or may not be a hallucination, but it's a hallucination I share with Merlin, and for some reason I can't help but believe in it. It feels so *right* to me. So true and so real. I could tell him about a flat-topped hill and an isle called Avalon and about the queen we both loved. I could tell him how it ended in the worst possible way—broken, unfinished, every last one of us betrayed—every last work unraveled by ambition and years-old hurt.

But I don't tell him, even though it's what I came here to do, because it still sounds too impossible even in my own mind. He'd never believe me. *I* barely believe me.

Instead, I let him kiss me, I let him hold me, and in the silvery dark, we make love one last time. He doesn't know it's our last time, but I can feel it in every kiss and whisper of flesh, singing as loud as a cathedral choir.

Last time, last time.

CHAPTER 28
ASH

NOW

IT'S CLOSE TO FOUR IN THE MORNING WHEN I GET TO THE White House, and Greer is tucked into our bed, softly dreaming with her hair webbed gleaming and gold over the pillows. I sit on the edge of the mattress, and I watch her for a long time. The rise and fall of her chest, the little twitches behind her eyelids, the rosy part of her lips.

And then I'm crying.

I thought it would make it easier to say goodbye separately, I thought I could minimize the pain to myself, but I'd indulged in a lie because this is no fucking easier. I've had so much practice saying goodbye to Embry, but to my Greer—

No, I'm as weak as a child right now, as lost as a lamb in the dark fields. How can I say goodbye to *her*? The keeper of my soul and my heart? The queen of broken glass?

My crying wakes her, and she stirs slowly, beautifully, a sleeping beauty straight out of a fairy tale. When her eyes flutter open and she sees me, she reaches for me, just like a kitten should reach for her sir, and I let her. I pull her into my arms and hold her as tight as I can and as I let my tears fall into her hair.

"What is it?" she whispers against my throat. "Do you need me?"

"Yes. God. Please."

"Then take me, sir," she says. Her words tickle the skin of my throat, and I tilt her head back, searching her eyes.

I wonder about telling her. Greer knows the myths and legends better than anyone, and unlike Embry, her self-worth and self-image aren't wrapped up in resisting me. She of anyone might be the most likely to believe all of it, as staggeringly impossible as it is. But then what would it change? If she did believe me? There's nothing I will do differently—I will still stand next to Embry tomorrow and I will still lay down my life if necessary. The only purpose it would serve would be to make her as miserable and as fearful as I am, and if I can spare her that at least, then I am delivering a mercy. Perhaps it's better to be her sir in this too and protect her from as much as I can.

Her eyes are searching mine right back. "What is it?" she asks softly. "What is it?"

I think I've finally found my right sacrifice, I want to tell her. *I think I've learned the day I'll be asked to set down my sword and my crown.*

It wasn't enough for me to live, and now I have to die.

I don't tell her that. Instead I kiss her lips as gently as I've ever kissed her, just enjoying the silky brush of her mouth against my own, and I turn her over on my lap so that she's draped across me and her ass is presented for my hand.

I spank her without warning, without warm-up. After each smack, I plump and soothe her stinging flesh, but I don't take it easy on her; I don't let up. I spank until I feel the sweat beading along my hairline, until she's crying into the sheets, until her bottom is the color of cherries in the summer. And I play with her pussy in between the abuses, since it's so available to me, swollen and wet and flushed and almost insolently peeking up through her ass cheeks. When I slide my fingers inside for the first time, I'm reminded that I am not the first man to use her body tonight, and oh, how that gets me hard. Especially as I feel the tender place in my own body where I was used by the same man.

I stroke her inner walls with demanding, cruel strokes. "It gets me off to feel you so slippery and messy from Embry." I give her ass a hard slap. "Do you like that? Having your husband feel how wet you are from another man? To be your sloppy seconds?"

She moans against the sheets, wiggling her ass higher, and I give her cheek a final slap before I toss her roughly across the bed and crawl over her. I pin her hips in place with my thighs, rising up to yank off my shirt.

"All I've ever wanted," I breathe, "from the first moment I saw you, was to cuff you to my bed and keep you forever. To trade my heart for yours, so that wherever we went, we were inside each other."

She offers me her wrists, and she's such a fucking picture right now with her nipples furled tight and her chest flushed and her delicious hair tangled everywhere. Offering herself. "Keep me forever, Mr. President," she begs. "Please, please, please."

God, how will I bear this? How will I disobey her tomorrow and let her go?

I unbuckle my belt and slide it free from its loops with a leathery hiss, cinching her wrists tight and threading the tail through the clasp. "Flex your fingers," I tell her, and she does. I pinch one of her fingertips, then I put my palm against hers. "Squeeze my hand." She does, her eyes glassy and her body trembling underneath me.

It was one of the sweetest discoveries of our relationship when it started—I'd already known she wanted the darkness—but her delight in the minutiae of kink gratified the careful dom in me. More than gratified—it fed me, nourished me in ways I never even knew I needed. She thrived on the smallest of cares and attentions, and I delighted in giving them to her, watching my lonely little princess bloom into a formidable queen as I tended to her the way she needed. Every safety check, every negotiation, every pre-scene discussion was foreplay to her, and every shower and snuggle and morning when I chose what I wanted her to wear was the most tender aftercare. There are as many ways of being a submissive as there are of being a human, and while Embry's brand of pugilistic submission was ambrosial in its own way, it was nothing compared to the intoxicatingly complete surrender of Greer's.

Greer *wants* to submit.

She *needs* to.

That young man dreaming of the Goblin King had never even come close to dreaming of this.

Satisfied that her circulation is good and we're not risking nerve damage, I give her hand a squeeze back. "Hands above your head, sweetheart."

She raises her bound wrists above her head, which serves the purpose of making her mouthwatering breasts jut closer to me with their tempting peaks. "What's your safe word?"

"Maxen."

I give one of her breasts a vicious slap, loving the arch of her underneath me as the pain sizzles through her body. Her eyes are still wet with tears from her spanking, and I know the blanket underneath her sensitive ass must feel sandpaper-rough. I lean down, one hand on her throat and the other running through her hair, and I have a moment when I'm frozen, hovering above her lips, the tips of our noses dancing together.

I'm frozen because it's too much, *she's* too much, she's too interesting, too intelligent, too slyly funny, too honest, too brave, too fucking beautiful for me to say goodbye to her. My hand at her head could spend weeks stroking her hair, my other hand at her throat could feel the thread and thrum of her pulse for years. I was born to sit with her body between my thighs, and my lips could spend eternity slipping and breathing against hers.

How could I have thought I could say goodbye in one night? When I could spend years and years and never get enough of her?

I'm crying again.

I kiss her hard, kissing down all the questions and worries I know she must have, and then I clap a hand over her mouth as I move my lips to her jaw, to her throat, to her collarbone. And there I do my goddamned best to make a farewell of her body, my hand stifling her moans and my body keeping hers still as I nurse at her breasts and lick into the little well of her navel. I don't pull my hand from her mouth until I'm moving down to her hips and her thighs, leaving no place unkissed, untasted, not even the backs of her knees or the rough pads of her toes.

I flip her over, making the same tour over her warm, spanked ass, over the dimples in her lower back, up to the angel wings of her shoulder blades. Kisses and bites and licks and sucks, anything a hungry mouth can do to a sweep of willing flesh, all the way up to her neck. I kiss her ears, the base of her skull, the winding loops of her cool, silky hair, remembering with pained fondness all the times I've rubbed that hair over the most private parts of me just to feel the cool silkiness on my most sensitive skin. Wrapped around my cock, sliding against my sac. Tickling my inner thighs. It would make her eyes glow with lust as she laid her head on my thigh and watched my face as I despoiled her hair. It would make her so wet that I could see the arousal shining on her thighs, so wet that I could smell the faint honey scent of it on the air.

Tonight, however, I move back down her body, kissing down the pearl necklace of her spine until I reach the spot I want to be. I grab her hips to hoist her up, and then I part her cheeks and give her a flat, long lick from clit to ass.

She cries out, rocking from side to side, and I give her a little swat. “Hold still, angel. This part’s for me, not you.”

“Mmph,” she says, pressing her face into the blanket as I return to her seam and begin fucking her with my tongue. *“Mmph!”*

I wasn’t lying though, because this part *is* for me. I can’t imagine dying without tasting her one last time; I can’t imagine leaving this life without the lingering memory of her on my tongue. She tastes so fucking sweet, with just that bit of salt and earth that makes her all Greer, and I’m so hard as I eat her, as I wonder which parts of her taste are uniquely hers and which are uniquely Embry’s.

I must have tasted her at least once a day since we’ve been married, but it will never be enough. Fuck. Never ever.

I make her come like this…then a second time, rolling her to her back so that I can see her face as I peer up at her over the rise of her pussy. It’s not a position I’ve used often, which is partly because it’s a very passive, docile way to eat a woman, although I meant what I said to Embry about positions being irrelevant to the heart of kink. No, it’s more that the temptation of her is too great like this, when I can see her lips working silently and her gray eyes massive with lust and love—and the minute I make her come again, I’m unfastening my pants and sliding home.

Every part of it I savor. Every part I commit to memory. The gasping way she says my name. The frantic rock of her hips when I slow down. The tremors in her thighs after I pinch her ass for being an impertinent slut and moving when I didn't tell her to.

The wet, sweet clench of her cunt as she comes a third time.

And finally, the look in her eyes as I surge over her and give her everything, everything of me.

Perhaps Embry's always had the part of me that wielded the sword, but she…she's always owned the part that wears the crown.

My little princess, my submissive, my professor and my angel.

My queen.

And maybe, if I've gotten to find her and Embry in a second life, I'll get to find them in a third. Maybe tomorrow I'll close my eyes and when I wake, we'll all be together again, starting all over, heartbreaks and wars and all. Because one thing's for fucking certain—while my heart beats, it will beat for them, no matter which life we're in.

I will find them again and I will love them again.

And if I have to, I will die for them again.

CHAPTER 29
ASH

NOW

GREER IS ATTENDING THE DEBATE WITH ME, AND I CAN'T find it in my heart to wish her elsewhere. I want her close, I want her near, and as much as I don't want her to see what comes next, I take a small cinder of comfort in knowing that Embry will be here. He will take care of her afterward, and she of him. I think back to my phone call with Merlin last night and swallow.

I should take pride in what will happen after I die. Take joy, even. This is all new, all different from my other life.

For once, at least two of us will have a happily ever after. And perhaps the letter I gave Merlin this morning to mail to Seattle will give Lyr some closure as well. I only had the chance to be his father for such a brief time, but I still want him to know that I treasured that time, that I loved him, and that I have every bit of faith in him and his future. All the things I never had a father tell me.

The pre-debate process is much the same. Makeup,

notes, bustling. Merlin is there, silent like me, as Belvedere and Kay talk. They don't know. No one knows except us, and I have a flash of empathy for Merlin. How has he borne it all these years, knowing things no one else did? Knowing horrible, ugly sins and terrifying futures?

It's a very lonely feeling.

Finally, Greer is kissing me for good luck, and she looks surprised but happy as I seize her close and kiss her hard, sliding my tongue between her lips and tasting her to my satisfaction. When I let her go, I take her left hand in both of mine and hold it to my chest. "I love you more than life itself," I say quietly, seriously. "And I always want you to be happy. Watching you and Embry love each other has been the greatest joy of my life. My love for the two of you exists inside your love for each other—when you love each other, you are loving me. Promise me you'll remember that."

"Ash, I—" Her brow is furrowed and her eyes are frantically searching mine.

"Say *Yes, sir, I promise.*"

She pulls her lips into her mouth, then lets out a long, worried breath. "Yes, sir, I promise."

I kiss her forehead and walk away. If those are to be her last words to me on this earth, then I can't imagine any better ones.

Yes, sir, I promise.

Thank God. If I go through the trouble of dying tonight only so that Greer and Embry spend their lives apart out of some misguided sense of honor, I'm going to be one furious sir. A dead sir, yes, but still a furious one.

And then it's time to go backstage and wait for our cue to enter.

Embry comes to stand next to me. "Brought enough Secret Service agents?" he asks quietly, so Harrison Fasse and the producer's assistant can't hear him.

"To keep you safe."

Embry lets out a huff, half-annoyed, half-amused. "You saw the metal detectors and pat-downs happening to the audience right? The agents in here sweeping the place? The background checks for the television staff?"

"There are ways of getting around metal detectors, Embry, and backgrounds can be forged well enough to pass a check."

"You're paranoid."

"Maybe." I move past the producer's assistant—a man about my age who looks distinctly irritated with my jostling and talking—so that I can angle my body against Embry's. So that no one can see me take his right hand and check for the ring I put on his finger last night.

It's not there.

My stomach twists in hurt even as I recognize I'm being ridiculous. What, did I expect he'd wear it on national television? The day after his wife's funeral no less?

But then he says quietly, "Wrong hand." And when he lifts his left hand, I see that he's replaced his other wedding band with mine.

My throat closes and I can't speak.

"It belongs there. It always belonged there, Ash. It should have been your ring from the beginning."

"Little prince."

"I know it's hard to believe that I love you, that I need you still, even as I'm fighting you, but can you? For me? Can you believe it? Because I do love you, and even if I still want to finish this race, I'll always kneel to you. Even if I *win*, I'll still kneel to you. We've always loved each other like this—alongside the struggle and the fighting. We can keep doing it… I want to keep doing it."

But this is the end, little prince. For me at least.

After tonight, I'll have to let you and Greer go.

I don't say that. Instead, as the moderator's voice comes over the sound system and the audience begins their wave of polite applause, I say quickly, "Promise me you'll love Greer as I do, that you'll take care of her."

For a minute, I think he doesn't hear me over the applause and the churlish hustle of the assistant toward the stage, and then he is looking at me with a genuinely confused expression, his eyebrows pinched together and his mouth pulled into an elegant frown. "Ash? What are you talking about?"

"Just say it," I beg, only a step away from the stage. "Just let me hear it. Please."

"Okay," he says slowly. "I'll take care of her. But, Ash—"

It's too late—the assistant is pushing me onto the stage and into the bright lights and there's no time to explain. There's only time to smile and to wave and to hope that Merlin is wrong about tonight, about everything.

Please, God, let him be wrong.

I think of this afternoon as I take my podium, as I smile, as I search the room for danger and as I make all the subtle adjustments you're trained to make—straightening your suit and finding the cameras and making sure your notes are in order. I think of how my hands shook earlier as I fixed my cuff links and slid my tie bar into place, how it took me three tries to put that damn flag pin on my lapel. I spent years getting shot at, waking up on muddy hills thinking that day might be my last, and yet I'd never felt fear like I felt it this afternoon getting ready to meet my end.

Maybe because, despite everything, I believe Merlin. Maybe because if I don't get this right, Embry could die.

Maybe because it means letting go of all that I've worked for—all the peace and prosperity I've tried to build—and having to trust it to the people I leave behind. I have to trust that they will hoist the banner for me after I'm gone, that they'll keep doing the work, that the world will be and stay a better place in their care.

It's the hardest thing to ask a dominant, to let go of his control, and certainly the hardest thing to ask of a king—and I suppose that means it's the most necessary thing to ask.

I think of the dreams that have been shining through my sleep lately, the dreams about that place over the water. The quiet lake and the drifting fog. I thought at first that it was Vivienne Moore's lake, but now that my new memories have surfaced, I think it's a different lake. One I've traveled over before, but not in this life.

Only I can't remember the place over the water. Even now, that memory stays hidden from me.

The first question comes, and the debate truly begins and…it's easy. Not like last time, when I couldn't find my own words, not like the time before when my heart was twisting at the sight of Embry after two years apart. It's almost like this really is a battle in truth, and the battle clarity falls over me like a cool cloak, and I feel light.

Free.

Ready.

Harrison makes a clumsy remark, which Embry leaps on gracefully, and it's easy to spin both arguments into my own point, easy to speak intelligently and clearly as I keep my eyes searching the periphery of the stage, the backlit heads of the audience. Merlin didn't know what to look for, and neither do I, so I keep my eyes open for anything. Someone skulking behind the risers the audience sits on or a cameraman acting strangely. Anything that triggers a sense of unease, of not-rightness.

There's nothing.

Everything is as it should be.

The debate rolls on—foreign policy, homeland defense, military spending—and they're things I could answer in my sleep. Embry too, although he still hasn't shaved the hawkish edge off his rhetoric—which, listening to him talk, I think is less about what he personally still believes and more about the practiced answers he hasn't had time to alter since his change of heart after Abilene's death.

I glance at my watch while Harrison Fasse answers the next question. We're forty minutes into the debate, and there hasn't been so much as an untoward sneeze in the room. A heady sense of relief begins to pound through me, almost dizzying in its strength.

Merlin was wrong.

Merlin was wrong.

Of course he was! Of course he was wrong, and all of this was just a delusion that I'd been weak enough to share. How silly of me to think one man could see the future, how foolish of me to believe any of this. There's only the here and now, this one life, and I don't even feel embarrassed that I believed it because I'm so fucking relieved.

Embry is safe.

No one has to say goodbye tonight.

Fasse is given the first chance at final remarks, and then it's Embry's turn, and I'm so full of relief and dizzy happiness that I'm smiling as he talks. I'll get to hear him talk as much as I want now; I'll get to stroke his hair while we both cradle Greer to sleep every night, election be damned. Fuck my pride. If he wins, I'll still be in his bed every night with my queen.

Nothing, not the White House or war or death, will break the three of us. Nothing.

When it's my turn, I feel as if all my relief and happiness and ease flow out into my words.

"I hope that I've been a good president for this country," I say, taking the time to look into each face in the audience. "I believe that I have. I've given this country all of my energy and all of my heart—first as a soldier and then as your leader. Mr. Moore and Mr. Fasse love this country as I do, and I'm proud to stand up here with them. I'm also proud to stand on my accomplishments. Everything I've done, I've done for peace, which might sound strange for a soldier to say, but it's the truth. When you vote next week—and when you're using your voices to keep who you voted for accountable—I hope you speak for peace each and every time. I hope you choose giving over taking. I hope you choose sharing instead of holding on, I hope you choose hope over fear. And I hope that together we keep choosing these things, not just once, but day after day—even when it's hard, even when we're angry and we're afraid. Choose each other. Believe in each other as I believe in you."

And then I add simply, "Thank you for having me as your president. It's been the greatest honor I can imagine."

There's a moment of quiet, of stunned silence. It's too short for a closing argument, too vague. I didn't even ask them for their votes, and I know somewhere backstage, Kay and Uri are gnashing their teeth in frustration that I went off script.

But then the applause starts, loud and rolling through the room like thunder, filling every corner, and I allow myself a single, quiet moment of pride.

Which is when it happens.

A cameraman, trying to wheel the camera around to catch the applauding crowd, realizes the dolly is trapped by some cords duct-taped to the floor and whips out a utility knife to cut the tape free and get his shot—and in a blink, the applause turns to chaos as three agents swarm him out of nowhere, grappling him to the ground and overturning the camera with an almighty crash.

I take a step forward, suddenly flooded with adrenaline, and perhaps it's the chemical rush or perhaps it's the lingering clarity from earlier or perhaps it's just always how it was meant to happen, but I see a flash of movement from backstage—the side Embry's on.

It's the producer's assistant.

And with all the Secret Service agents trained on the cameraman, no one sees, and Embry himself has his back turned to the assistant—like me, he was getting ready to move toward the commotion, the soldier in him unwilling to hold back from jumping in.

I'm so close to him.

As I was meant to be.

It comes together in something faster and neater than an instant, every single piece of our story, every moment that the three of us have ever lived, and if this is the least of what I can give, then I'll give it gladly.

It's not fear I feel in this final second, but love. All along it was me who had the whole world in his eyes.

There's barely time to catch the white glint of a ceramic knife before I've taken the two steps necessary to shove my way between the attacker and Embry, and the arcing blade is aimed right for Embry's ribs.

I'm there. I'm there just in time, and I manage to knock the blade aside with an elbow and the side of my arm. There's a bright slash of pain along my triceps, a shove to my shoulder that staggers me back, and then we're wrestling for control of the knife.

All of this happens in a split second, and I feel Embry turning in shock behind me. I can sense the rush of Secret Service agents toward us, and I land a knee in the attacker's groin right as he kicks at my foot, and our tangled legs send us both falling to the floor, me on top of him.

I land with my forearm on his throat and my hand groping for the wrist of his knife hand, grunting as his knee or elbow or something digs into my stomach.

"It's over," I say.

"Strength in the Mountains," he wheezes underneath me. "Strength until Death."

The Carpathian motto.

"There's strength here too," I tell him. "You're done."

I finally find his knife hand as Embry drops to my side to help me wrestle the would-be assassin and the Secret Service agents surround us, shouting and grabbing for the attacker. And as I'm gently pulled back to my knees and the attacker is pinned down, there's one thing I'm very, very aware of.

The attacker no longer has the knife in his hand.

I look down.

"*Ash*," Embry says, his face going pale. His eyes are on my stomach, and it's not the pain I register first, but the hot spill of my own blood.

Somewhere someone screams.

And then I'm so dizzy I can't breathe, can't think properly, and I feel myself slumping—against Embry. It's my little prince's chest I'm against, and it's so solid and so warm, and all those years I spent holding him, I should have made him hold me too, because it's so nice, so very nice. He's so strong. So good.

"The ambulance outside is ready, the paramedics are coming now," someone says nearby. Belvedere.

Then a cloud of soft gold. "You stay here," Greer says fiercely, her hands tight around mine, her lips near my ear. "You can't leave me, you can't leave *us*, Ash, please—"

She's crying, and Embry's chest is heaving behind me, and his hands are everywhere, trying to staunch the blood and cradle my face, and when I force my eyes open, I see the two of them. And I see Morgan, her face pale with horror and her hands pressed to her mouth, and Vivienne Moore barking orders at anyone who will listen, and for a minute the three women—Greer and Morgan and Vivienne—are different, dressed in gowns and crowns, and there's a fourth woman, a woman I've never seen before, but I know her name.

Imogen.

My birth mother.

Behind her, the lake beckons, still and clear as glass. The four of them will go with me, but I know only my mother will take me to whatever waits after the lake.

And then I blink again and I'm back in this life, back among Greer's desperate pleas and Embry's broken sobs and so many hands are lifting me—a backboard or a gurney maybe—and there are so many screams and so much shouting, and at the last, before my vision dims completely, I murmur hazily up to Greer and Embry, "You have to kiss me goodbye before you go."

And then there are frantic kisses and tears, and hands warm with my own blood.

There's a boat waiting for me.

There's a better place, over the water.

The Place Over the Water

CHAPTER 30
GREER

THREE MONTHS LATER

"I, EMBRY LANCE MOORE, DO SOLEMNLY SWEAR THAT I WILL faithfully execute the Office of President of the United States, and will, to the best of my ability, preserve, protect, and defend the Constitution of the United States."

The cold wind whips around my ears as I look up at the dais where Embry stands with the chief justice of the Supreme Court, looking sober and painfully handsome in his long wool coat and leather gloves, his hand resting on a Bible that's all too familiar.

It's Ash's Bible.

I don't realize I'm crying until the wind gusts again, freezing the tears right off my face. Ash kept that Bible on his end table always; it wasn't unusual for me to crawl into bed and find him already there, shirtless and absorbed, the heavy book propped against one pajama-clad knee. Many nights I fell asleep to the sound of those onion-skin pages turning carefully, to his steady breathing as he shut the Bible around his finger and closed his eyes to pray about what he'd just read.

My faithful king.

Merlin wraps his arm around me, handing me a handkerchief to try to minimize the danger of tear-induced frostbite. I lean into him, his body strong and slender under his own wool coat, and I remember a time as a little girl when I was terrified of him. Now, after the last three months, I count him as one of my dearest friends. Nimue too, his new wife, who is on the other side of me. And on the other side of her, her adopted son and heartbreaking reminder of all that I've lost, Lyr.

I steal a glance at him, and even at seventeen, he has so much of Ash in his face, in his bearing, all black hair and serious features and green eyes that already promise honor and dignity.

I turn back to Merlin and try to stop crying.

Up on the dais, the ceremony concludes, with Embry waving at the people and then giving Galahad—snuggled tight in Vivienne's arms—a kiss on the forehead. A ripple of adoration goes through the crowd.

I cry some more, and this time Lyr himself reaches across Nimue to hand me a fresh handkerchief.

I don't remember much from the night my husband died. I don't even know if I want to—what I do remember is horrible enough.

Being pulled away from Ash after I kissed him goodbye.

The paramedic saying, "Shit, he's fading—he's going—" as he struggled to get an IV.

The smell of blood like salt and metal and the white knife sticking out of his body like a bone.

The Secret Service agents yanking me away as I screamed,

and they had to wrestle Embry back too—I saw him swinging at the agent trying to move him away. Eventually he was carried; he was kicking; he was screaming too, both of us screaming and fighting to get back to Ash's side.

It was protocol, see. To get us all to different secure locations in case the attack wasn't finished, in case there was more…

Neither Embry nor I were there when Ash died. It was Merlin.

Fitting, I guess. Merlin was there when Ash's life began… and then he was there as it ended.

By the time the protocol had been satisfied and the Secret Service pronounced us all safe, Ash was dead, his body en route to the funeral home, and the nation was in shock. A president had just been killed on live television. And not just any president, but *Maxen Colchester*—the hero, the handsome king who had won a nation with his honesty and goodness and bravery. He'd died to save his own opponent, who was also his best friend, and it more than humbled everyone to witness. It shook the country, rattled the country right down to its bones. Here was a man who not only said good and brave things, but acted on them even until the very last, who carved a new definition of honor and courage into the dictionary with a white knife and red blood.

I should have listened, Embry said over and over again. *I should have listened. It's my fault.*

His guilt filled him like water, like blood.

And I—I was nothing. A ghost. A vacancy of grieving air. I sleepwalked through the funeral, through the interment of the ashes. Merlin asked if I wanted to keep the cremated remains or scatter them, but my mother-in-law wanted her son in the family cemetery in Kansas City where she could visit him, and no one had the heart to refuse her.

My heart had been burned up alongside my husband's anyway.

Kay was sworn in the night Ash died, and also became the lead name on the ticket, naming Trieste as her vice presidential candidate. It was a close race, with Ash's death casting a huge confusing pall over everything. Did the sympathy vote go to his sister? Or his best friend and fellow soldier?

It went to Embry in the end, but only by the skin of his teeth. When he got the call, I was standing in his hotel room; the watch party was in the ballroom down below.

"I have to go down and give the speech," he said, swallowing. His hands were shaking. "Will you come?"

I would come. Somewhere deep inside my hollow form, there was a memory of a girl who had been groomed for such moments, and that girl knew the importance of continuity. Whoever won, having Ash's widow at their side would show the country it was okay, that the transition of power was good and necessary, and would hopefully lend an air of something like postmortem endorsement from the fallen president. I would have done the same had Kay won.

Embry gave a beautiful speech, mostly about Ash and what a leader Ash had been. How much he intended to honor Ash's wish for peace. And for the first time, he told the world that he'd loved Ash not only as a brother in arms, but as a man.

All Ash had ever wanted was to publicly call Embry his own, and now Embry was giving him that at last, even if it was after Ash was in the ground.

I suppose there was some media furor around it, but it was mild, over quickly. That Ash had been queer as well only seemed to add to the ways that the nation grieved, not subtract from it, and that the new president-elect was openly bisexual merely added to the energy of his election. Aside from a few men stepping forward to sell tell-alls of torrid nights with either Ash or Embry, the truth of their love floated up into the air like a balloon and drifted easily into the horizon. The world was ready to know it and mostly be okay with it. Ash would have been proud of that—he did always like to believe the best of his people, and here they were, being the best about one of the most personal, intimate parts of his life.

The day after Embry won the election, with the November cold creeping in through the corners and windows, I found out I was pregnant.

I texted him—who else would I text?—and he came to the White House right away, finding me sitting on the bathroom floor, staring at the pregnancy test like it might bite me, with citadels of cardboard and packing tape closing me in like a prison. I was supposed to move out that week, make room for Kay, who would live there until Embry moved in after his inauguration, and I'd insisted on packing up all of our personal effects myself. Ash's toothbrush and half-empty bottle of mouthwash. His comb, with a single black hair caught in the teeth…now the only hair of his that existed on earth.

The pregnancy test sat surrounded by it all like some kind of mythic relic, the Holy Grail I'd been striving for these past three years. How long I'd waited to behold this one thing, these two blue lines, and now seeing them made me electric with fear.

Embry scooped me easily into his arms and carried me to the bed—my marital bed, Ash's bed—and arranged me against his chest. I felt like I couldn't breathe for either joy or grief or both.

"I don't know whose it is," I said numbly. "Yours or his."

"It doesn't matter, Greer. I'm yours either way."

He pressed his hand low on my stomach. He took a breath. "And if it is Ash's—" He broke off, but he didn't need to finish because I knew what he was thinking.

If it was Ash's, then it might be the only part of him we had left.

Three months after Embry's inauguration, we marry in a quiet ceremony by Vivienne's lake. It's late April, with a fresh spring breeze rustling along the shore, and as Embry and I say our vows, he keeps one hand in mine and the other on my belly, which pushes through my simple white dress in a taut curve. The baby kicks as I say *I do*, and we both laugh. When we exchange rings, we exchange the same ones we already had, so that I'm wearing the wedding ring I married Ash with and Embry is wearing the band Ash gave him the night before he died.

My love for the two of you exists inside your love for each other—when you love each other, you are loving me.

I have to believe that's true. I have to believe that this is what Ash would have wanted, and anyway, there's no other way it could have happened—Embry and I were magnetized together by our hurt. Who else could understand my loss? Who else would miss every part of Ash, not just the leader or the friend, but the cruel, demanding lover and the devout Catholic and the tired soldier who still had trouble sleeping at night?

With each other, the pain seemed bearable because we could share it and nurse it and tend to it, and keep our memory of Ash alive and thriving. The first time we fucked, the night of Ash's funeral, each pretending he was still there with us, it felt like the first time I could breathe again, and I hoped and prayed to God it was what Ash had meant the night he died. That no matter what happened, he would want Embry and me to be happy together.

Happy would be a stretch without Ash. But being together…yes, we could do that at least.

And for the sake of the child in my belly, I hoped that happiness would come again, even if I doubted it could ever come for me. But for Embry and this baby, I wished all the happiness in the world.

Strangely, the biggest advocate for our relationship was Merlin. Merlin who had once admonished us to keep our ménage a secret, who had once pressured Embry to keep his relationship with Ash hidden. It was as if something broke free in Merlin after Ash's death, like a great burden had been lifted, and for the first time I saw how truly capable of compassion and friendliness he was.

"Let the public gawk," he said with a dismissive gesture when Embry and I told him about the baby. "I daresay they'll ultimately find it romantic that you found comfort with each other. And if they point back to the Melwas video and cry *affair*, who cares? You have more than enough PR capital to spend on it."

And today, at our wedding, he is in the very front row. He was there at the private wedding Mass Embry and I had first thing this morning, the only one sitting in the pews as we made our vows with the Church. And here at the ceremony we are having for our friends and family, he walked me down the aisle to give me away. He beams at us as we exchange our vows for the second time today, and for a moment I have to absorb how strange I would have thought this wedding years ago. Behind me, Morgan stands as my matron of honor, in front of me stands Nimue performing the ceremony, and behind Embry stands Lyr, straight and manlike in his tuxedo, so very like Ash that it hurts and it heals to see him here in this moment. And between us both sits Galahad in his own miniature tuxedo. He's found a stand of early dandelions and he's busy plucking them in his little toddler fists and blowing the seeds at our legs. And in his happy laugh, I hear both Embry and Abilene. Whatever her faults, he has the best parts of her—the spontaneity, the courage, the determination—and now he is my son too, and I love him as I will love my unborn child once they are born. Embry and I are waiting until the birth to find out the sex.

In the small spread of chairs along the shore, all the people I care about and love are here, with nothing but blessings in their hearts for Embry and me—Vivienne, Kay and Althea Colchester, Trieste, Belvedere, Uri, Gawayne, Percival Wu and Emily Gareth, and Lynette my assistant.

With all of them watching, and for the second time in my life—and technically the second time today—I marry the president of the United States.

After the ceremony, we have the reception on Vivienne's wide lawn—surrounded by mountains and with the water glinting teasingly through the trees—and Merlin finds me after the cake and dancing.

"Would you mind taking a stroll with me?" he asks. "The sunset will be quite pretty over the lake, I think."

I kiss Embry goodbye for now, and he slings his tuxedo jacket over my shoulders when I tell him where I'm going, and then Merlin and I step out on the smooth path down to the lake.

"Congratulations," Merlin says. "It was a beautiful wedding."

"Thank you. I wish…"

But I don't actually know what I want to wish for. That I didn't need to have a second wedding because my first husband was still alive? Obviously, yes, of course, that an infinite amount of times over.

Still, these last few months Embry and I have shared…I don't know that we could have shared them at any other time. Even after Chicago, when we were both still technically unattached, I don't know that we could have built something lasting and real, because we would both have ached for the man we really wanted, possibly to the detriment of loving each other. It's only been in the shadow of his death, in the real chasing of his ghost, that we've been able to offer ourselves naked and unconditionally to each other. Because we are all that we have left—and all that we have left of Ash. Our love has finally grown from a sapling in the shade of Ash's mighty heart into something powerful and eternal in its own right.

So I can't wish things the same, but I also can't wish them different. I will always be half a heart without Ash, but sharing the remains with Embry has been beautiful too—all the more beautiful for his own pain.

Thankfully, Merlin seems to know what I'm struggling to convey. He nods as he takes my hand to guide me over the rocky rise that leads to the shore path, and again I notice how strong he is, how still young he is. He's barely touching fifty, and his hair and eyes are as dark and fairy-tale like as ever. I get the sudden sense, just from the warmth of his hand holding mine, that behind all that urbane sophistication, behind all that mystery, is a surfeit of carnal and deep power. Nimue is a lucky woman.

"I have a wedding gift for you," he says, "but first I wanted to tell you a story. And I've been waiting to tell it to you for a very long time."

"Is that right?"

"But I think you know the first part. You're about to publish a book about it."

I look up at him with some surprise. "The book about kingship in the Dark Ages?"

"The very same."

He helps me over a log—help I wouldn't have needed just a month ago, but the baby nestled in my belly has grown enough to shift my center of balance now, plus I'm still in my wedding dress—and then we are at the shore itself. The water laps clear and quiet at the multicolored stones, and the music and merriment of the reception fade behind us. It's almost like we're in a different world now, a world apart from time, from the usual grinding on of events and history.

"I suppose you've never noticed, in all of your research, how many parallels there are between the stories about King Arthur and your own life?"

I laugh a little. "It's hard not to notice, talking to someone named Merlin." I say it mockingly, teasingly, but he doesn't respond in kind.

"Greer, think. Not about my name, but about everything else. Your affair with Maxen's best friend, his son with his sister—all of it. Has it never struck you as odd?"

I pull back and stop, looking at Merlin to see if he's truly serious. "It's never struck me as odd because King Arthur as we know him isn't real. There's a historical figure we can point to as the source of the legend, but everything else—the incestuous son, an unfaithful queen—they're all just stories. They didn't really happen."

"They did happen," Merlin says quietly. "I know because I was there."

I stare.

He stares back, eyes like obsidian mirrors reflecting my own face, my own uncertainty, and revealing nothing of his own.

"Some things happened differently," he continues softly. "And the legends have confused a lot. People have changed names, changed roles, but the heart of it is the same: once upon a time, there were two warriors who loved the same woman as much as they loved each other. And everything that happened afterward led inevitably to tragedy."

"You can't expect me to believe that," I protest, but my protest sounds hollow, even to my own ears. It's something about the lake right now, something about his eyes. Something about the fog creeping in from the edges of the forest, like a memory from another world. I struggle and search for all the reasons why this is impossible. "You scared me with a story like this when I was a girl too. Remember? *Keep your kisses to yourself.*"

At that he touches my chin, making sure our eyes meet. "Greer, I told you everything that you needed to hear to make things happen the way they needed to."

"I don't believe you."

"And not just you. I told Embry what he needed to hear, and Maxen as well."

"No."

Merlin continues gazing at me in that way of his that reveals nothing—well, almost nothing. There's something in those depths that reassures me, and I'm not sure what it is. Benevolence? Sincerity?

"When I told Embry all those years ago that he had to sacrifice his relationship with Maxen in order for Maxen to do great things…when I told Maxen that there was no way he could accomplish everything he wanted to do in a single term—I didn't say those things because I believed them, Greer. I said them because they were what they needed to hear, just as I said the things you needed to hear. Everything I told you, every warning or request or piece of advice, was all designed to bring us here. To this."

"To what?"

Merlin looks up at the sky for a minute, the sunset painting vivid color in his onyx eyes. "Peace."

"I—" I don't have a response to this. I'm confused and stunned and a little angry and still disbelieving. And as I'm cycling through all of these feelings, Merlin leads me to a nearby log and bids me to sit.

"It had to happen this way," he says gently, peering down at me. "Every part of it. The way he loved Embry during the war, the way he loved you, the heartbreak over both of you.

Jenny. Your wedding and then your abduction. Every single thing drove Ash to become more than a leader. He became a king, a legend, and the work he did is going to stand for the next century. His sacrifice ensured that—the memory of his heroic death is going to protect all that he's built. But none of it—not the peace or the prosperity or the progress—could have happened without the three of you loving and hurting for each other as you did."

I still can't find any words—thoughts, feelings—anything. It's as if someone has come to tell me that the sun is dark and the sky is below my feet.

"It was all necessary, Greer. Every moment of it. And I'm happy to say that this time I got it right."

"Got what right?" I whisper, looking up at him.

He smiles kindly and sits next to me, glancing meaningfully at my belly, at the hand that curls protectively over it, where Ash's ring winks in the scarlet and orange light. "There is a happy ending this time. Last time, you and Embry chose the memory of Ash's grave over each other, and last time, there was no child of Ash's body inside you."

This provokes the first real flash of feeling from me other than shock. My heart flutters in my chest to match the hard flutters in my stomach. "The baby is Ash's?"

"Yes."

My eyelids burn and I look away. Embry and I had decided not to do a paternity test because we knew it didn't matter to our future—in another, better life, I would have carried both their children regardless—but still, I had wondered. Wished for this one last piece of him.

Merlin is still smiling, his eyes on the lake now. "There's so much ahead of you."

The sun finally drops below the mountains, kissing everything green and gold and foggy, and I decide to believe him. I decide to push away how impossible it all is, how thoroughly surreal, and just accept what the quiet water and Merlin's dark eyes already seem to know.

"Another eight years in the White House?" I ask, looking at the lake too. "More children?"

"More children for sure. Too many, some might say," he chuckles. "But not another eight years in the White House, only four. Embry could easily win if he runs again, but he won't want to. The next fight will fall to Morgan and Kay, and whoever wins will safeguard Maxen's legacy just as carefully as Embry would. The future will go to Maxen's sisters."

"Embry won't want a second term?" I ask, confused. "Even if it's obvious he could win?"

"There will be something else he wants more. Which reminds me, I have your wedding gift right here." He reaches inside his pocket, withdrawing a small envelope with long, elegant fingers.

"Shall I open it now?"

"Why not?" he says, standing up and smoothing his jacket. "It is for you and Embry both, of course. That's how wedding gifts work."

I open up the envelope and a key falls out. Just a plain silver key, the ordinary size and shape of a house key. It glitters orange in the fading light.

There's a small piece of paper inside as well, with an address I don't recognize and a string of numbers at the bottom.

"You'll find the necessary travel plans already made," Merlin says briskly. "And Embry's schedule cleared for the next week and a half."

I blink up at him. Embry and I hadn't planned on taking a honeymoon—partly because my last honeymoon had ended with an abduction, and partly because we still didn't have the heart to celebrate our marriage without Ash.

"You planned us a honeymoon?"

Merlin smiles but doesn't answer, turning to walk back to Vivienne's house.

"But why did you give us a key?" I call after him.

He pauses and looks back at me. "I only said it was a gift, Greer. I didn't say it was from me."

CHAPTER 31
GREER

"I DON'T THINK I'VE EVER BEEN HERE BEFORE," I SAY THE next day, peering out of the window. "Strange to think this is only an hour outside DC. It's like another world."

The car noses down a curving ribbon of road, green mountains swelling prettily in the distance, the road limned with heavy, old trees and punctuated with bursts of sunny fields. We'd flown in this morning and then driven toward the address in the envelope, our usual convoy of black cars snaking through the spring-green foothills to take us there. I'm looking forward to some freedom after we arrive; Merlin worked his brand of twenty-first-century magic, and apparently this location is secure and outfitted with everything Embry will need to work while we honeymoon. Which means privacy similar to Camp David's, where the agents are on the perimeter and we are free and mostly alone within.

Thank God.

We come to a large gate, tall, simple, and strong, and the string of numbers at the bottom of Merlin's paper sends the gates swinging silently inward. We turn onto a narrow drive, lined with even more trees and low pasture fences, and crawl slowly through the tunnel of green.

"Horses," says Embry in a strange voice. And I look out my window to see that he's right—at least two of the pastures we drive past have horses grazing and stamping around. They're gorgeous animals, proud and rippling with muscle, their coats sleek in the afternoon sun, and I'm so taken with them that I don't see the moment that the drive opens up to a massive house. But Embry does and gives a sharp inhale.

"Wow," I breathe. It's like something out of a storybook—three stories stretching into the blue Virginia sky, sprawling symmetrically into cupolas and gables and conservatories. It's white and many windowed, so that the whole thing seems to shine and glitter, a fairy-tale castle with all-American touches—the black shutters, the peaked roof, the Colonial architecture. Behind the house, I can make out the splashing glint of the Shenandoah River. A new-looking stone sign in the center of the drive proclaims the house to be called New Camelot.

Oh, Merlin.

We step out of the car when it stops, and when we get to the front door, it's locked. I use the wedding gift key to unlock it; the lock is new and the key is new, and it clicks and slides open easily as we step inside.

Even though we knew Merlin had prepared the property ahead of time for us, I'm still surprised at how fresh and welcoming it feels inside. We step into the large foyer, marked by a gorgeous curving staircase, and the drapes near us flutter—the windows were left open for us. And on the tables and stands, fresh-cut flowers fill the space with the delicate smell of spring. We walk through the foyer to the back of the house and stand at the tall windows overlooking a sloping green lawn that ends at the river. Near the river shore, a groundskeeper is splitting wood, and I think of how lovely a fire would feel in the cool mountain evenings.

"Fuck, this place is pretty," Embry murmurs, wandering back to the front door to help the agents with our luggage. I hear him talking with them about security arrangements, but I tune it out, choosing to gaze out at the river instead, and the trees, and the mountains, all of it. I think back to all the fairy tales I loved as a girl and decide those princesses can keep their musty castles and Baroque chateaux—I'd take the gables and flashing windows of this American Arcadia any day.

There's a chair next to the window, as if someone else loved this view as much as I do now, and I wonder who it was. Is this Merlin's personal property? Is it a place he loans out to different people? His diplomatic friends, perhaps, or maybe the senators or lobbyists he likes to woo behind the scenes. Either way, I can see myself spending the entire next week in this chair, when I'm not in Embry's arms of course, and I'm turning around to tell him so when I notice the small table next to the chair. It has a Bible on it.

A very familiar Bible.

My heart hammers in déjà vu and grief as I take in the worn leather spine, the dented corners. The gold script stamped at the bottom.

Maxen Ashley Colchester

It's Ash's Bible, the same one on which Embry swore his oath. Merlin told us after the inauguration that he'd sent it to Althea Colchester, and we all thought it a kind gesture, since she'd given him that Bible herself when he was confirmed as a teenager.

But the Bible's not with Althea Colchester in Kansas City. It's here, in Virginia.

In a house that Merlin sent us to.

I touch the cover with my fingertips, the pebbled leather

soft and cool just as I always remembered it being. The baby inside my body stirs, as if answering the living reminder of his or her father's piety, and unshed tears sting my eyes as I lift my gaze to the window, desperate to look at anything but that Bible.

Why does it have to be *here*? Why couldn't someone have warned me, prepared me, told me that my honeymoon would start with my heart breaking all over again?

And now I see and feel Ash everywhere—in the strong mountains and the towering trees, in this majestic house furnished as cleanly and modestly as he furnished his bedroom at the White House, even in the muscled swing of the dark-haired groundskeeper down by the river, who is now burying the axe in the ground at his feet and taking a minute to stare at the river. Even from here, I can see that he's rubbing at his forehead.

Rubbing at his forehead with one thumb.

I didn't say it was a gift from me.

Merlin's words echo through my mind as I'm pushing my way out of the back door and onto the expansive patio. And before I know what I'm doing, I'm tripping down a long set of shallow stone stairs to the lawn. I'm holding my belly as I half walk, half stumble down the soft, grassy hill. I know I'm being foolish, I know I'm being absurd and stupid, and part of my mind keeps thinking of what I'll say to the poor groundskeeper once I reach him—maybe that I was simply wild to see the river. So wild that I'm crying with it, nearly blind with it.

But the other part of me doesn't care, doesn't care at all, because if Merlin can believe that I'm a reincarnated Brythonic queen, then aren't I allowed to believe only for a few moments that a strange dark-haired man could be Ash?

Is that so aberrant, is that so wrong?

God, I can't breathe. It's like all the air has frozen into

place, like the world is cut out of diamond, and above and behind me, I hear Embry call my name, but I don't care, I don't care. And oh God, at the sound of my name, the man on the shore turns; he turns and looks at me, and I don't know what kind of cruel trick this is, what kind of magic, but that man has Ash's shoulders and hips, Ash's powerful arms, Ash's black hair and strong nose and square jaw. That man is walking toward me like he knows me, he is running and I'm running, and then we are close enough that I can hear my name on his lips, I can hear the harsh draw of his own breath, and then his mouth is on mine, his arms are banding around my back and his hands are huge and possessive everywhere, as possessive as his mouth, which takes and takes and takes and never stops.

Until we break apart, panting. On every gasping breath I smell the smoke and leather smell of him, his mint taste still on my tongue, and when our eyes meet and I see the green eyes of my sir, my knees buckle and I drop.

"Easy, easy," he croons, catching me as if I weigh nothing and lifting me into his arms. "I've got you, angel. I've got you."

"You—you're—"

"I know," he says, his eyes crinkling in a smile.

"But…how?" My hands are on his face, making him look at me, holding him still so I can look at him, and I'm so greedy for all of him, and my heart is still thumping hard against my ribs because I'm witnessing a fucking miracle and my sir is here, my king is here, my husband is here—Ash is alive.

"Merlin," Ash answers. "And a little bit my own work too. I thought I was going to die, but—and I hope you'll forgive me for this—I wanted to plan on living too. Despair is a sin, and I've always preferred my sins to be more enjoyable." His eyes darken mischievously. "As you might recall."

I'm pressing my fingertips to every crease and rise of his face, the face I thought I'd never seen again, the face I last saw pale and near dead on a gurney. Every part of him was and is so precious to me, and God, how have I lived without these full, soft lips in my life? The dark fans of his eyelashes? The faint cleft in his chin? How can I be in his arms right now? Cradled against his solid, muscled chest? With his child nestled between us—oh God, his *baby*, he doesn't know—

"I asked Merlin," Ash continues, gazing at me just as hungrily as I'm gazing at him, "that if I somehow lived, if there was a way he could hide me. Make it so everyone thought I was dead. I did manage to live—it was a near thing, though—and Merlin worked his magic and made it so the world thought I died."

My joy and awe are still so fucking real I'm throbbing with them, but for the first time, I feel a surge of vivid, gnawing hurt. "Why?" I whisper. "I thought—Ash, we thought you were dead. Embry blamed himself for *months*. I buried you, I—"

"Shhh," he says softly, pressing his forehead against mine. "I know. And I'm so fucking sorry, I really am, except...I'm also not. I did it for a reason."

"What possible reason?" I cry. "What possible reason could there be?"

"You," he says simply. "And Embry."

"I need more than that," I tell him, a little fussily, which makes his eyes crinkle again. He hoists me a little tighter in his arms, holding me so easily, so gently, and even in my hurt and anger, I never want him to let me go.

"I realized the night before—" He has to close his eyes a moment before he continues. "The night before it happened. How much I loved you both...and how much I had wronged you both, however inadvertently."

"Wronged? How could you think that?"

He sighs. "I had the privilege of meeting you and Embry at different times, having you both all to myself; I got to fall in love with you separately. But you and Embry have always had the shadow of me hanging over your love. I was present inside it even from the beginning." He smiles sadly at me. "You never had the chance to love each other without me in between."

I want to argue with him, I want to tell him that he's wrong, but I think of the new, deep commitment Embry and I have hammered and forged since Ash's absence and how different it is from what we had before. Mature. Tailored to each other.

"If I survived, I knew that I wanted us to live forever as a three. And you and I had time as man and wife, and Embry and I had time as—well, as *something* anyway—but you and Embry needed that time too. And so it was my last gift to you. The time that I've gotten to have with the both of you, I wanted you to have with each other."

"Your last gift to us," I echo.

"Yes," he says fiercely, "because I'm done giving now. I'm ready to take." And his lips are hot and urgent on mine, setting my skin on fire and my pulse chasing through my veins. I'm suddenly terribly, squirmingly aware that I haven't been spanked or bound or dominated in any way since my last night with Ash, and I'm going to combust without it.

Ash sets me down onto the grass so that he can kneel in front of me and press his head against our unborn child.

"Did you know?" I ask, running my hands through his thick black hair.

"Merlin told me after Embry's inauguration, and it killed me to stay away," he says. "I'm not going to lie, Greer, if I'd known that you were pregnant when I was recovering from the stab wound, there's no way I could have stayed hidden. But I also wanted you and Embry to marry first, before we all found each other again. That was very important to me."

He looks up at me with a smile. "And I'm a bit of a prisoner here," he says. "Since the world at large believes me dead and it's better that way for all I've built if they keep believing it. But I didn't want to wait a moment longer to see you again. To see this baby."

"It's yours," I tell him softly.

The sunlight catches the tears glassing his eyes, and I catch them with my fingertips as they fall. "I don't know if I can forgive you for staying away," I say in a choked voice. "For leaving me. For the pain."

He looks up at me through those long, perfect eyelashes, now sparkling with tears. "Just promise me that you'll spend the rest of your life trying."

Now I feel my own tears spilling to match his. "Deal."

"And answer me honestly—did it work? Your new husband, do you love him as deeply as you love me?"

"Yes," I admit, and the confession is all at once freeing and gutting. "Yes. I love him just as deeply."

"Then I'll take your rage and your hurt. I will gladly pay any price, because to know the two of you love each other as I love you is all I've wanted since the day we came together. Since that first night—Oh."

He breaks off and I turn to see Embry standing several feet away, his hands by his sides and shell shock etched on his face.

"Achilles," Embry says numbly.

Ash rises from his knees, and for the first time I really notice what he's wearing, ragged jeans and a soft, tight T-shirt, and even dressed like that, even coming up from his knees, he still looks every inch a king.

"Patroclus."

They stand there staring at each other for a minute,

and then Ash crosses the distance to Embry in several long, powerful strides. There is a single second when the two of them seem to breathe in heaving, muscled tandem, and then their mouths are crashing together, Ash cradling Embry's face, and Embry's hands fisted violently in Ash's shirt.

"How?" Embry keeps mumbling against Ash's lips. "How?"

"I want to spend the rest of my life telling you," Ash says. "Will you let me?"

And Embry nods and nods, his nodding turning into more kisses, and then the three of us are together, sharing one kiss, the same kiss

breathless

wet

equal

alive

And then we're falling to the ground, and there's no time to go to the house, no time to care about who might see; there's only time to share what we've been missing all this time, what our bodies have been yearning for, and right there on the soft grass, in the warm sunlight, our three hearts beat as one once again and we share every breath, every kiss, every single drop of our love. Equal and alive.

Three.

When I was twenty-nine, I saw a king come back to life.

And we've been living happily ever after ever since.

EPILOGUE
ASH

FOUR YEARS LATER

"WELCOME HOME, LITTLE PRINCE," I SAY AS EMBRY WALKS through the door, stamping the snow off his dress shoes, followed by three sets of small snowy boots behind him.

"Daddyyyyyyy!" screams Galahad, racing through the door after Embry and launching himself into my arms. Little Imogen, almost four, follows suit, followed by Arthur who, at barely two, still has a binky stuck firmly in his mouth. Soon I'm on the floor with my three children crawling all over me, my phone still warm in my pocket from my weekly phone call with Lyr, who's settling into his off-campus apartment in Manhattan.

"You are going to get covered in snow," Embry warns, hanging up his coat because—sure enough—all the kids appear to have rolled from the car in the snow rather than walked, but I don't care. It's only been three days since I've seen them, but whenever they're gone, I miss them like my skin is flayed raw. Same with Embry and Greer.

But that's all about to change.

"How did it go?" I ask, helping my stepson out of his coat and boots before moving on to my daughter.

"Surely you were watching on TV—"

The door blows open, bringing Greer inside in a gust of white wool and long blond hair. Snow is caught in her hair and eyelashes, and already my blood is warming as I think about licking the snowflakes off her skin. Maybe tonight after we put the kids to bed, I can bring in some snow from outside and Embry and I can take turns teasing her with the cold...

And then she opens up her coat and I see something fuzzy and wriggling and alive cradled against her chest.

A kitten.

"What is that?" I ask with some amusement.

"Kay sent it home," Greer says, toeing off her snowy high heels. "She said the kids would need something to remember the White House by, so she got them a white kitten. Imogen's already named it Jana, by the way."

Imogen nods solemnly at this, pattering over to her mother to carefully take the kitten and crush it to her chest. Arthur trails after her, not reaching for the kitten, just keeping watch with his bright blue eyes and his binky moving in thoughtful sucks. Even though he's the baby, he's the protective one, constantly following Galahad and Imogen around with a concerned look on his face.

"Kay was magnificent, of course," Embry says, unwinding his scarf and pulling off his gloves. "And I froze my balls off."

"I hope not. I have plans for them."

Even now, more than two decades later, my tone makes him flush, which sends Greer's eyes flaring with interest. Which makes other parts of *me* flare with interest.

But first, bedtime.

Between the three of us, we get the three kids bathed and brushed and swaddled in warm footie pajamas. "Can we sleep in your bed tonight?" Galahad asks, and then cannily nudges Imogen, who looks up from her kitten prisoner to blink at us with huge, soft green eyes, which none of us can say no to. So we end up all piled in bed, the snow falling heavily outside, the three adults still dressed and watching the news as our kids slowly melt into sleep snuggled against us. The kitten kneads little kitty biscuits on my thigh, and then curls up in my lap in a tiny, fluffy ball.

"Did you talk to Kay at all today?" Greer asks after a while. "I wondered if you'd get a chance."

"I did. Mom stayed here last night before she went on to DC too."

Both Kay and my mother know I'm alive, as do Lyr and Morgan and Vivienne and Nimue. I told them all after Greer and Embry found me again, and my mother in particular was furious with me, but when I explained to her why I did it—not just for the two people I loved but because I hadn't known if I would live or not, and it seemed the best way to save my legacy in light of that uncertainty, she began to understand. Even now, four years later, she is still working on forgiving me, but I can handle being unforgiven so long as I am allowed to love her anyway.

There are boxes all over the normally neat room—the movers came from the White House earlier today while I made myself scarce on a long, snowy hike. The price of being dead is that I have to stay dead, which means I don't get to leave New Camelot very much, but thanks to Merlin's modern magic and documents of dubiously legal origin, I've been able to go some places, provided I've grown a beard and I'm wearing contacts to hide the distinctive green of my eyes. But mostly I don't want to leave. Merlin chose this place for its proximity to the capital, and at least twice or thrice a week, Embry and Greer and our children are able to come to me. All of them have only ever known New Camelot as their other home, and me as Daddy.

And now this is their *real* home. Our real home. Embry declined a second term, and Kay has taken his place, and now there's nothing ahead of us but the rest of our lives.

"I think they're asleep," I whisper. "Should we go downstairs?"

Greer and Embry nod, and we all get up—I move Jana the kitten, who gives a protesting squeak as I do—and nestle her close to Imogen. Then we tiptoe out of the room and go downstairs; I grab a baby monitor on the way out.

"I can't believe it's finally over," Embry murmurs as we walk down the curved staircase to the main floor.

"I can," says Greer. "It feels like I've been waiting forever."

I privately agree, although I don't say so as I pull a plain silver key from my pocket, a twin to the one I gave Greer and Embry four years ago. Both my husband and my wife change as I unlock the door to the basement. They grow quieter, more excited, even the sound of the key in the lock getting their blood hot.

I gesture for them to go first so I can lock the door behind us and give the doorknob a sound shake to make sure it will hold. The children seem to accept having three parents as a matter of course, but I think it's best to wait on explaining the kink to them. Maybe when they're thirty. Or never.

The other reason I make them go first is so that I can have the private pleasure of watching them walk in front of me, Embry's head near to Greer's, his strong, elegant hand at her back to guide her safely down. It's been agony living apart from them; I've had to remind myself often that I might have died that night—that I get to see them at all is a blessing, and that I get to have tonight and every night for the rest of our lives is more than a blessing; it's the touch of God.

But even though I've missed them like air itself when they can't be with me, watching their marriage grow and solidify has been worth every night in a cold bed, every day with an empty nursery. It may have taken them a long time to forgive me, but there's no way I can regret it now, when the three of us are stronger for the past four years they've spent together. Each side of our triangle is now tempered with time and trust and wisdom, each point where the triangle meets is fused watertight.

And I'm a patient man. I knew that I would have all the time in the world to demand back every kiss and touch and stroke that I missed. I plan to start demanding right now, actually.

When we reach the foot of the stairs, I snap my fingers and feel the familiar heat in my blood as Greer drops to her knees. My cock, already lazily stirring, thickens and swells at the sight of her. Embry makes it worse by dropping his gaze to where the thin wool reveals the shape of my erection and he licks his lips.

"Ready to kneel, little prince?"

"Never," he says, in a voice that means *always.*

We walk through another doorway into our private playroom, Greer crawling behind me and Embry walking a few steps behind her, admiring the view.

"Undress," I command them both, and they hurry to obey as I look on with crossed arms and my cock tenting my pants.

I spend a few quiet moments taking in their bodies, which are now exposed and offered up. I met and loved both of them when they were young, but all these years later, I find their bodies more perfect and dear to me than ever. The faint stretch marks on Greer's belly, the silver salting through Embry's hair. She's in her thirties now, both Embry and I are brushing up against forty-five, but like Embry said once to me, we make each other feel young.

And down here, where I am sir and king, we make each other feel alive.

"I think Embry deserves a little reward after today," I say, stroking the crown of Greer's head after she drops back to kneeling. "Don't you think so, pet?"

She nods.

"Then up on the bench."

Embry groans as our wife stretches out along the length of the bench, her hands going over her head in anticipation of being tied and her legs spreading wide in anticipation of being used. Her pussy gleams pink and wet in the soft light of the playroom.

"Can I touch myself?" Embry asks in a needy voice as I take a set of silk ropes off a nearby hook. "Please?"

"No, you may not," I answer, starting on Greer's wrists.

He gives a plaintive groan, his hands flexing wildly at his sides, which only serves to amuse me and harden my cock even further. Denying him is so very sweet, especially when the thing I'm denying him is already wet and arching under my ropes. With the ease of years of practice, I secure her to the bench with wraps under her breasts and around her waist; with a simple frog tie, I have her legs bent and bound, her cunt opened up for me and Embry like a blown flower.

"Oh God," Embry says in a strangled voice. "Jesus fuck."

"Yes?"

"Please," he begs. "Please let me fuck her."

"You want to fuck that pussy? It's mine, though."

Embry's breathing hard enough that I can see the muscles jerking around his stomach and ribs as he struggles for air. Below his navel, his cock is a livid plum color and hard enough to hammer nails.

"I'll let you fuck her," I say, running a finger up Greer's slick folds and then sliding that finger into her mouth for her to clean. "If you give me something."

"Anything," Embry vows.

"Mm, *anything*. I like the sound of that. Okay, then. Climb between her legs and tell me how that cunt feels."

Embry obeys as eagerly as a youth, clambering on the bench so fast he bangs his knee against the edge. He doesn't care, he needs it too much, and he lets out a wild grunt as it takes him longer than he can stand to press the tip of his dick against her entrance and nudge inside. But when he does finally push into her heat, he gives an almighty groan and slumps over our helplessly bound wife, resting all his weight on her and burying his face in her neck as his hips pump furiously into her spread pussy.

I squat next to the bench so I can stroke Greer's face as she's being used. "Is Embry making my wife feel good?" I ask.

"Yes," she breathes, color high in her cheeks and her teeth digging into her lower lip.

"Is he going to make that pussy come for me?"

She gives a tiny whine, nodding and closing her eyes. I slide my hand between their bodies and tuck my fingers around Greer's clit to add to the pressure. I catch the gleam of my wedding ring between the lean ridges of his stomach and the soft curves of Greer's belly, and my heart does that thing again, where it feels so full I can't stand it.

My husband and my wife.

My prince and my queen.

"Show him how good that pussy comes, angel," I murmur to her, kissing her temple and watching where my hand moves between them. "Show him how wet it gets."

With an abrupt, pained cry, she obeys, writhing hard against her ropes as Embry rides her hard through it all, grunting every time her cunt squeezes around his cock. I keep massaging her clit until she's done, and then I make her lick my fingers clean as I watch.

God, her lips are so pink and pretty around my fingertips…her tongue so wet and clever…and those silver eyes sparkle with the same curious light I saw in a submissive teenager once upon a time, as she begged a soldier to wreck her under a full English moon.

When she's finished, I tuck away her hair so it won't tickle her face and lean in to kiss her tenderly. "Welcome home," I whisper against her lips. They taste like her now, a hint of salt, a hint of tart, lots of sweet. "I'm ready for forever now."

"I'm ready for forever too," she whispers back.

Embry lifts his head, slowing his thrusts so he can kiss each of us in turn, mumbling his own things about forever, but his words are broken across the shore of his pleasure and he can barely get them out.

That's okay. I have other plans for his mouth.

I stand up, take the baby monitor out of my pocket and stand it on a nearby table, checking to make sure the volume is dialed all the way up and the video feed is live and showing three snoozing lumps of footie pajamas and binky…and one white kitten.

Babies safely asleep, I turn back to my husband, who is still working his cock in and out of our wife's cunt and who is also eyeing me with hunger. And when I reach for the back of his head and unfasten my pants with my other hand, he already has his mouth open like the good little prince he is.

The moment the crown of my cock brushes against his satin tongue, I forget to go easy. I force my length all the way down his throat, admiring the hollows of his cheeks and the way his lashes lay long and thick on his cheekbones before I pull out and give him a chance to breathe.

"Mmm," Greer says from below us. "Fuck, that's hot."

"Dirty little queen," I tell her. "You like watching me fuck his mouth? You like watching me use him?"

She has to swallow before she answers, and I see she's close to coming again. "Yes. Yes, I do."

"What should I do next?"

"Fuck his ass," she says, and her voice is full of all the best kinds of filth and prurience.

I pull out of Embry's mouth and give his face a playful slap. "I never like to say no to a lady," I say, stripping off my thin sweater and pants and then reaching for the lube.

Embry shivers as he feels the push of my knees as I climb behind him, and then he says, "Wait, Ash. Wait."

I have two fingers covered in lube, one hand on his ass, and a cock that's so ready to fuck it's a miracle I haven't fucked them both twice over already. But at the word *wait*, I immediately settle back on my heels and drop my hand. "What is it, Embry?"

"I don't want you to stop," he says quickly. "I just…I wanted a minute to savor this. So I can remember what it felt like the first time you fucked us when we were all yours again."

"*Oh.*" His words burn a happy glow in my chest.

"Embry and I have loved our time together," Greer adds, looking up at me with those moon-sea eyes. "But this is where we belong. Under your care. At your feet."

"Yes," I say, because it's the simple truth. It's where they belong, and in return for their love, I'll give them everything of me forever. I already have. I always will.

Embry looks over his shoulder at me. "Are you going to fuck me or what?" And I have to laugh because he might as well be twenty-one again, petulant and impatient. Spoiled.

And I might as well be twenty-two again, consumed with all the ways I'd like to fuck the petulance right out of him.

I prepare him with all the humiliating and examining probes and presses that he likes so much, and then I press my thighs to the backs of his. His asshole is a ring of taut heat at the head of my cock, and it feels like I'm being swallowed whole as I slick and shove my way inside.

"Don't I get a reward too?" I say into his ear as I fuck him with slow pushes and pulls. "For being so patient?"

"Yes," he moans. "Yes. Anything."

"How about everything?"

"Everything."

And then the three of us fuck for a long time in silence, my every thrust pushing his cock deeper into Greer, our every moan reverberating through each other's flesh and filling the room.

"Come inside our princess, Embry. Show her how much you can give her."

I highlight my words with a wicked roll of my hips and then Embry is shuddering and gasping, his ass clenching around my cock as he drains his body into Greer's, and then I come with a sharp grunt and an agonizingly delicious clench low in my groin, spilling deep, deep into his most secret place.

We stay in a heap for a minute, all of us breathing hard and relishing the trickles and flutters of post-sex bliss, and then in tandem, we all turn our heads to the baby monitor, unable to believe our luck.

The lumps are all still curled and cuddled and fast asleep.

"More?" I ask my spouses.

"More," they agree.

I untie Greer, we shower quickly, and then we spend the night celebrating the rest of forever. Embry and I share Greer between us, we make her crawl, we make her suck on our cocks until we can't stand it anymore and then we share her again. At the end, I let Embry have my ass as Greer and I kiss in languorous, tender kisses and she traces the jagged scar on my stomach, and eventually Greer begs to ride me as I'm being fucked. We turn into a tangled mess of limbs and cocks and hair, and it's perfect, it's everything, and when we come, we come together. One heart. One life.

The snow is still blowing in reckless swirls past the windows when we climb, sated and spent, upstairs, as we shower and brush our teeth and contemplate the limited room on the bed—a bed I even had custom made to accommodate three adults and some children smashed between.

"Oh," Greer says suddenly, looking pale. "I don't feel well." And then she turns and walks back to the bathroom. A few seconds later, we hear the unmistakable sounds of retching.

Embry and I look at each other.

Then we're both bolting to the bathroom.

"There are tests somewhere in here," Embry mutters, rifling through the bathroom drawers. "We ought to start buying them in bulk, really."

I smile at that, kneeling behind Greer so I can sweep her hair up off her neck while she's sick. "Are you late, princess?"

"Just by a couple of days," she whines. "And maybe it was just some bad seafood or something."

I hear a phone ding from the bedroom, and Embry trots back to get it—force of habit from being the president, I suppose; there's no call or text that goes unchecked—and then I hear him laughing.

"Who would be texting at this hour?" our wife grouses.

Embry is walking in as she says this, and he holds the phone so we can both see the screen. It's from Merlin.

Congratulations.

I can't help it, I laugh too. And then harder as the second text comes in.

You might want to consider buying twice the usual amount of clothes.

"Fuck," Embry says in wonder as he reads it. He looks down at Greer and me as I rub soothing circles on her back. "Twins?"

"Twins!" wails Greer, right before she's sick again.

"Why not?" I say, my heart so warm and happy that I think it might light up the snowy darkness outside. "We have the rest of forever to figure it out, right?"

"We do," confirms Embry as he gets to his knees to comfort Greer. She slumps into me, and soon both of them are in my arms, between my legs, as I sit against the bathroom wall, rubbing warm caresses on their backs and necks, feeling them both cradle each other as I'm cradling them.

And I can't help but think of how fitting it is, that my forever will start right here. Not on that flat-topped hill in Somerset, not on the shore of a lake that beckons me to some other fog-haunted world. Not on a field of bloody victory or in the White House.

No, forever starts right here, with the two people I've loved through every lifetime, with the two people that I will love in every lifetime after this. Here on a bathroom floor, with the promise of new life between us, with our other new lives slumbering sweetly nearby, with our bodies still loose and aching from loving each other so much.

Forever starts here. With my husband and my wife. My prince and my queen. The three of us sharing one heart, which beats together, and which will beat together in every lifetime yet to come.

AFTERWORD

There's a story I've loved since high school, and it goes like this. John Steinbeck (yes, that John Steinbeck, *The Grapes of Wrath* guy) was obsessed with King Arthur from a young age and decided he was going to translate Thomas Malory's *Le Morte d'Arthur* for a modern audience. But he could never bring himself to get any further than Guinevere and Lancelot's first betrayal. Every time he got to the place where the two lovers finally became unfaithful to their king, he despaired and couldn't make himself go on.

I'm like 99 percent sure that story is apocryphal, and now I don't even remember where I heard it, but to a teenage Sierra that didn't matter. What mattered is that I felt the same way as John Steinbeck, and I was violently relieved to hear I wasn't the only one who hated the love triangle between Arthur, Guinevere, and Lancelot.

See, I've also been obsessed with Arthuriana from a young age, starting from the time my mother handed me a copy of *The Once and Future King*, yellowed and smelling like must and cigarettes. (Even now I can't smell a cigarette without thinking of Archimedes the Owl.) It was my first exposure to King Arthur, and a better introduction I can't imagine, and it was followed by all the staples of the Arthur genre in my teenage years: Mary Stewart's Arthurian Saga and the wrenching *The Wicked Day*, Nancy McKenzie's *The Queen of Camelot*, Susan Cooper's *The Dark is Rising*, Rosalind Miles's *Guenevere, Queen of the Summer Country*, Bernard Cornwell's *The Winter King: A Novel of Arthur*, John Boorman's *Excalibur* (which is ridiculous and amazing), Antoine Fuqua's *King Arthur* (which features a very stoic Clive Owen and a very broody Ioan Gruffudd and also Hannibal and Will Graham (by which I mean Mads Mikkelson and Hugh Dancy with long, Dark Ages-esque hair) and Keira Knightley in a leather bra—I don't know that it's a *good* movie but you should definitely watch it), and finally in college, I went back to the sources and read Malory and Tennyson and Chrétien de Troyes and that wacky Geoffrey of Monmouth. I also read all the nonfiction—Geoffrey Ashe and Leslie Alcock and anything my broke college hands could dig up at second-hand bookstores.

From these books I learned that Lancelot was a late French invention designed to entertain listeners who gobbled up tales of courtly love; that in the oldest stories, it seems to be Mordred that Guinevere betrays Arthur with; that every version of Arthur's story from *Culhwch and Olwen* to Meg Cabot's *Avalon High* is a vehicle to reflect the anxieties and beliefs of the society that produced it. The King Arthur legend is a mood ring—it can be a glittering tale of chivalry and brave deeds or it can be a gritty war narrative or anything in between—and it's up to us to decide which it is.

In fact, the very first book I ever wrote—a high school project that leaked into my early college years—was my own Arthur retelling, and into it I poured all of my frustrations and hopes about the characters. And chief among those frustrations was the one I shared with John Steinbeck—how could Lancelot and Guinevere betray Arthur like that? Why? If you served the bravest, kindest man you'd ever known, how could you scamper off to be unfaithful to him?

In fact, despite the best efforts of T.H. White, with his closeted sadist Lancelot, and Nancy McKenzie, with her loyal-but-conflicted take on the knight, I never could find myself caring about Lancelot at all. It's like offering someone a hot dog when they're eating steak—who would take the knight when they could have the *king*?

But in my (admittedly perverted) teenage mind, I *could* understand falling in love with Mordred. He was dangerous and brooding and misunderstood and usually wanders around in lots of black clothes making acerbic comments, and that sort of Hamlet-esque type has been my jam for as long as I can remember. And so in my teenage retelling of the legend, I dispose of Lancelot and make the real love triangle between Mordred, Arthur, and Guinevere. (This book is forever hidden, by the way, because it's trash, but I'm telling you this so I can explain how and why I've had Ash, Greer, and Embry's story in my head for so long and why I wrote it the way I did.) See, I wanted to fix the romance part of the story. I wanted for my own selfish reasons to straighten out the betrayals and the infidelity and then rearrange them in a way that suited my own (again, perverted) heart.

First of all, the only thing that made sense to me was to make the three of them love each other. On the face of traditional wisdom, King Arthur's legends seem to be the practicum of heterosexuality—men being *men*, ladies being either foul temptresses or helpless damsels, not to mention the entire tragedy ultimately turns on a straight love affair. Yet as a bisexual teen, it never escaped my notice that beneath the surface, there seemed to be a lot of things that hinted at queerness—T.H. White, famously closeted himself, made his Lancelot hero-worship Arthur to the point of something tantalizingly close to love. But beyond the modern retellings, I saw it in the old texts too. There's the strange kiss-sharing game Gawain plays with the Green Knight and the Green Knight's wife, the time when Sir Lancelot puts an unconscious Sir Dinadan in a woman's dress, and then let me present this little tidbit to you from *Le Morte d'Arthur* itself:

> "Dinadan went unto Palomides, and there either made other great joy, and so they lay together that night. And on the morn early came Sir Tristram and Sir Gareth, and took them in their beds, and so they arose and brake their fast."
>
> —Thomas Malory, *Le Morte d'Arthur,* vol. II, pg. 81

I don't know about you, but making great joy in a shared bed sounds delightfully eyebrow-raise-y to me.

Secondly, I knew that no Arthur of mine (or Guinevere of mine) could love the fussy, weak Lancelot of the legend, so I took a little artistic license and I fused my conception of Mordred into my Lancelot character. Embry occupies the same space as Lancelot (because even Sierra isn't bonkers enough to have a polyamorous love triangle between a father and a son) but I imbued him with all the things I loved best about Mordred. Embry is brooding and a little tortured, he loves imperfectly, he's the one ultimately to betray Ash. But also—and I refuse to apologize for this—a secret son was just too much fun for any writer to give up, so that's why we have Lyr along with my Mordred-ish Lancelot.

Thirdly, I knew that I was going to give Arthur the happily ever after he deserved. In the legends, Arthur and Mordred kill each other on the field of battle, and Arthur clings to life long enough for there to be an extended narrative about him trying to get Sir Bedivere to throw Excalibur back in the fucking lake and Bedivere just cannot follow instructions (unlike my version of him, Ryan Belvedere, who is *excellent* at following instructions). Lancelot and Guinevere respectively become a hermit and a nun after Arthur's death, and so everyone dies alone. Womp womp.

Not on Sierra's watch.

Fans of the Arthur story will recognize a few things. Carpathia serves the same function as the Saxons in the legends, for example, and the burning of the boat in Glein echoes a crime that either Morgause or Arthur himself commits in the story, in order to hide the birth of Mordred. The names of the battles—Glein and Caledonia and Bassas—are taken straight from the legend. Melwas, in the stories, is Meliagrance (or Meleagant or Meliagaunt—names are wiggly in the legends sometimes), who kidnaps Guinevere and later challenges her fidelity to King Arthur at Camelot, using the bloody sheets leftover in his dungeon as proof. (For all of you who were stressed reading Embry and Greer's sex scene in Melwas's stronghold, blame Thomas Malory! He did it first!)

You will recognize Morgan Leffey as Morgan Le Fay, of course, and I'm sure you recognized Vivienne as my own modern-day Lady of the Lake.

Abilene Corbenic is a combination of Elaine of Corbenic and the Lady of Shalott (also called Elaine of Astolat). Readers familiar with the legends will see Elaine of Corbenic's deceptions echoed in Abilene—in the original stories, Elaine tricks Lancelot into sleeping with her by pretending to be Guinevere, twice actually, which is how she ends up marrying Lancelot and carrying his son, Galahad.

Why did I make her the chief villain, as opposed to Mordred or Melwas? In the legends, the final climactic conflict is between a father and a son, and it's a war for a kingdom. It's usually portrayed as a man's narrative, but it doesn't have to be. I rather liked the idea of sending in some women to disrupt the traditionally masculine power struggle, and even though it's a departure from the legend to locate the source of the chaos inside the Elaine character, to me it made the most sense within the world I'd created. The New Camelot series is about love and pain and the intersection between the two. I show how powerful that intersection is with the Ash-Embry-Greer triad… and I wanted to show how destructive it could be in the character of Abilene. She is the reverse of our lovers; she is the distorted reflection of obsessive love. And I think that the Lady of Shalott and Elaine of Corbenic have this quality too—the Lady dies of unrequited love and Elaine of Corbenic (let's be frank) commits something on the spectrum of sexual assault and rape. These women allow obsessive love to swallow their identities and moralities whole. *That* is chaos. And to me more interesting than the traditional motives of ambition or revenge given to the usual slate of Arthurian villains.

Also, I liked Morgan too much to make her the bad guy.

Anyway, all that being said, making the villain a woman carries its own price. I hope that Morgan and Greer and Vivienne are layered and complicated enough to offset Abilene's role in the story.

As for the kink—well, I could write another two thousand words about that alone—but the simplest explanation I can give is that the King Arthur story is a story about love, power, and the experience of being human. I would say kink is the practice of those same things.

Besides, how fun is it to say the words "Kinky King Arthur"? It's so much fun, admit it.

I hope that I've done my love of the Arthurian genre justice with my kinky, queer, polyamorous books. I hope

I gave Arthur the ending he deserves. I hope my clumsy attempt at translating the legend has been, at the very least, fun for you to read, and I hope that if John Steinbeck were raised from the dead and forced to read it, he'd finally be able to get past the first kiss. All the fun stuff's after the first kiss anyway.

xoxo,
Sierra Simone
October 2017
Olathe, Kansas

ACKNOWLEDGMENTS

In the words of my prophet Britney Spears: oops, I did it again. I promised everyone I wouldn't write a book that wrung me out and wasted me like *American Queen* did, but Ash had different plans for me, and so this is the place where I say *thank you thank you* and also *I am so fucking sorry.*

Sorry and thank you to Laurelin Paige, who always gets the brunt of my angst somehow and who has midwifed enough books for me to do it with a deft and compassionate hand. You are Ash, for real.

Sorry and thank you to Melanie Harlow and Kayti McGee, CPs and cheerleaders and lake walkers that you are.

Sorry and thank you to Julie Murphy, who talked through all sorts of thematic and social issues with me, and also helped me stress-shop for clothes, and also remotely organized my thirtieth birthday party when I was too scattered to do it myself. Also she is my Instagram boss. Teamwork makes the dream work, my friend.

Sorry and thank you to Tessa Gratton and NCP, who are the smartest people I know and somehow always have Tank

7 in their fridge and I probably made a hash of talking about sexuality and power, but anything I did right is a credit to what they've taught me.

Sorry and thank you to Ashley Lindemann, who has known me since I was fourteen, and has shepherded me gently through every tantrum and tornado these last sixteen years (but especially with this book, sorry about that lol). Being my best friend is hard work.

To the rest of the crew that keeps the world spinning while I'm in the writing cave—Serena McDonald, who gave me so many amazing pep talks and keeps my lambs happy; Melissa Gaston who is not only a graphic genius but some kind of organizational wizard, and hilarious to boot; Candi Kane who can whip up Google docs faster than I can sneeze and knows everything there is to know about Getting Shit Done.

To Rebecca Friedman, my agent, who gives the best advice, the best encouragement, and is overall the warmest, kindest, smartest mentor I could have ever asked for. To Flavia Viotti and Meire Dias of Bookcase Literary—thank you for all of your tireless work being my champions internationally!

To Jenn Watson, publicity goddess, along with the rest of the Social Butterfly team—you make releasing a book smooth and easy work and the best kind of fun.

To Nancy Smay of Evident Ink, who is not only a sharp-eyed editor, but who is also a fount of insight and kindness and a good friend. Also Michele Ficht and Erica Russikoff, my proofreaders, for their time and eagle eyes.

To Braadyn Penrod at ByBraadyn Photography, who gave me a gorgeous picture, Endi Zalic my cover model, and then Hang Le for giving me yet another stunning cover (and being very patient with me, I owe you dessert sometime).

And to all of the authors who listened to me fuss and helped me along the way, either by talking about King

Arthur or by being an awesome human or by just giving me another drink on a writing retreat: Nana Malone, who made me a project plan and held my hand through the shaky final days; Christine Reiss, who helped me figure out a way to Ash's voice the day before the eclipse; Jessica Hawkins, Kennedy Ryan, Stacy Kestwick, Becca Hensley Mysoor, Robin Murphy, Sarah MacLean, Carrie Ryan, Zoraida Cordova, Tara Hudson, Dhonielle Clayton, Sophie Jordan, Rachel Hawkins, Ella James, and all of the Shop Talkers and 1001 Dark Night Authors and everyone in the *Glamour* Anthology.

And Jana Aston, who will now live eternally as a little kitten making kitty biscuits on Ash's lap as the snow falls outside.

To all of the bloggers on Facebook and Instagram who take the time and energy to talk about my books—thank you so much, and I'm in awe of your generosity and organization! (And also how pretty your Instagram pictures are!)

To all of my readers—this has been a bit of a ride, hasn't it? I can't tell you how fucking grateful I am that you were willing to take a chance on my bananas King Arthur kink, and your enthusiasm and energy for Ash, Embry, and Greer have been the fuel in my tank this last year. So thank you. Thank you a thousand thousand times. I don't deserve your affection but I'm selfish enough to take it anyway…

And finally to my husband, who is my actual once and future king, who is a patient father and generous partner and who knows his way around ropes and riding crops better than President Colchester. Yes, I can come down to watch TV now. I promise to kiss you goodbye whenever I leave (even though it's usually just to get more scotch).

About the Author

Sierra Simone is a *USA Today* bestselling author and former librarian who spent too much time reading romance novels at the information desk. She lives with her husband and family in Kansas City.

Sign up for her newsletter to be notified of releases, books going on sale, events, and other news here: subscribepage.com/sierrasimone.

thesierrasimone.com
thesierrasimone@gmail.com